June
Best wishes
with love,
John Ristine

MESSIAH

A Journey From Galilee To Golgotha

John Dennis Ristine

Printed in the United States of America
First edition

Quotation from the Gospel of Thomas taken from "The Other Bible"
published by Harper and Row.

Quotations from Josephus taken from "The Works of Josephus"
published by Hendrickson Publishers.

Map of Israel 30CE

ACKNOWLEDGEMENTS

I thank the late Bill Guelcher who spent countless hours working with me to construct a story that would make sense literally and practically.

The late Bill Beckfeld read the first draft and offered many suggestions to improve the story.

Two friends from the Cursillo Movement, Ed Pehoski and Mike Robertson listened to my ideas every Thursday morning for fifteen years and offered encouragement and suggestions.

Kevin Jents and Al Jirele convinced me that this was a book that would provide tools people could use to better understand the message of the four Gospels.

Wally Woehrle read the last drafts and contributed to the writing of the Epilogue.

Father Robert Monaghan tutored me in practical spirituality and introduced me to the writings of Bishop John Shelby Spong.

Dr. John Stoll, Biblical scholar and teacher.

My friends from Writers Unlimited (Birchwood, Minnesota) who patiently critiqued several chapters in the book.

My children, Debbie, Kevin, Renee, Theresa, Marilyn, and Kathy; all of whom helped with this effort.

My granddaughter, Jennifer Corazzo helped with the final edit.

Finally, my wife Janet who read all the drafts of the book and acted as my in-house editor. She is an avid reader who knows the difference between a good story and a bad story. I could not have written the book without her help and encouragement.

To Red
For her support and patience

PREFACE

I grew up Catholic which meant that my exposure to the Bible was limited to looking inside the front cover to check important family dates. Our Bible did have pictures to illuminate certain passages and I occasionally scanned them much as I would with an illustrated novel. I played with my Protestant neighbor children but I was never exposed to their reverence for the Bible. We went our separate ways on Sunday morning. They to their houses of worship and I to a cavernous church where two or three short readings constituted my total weekly exposure to the Bible. I remember a night in a motel room years later where I was wrestling with my dysfunctional spiritual life. I opened the Gideon Bible placed on my night stand. Randomly, I opened it to Paul's Letter to the Galatians. I didn't understand a word I read and tossed the book back on the table.

Things changed in 1979 when I had a born again experience. It was short and powerful. A curtain opened and I was treated to a beautiful light. As I recall, it lasted less than three seconds but the gift that came with the light has stayed with me for thirty-three years. The next time I picked up a Bible the words jumped out at me. I understood what I read no matter where I looked. I came to understand that the Bible is the greatest piece of literature ever written. I was filled with raw knowledge which was good, but I wanted more; like what's the story behind the story?

I looked for a Bible study that would broaden my understanding of scripture. That brought me into contact with a number of Evangelical communities. From there I was led to a weekly Bible study hosted by Dr. John Stoll. We met every Monday morning for more than five years. Dr. Stoll answered many of my questions while teaching our group how to study the

Bible. Our family started a home Bible study program and I started to teach the Bible to people in our local Catholic community. People were impressed with my understanding of the Bible but I knew there was a world of Protestants who had more knowledge than I. But I was surprised to learn that many of them had no better understanding than the average Catholic.

The problem with studying the Bible is that the reader needs to fill in the blanks – the information not given. We need to know the social and political environment of the First Century to understand the challenges faced by Jesus and his followers. We need to know how people lived in the First Century. Like us, they worked to provide food, clothing and shelter for their families. But where did they work? Perhaps they spent a great deal of time looking for work. What was the relationship between the religious leaders in Jerusalem and the average man in Capernaum or the Emperor in Rome?

Most Christians believe that Jesus was both God and man. Do we see the *man* in the Gospels? Sometimes. Do we see him angry, happy, or even in love? Seldom. The Gospel stories present Jesus as a kind of superman who always has control of his emotions and the situation around him. This book tries to put a more human face on Jesus and the people who followed him. After all, the followers of Jesus had no idea that he was the Messiah until after he died.

One confusing part of the New Testament is the number of people in the stories, many who share their name with others. We see James bar Zebedee, James, the brother of Jesus, and James bar Alphaeus. There are five Mary's and at least four Judes' or Judases in the Gospels! It gets worse when we read about members of the Herod dynasty. Herod the Great ruled when Jesus was born. Herod Antipas ruled when Jesus died. Herod Agrippa I ordered the death of the apostle James. There are at least three additional Herods in the Gospels to confuse us even more.

When you go to the back of the book you will find a list of apostles, a list of Gospel characters and a short summary of the Herod dynasty. At the very end there are questions you can use for discussion in readers' groups. I pray that this book will open new vistas in you Bible studies.

CHAPTER ONE

"I will send my messenger ahead of you, who will prepare your way" — "a voice of one calling in the wilderness, 'Prepare the way for the Lord, make straight paths for him.'"

And so John the Baptist appeared in the wilderness, preaching a baptism of repentance for the forgiveness of sins. The whole Judean countryside and all the people of Jerusalem went out to him. Confessing their sins, they were baptized by him in the Jordan River. John wore clothing made of camel's hair, with a leather belt around his waist, and he ate locusts and wild honey. And this was his message: "After me comes the one more powerful than I, the thongs of whose sandals I am not worthy to stoop down and untie. I baptize you with water, but he will baptize you with the Holy Spirit."

Mark 1:2b-8

On a late spring afternoon, Jesus of Nazareth and Andrew, the son of Jonah reached the brow of a hill overlooking the Jordan River. There they saw a small group of people standing around a tall man. Jesus and Andrew quickly moved down the hill and stood with the people, listening as the man preached to them. Jesus recognized the man. He was John, the son of Zechariah and Elizabeth. Jesus had not seen John for more than six years and hardly recognized him, full bearded and dressed in clothing suited for the wild. Elizabeth and his mother, Mary, were cousins and there were times when Jesus and John played together when his family went to Jerusalem for holiday celebrations. But they drifted apart after the death of John's elderly parents and Jesus later heard that John went to the monastery at Qumran to live in the Essene community.

Jesus noticed that some of the people were soaking wet, shivering from the cool afternoon air sweeping in with the long shadows from the west. John looked at Jesus and Andrew. "Did you come to be cleansed of your sins?" he asked.

Jesus pointed toward the people. "Do you want us to bathe as they did?" he asked.

It was then that John recognized Jesus. "Do you wish to be baptized, cousin?"

"Yes."

John smiled. "Your friend Andrew has already been baptized and I recognize that you are a man gifted with holiness. It is I that should be baptized by you."

"Never the less," Jesus replied, "I wish to be baptized by you."

So John invited Jesus to the water's edge and walked with him into the Jordan River. When they reached waist high depth, John asked Jesus to kneel and he held his head under the water. Water sprayed from his hair as Jesus jumped up and shook his head. John laughed and embraced Jesus. "Now you are ready to do God's work," he said as they waded back to shore.

A few people stayed with Jesus, John, and Andrew as the evening wore on. They warmed themselves around a fire and listened as John and Jesus talked about their lives since they last saw each other. "I assume you attended the Passover celebration in Jerusalem before coming here," John said.

"Yes, I came with my mother and friends from Galilee."

"Where are they now?"

"They left for Galilee two days ago. I chose to stay back for a while."

John glanced at Andrew then looked back to Jesus. "Why?"

Jesus rubbed his chin. "I'm not sure why. It just seemed that I needed to move in a new direction."

"What does that mean?"

"I am a carpenter and I have had rabbinic training." Jesus looked in the distance as he continued. "But I feel unfulfilled, as if my life is going in the wrong direction. I'm not married, I have no children, and I seem more suited to wander from place to place than settling down with a family."

John leaned close to Jesus. "Perhaps you should be doing what I am doing. A commitment to this life does not leave room for wives and children."

"What are you doing?"

"I am calling people to repentance. You might say that I am a prophet."

"Not the Messiah?"

John laughed. "Not I. There will be a Messiah in our time, but I am not the one."

"Do you know who that might be?"

"Jesus, I baptize with water. The Messiah will baptize with fire and the Holy Spirit."

John looked at Andrew. "My friend, what is your reason for staying here while your family travels home?"

"Business," replied Andrew. "I used this occasion to find someone who will sell our fish in Judea."

"Did you find a person?" John asked.

"I met with a merchant from Kerioth who says he can sell all the fish we catch. His name is Simon. He has a partner in Caesarea who sells salt, spices, and fine fabrics in Galilee and Samaria."

John glanced at Jesus. "Merchants…the curse of mankind."

"People have to eat," Andrew interjected.

"Merchants have no conscience. They fleece the poor, the widows, and the orphans." John stood and stretched. Yawning, he added, "This is not a time to solve the problems of the world. You are welcome to stay here with me tonight. It is safer than traveling on the Jordan Road." Jesus, Andrew and the remaining few pilgrims expressed their appreciation and prepared to bed down for the night.

* * *

Early the next morning the small encampment rose and shared a breakfast consisting of dry bread and fresh fruit picked from trees near the river. Later, Andrew agreed to join the others on their journey to Galilee. Jesus did not join them, instead choosing to spend time alone in the Judean desert.

It was during his forty days in the desert that Jesus came to understand his calling. He remembered John's words about the merchants: "They fleece the poor, the widows, and the orphans." Jesus understood that the political and religious leaders of Galilee and Judea robbed people of their basic human needs and more importantly, leave them without hope, and without a future. He realized that to be a parent and not have a vision of who your children can be, leads to hopelessness.

Sometime later, Jesus told his followers about his experience in the desert. He was so deprived of food and water for those forty days that he began to dream visions of God and Satan in conflict because of him. But it was through this experience that he saw the need to lead people from perpetual spiritual and physical poverty to the Kingdom of God. Using this knowledge and working with a small group of disciples he would strike fear in the hearts of the Temple crowd before he was done.

CHAPTER TWO

"For if you forgive others when they sin against you, your heavenly Father will also forgive you. But if you do not forgive others their sins, your Father will not forgive your sins."

Matthew 6:14

Two men sat on benches at twilight looking past the short walls of a small Judean outpost called Kerioth-Hezron. Located in the Judean foothills, eighteen miles from Masada and the Salt Sea, Kerioth served as a commercial center for the seven small towns located within a full day's walk.

"I am glad to be leaving here. This is no place for an ambitious man like myself," Judas bar Simon[1] said to his Greek friend, Gallus.

"Kerioth isn't that bad," Gallus replied.

"Not for you, you're only a visitor here," Judas countered as he gazed at the sand swirling around the courtyard.

Gallus asked, "Why does your father still live here?"

"Tradition!" Judas hissed. "He was born here and he wants to die here." Judas sipped wine from his cup and continued, "Gallus, you've traveled to many places in the Roman world. The only places I go to are Jerusalem during our feast days and Herod's fortress at Masada when our guests want to see something other than sand."

"That's all?" Gallus asked.

"Well, my father has a business partner in Caesarea. I went there a few times and I went to Tiberias once." Judas filled his cup with wine. "Caesarea is a beautiful city, said to rival Alexandria, but Tiberias is a typical northern city--dusty, hot, and full of rude Galileans." He offered more wine to Gallus. "Help me finish our wine. Let's see, two cups of wine at the dinner and..."

"Three cups since."

---

1 'bar' and 'ben' refer to the lineage of the person. It means 'son of…' John bar James reads as John son of James. Women use 'bas' as their identifier.

"Who's counting?" Judas asked with a hiccup. Catching his breath, Judas said, "Tell me about Athens and Rome."

"They're like most cities, dusty and hot in the summer and cold and wet in the winter, just like Tiberias."

Judas beckoned Gallus to join him outside their courtyard, near an acacia tree. There they sat looking at the transparent night sky. "Anything is better than Kerioth," Judas mumbled between his hiccups.

"You've never been in the other provinces," Gallus replied with a hint of irritation. "This is the seat of luxury compared to some of the places..."

"Words come easy to you," Judas interrupted with a snap of his fingers. "As I said before, I'm glad I'm leaving here. My father arranged a position for me with his partner in Caesarea. I understand that this--what do they call him--Roman procurer, Pontius Pilate, lives in Herod's palace in Caesarea."

"Procurator."

"Procurator?"

Gallus laughed. "Yes, he's the procurator. Pontius Pilate has quite a reputation in Roman circles." Waving his cup at Judas, Gallus added, "Listen, Judas, you'll have to learn Roman names and customs if you intend to live in Caesarea, or any other city controlled by the Romans."

Judas gave Gallus a sideways glance. "Is that how you survive?"

"Yes. I learn everything I can about people who are important."

"That's why I like you Gallus; you're wise in the ways of the world."

"Thank you, Judas," Gallus replied with raised eyebrows. "I only wish that were true."

* * *

Judas woke the next morning with a pounding headache. The crowing roosters outside his courtyard and the bright sunlight streaming into his room aggravated his condition. Opening one eye, he cursed himself for drinking too much wine the previous night. Later, he went to a corner stand, splashed a few handfuls of water on his face, and took a small chest from underneath the table. He poured a dash of opium powder from a leather pouch into a cup, added water, and drank the concoction. Following that, he washed, dressed in a light linen tunic, and hurried to the courtyard for breakfast with his father Simon and Gallus.

Judas said little as he picked through his breakfast of ripe red berries, fresh orange juice, and wheat bread left from the previous day. After a few minutes, Simon raised his cup. "I pray, Judas that you don't fall in love with a Galilean woman while you're in that place."

This was a subject Judas didn't want to talk about, but forcing a smile, he explained to Gallus, "My mother was a Galilean. She met my father in Jerusalem during the Feast of Purim. They married and, a year later I was born."

Simon continued the story. "My Rachael longed for her friends and relatives. One day, when Judas was three years old, she left to visit her family in Galilee and never returned."

"When did that happen?" Gallus asked.

Simon shrugged. "Almost seventeen years ago." Eyes misting, Simon leaned against a post. "I went to Galilee to find her. When I reached her home, her family claimed she was still in Judea. I searched everywhere; for in my heart, I thought I would find her in Galilee. One day I saw a woman who looked like Rachael working in a field near the Jordan River. I left my donkey on the road and dashed into the field but she ran from me when I called to her. That was the last I saw of her. I kept walking through the field until I reached a clearing. There I found some men and boys sitting around a fire. "Had they seen a woman pass by?" I asked. "No," they replied."

Looking at the floor, Simon continued, "That was the last I remember. I woke a few hours later, lying next to the clearing. I was certain the men found my donkey and took my baggage. Now, I would be dependent on the good will of other travelers on the Jordan Road." He looked at Judas and Gallus. "Not a good feeling!"

Gallus whistled. "I understand."

Visibly moved, Simon paused for a moment before resuming his story. "I stayed next to a clump of lilac bushes near the road and shouted for help to people passing by. A few hesitated, but who wants to help a man looking like a tramp next to the road? Finally, a man stopped. He treated my wounds, and gave me a ride on his donkey to the next city." Simon looked at Gallus. "This might surprise you, but the man was, or I should say is a Samaritan."

Gallus smiled. "Judeans think they're the only ones who help other people. Don't you know people help each other all over the world?"

"Yes," Simon replied. "What you don't understand, Gallus is that I'm a Jew and he is a Samaritan. Jews and Samaritans have been enemies for six hundred years." With a wave of his hand, Simon continued, "But in this case, we are lifelong friends. In fact, the man who found me is now my business partner, Abiram, the man Judas will work with in Caesarea and Galilee." Looking at Gallus, Simon added, "Abiram sends fruits and vegetables to southern Judea and I ship salt and imported goods from the territories east of Sinai." Simon lifted his cup. "Now we have decided to expand our business to include the sale of fish caught in the Sea of Galilee." He glanced at Judas. "Judas will share in our partnership. He will travel to Galilee to finalize a deal I made with a fisherman named Andrew bar Jonah. He fishes with a group of boats owned by a Zebedee of Capernaum."

Placing his cup back on the table, Simon put his hand on Judas' head. "Remember always, your dependence on Yahweh. Be true to the Torah and the words of our prophets and patriarchs." Tears rolled down Simon's cheeks, fading into his beard as he embraced Judas. "I sent a message to our friend, Joseph of Arimathea, asking his permission for you to stay at his house in Jerusalem before you travel to Caesarea." Then Simon's mood brightened. "Meantime," he said, "I'll look for a fine Judean girl for you to marry." Responding to Judas' glare, he added, "Alright. I won't make a commitment until you see her."

Judas grasped his father. "That doesn't worry me. I'm afraid you'll keep her for yourself if you feel she's good enough to marry me."

"No, son, I wouldn't do that. After all these years, I still love your mother. I didn't divorce her, though I have the right to do so. And I certainly don't believe in marrying more than one woman."

Judas gazed into his father's eyes. "I'm worried about you, living alone now that I'm leaving."

"I have my friends."

"It's not the same."

"I know, but don't trouble yourself over me. You have your life to live." Looking at the sky, Simon added, "You better hurry if you want to reach Hebron by sundown."

Judas bar Simon finished his breakfast, excused himself, and went to his room to prepare for his trip.

In the courtyard, Simon told Gallus, "You will reach Hebron by sundown. Tomorrow, you should be able to catch on with a caravan of merchants traveling from Hebron to Jerusalem."

When Judas returned to the courtyard, Simon wept over him, saying, "May God leave the sins of our fathers at my doorstep, and bless you with a safe journey." Then he gave Judas a robe. "Let this be a symbol of our love for each other. It's the finest robe I own. I pray it will protect you until you return home."

* * *

Judas and Gallus spent their first day traveling an isolated road that was no more than a narrow path blown over with sand. Fortunately, Judas knew the landmarks and led them to Hebron well before dusk. They stayed the night in a house belonging to a cousin of Judas, then left for Jerusalem the next morning with a group of traders and soldiers. It was an interesting trip for Judas and Gallus. Their traveling companions were coarse men who enjoyed food, wine, and lusty stories. Gallus, for his professed ways of the world, sat in awe as the men exchanged stories during their mid-day meal. It was several days before Judas, upon reflection, realized there was a liberal sprinkling of lies mixed with the narratives.

* * *

Joseph of Arimathea arrived home from the Temple and spotted his son Reuben talking to Judas in the courtyard. He greeted Judas and said, "I received your father's message and look forward to spending some time with you." He stepped back to observe Judas and asked, "When did you arrive?"

"Almost mid-day," Judas replied.

Joseph glanced in the direction of the Upper City. "Then you missed the crowds at the market. For some reason the usual shipments of food and milk were delayed until late afternoon."

Reuben invited Judas to a comfortable cushion and gestured to a servant standing nearby. The servant quickly poured a cup of wine for each man.

Judas offered a toast to Joseph. "My father sends his greetings and prays for your continued good health."

"Thank you and my best wishes to him as well," Joseph replied. After drinking from his cup, he asked, "What brings you to Jerusalem?"

"I'm on my way to Caesarea...to work with my father's partner, Abiram." Judas carefully measured his words for he felt the effects from wine he drank earlier with Reuben.

Joseph's eyebrows rose. "Abiram?"

"Yes."

"So you will work for a Samaritan in a Roman city."

"It sounds bad, doesn't it?" Judas drained his cup. "I...I hope..." Judas burped. "...I have a mission." He hiccupped.

"Hold your breath Judas," Reuben said.

"What?"

"Hold your breath. That'll cure your hiccups."

Judas snapped to attention and held his breath. "What a curse," he complained. "I get...hiccups every time I...drink wine too fast."

"There are worse curses," Joseph remarked.

"Do you know Abiram?" asked Judas.

"I met him a few times," Joseph replied. "He's honest; he keeps the Sabbath and obeys the Law of Moses." Joseph winked. "Samaritans aren't quite as bad as people would like us to believe."

Judas frowned, "I don't trust Samaritans."

Joseph got up, drew a cup of water from a small brass jar and handed it to Judas without comment. Judas sipped the water until his hiccups subsided.

Joseph continued, "Abiram is an ambitious man. My friends tell me he intends to expand his business to all of Galilee."

Judas groaned.

"What's wrong?"

"I don't think I will like Galilee," Judas replied.

Joseph laughed. "Let's see, you once told me you don't want to live in Kerioth. Now you say you don't trust Samaritans and you don't like Galilee. You're going to run out of places to live." Joseph's face sparkled.

Judas' face reflected a different emotion. "Why don't people take me seriously?" he retorted.

"I'm sorry," Joseph replied. "If Abiram intends to expand to Galilee, he'll need a few Jews, heh? Besides, your mother was a Galilean."

"Don't remind me," Judas mumbled. "Surely you know there are better places to live than Galilee."

"Maybe." Joseph grinned. "It wouldn't hurt any of us to spend some time in Galilee. After all, Galileans are Jews." Joseph gestured to the servant who refilled their cups.

"With respect, father," Reuben interjected. "They are Jews, but they're not like us."

Eyebrows raised, Joseph asked, "Don't you think God created us the same underneath?"

"Even Romans?" asked Reuben.

"Even Gauls?" queried Judas.

"Perhaps all men." Joseph replied.

Judas licked his lips. "Did you resign from the Sanhedrin?" he asked cautiously.

"Why do you ask?"

"You sound more like a Greek or Egyptian than a Jew."

"I don't share my ideas with everyone," Joseph replied. "Give me credit for some prudence."

The younger men raised their cups. "Here's to your sense of prudence, whatever that is."

Joseph looked up when a servant signaled him. "It's time for supper." Then he paused and sniffed. "I smell the aroma of fresh fish from the Sea of

Galilee," he said to Judas. "I hope you enjoy it." Joseph's humor was lost on Judas.

They reclined on several cushions placed around a low table and began their meal with a traditional blessing. Then Joseph drew the steam from the fish toward him. "Olive oil and almonds, that's the best way to cook fish," he commented as the servants brought steaming bowls of beans, chickpeas, and barley bread.

Later Joseph asked Judas, "How are you traveling to Caesarea?"

Judas dipped a piece of bread in a bowl of honey before answering. "By caravan," he muttered. The honey dripped on his fingers and soon stuck to everything he touched.

"I'm going to Arimathea...maybe in a week," Joseph said. "You could travel with me that far, then go to Joppa and catch a boat to Caesarea."

Judas licked his fingers and reached for the dish filled with grapes and figs. "I promised my father that I would try to arrive in Capernaum early next week," he replied as he nodded his approval of the mint flavoring on the dessert. "I'm not even sure where Capernaum is, but I expect that Abiram will show me the way."

"Capernaum is in the north, near the Sea of Galilee." Joseph went to his writing table and unrolled a scroll with a map inscribed on it. He showed it to Judas. "Here, on the northwest corner of the Sea. It's a fishing town."

Judas shook his head. "See, the Galileans are different. They fish. Who ever heard of a Judean fishing?" He looked at Joseph and Reuben. "Do you like water?"

"I use water for my bath," replied Joseph.

"I'm afraid of the sea," answered Reuben.

"There you are; normal people don't like water." Judas looked over Joseph's shoulder. "How close is this Carpon to Tiberias?"

"Capernaum, Judas, Capernaum. It is north of Tiberias, on the other side of the mountains from Caesarea."

They returned to the courtyard after the meal and lounged on cushions, each caught up in their own thoughts. After a while, Joseph raised a finger. "I didn't expect you to spend such a short time with us. I was hoping to take you to the Temple, but that can wait until the next time you are in Jerusalem. Maybe then we will have a chance for you to meet some of our leaders."

"I would like that," Judas replied.

CHAPTER THREE

Jesus returned to Galilee in the power of the Spirit, and news about him spread through the whole countryside.
He was teaching in their synagogues, and everyone praised him.
He went to Nazareth, where he had been brought up, and on the Sabbath day he went into the synagogue, as was his custom. He stood up to read, and the scroll of the prophet Isaiah was handed to him. Unrolling it, he found the place where it is written:

"The Spirit of the Lord is on me, because he has anointed me to proclaim good news to the poor. He has sent me to proclaim freedom for the prisoners and recovery of sight for the blind, to set the oppressed free, to proclaim the year of the Lord's favor."

Then he rolled up the scroll, gave it back to the attendant and sat down. The eyes of everyone in the synagogue were fastened on him.
He began by saying to them, "Today this scripture is fulfilled in your hearing."

All spoke well of him and were amazed at the gracious words that came from his lips.
"Isn't this Joseph's son?" they asked.

Jesus said to them, "Surely you will quote this proverb to me: 'Physician, heal yourself!' And you will tell me, 'Do here in your hometown what we have heard that you did in Capernaum.' "
"Truly I tell you," he continued, "prophets are not accepted in their hometowns. I assure you that there were many widows in Israel in Elijah's time, when the sky was shut for three and a half years and there was a severe famine throughout the land. Yet Elijah was not sent to any of them, but to a widow in Zarephath in the region of Sidon. And there were many in Israel with leprosy in the time of Elisha the prophet, yet not one of them was cleansed—only Naaman the Syrian."
All the people in the synagogue were furious when they heard this.

They got up, drove him out of the town, and took him to the brow of the hill on which the town was built, in order to throw him off the cliff.
But he walked right through the crowd and went on his way.

Luke 4:14-30

Fearing the anger of the people in Nazareth, Jesus went to Capernaum and spent time with James and John, the sons of Zebedee. He told them about his baptism in the Jordan as well as the time he spent in the desert. One day Jesus shared a mid-day meal with James and John after they returned from morning fishing. "What did you decide to do after the time you spent in the desert?" asked James.

Jesus smiled. "It's hard to explain."

"Are you telling us something different than what you have talked about during the past five years?"

"Is it possible for a small group of people to change the world?" Jesus asked.

John grunted. "Only if you kill the Romans and that would take a large group of people…like an army." He tossed the core from his pear at to a dog standing nearby.

"I hadn't considered murder or war as a practical plan."

"What exactly do you want to do?" asked James.

Jesus stroked his beard. He had a thin light beard, unlike the thick, dark beards seen on Judeans. "Don't you notice how people are treated?" he gestured as he continued; "It's not just the Romans or the Greeks. Our own leaders; the high priests and scribes rob the poor and oppress them with laws and rules that have nothing to do with our covenant with God."

"We have noticed that," James replied. "But what can we do." He looked at John. "I don't know much about these things, but I think John may be right. Only the people with power can change how the world works."

Jesus shook his heads. "We have the power to change the way things are done."

"We are fishermen," John responded. "We barely have enough time to repair boats, catch fish, and eat our meals. Also, James has a family. Can you imagine how his wife would react if he decided he wanted to change the world?"

"Don't forget our father Zebedee," added James. "He thinks we spend too much time with people like you as it is."

"People like me?"

"He says that you should stick to working like the rest of us."

"But I do work. I am a carpenter. He knows that."

"You are also a rabbi. He says you should spend more time earning an honest living and less time telling others how they should live their lives." James pointed a finger at Jesus. "What do you think about that?"

Jesus face reddened. "If that is so, why are we having these discussions?"

"I'm not sure. There's something about you that is different. Something that draws me to you."

John nodded in agreement. "He also wonders why you never married."

Jesus looked at John. "Why aren't you married?"

John shrugged. "I have time. You are at least fifteen years older than I."

Jesus laughed and put his hand on John's shoulder. "Surely you have the temper and intensity of your father. I like that."

James and John started to leave, but Jesus called them back. "One more thing. We could start by helping poor people find work...work with honest pay. Think about it."

They both nodded their agreement but as they walked away, John looked at James and said, "We have enough trouble getting honest pay from our father. What can we do about the rich merchants in Galilee?"

* * *

On the following week, Jesus found work with his friend, Philip, a stone mason from Bethsaida. They were hired to repair some buildings damaged by fire. At night he would meet with Philip, Andrew, and his brother Simon.[2] Andrew and Simon fished with Zebedee's fleet off the coast of Capernaum. Sometimes the fishermen brought their wives and children to these sessions and they would eat their evening meal sitting around a fire listening as Jesus talked about God and the prophets.

One night Simon asked Jesus if he intended to continue preaching in Galilee.

Jesus replied, "Why do you ask?"

Simon looked straight into his eyes and said, "It seems that you are having no effect on our people. Nothing changes after you preach in the synagogue or even when you seem to cure people who are sick." He waved his hands dismissively. "People either walk away shaking their heads or they become angry and send you away."

"People have trouble understanding what I am saying. For some, it doesn't fit their deep set ideas; for others my words differ from those of others who preach to them."

"What makes you so sure you are right and they are wrong?" Simon continued as the others nodded.

Jesus pointed to Simon. "Make no mistake about who I am or what I am trying to do. Do not think that I have come to do away with the Law of Moses or the teachings of the prophets. I have not come to do away with them, but

2 Later to be known as Peter or Simon Peter.

to make their teachings come true. I will choose people from among you who will help me do this!"

"What do you mean by that?" Simon asked in a quiet voice.

"I need people who will go into the world to spread the word of God. Those who follow me will drive out evil spirits, heal diseases, and show people that common men have more wisdom than the learned scribes who live in the Temple."

Simon smiled. "In between catching enough fish to feed my family?" His wife Naomi nodded when she heard his words.

Jesus responded, "Simon, you and the others I choose will become fishers of men. Your catch will be bountiful and pleasing to God."

For the first time, Andrew entered into the conversation. "It is time for a change. There are some who believe that the coming of the Messiah is close at hand. Perhaps he walks among us already." Looking at Jesus he added, "And perhaps John the Baptizer and Jesus the carpenter are anointed to be his prophets."

Simon shrugged and looked at Andrew. "Brother, you spent too much time in that monastery at Qumran. Those radical dreamers fill peoples' heads with wild talk about Messiahs and a war between good and evil. Stick to fishing and let Jesus save souls."

Andrew laughed. "Where did you get all that information?"

"I'm no fool. I hear the talk going on in town and on the lake." Simon yawned, looked at Naomi and said, "It's late and we need to be on the lake early in the morning. Let's go."

Andrew rose to his feet and clasped Simon's arm. "You're right; I expect that the merchant's son from Judea will be here any day now to make arrangements to ship fish to Jerusalem." Then he turned to Jesus and said, "There are many people gathering followers who are willing to cling to their interpretation of the Scriptures. From what you told me so far, it seems you want to form a community that will follow your version of what has passed and what is to come. I'm willing to work with you if you wish."

Jesus embraced Andrew. "Thank you, my friend. I accept your offer." As they parted Jesus added, "Perhaps you can convince your Judean friend to join us as well."

"That would be interesting," replied Andrew as he headed for home.

* * *

Jesus shared living quarters with Philip while they worked in Capernaum. They talked almost every day about the Kingdom of God and Jesus' vision that the Kingdom was at hand. Philip knew the brothers James and John, the sons of Zebedee, as well as Andrew and Simon, the sons of Jonah. He asked Jesus if those men had agreed to join him.

Jesus replied, "Andrew will but Simon, James, and John have not made a decision."

"Do you think they will?"

"Yes, but they need to work it out with their families and Zebedee. It's possible that our work will take us far from home. That will disrupt their work and families."

"Simon told me that you have angered people with your talk. That you are nothing more than a magician with all that fancy talk and supposed miracles. Wouldn't it be easier if you just settled down as a carpenter and perhaps a husband?"

"And leave God's work to others?"

"Yes. Who ordained you to take the place of the priests and scribes?"

"I was anointed by God in the desert after the last Passover. The Spirit of God touched me." Jesus sighed, "I knew from then on that I have to follow the Word of God to whatever place it will take me. But I cannot do this by myself. That's why I need Simon, James, John and you!"

"ME? What do I know about kingdoms and the other things you talk about?"

"Those who follow me will know these things when the time is right. They will go out into the world and announce that the Kingdom of Heaven is near! They will heal the sick, bring the dead back to life, heal those who suffer from dreaded skin diseases, and drive out demons."

Philip shook his head. "I don't know much, but I do know that our people have a long history of killing our prophets. Is that what you want?"

"My followers will go out like sheep among wolves. There will be men who will arrest them and whip them in the synagogues. They may be brought before rulers and kings to tell the Good News to them and to the Gentiles. But remember one thing; the words spoken to them will not be our words, they will come from the Spirit of our Father speaking through them."

Philip shook his head. "No wonder you are having trouble convincing your friends. Not only will they risk their job and family, but they may end up dead or in prison."

"I will not lie to them, or you. I am well aware of the history of our people, their intolerance for the words of the prophets, and the danger we will face."

* * *

Jesus spent the summer working as a carpenter by day and teaching the people he choose as his disciples at night. He also preached in the synagogues in Northern Galilee when the opportunity presented itself. By fall, his cousin Thomas joined his small group of followers along with Philip, James, John, Andrew and Simon. Later Nathanael, a friend of Philip, and Levi, a tax collector, joined the group. Levi later became known as Matthew.

Matthew (Levi) held a great banquet for Jesus at his house, and a large crowd of tax collectors and others ate with them. But the teachers of the law complained, "Why do you eat and drink with tax collectors and sinners?"

Jesus answered them, "It is not the healthy who need a doctor, but the sick. I have not come to call the righteous, but sinners to repentance."

CHAPTER FOUR

"You have heard that it was said, 'Love your neighbor and hate your enemy.' But I tell you, love your enemies and pray for those who persecute you, that you may be children of your Father in heaven. He causes his sun to rise on the evil and the good, and sends rain on the righteous and the unrighteous. If you love those who love you, what reward will you get? Are not even the tax collectors doing that? And if you greet only your own people, what are you doing more than others? Do not even pagans do that? Be perfect, therefore, as your heavenly Father is perfect.

Matthew 5:43-48

Judas of Kerioth arrived in Capernaum and met with Andrew and Zebedee. Judas provided the details regarding requirements for the preservation and shipment of fish from Galilee to Judea. They also finalized plans for his father Simon and their partner Abiram to ship salt, fine fabrics, and other products brought from east of the Great Salt Sea.

Andrew arranged for Judas to stay at a small inn located on the east edge of Capernaum. Judas felt that the inn was no better than a run down shack in Judea but his room did have a bed and a wash basin which suited his immediate needs. He accepted the arrangement, knowing that he only planned to remain in Capernaum for a month or two, or until he was satisfied that these crude fishermen would do their job properly. It was a lonely time for Judas in this unfamiliar province and he soon longed to return home.

One day Andrew invited Judas to what had now become regular evening sessions with Jesus. Judas welcomed the opportunity to sit near this man and listen to him talk about God and man. Judas did not consider himself to be a religious person but he did have a curiosity about what these preachers had to say. This was new for him because Kerioth was too small and set in its ways to attract people like Jesus.

That night changed Judas' life in a way that he would never understand. He could tell that Jesus was no ordinary preacher; that he had a special gift of perceiving and explaining the mysteries of life. But later, before he went to bed, he shook his head. "I must have been dreaming," he said to himself, "or maybe I drank too much wine with my evening meal. Jesus is just another preacher who knows how to influence these ignorant Galilean peasants."

None the less, Judas continued to find reasons to spend time with this group of people with whom he had nothing in common. One night Judas stayed near the fire until only Jesus remained.

Jesus started the conversation by asking how long Judas intended to stay in Capernaum.

"Maybe a few weeks," Judas replied absently.

"I sense that you don't like it here."

Judas shrugged. "How can you tell?"

"Well," Jesus replied, "you make very little effort to talk to the people around the fire. You sit away from everyone but Andrew. Do you share the common Judean belief that Galileans are uneducated and relative newcomers to true Judaism?" He waved his arm and added, "Perhaps we are uncivilized compared to our brothers from Judea."

Judas face reddened. "Why…why no. Why do you say that?"

"Because it is true. Judas, I can read your soul."

"What do you see?"

"I see a man looking for answers but he does not even realize it. It's possible that someday you will do great things." Jesus put his hand on Judas' shoulder. "Perhaps you will be remembered long after we are both gone."

Suddenly feeling uncomfortable, Judas replied, "You don't know me, you don't know my family, and you don't know what I think."

"Then my perception of you is wrong?"

"Maybe. Would it surprise you if I told you that my mother is a Galilean?" Judas lost his breath momentarily when he realized what he said.

Jesus smiled. "It does surprise me. Is she still alive?"

Judas looked at the ground. "I don't know."

"How long has it been since you last saw her?"

"I don't want to talk about it."

"I understand." Jesus picked up a stick and poked at the fire's dying embers. "Are you interested in what I am doing and why I am doing it?"

"I'm willing to listen."

"Let me ask a question. Do you feel that our leaders are fulfilling the spirit of the Law?"

"I guess they are. How would I know?"

"Aren't we taught to care for those in need?"

"I think so."

"You are half right. Pharisees outside of Israel take care of those in need. But Pharisees and Sadducees in Judea and Galilee willfully ignore those in need."

"Perhaps those people in Israel who are in need would be well advised to work hard enough to support themselves and their families."

Jesus noticed an air of indignation in Judas' voice. "I won't argue with that, but I know people in Capernaum and Bethsaida who are willing to work hard all day, all week, and all month to support their families but there is no work for them."

"Why not?"

"Galileans are farmers and fishermen. Farmers and fishermen usually earn only enough money to support their families. They seldom need extra people to help them do their jobs. There are also people unable to work because of bad health or physical limitations. We are a poor country with more people than jobs."

"What can we do to solve this problem?"

"We should strive to change society so that every person is treated with respect and compassion." Jesus raised a finger. "*And* reduce the poverty rising from the inequality of the rich and the poor."

"I need to think about that," replied Judas. He yawned and added, "It's late, I plan on leaving early tomorrow morning, but I will return in a few months. For now I need sleep but I would like to talk more when I return"

Jesus nodded his agreement and they went their separate ways.

Judas left for Caesarea the next day satisfied that he had fulfilled the expectations of his father and Abiram. He was also left with the feeling that he had not seen the last of this Galilean preacher.

CHAPTER FIVE

On the third day a wedding took place at Cana in Galilee. Jesus' mother was there, and Jesus and his disciples had also been invited to the wedding. When the wine was gone, Jesus' mother said to him, "They have no more wine."

"Woman, why do you involve me?" Jesus replied. "My hour has not yet come."

John 2:1-4

During the time Jesus was on earth, there were two events that gave the average person a chance to celebrate; holidays and weddings. Holidays were traditionally celebrated in Jerusalem, but weddings were celebrated near the home of the bride and groom. The average person didn't always have the time or money to attend holidays in Jerusalem but they usually found a way to attend a wedding in or near their home town. Such was the wedding at Cana. By anybody's standard, this was a very large wedding with sisters, brothers, aunts, uncles, cousins, and friends attending. Guests from as far away as Jerusalem and Jericho came to Cana to celebrate this marriage of two first born children from different clans. Jesus came to the wedding personally as a guest and officially as a rabbi. His mother, Mary, came with her sister Salome as guests and caterers. John and James, the sons of Zebedee and Salome, functioned as ushers and servers.

The ceremony began when the bride and groom began their short procession at dusk through the street that led from her father's house to their new home. Musicians, dancing as they played, led the way. They were followed by the wedding couple, guided by lamps held along the route by the wedding guests. The bride's braided hair, radiant with semi precious stones, seemed to reflect the light from each lamp, creating an aura of beauty and mystery about her face. Her attendants followed, lighting the way for the guests who joined the procession. Spectators found themselves caught in the swaying crowd and began to feel a sense of exhilaration and followed the parade snaking through the community.

When the procession reached the home of the bride and groom, the musicians parted, making a path that led the bride and groom to a large canopy in front of their house. Jesus came to bless the couple, the meal, the house, the wine, the guests, and anything else that was part of the ritual. Then the newlyweds sat on large cushions where they presided over the wedding feast like a king and queen. They watched the pulse of the celebration quicken as if the guests intended to party late into the night.

Jesus and John watched the activity, drinking wine and aimlessly eating canapés made from fruit, vegetables, and flat bread. Andrew's brother Simon joined them, bringing an attractive woman and a young boy. He drew the woman close to Jesus and said, "This is my friend Mary Marcia. She is from Jerusalem." Pointing to the boy, he added, "And this is her son, Mark. Her daughter Rebecca is somewhere in this crowd, probably playing with relatives she hasn't seen in a while."

Jesus smiled and said, "Welcome to Galilee. Have you been here before?" He noted the warmth radiating from her dark brown eyes.

"Once several years ago…before my father died. Celecia, the bride's mother, is my cousin."

"Cana is a long journey to visit a woman you only saw once several years ago."

"Celecia has often stayed at our home when her family came up to Jerusalem to celebrate our holidays."

Jesus looked at Mark. "And how old are you, young man?"

Mark shuffled his feet. Mary Marcia answered, "He's thirteen."

"Fourteen."

Mary Marcia looked at Mark. "Not until next month." She looked at Jesus. "They want to grow up in a hurry."

Then Simon said to Jesus, "I wanted you to meet Mary Marcia because she has a large home in Jerusalem. Andrew and I have stayed there on several occasions."

Jesus nodded and looked at Mary Marcia. "So you rent rooms to people traveling to Jerusalem?"

"I rent to people I know and trust," She replied. "Although, I generally do not charge rent as my friend Simon implies."

"How does your husband feel about this?"

"I am a widow."

Jesus looked at Simon. "A widow? Did you know?" He smiled. "Of course you did."

Mary Marcia and Simon both blushed.

Jesus said, "I'm sorry to hear that. Who was your husband and when did he die?"

"His name was Veturius Marcius," she replied. "He was an officer in the Roman army. He died five years ago when his ship was attacked by pirates."

Jesus turned his attention to Mark. "Do you want to be a soldier like your father?"

"I did when I was younger but not now."

"What then?"

Mark hesitated for a moment, and then replied, "I want to be a historian like those who work in the Library at Alexandria."

"I have a cousin living in Alexandria," Mary Marcia added. "Mark already spent a summer at the Library."

"I am familiar with the Library," Jesus replied. "It is a remarkable institution. Mark will learn a lot from those scholars who have dedicated their lives to learning." He put his hand on Mary's arm and felt a slight tension. "I must leave now but I look forward to visiting you the next time I travel to Jerusalem."

That night, the guests slept in tents erected wherever there was a spot of land available and left for their homes the next morning. Mary Marcia stayed on for a few days visiting with her cousin Celicia.

CHAPTER SIX

The LORD takes his place in court; he rises to judge the people.
The LORD enters into judgment against the elders and leaders of his people:

"It is you who have ruined my vineyard; the plunder from the poor is in your houses. What do you mean by crushing my people and grinding the faces of the poor?" declares the Lord, the Lord Almighty.

Isaiah 3:14-15

On the following Sunday, Jesus took James, John, and Simon to an encampment a short distance south of Capernaum. It was a Paupers' Camp sprawled at the foot of a hill located beyond a scraggly bean field. A barefoot woman dressed in a shredded tunic chased crows and dogs away from the vegetables. John noticed her feet, black and hardened from the sharp stones littering the hillside. The trees that once shaded the hill were long ago cut for firewood, leaving only isolated stumps that reminded him of an army of shrunken sentinels. When John looked down on the camp, he saw half a dozen roofless shacks and a few moldy tents.

Jesus looked at John, Simon, and James and asked, "What part of your world looks like this?"

John looked at the litter scattered around and replied, "This is not part of our world."

"We can change their lives if we change the way we think about them," Jesus replied.

"How?"

"They're here because we treat them as if they're not human. Do you know what that means?"

"I'm not sure."

"It means we can ignore their suffering and not worry. We can call them names and condemn them to a life of poverty and despair." Jesus continued, "Do we worry when dogs or pigs suffer?"

“I don’t,” John answered without thinking. Remembering Jesus’ earlier comments he braced himself for a parable.

Instead, Jesus spied his cousin Thomas near a shack made from twigs and rags and hurried through the beaten underbrush to reach him.

Simon and the others stayed in the background as Thomas greeted them.

“Did you find someone to help clean this place?” Jesus asked.

“There’s a boy named James bar Alphaeus.” Thomas pointed to a hill behind them. “He lives in one of those caves with his mother.”

“Who else?”

Thomas put his hands on his hips. “Do you remember the woman, Mary, from Magdala--the one you cured?”

“I do,” Jesus replied.

“She came looking for you a few days ago. She says she wants to live here.”

Jesus raised his eyes to meet Thomas’. Thomas returned an intense gaze. Then Jesus nodded and looked at Simon. “See? Some people...”

“What happened to her?” James interrupted.

“She was possessed by demons,” Thomas answered.

John laughed. “Don’t tell me you believe in de...” He saw from the look on Jesus and Thomas’ faces that they did believe.

“You should’ve heard what Zebedee said about you this morning,” Simon mumbled.

“I probably will someday,” Jesus responded. Then he looked at Thomas. “Is she...Mary, well enough to survive here?”

“I think so. She seems more settled than before.” Thomas relaxed his gaze, the tension of a moment before passed.

Thomas pointed to a young man walking toward them. “That’s James I told you about...James bar Alphaeus. His mother is also called Mary.”

“Where is his father?”

“She said he died fighting the Romans at Hazor.”

Simon looked at the boy as he approached. “I’ve seen him before, begging for food at the harbor. His mother is very poor.”

* * *

Jesus and the four men left the Paupers’ Camp, heading for their homes in Capernaum and Bethsaida. On the way Thomas told Jesus that he heard that Herod Antipas imprisoned John the Baptist.

“Why?” Jesus asked.

“They say that John was preaching in the streets of Machaerus, condemning Herod for marrying his niece Herodias.”

Jesus smiled. “That shouldn’t bother John. The Herods deserve each other.”

“John also condemned them because both Herod Antipas and Herodias were previously married. In fact Herodias was married to a half brother of Herod Antipas.”

“It runs in the family. How many times did Herod the Great marry?”

Thomas shrugged. “I don’t know, maybe nine or ten times.”

“Well, there you are,” he replied, giving Thomas a light shove. “I hope he doesn’t irritate that fox Herod any more. There is important work to be done.”

“You said John is a prophet. You know what we do to prophets.”

“Yes, we kill them,” Jesus answered with a frown. “I wonder if there is anything we can do to help him?”

“Machaerus is too far from here. I doubt whether we could reach there in time to do any good.”

Jesus stroked his beard. “I wonder why John was there in the first place. I thought he was going to concentrate on Judea?”

“Who knows?” Thomas muttered.

Their companions listened to the conversation between Jesus and Thomas as they headed for home and wondered what all the fuss was about.

CHAPTER SEVEN

Be joyful at your festival—you, your sons and daughters, your male and female servants, and the Levites, the foreigners, the fatherless and the widows who live in your towns. For seven days celebrate the festival to the LORD your God at the place the LORD will choose. For the LORD your God will bless you in all your harvest and in all the work of your hands, and your joy will be complete.

Deuteronomy 16:14-15

There were several holidays celebrated in Jerusalem by believers from the entire known world. Passover was one of the most important holidays and usually drew a sizeable number of pilgrims. This city of seventy-five thousand often grew to a metropolis twice that size when the pilgrims were present. At night, people stayed with friends and relatives in Jerusalem, in tents outside the walls of the city, or in small towns located within an hour's walk to the city. Mary Marcia owned a house large enough to include a courtyard and living quarters on the lower level and an upper room large enough to provide sleeping quarters for several people. It was to this house that Jesus, John, Andrew, Philip, and Aaron, the son of James bar Zebedee came to celebrate Passover.

Two nights before their Passover celebration, the guests at Mary Marcia's house heard loud sounds and watched smoke rise above the city. The next day Amos, a neighbor, ventured to the market for fresh fruits and vegetables. Returning a short time later, breathless and excited, he came to Mary's house and told everyone what he heard.

"Yesterday, several construction workers were injured when a section of a building they were repairing collapsed," he gasped. "I think they were Galileans. Then last night, a group of Galileans started fighting with the other construction workers near the market in the Lower City."

Amos leaned against the wall to catch his breath. "A Roman patrol came to stop the fighting," he continued with short bursts of words. "But both groups turned on the soldiers and drove them back to the fortress. I heard they killed at least six soldiers. That's the last time anyone will see a Roman soldier in the streets of Jerusalem." Amos puffed his chest as if he had personally driven the soldiers back to the fortress. "This is the part that really surprised me. Apparently some Zealots saw the men fighting and decided to attack the places in the Lower City where the Romans and Greeks have their shops. The Zealots smashed their pagan idols and burned their buildings. I heard several Romans and Greeks died in that riot."

Andrew, numbed by what he just heard, said, "Our people did that? Why?" He shook his head. "I can't believe it happened."

"Don't doubt it," Amos advised. "Tonight they'll take control of the city from the Romans."

"They?"

"The Zealots, the rioters. The soldiers are in the Antonia Fortress and the Zealots will kill them if they try to leave." Amos beamed. "The one who told me these things said they'll burn the fortress tonight if they have a chance."

"How can this happen?" Andrew asked with more than a little disbelief in his voice.

A shout from the other side of the wall followed by a staff banging at the gate interrupted them.

"Who is it?" Mark asked.

"Let me in!" a voice growled. "Are you going to make me stand in this heat all day?" Mary nodded to Mark and he opened the gate wide enough to allow a very short, fat man totter into the courtyard. The man slouched as he walked, as if he were looking at the ground for money.

Mark flinched when he saw the man's long gray hair and untrimmed beard. The man shuffled over to greet Mary, and then looked at the others. "What are you staring at?" he muttered. "Haven't you seen an old man before?"

"We were talking about the riots," Mary replied.

"What riots?" he asked.

"There were fights last night between the construction workers," Mary said. "Then some Zealots fought a Roman patrol. Apparently the Zealots killed some of the soldiers and set fires in the Lower City."

"I didn't see any fires," the man said.

"But we heard the sounds and saw the flames from our windows, and this morning Amos heard stories in the marketplace."

The old man put his finger to his lips. "Be careful, my child; Fires look brighter and sounds are louder when you view them through a window. I walked through the city this morning and saw nothing of what you describe."

"What about the Romans?" Andrew asked.

The man sniffed, "Everywhere! Everywhere! I think the whole Roman army is in Jerusalem."

They looked at Amos, who gazed at the sky. "I only told you what I heard," he mumbled.

The old man pointed to young Aaron. "Who is this?"

"My nephew," John answered. Pointing to Andrew and Philip, he added, "We came here from Galilee."

"Good looking boy," the man observed. Aaron winced.

"He's no longer a boy," John said. "Who are you?"

"Rabbi Joachim ben Eleazar--from Antioch," Mary interjected.

Aaron cautiously observed the old man. For the first time he noticed the man's bare feet were black and calloused.

"My cousin Barnabas studied at his synagogue," Mary said.

The sight of the man left Aaron speechless.

"He comes to our house every year for Passover," Mary continued. "Except last year."

Gray hair poked through the holes in his skull cap.

"He walks the entire distance from Antioch to Jerusalem."

The man's back was round, like a fat wheel.

Aaron continued to stare.

The Rabbi's tunic hung almost to the ground.

Aaron struggled for composure. He wanted to stare at the man forever, but finally walked over and stood next to John.

* * *

Philip and Andrew spent most of the day at the Temple. "There were riots last night," Philip reported after he and Andrew cleansed themselves and returned to the courtyard.

Amos looked pleased.

"And some fires," Philip continued. "They weren't widespread or particularly destructive." He picked a pear from a tray and tossed it in the air. "The flames we saw from the window were from bonfires built by people trying to keep warm in the open fields near the arena. It's still cold at night on the countryside. A man at the market told me the Romans caught a few rioters. He said the Romans will execute them."

"Were any soldiers killed or injured?" Amos asked.

"I don't know." Philip bit into the pear. "Apparently the Romans are worried that there will be more problems. A man told me Pontius Pilate is in

Caesarea and he sent a message to the Tribune in charge of Jerusalem to keep order at any cost."

"Pontius Pilate?" Mark whispered.

"Is something wrong?" Philip asked.

"My father talked about him once. He said that the Romans removed Pontius Pilate from his last post because of his intemperance." Mark continued, "My father said that Pontius Pilate has a violent temper."

"What will the Romans do?" asked John.

"Execute a few Jews," Joachim answered as he shuffled toward a bench. "Apparently, the Zealots killed three Roman soldiers last night," he muttered. "The Roman tribune in charge of the Jerusalem army announced this morning that they will retaliate by executing six Jews."

Later that day, Mark, Philip, and Andrew went to the market. People with scarves covering their faces hurried from stall to stall, eyes darting at the soldiers casually strolling through the main street. Mark heard rumors every place they shopped. One man said, "The Romans will execute thirty Jews, ten for each soldier." Another added, "The Romans will close the Temple during the Passover celebration."

The people at Mary Marcia's house learned later that the Romans had decided on several courses of action. First, they would torture and execute the men they caught the previous evening. Second, they planned to close the city gates at noon each day during Passover week to control the crowds. Finally, they decided to suspend construction activities during the week of Passover and keep the workers outside the city walls.

Because only a limited amount of people were allowed in the city at one time, it was left to the Jewish leaders to decide who would worship at the Temple and when they would worship.

* * *

The next morning, the day before Passover, Jesus and John left early to visit with friends while Andrew and Philip went to the Temple with young Aaron. Once there, they mixed with the crowds underneath the Temple esplanade where the merchants exchanged money and sold animals for sacrifice.

"Get out of my way!" a swarthy slave screamed when his cart bounced against Aaron. "Move! Move! Move!" he hollered as he wiggled through the crowd. Philip felt uncomfortable with the crowds of people and animals jostling against each other. To him, Temple worship was a messy way for the Jews to pay homage to God.

Later, while he and Andrew waited to purchase their offering, Aaron asked, "Why do you do this?"

Andrew shrugged. "The Law commands us to offer a living sacrifice to Yahweh during Passover. That's why we have animals and birds for sale at the Temple."

Philip stepped into a muddy rut and shook his foot, but the mud stuck to his sandal. Within minutes, another cart splashed water on him and Andrew. Andrew shook his fist and cursed the driver. Philip smiled. Mild mannered Andrew seldom lost his temper.

Andrew took a handful of sesterces from his pouch and handed them to the merchant when they reached the front of the line. Then they inched through the crowd with a cage containing a small ewe. Philip wiped his nose with his sleeve asking, "Why didn't you bargain with the merchant? I never saw you buy something for the asking price."

Andrew sighed, "There are times when you ask too many questions. In this case, we have no choice. The merchant would brush me aside and serve the next customer if I tried to bargain." Andrew jumped backwards when a man smelling of too much wine swayed toward them and cursed. Ignoring the man, he continued, "There always seems to be a shortage of animals and birds during our Passover season. By this afternoon, as many as twenty people may have to share a sacrifice."

"At least that spreads the cost," Philip noted.

"Yes, but Yahweh gives us greater blessings when we make individual sacrifices."

Aaron asked, "Why does God want us to sacrifice living animals?"

"We are commanded to do so by our Law," Andrew patiently replied.

"To me, it looks like a way for greedy merchants to make money."

"What do you mean?"

"Somebody is making money because of our rules and I think it's the people selling animals."

Andrew frowned and gestured for Philip to keep his end of the cage off the ground. "Be patient, it will soon be time for us from Galilee to present our offerings."

* * *

As they left Andrew looked at the southwest tower of the Antonia Fortress as he walked toward the Court of the Gentiles and noticed the soldiers watching the crowd. He looked the other direction, toward the Lower City and saw empty streets.

Andrew looked up when a priest sounded the shofar from the roof of the Temple. As he pulled Aaron toward the gate, he said, "That's the signal for us to leave and the Greek Jews to enter."

Andrew had hardly spoken when they found themselves in the midst of a group of tense, sweaty worshippers jostling each other as they left the Temple grounds.

Andrew gestured at the crowd. "Most of these people are pilgrims, but there are thieves and prostitutes among them as well. Also, merchants come to sell their trinkets." Looking at Aaron, he added, "You're right about people making money from these celebrations."

Pushing Aaron, he pointed to the west wall of the Temple. "Here, walk quickly. I want to leave before the Romans start prodding us. This overpass will take us directly to the Upper City."

* * *

Rabbi Joachim returned from the Temple in the early afternoon with an anxious look in his eyes. "Buy the food you need for the Passover celebration as soon as possible," he warned Mary. "Buy enough to last for the Sabbath. When you are done, bar the gate and cover your lamps." Rabbi Joachim looked at the people in the courtyard. "The Romans are losing control of the city. Do as I say!" Rabbi Joachim gestured to the people in the courtyard. "The stalls are empty. There are no more sheep and birds. The authorities shut off the supply when they closed the gates. Now, for a reason unknown to me, the High Priests refuse to accept single offerings by more than twenty people."

"Surely they will correct that situation," Andrew argued. "Do you really believe there'll be trouble again tonight?"

Rabbi Joachim stiffened and rapped his staff on the ground. "Of course! Why do you think I told you these things?"

"Sorry." Andrew shook his head. "We'll do as you say," he replied as he exited the courtyard.

Mary Marcia met Andrew in the atrium. "Everyone is safely here except Jesus and John. I have to finish our Seder preparation. All we've done so far is kasher the special pots and bowls reserved for Passover."

"And the matzah?"

"We're baking it now. First we need to dispose of the hametz--then we'll be ready." She looked toward the gate. "Oh, I hope we get ready on time"

"Don't worry," Andrew whispered. "Everything will be fine."

She gave him a stern look. "You only have to worry about the Haggadah. I need to finish cleaning the house, dispose of the hametz, supervise the meal, and prepare the..."

"Wait, you don't have to do those things by yourself."

"Yes, but I need to make sure..."

"It runs right."

"Stop interrupting me," she snapped. She looked at the gate once more before she disappeared around the corner.

Jesus and John bar Zebedee returned shortly before sundown, out of breath and drenched with sweat. Mary quickly gave them towels and a bowl of water to cleanse themselves. As he dried his hands, Jesus said to Andrew, "It's chaos out there. There are no animals or birds left for sacrifice, yet I saw swarms of people streaming toward the Temple when we left."

"Then there will be trouble," Andrew observed.

Philip nodded. "There's talk that Pontius Pilate sent his Praetorian Guard here from Caesarea,"

Mary Marcia looked at the sky and gestured to John and Philip. "It's almost sundown, stop gossiping and prepare for our Seder."

CHAPTER EIGHT

"This is a day you are to commemorate; for the generations to come you shall celebrate it as a festival to the LORD—a lasting ordinance. For seven days you are to eat bread made without yeast. On the first day remove the yeast from your houses, for whoever eats anything with yeast in it from the first day through the seventh must be cut off from Israel. On the first day hold a sacred assembly, and another one on the seventh day. Do no work at all on these days, except to prepare food for everyone to eat; that is all you may do. Celebrate the Festival of Unleavened Bread, because it was on this very day that I brought your divisions out of Egypt. Celebrate this day as a lasting ordinance for the generations to come."

Exodus 12:14-17

Their candles cast wavy shadows on the walls as they marched to the upper room to celebrate the Seder. Once there, they placed the candles around the table and sat on their cushions. The Seder plate, k'arah, held the only food on the table.

Andrew and Mary arranged the ancient symbols of Passover in a carefully prescribed order. First they placed the green vegetable called karpas on the plate. Karpas symbolizes spring and rebirth. Then Mary prepared a bowl containing a mixture of chopped dates, apples, nuts, wine, and spices. "Do you remember haroset from previous seders?" she asked Mark. Without waiting for an answer, she continued, "Haroset represents the mortar the Hebrew slaves used for bricks in Egypt."

A plate of bitter herbs was placed next to the haroset. The herbs, called maror, would remind people of the bitterness of slavery. Mary asked her daughter Rebecca to put a roasted egg on the plate as a sign of the sacrifice offered by each Jew going up to the temple. Rebecca finished the plate by putting the zeroa, or roasted bone, on the plate as a further symbol of sacrifice.

Jesus wore a white robe, called a kittel, over his shoulders and asked Mark to fill the Elijah cup. Then he addressed the group. "As you know, we wear a kittel several times in our life. This is the first time for me. Someday my friends will bury me in a kittel. The kittel represents for us, the dying of the old as the new is born. It helps us to remember that the older generation from Egypt perished in the desert when the new generation approached the Promised Land."

He continued, "We fear dying and often deny its reality. Yet death is the price of liberation now, as it was for our ancestors in the Sinai. This kittel reminds me of that truth, and perhaps helps me fear dying less."

Jesus had no sooner finished speaking when they heard a roar from the Lower City. They ran to the narrow windows of the upper room but saw nothing.

Jesus recited the Kiddush over the first cup of wine and concluded with the she-he-heyanu blessing. Following that, they carefully washed their hands to symbolize their cleansing from ritual impurity. They followed with the karpas, the yahatz, and the breaking of the middle one of the three matzot.

After eating from the K'arah, Joachim ben Eleazar stood to begin the Haggadah, the story of the Exodus. He raised a piece of matzah and said, "This is the bread of affliction that our ancestors ate in Egypt. We invite all who are hungry to join our celebration."

The noise from the city increased. Now they saw flames rising from the vicinity of the Temple when they looked through the windows.

Jesus called them to return to the Seder table. "Do not profane this sacred night with your concern about the outside world," he counseled. "The Lord our God will protect us whether we worry or not."

Andrew continued with the four questions until he realized he had forgotten their traditional declaration. Red faced, he stopped, raised his cup and said, "This year we are slaves, next year we will be free." He paused for a moment. "We are indeed slaves and long to eat the bread of freedom."

After the Haggadah, Jesus took the matzot and recited two blessings, one for bread and a special one for matzot. Then each person took a piece from the bottom matzah, made a sandwich with maror, and ate it. Jesus raised his arms and declared; "Now we are free to eat our joyous meal."

The sounds outside their walls provided a continuous backdrop to their meal. Sometimes it sounded like people fighting, other times like a swarm of bees buzzing over the upper city. Mary glanced at Andrew and Jesus when the noise grew louder. They nodded to reassure her. Later, Andrew rose and drained the fourth and last cup of ritual wine. Then he led the group in the traditional poem called "Hasal Siddur Pesah."

Philip played the lute to accompany the traditional songs depicting the Passover themes. The group sang with laughter and gusto even though the words were often terrifying. Andrew, Philip, and the others cheerfully sang about death after death and destruction after destruction because they knew the ending. The Holy One would come to slaughter the Angel of Death and bring complete redemption to Yahweh's people.

"And that," said Joachim ben Eleazar at the end, "is how the Haggadah reassures us. That is how the story ends." Sounds of violence, now closer to the upper room, seemed to overwhelm his closing prayer. Andrew looked at Mary and whispered, "I wonder, is this the night of the Angel of Death?"

Mary shook her head. "No, I believe it's the night of the young rebels. Keep the gate locked and extinguish your lamps. We will survive this evening if we trust Yahweh to protect us."

* * *

Philip and Andrew stared through the windows of the upper room the next morning and saw wisps of smoke straying from several parts of the city. Later, Amos came to their house and told them the story of what happened the previous night. Looking at the people gathered in the courtyard, he said, "The trouble started when a mob of worshippers from Greece went to the home of the Chief Priest, Caiaphas. They were angry because there were no sacrificial animals left for sale at the Temple. Also, the Temple authorities decreed that no more than twenty people could share in a sacrificial offering."

Andrew said, "The people have a choice. They can offer something other than an animal."

"True, but there were no birds left either." Amos looked at Mary. "Where did I stop?"

"The mob?"

"Oh yes. A large crowd surrounded Caiaphas' house and demanded he explain why they had to risk Yahweh's wrath because of his rules. But Caiaphas stayed inside until his guards scattered the crowd."

"That should have ended it," Andrew interjected.

Amos stared at Andrew as if he were an apparition. "That's true--if it would have stopped there," Amos continued. "But some of the people went back to the Temple and sacked the merchant's stalls--the ones that sell trinkets outside the walls. Others gathered near the old Hasmonean palace." Amos made a helpless gesture. "It was as if someone was provoking the mobs. They went from there to the Lower City where they trapped several Roman soldiers in a street with no exit."

Amos' next statement startled them. "They killed several soldiers."

"Are you sure this happened?" Andrew asked.

"Yes. I was at the Temple when the people started for Caiaphas' house. I ran to a friend's house near the temple to hide until the situation calmed. I watched from his roof and saw the reinforcements running to rescue the soldiers trapped in the Lower City. Even when they were outnumbered, the people taunted the soldiers and threw stones until the soldiers retaliated with a volley of arrows. That stopped the mob long enough for the soldiers to gain control."

Amos sipped wine from a cup Mary gave him. "We thought the trouble ended when the crowd dispersed and the soldiers retreated toward the Antonia Fortress. But another group of men hid on the west wall of the Temple and dropped boulders on the soldiers when they passed underneath." Aaron shook his head. "I don't understand why the Romans took that route."

"I don't understand why those people chose last night to fight with the Romans," Andrew muttered. "Why didn't they honor Passover as we did...as did all sensible people in Jerusalem?"

"They're not all Jews. You know there are Gentile workers in the city. What do they care about Passover? They don't care about us; they just want a good time." He sipped from his cup and continued, "Then there are the zealots, animals looking for a chance to riot. They run away after they're done and leave others to stand the wrath of the Romans."

Signaling for silence, Amos said, "Let me finish. Someone told me there are several hundred extra soldiers in the fortress. We watched from the roof... my God; they poured out, some on horseback, the rest on foot."

"They caught several men near the Temple and dragged them to the fortress. Then they went to the Lower City and barricaded the streets. I couldn't believe my eyes, some people still tried to attack the soldiers with rocks. The soldiers captured them as well and took them to the fortress."

"What about the fires?" Andrew asked.

"Some of the mob at the house of Caiaphas fought with the soldiers, and then escaped through the Zion Gate." Amos pointed to the south. "The soldiers caught them near an area used for storing construction materials. The mob started some pilings on fire and escaped into the valley. There was another fire near the fortress. The soldiers trapped some men in an old building and started it on fire to drive the rioters out."

"Is that it?" Andrew asked.

"Isn't that enough?"

"I didn't..."

"I know," Amos sighed. "I stayed with my friend and worried all night about my family, and they worried about me. Some Passover." He glanced around the courtyard. "I have to go; I only came to warn you to stay off the streets today."

Mark looked at the others after Aaron left. "Why?"

"Why what?" Andrew asked.

"Why do people cause all that trouble? Where is the God of the Jews--you know--the one you say will deliver us? Why do..."

Andrew waved his hand. "We have no time to discuss why these things happen. Right now we have to prepare for the second day of Passover, and then make plans for the rest of the week."

* * *

Within an hour, the porter responded to another knock on the gate. He looked through the eyehole and immediately yelled for Mary. "Who is it?" Mary asked.

"Open this gate," came an authoritative command from the outside.

"By whose order?" she asked.

"Tribune Vehilius Gratus."

She put her hand to her mouth and looked around the courtyard. "Romans," she hollered at the porter. "Let them in! Let them in!"

Four soldiers in armor came through the gate. A centurion quickly scanned the courtyard, and then gestured to Mary and attempted to speak in Aramaic. "Is this your house?"

"Yes it is," she replied after discerning his question. "What do you want?" She spoke to him in perfect Latin.

He grinned and asked using Latin, "I want you to assemble the people who live in this house here, in your courtyard."

She looked at him for a moment, not moving.

"Now!" he bellowed.

She beckoned to the porter and within moments, the residents and tenants came outside.

The centurion scrutinized them, then looked at Mary and asked, "Is this it?"

"Yes." she replied tersely.

He instructed his men to conduct a search of the house, and then pointed to Philip. "Where do you live?"

"Bethsaida." Philip replied using a Greek dialect.

He looked at Andrew and Jesus. "What about them?"

Philip pointed to each one in turn and named their city.

He stared at Rebecca, then at Mary. "What are you running here...a house of prostitution?"

She shot a burning glance at him. "What do you want?"

"Our patrols spotted some suspicious people near this house. We're looking for the men who looted this part of the city last night. Isn't..." he looked at Philip, "Is Bessedda located in Galilee?"

Philip swallowed a grin. "Yes, why?"

The centurion moved closer to him. "I'll ask the questions. Our tribune told us to watch you Galileans. You people are agitators."

Approaching the centurion, Mary said, "I am Mary Marcia Africanus, the wife of Veturius Marcius Africanus. Last night we observed our Passover celebration in this house." Jesus was surprised to hear her use her full Roman name.

The centurion's eyes darted between her and the people in the courtyard.

She looked into his eyes. "I swear on the name of Tiberius Claudius Nero that everyone spent the entire afternoon and evening in this house."

"Where is your husband now?" the centurion asked.

"Dead," she replied in a low voice.

The centurion looked at the people then pointed to Mary and said, "My men are responsible for this section of the city. They have orders to kill anyone outside these walls after sundown. Don't go outside these walls even to relieve yourself." With that, he and his men left the courtyard.

Mary Marcia and her guests celebrated their second night of Passover at sunset. They heard no noise from the city and saw no fires. It seemed the Romans were back in control.

* * *

Andrew and Mary went to the market the next morning through deserted streets that normally bustled with activity. There was little food at the market because the Romans had kept the gates closed since the previous afternoon. The farmers, content with remaining outside the gates, sold everything they had to the people camping outside the city.

One merchant told Andrew, "The Romans have several prisoners in the fortress. They'll go on trial this afternoon and probably will be executed tomorrow morning."

"What about the Romans," Mary asked. "How many soldiers did the rioters kill?"

"I don't know for sure," he answered. "Some say ten or fifteen."

"They'll hang twenty or thirty," Mary muttered.

"Yes, and I hope they hang the Zealots," the merchant declared. "They're no friends of ours."

"Is it safe to travel?" Andrew asked.

"Maybe tomorrow," the merchant replied. "I stood on my roof this morning and watched columns of people on the roads leaving Jerusalem. They're not staying for the week as they usually do. People are afraid," he added with raised eyebrows. "There was at least one killing last night at the Olive Mount."

Mary looked at Andrew. "Maybe I won't need as much food as I thought."

* * *

On the last full day in Jerusalem for the guests at Mary Marcia's house, Jesus and Andrew were talking casually in the courtyard when Jesus said, "I want to see the trial before I return to Galilee."

"Trial?" Andrew asked.

"Yes," Jesus replied. "The rioters they caught the other night. They're trying them today at the open square outside the west wall of the Antonia Fortress and I know the Romans speak Latin during their trials and I know little about the language. I need someone to translate for me."

"How about Mark?"

"Why him?"

"His father was a Roman soldier. He should know Latin."

Jesus found Mark and asked him to go to the trial.

"Why do you want to see the trial? From what I've heard, they intend to punish the Jews they caught. They've already released the Gentile workers."

"It will give us a chance to see Roman justice."

Mark looked around the courtyard. "There isn't much to do until later," he said. "But I want to leave the fortress no later than mid afternoon. I have to get ready to go to Alexandria tomorrow."

As they walked to the Antonia Fortress, Mark asked, "Are you pleased that those men killed Roman soldiers, or happy the Romans caught them?"

"I cannot be happy when one human being kills another. Our Law condemns taking someone's life."

"I once wanted to be a soldier?"

"But not now?"

Mark nodded. "I want to study and write about history."

"I remember you telling me about this when we met at Cana. So you haven't changed your mind since then?"

"No," Mark replied as they followed a small group of men heading toward the fortress.

"What will you write about?" Jesus asked.

"My teachers at the Alexandria Library want me to write about life in Galilee."

Jesus laughed. "Why would anyone want to know about life in Galilee?"

Mark shook his head. "The scholars want to know about everyone and everything. I suppose they might even be interested in learning about life in Antioch."

* * *

Once at the Antonia Fortress, Jesus and Mark listened at one end of the immense square as a centurion read a proclamation in Latin. Six men, naked and tied to each other with ropes heard their death sentence read in a language they didn't understand. Mark flinched when he realized three were about his age. Four nights earlier, these men now standing naked and bleeding in front of their accusers swaggered through the city terrorizing people. Now vacant eyes stared from swollen faces as they listened to the decree signed by Tribune Vehilius Gratus. Some people tried to ease their way out of the crowd, but most pushed forward for a closer look.

A group of soldiers surrounded the men and raised their spears to control the crowd. A guard whispered in a prisoner's ear. The prisoner raised his head and spit in the guard's face. The soldier wiped his face with his sleeve and with the same motion slammed his forearm across the prisoner's nose. The condemned man staggered, but remained standing, held in place by the ropes that tied him to the other men.

The centurion read the same decree in Greek. "These men murdered Roman soldiers. They rioted and burned public buildings. I therefore decree that they be sentenced to death by crucifixion."

Mark started to leave the square when the centurion ordered the guards to take the men away, but Jesus pulled his sleeve. "Let's follow them."

Mark shook his head. "I have no interest in watching a crucifixion," he said gravely. "It's a terrible way for a man to die."

Jesus and Mark turned toward Mary's house as the guards whipped the prisoners and screamed warnings at the crowd as the procession trudged toward the Genneth Gate.

* * *

As Jesus left for Galilee the next morning, he counted six crosses on the hill outside the Genneth Gate and shuddered as barely visible figures wiggled like worms on a stick. He thought he saw a crowd of people jostling near the crosses, but the activity faded in a cloud of dust.

Judas of Kerioth also came to Jerusalem with his father to celebrate Passover. They left Jerusalem on the same day and saw the six men hanging on the hill outside the Genneth Gate. Judas averted his glance as much as possible, yet he was mesmerized by the spectacle of human beings condemned to such agony.

As they prepared to go their separate ways; Judas to Galilee and his father to Kerioth, they embraced and wished each other a safe journey.

CHAPTER NINE

"The country also that lies over against this lake hath the same name of Gennesareth; its nature is wonderful as well as its beauty; its soil is so fruitful that all sorts of trees can grow upon it, and the inhabitants accordingly plant all sorts of trees there; for the temper of the air is so well mixed, that it agrees very well with those several sorts, particularly walnuts, which require the coldest air, flourish there in vast plenty; there are palm trees also, which grow best in hot air; fig trees also and olives grow near them, which yet require an air that is more temperate. One may call this place the ambition of nature, where it forces those plants that are naturally enemies to one another to agree together; it is a happy contention of the seasons, as if every one of them laid claim to this country; for it not only nourishes different sorts of autumnal fruit beyond men's expectation, but preserves them a great while; it supplies men with the principal fruits, with grapes and figs continually, during ten months of the year and the rest of the fruits as they become ripe together through the whole year; for besides the good temperature of the air, it is also watered from a most fertile fountain. The people of the country call it Capharnaum. Some have thought it to be a vein of the Nile, because it produces the Coracin fish as well as that lake does which is near to Alexandria. The length of this country extends itself along the banks of this lake that bears the same name for thirty furlongs, and is in breadth twenty, And this is the nature of that place. "

Josephus Flavius (Wars - Book III, 10, 8)

It was late afternoon when Judas walked into Capernaum along the single road that divided the houses from the synagogue, harbor, and market. He went directly to the inn he had stayed at in his previous trip. He dropped off his bags and told the proprietor, Nahum, that he would return in time for the evening meal. Then he went looking for Zebedee and Andrew.

He went to the lakeshore where a row of piers sat protected by a break-water jutting into the lake. Only three boats bobbed in the water next to the docks. He went up to a man cleaning one of the boats and asked whether Andrew was still out on the lake or at home.

"I haven't seen Andrew all day," he replied. "In fact I haven't seen Simon or the sons of Zebedee either." With that he turned his back on Judas and continued to clean the boat.

"Have you seen Zebedee?"

"About two hours ago," the man replied impatiently. He turned back and looked at Judas. "I wouldn't talk to him right now. He is very angry with Simon and his sons James and John." With that, the man returned to his chores.

A short time later, Judas spied Andrew walking toward the piers. He called to Andrew and hurried over to greet him. "I've been looking for you," he said. "That man over there said he hadn't seen you all day."

"I didn't fish today," Andrew replied. "My brother Simon disappeared along with James and John."

"Where did they go? Do you know?"

Andrew shrugged. "Jesus seems to have disappeared as well so I assume they are with him."

Pointing, Judas said, "That man told me that Zebedee is upset."

Andrew smiled. "You don't want to be near Zebedee when he is upset."

"What is this all about?"

"I don't know."

"What are you going to do?"

"For now, I'm going to see what Simon's wife has to say about this. Would you like to come with me?"

"Something tells me I should stay here but I have nothing else to do so I'll go with you."

* * *

Judas and Andrew hurried toward a cluster of modest houses near the road. As they drew closer, they saw women working in small gardens and hanging freshly washed clothes over retaining walls. The women stopped and waved when they saw Andrew.

As they approached a well worn house fronted by a small dirt courtyard, Andrew called to a sullen looking woman sitting on a bench next to her door. She looked up when they arrived at the house.

Andrew glanced at Judas. "Do you remember Naomi, Simon's wife?"

Judas nodded and reached to greet her, but pulled back when he saw her frown. Naomi stared at Judas then asked Andrew, "What is he doing here?"

"He was here a few months ago to finalize an agreement with Zebedee. Judas' father and Zebedee are in business together. Judas' father ships spices and cloth to Galilee and Zebedee ships fish and fruit to Judea. Judas will be coming here from time to time to help organize our shipments."

Naomi rolled her eyes. "Zebedee will do anything for a shekel, even if he has to deal with a Judean."

Andrew ignored her comment and gave her his best smile. "You look angry."

She lifted her robe over her ankles and sighed, "Everything is wrong. I can't believe how messed up our lives are."

Andrew looked around for some obvious signs of trouble. "Tell us..."

"Your friend!" she rasped. "He took Simon and the sons of Zebedee and left town."

"My friend?"

"Jesus!" She spat the name out like a rancid date.

"Where did they go?"

She glanced to the north. "That way."

"When did they leave?"

She gestured helplessly. "I don't know."

The men stood in the courtyard for a few minutes, unsure of what they should say or do. Finally Naomi broke the silence. "I suppose you're hungry."

Andrew looked at Judas. "I am. I haven't eaten since this morning."

Naomi went into her house and returned with a wineskin and two cups. "Here's some wine. I'll get some food." Within moments, Naomi came outside carrying a dish of barley bread and smoked fish in one hand and a dish of fruit in the other. The men sat on the ground, leaning against the short retaining wall, and quickly ate the food. After a few minutes, Andrew waved a piece of bread in the air, saying, "I didn't know how hungry I was until I started eating." When he finished, he put his cup next to the empty plates and said, "Now back to my original question..."

Naomi raised her arms. "I know, I know. Where did they go and why? People keep asking and I don't know the answers. They come to my house and say, `Oh you poor woman, you have a young child and that man runs off like a fool and leaves you to care for yourself.'"

"Maybe they're right," Andrew interrupted.

"No one knows better than I." She swirled the juice left on the fruit plate.

"Do you think they decided to go to Jerusalem?"

"No--no, they went north," she answered impatiently.

Andrew scratched his head. "I don't understand how they could leave and not tell anyone where they were going."

Naomi scraped the dishes in front of a goat standing near the door and put them on a stand next to the water basin. Just then, they heard a groan from inside the house. Naomi put her finger to her lips. "It's our daughter, Jepthania," she whispered. "She's had a fever for a week."

Drawing them closer, she continued, "Jesus came one day for supper when my mother was sick. He prayed over her and before I knew it, she was well. So Simon took me aside and said, `See, I told you he could do miracles.'" She tugged on Andrew's sleeve. "Do you know what I told him?"

"No."

"Ha--well I told him that it was no miracle that an old lady felt better after a bowl of hot soup."

"Did Jesus give her hot soup?" Judas asked.

"*I* did...a few hours before Jesus came to our house. Anyway, she was up and ordering us around the next day. I don't know, maybe he did heal her." She looked into Andrew's eyes and said, "But I'll tell you something, Jesus is taking Simon and the Zebedee's away from us. You'll probably be next." With that, she disappeared into the house to care for her daughter.

Following that, Andrew and Judas returned to Nahum's inn.

* * *

Judas took his bags to the same small room he occupied the last time he was in Capernaum. Then he went outside and stared through the last strands of sunlight reflecting off the jagged stones on the beach. He remembered how the fine sand on the Mediterranean beaches sifted between his toes when he walked next to the water. In Galilee, a man needed sandals as to walk the beaches.

Later, as he and Andrew sat around a small fire near the beach, across from the inn, Judas asked about the men who fished the Sea of Galilee.

Andrew threw a piece of wood on the fire and leaned back on his elbows so he could see the sky. "As you know, we work for a man named Zebedee and his partner, Aaron Yohaz. Zebedee owns most of the boats and hires them out to us. In turn, we sell our fish to him."

"Will you tell me what you know about Jesus?" Judas asked.

Andrew stroked his beard. "It's too late to tell you tonight. Perhaps we'll talk tomorrow."

* * *

The next morning, Andrew and Judas arrived at the harbor in time to see the flickering oil lamps on the ships' masts disappear over the horizon. As he approached his boat, Andrew spotted a small figure, robed from neck to ankles, emerge from the shadows. Stroking his beard, Andrew muttered, "Oh--oh."

"What is it?" Judas asked.

"Zebedee--He's coming over here," Andrew whispered.

A short, wiry man walked toward them carrying a staff almost as tall as its owner. He thrust a thin forefinger at Andrew as if he were delivering a bolt of lightening. "Why aren't you with those fool sons of mine? After all, you're the one who brought that preacher to Capernaum." Zebedee lifted his staff in the air. "Why I should..."

Andrew raised his hands. "What's wrong now?"

"What's wrong? I go to Jerusalem for Passover and half my men run away with that lunatic. Now you're standing on shore watching the boats sail when you should be with them. Why are you doing these things to me?" Before Andrew could answer he added, "Or are you going to stop fishing and chase that dreamer too?"

"Jesus?" Andrew asked.

"Yes, Jesus."

"I don't know, he didn't ask me this time," Andrew replied.

Zebedee's face turned a deeper shade of red as he walked across the dock, thumping his staff with every step. "I have customers waiting for fish and they run off to..." For the first time he noticed Judas standing next to the boat. Icy blue eyes flashing like darts, he walked toward Judas and said, "When did you get here?"

Judas tried to respond, but the words caught in his throat.

"Speak up!"

"He arrived yesterday." Andrew said.

Zebedee snarled. "At least he's here and that's all that counts." Zebedee tugged at Judas' sleeve. "Your father sent you here to make sure we did our job right. Well you can start by fishing with Andrew."

"But I don't know how to fish."

"Andrew will tell you what to do." Zebedee grinned. "Just make sure you don't drown."

Andrew shrugged.

Zebedee continued, "Fish in that boat until I tell you different. Now get going!"

Judas stood petrified at the sight of this small man with a large voice capable of reducing Andrew to a stammering boy.

Zebedee looked at the water, and added, "It's too late to catch the others. Take a trawling net from John's boat and fish south, near Magdala." Zebedee waved his staff. "Now get going!"

Andrew and Judas raised the mast, secured the lines, and shook the sail. As the boat slipped out to sea, they watched Zebedee pacing the shoreline until a blanket of fog covered him. Andrew welcomed the light wind that pushed his boat away from Zebedee's wrath and toward the fishing area south of Capernaum.

Once they reached open water, Judas said, "I don't know how to sail a boat or how to catch fish."

Andrew gave the tiller to Judas and leaned against the side of the boat. "I'll teach you as much as you need to know to stop us from drowning. Just make sure you stay out of my way when we find the fish. For now steer the boat as I tell you. As I told you last night, we work for Zebedee. When we don't sail, he doesn't sell fish." Andrew waved his hand and added, "Don't worry about him; he's not always this way."

"Was he talking about Jesus?" Judas continued.

"You mean the part about dreamers?" Andrew looked at the first shafts of daylight cutting across the sky. "Zebedee thinks it's wrong to ask questions about our faith," Andrew added as he carefully coiled the ropes attached to the nets.

Judas changed the subject. "I heard that you once lived near the Salt Sea."

"I lived with the Essenes in Qumran," Andrew replied.

"What did you do there?"

"I studied with them and copied scrolls..."

"Then you can read and write?" Judas interrupted.

"A little, but not like a teacher or scribe."

"How did you copy scrolls if you..."

Andrew waved his hand. "I copied symbols. I didn't always know what they meant."

"What did you copy?"

"Mostly sacred writings from Moses and the prophets." He tugged his beard. "Although I don't think too many people want to read about the Teacher of Righteousness and the coming of the New Age."

They held on to the railing when a large wave hit the side of the boat. Judas signaled his apologies and steered the boat into the waves. "What is a Teacher of Righteousness?" he asked after he caught his balance.

"A Messiah," Andrew answered.

"Jesus...do you think he's the Messiah?"

Andrew smiled. "Maybe..." He seemed lost in thought as his gaze shifted to the horizon.

Judas noticed that Andrew became more guarded during their discussion, as if he were afraid of revealing a secret. "You said you would tell me about him," Judas persisted.

Andrew picked some stones off the deck. For the first time, Judas noticed Andrew's limp. "Does your foot hurt?" he asked.

"Why do you ask?"

"You're limping."

Andrew looked at his feet. "I, ah...my left leg is shorter than my right. I limp when my leg is tired."

Andrew sat on the foredeck and gestured for Judas to sit next to him. "We can't go through life ignoring the things that happen around us," he said.

"What about Jesus?" Judas interjected.

Andrew threw the pebbles in the water, one at a time. "My brother Simon and I have known Jesus since were boys. Two years ago I saw Jesus at the Essene monastery at Qumran near the Salt Sea," he said. "But it was near the end of my stay so I only talked with him a few times. This year I went to Jerusalem on a combined celebration of Passover and business trip. Zebedee sent me to find a storehouse to keep the fish and fruit he was sending from Galilee. On the way back, I met Jesus near Jericho and he told me he had heard that a man from Qumran was preaching near the Jordan. I wanted to see who it was; I thought I might know him. So Jesus and I traveled north of Jericho until we spotted a crowd of people following a man dressed in a loin cloth, tunic and sandals. When we came closer, we realized he wasn't wearing a tunic." Andrew's eyes opened wide. "He just had a hairy chest."

"Did you know him?" Judas asked.

"I knew him from the monastery," Andrew replied. "The crowd knew him as John the Essene, but at Qumran we called him John the Baptizer."

"This isn't Jesus you're talking about?"

"No. There's no resemblance between Jesus and John the Baptizer." Andrew gestured for Judas to alter his course as he continued talking. "First, the Baptizer talked about personal sacrifice. Then he ranted about the Herods, the Romans, and the high priests. All of a sudden I saw Jesus standing next to the Baptizer. John--how do I say it? John turned to the people and said, `This man is the promise of our generation. He is the Anointed One.'" Andrew gave a helpless gesture. "I wanted to leave, but I was captivated by the scene."

"John the Baptizer led Jesus down the hill where he stripped to his loin cloth and together, they walked into the water. When Jesus' head was almost in the water, John pushed him the rest of the way and held him. When he let go, Jesus jumped up spitting water. Then John yelled that Jesus was purified--without sin."

"That sounds like a trick."

Andrew laughed. "That's what I said." Then his eyes narrowed. "I wasn't ready for what happened next."

Andrew stopped when he heard a commotion in the water. "Over there! The fish are over there!" Within seconds, Andrew unhitched the sail and let it fall, then gripped one end of the trawling net. Andrew sent Judas to the bow where he took the other end, and together they heaved it over the side of the boat. Then Andrew yelled for Judas to tie one of the middle ropes to the railing. Judas pulled the rope just as a wave caught the boat and spun it away from the net. The rope sped through his hands and slapped over the side of the boat.

Judas doubled over and shook his burning hands while Andrew pushed him aside and secured the second rope. Returning to the tiller, he stabilized the boat and pulled the sail tight. Finally Andrew tied the last rope.

Andrew clapped his hands "That'll hold for a while."

Judas' hands and pride stung, but he forced a weak smile, saying, "Fishing isn't as easy as I thought it would be."

Andrew nodded. "You better watch next time when we pull the nets in. I don't want you to hurt yourself." Now Judas' pride stung worse than his hands.

They started back to Capernaum a few hours later with a catch of silvery musht flopping in the bottom of the boat. "We usually fish for these at night," Andrew said. "This is a small catch compared to night fishing."

Judas tried to show his interest with a knowing nod, and then changed the subject. "Will you finish your story now?"

"Sure, where was I?"

"This John Baptizer pushed Jesus under the water."

Andrew continued, "Jesus seemed to radiate light when he came out of the water. His eyes...I remember he looked right at me--almost through me. Suddenly, I heard birds singing more clearly than ever before. It was if the heavens opened and God himself stood in the water."

"Maybe you imagined that."

"Maybe, but to me it was real." Andrew looked over the side of the boat, and continued, "John the Baptizer started talking. What a voice, I'll bet they heard him in Jerusalem. 'Submit to God's Law!' he said. 'This water will cleanse your flesh and bring the spirit to your hearts.'"

Judas shook his hands to relieve the last tinges of pain from the flying rope. "How do you remember what he said?"

"I'll never forget."

"What was John the Baptizer trying to do?"

"He used water as a sign of repentance."

"I remember when the rabbis talk about the Day of Atonement. Doesn't that take care of...repentance?"

"Not according to John the Baptizer. One day...one year. That's not enough, he said. God doesn't ask us to act like the Gentiles."

Judas waved his hands. "What happened next?"

"Only a few of us remained after the crowd left, so John the Baptizer asked us to camp with him for the evening." Andrew looked past the bow and said, "I realize now I didn't go to the Jordan River that day by accident. The experience changed my life."

"How?"

Andrew tugged at his beard. "This might sound strange...but I saw...a light."

"A light? When?"

"When Jesus went into the water."

Judas shook his head. "Water? Light? Essenes?" He looked at Andrew. "This is interesting."

"I wish I could explain it better."

"Is that the end of the story?"

"We talked most of the night. First John the Baptizer talked, then Jesus."

"I can hardly wait to see Jesus again," Judas declared. "When is he coming back?"

Andrew waved his hand. "I hope in a few days."

"Do you know where they went?" Judas asked.

"Not exactly. I think they went where they could be alone, to pray and meditate."

"What good does that do?" Judas asked.

"Jesus says it helps us to understand God's will," Andrew replied. "One more thing, there was a word that John the Baptizer used. It's spirit. He says it exists inside us."

"I don't understand."

"Neither did I at the beginning." Andrew stopped talking when Capernaum came into view, signaling for Judas to steer the boat toward the harbor.

"Then what's the point if you don't understand?"

Andrew looked at Judas. "I'm not sure. I'm not sure why we should worry about the things Jesus and John the Baptizer talked about. All I want to do is fish, marry a pleasant woman, and raise children. And if I lead a good life, someday join my forefathers. That's all I ever wanted."

"Then do it."

"I can't. God planted a seed in me that day in Jericho. I'll never forget or turn back." Andrew looked toward the city. "Some of us must search for... maybe like John the Baptizer said, search for the spirit within us. Jesus said we'd find God there, the spirit of God--nephesh."

Andrew closed his eyes. "What right do I have disrupting Zebedee's fleet, our families, and my own life, with these ideas?" He looked away, as if embarrassed. "I'm a fisherman, not a rabbi or priest."

Shortly before they reached shore, Andrew made a statement that Judas remembered for a long time. "I never told anyone that I had visions that night," Andrew said. "I felt myself floating in the air, supported by the angels. I saw my parents around me and we floated over the sea. For the first time in my life, I was free."

"Free from what?"

"The things that tie us to the earth. Is it wrong to believe we need to escape the mud we're made from?"

CHAPTER TEN

As they were coming down the mountain, Jesus gave them orders not to tell anyone what they had seen until the Son of Man had risen from the dead. They kept the matter to themselves, discussing what "rising from the dead" meant.

Mark 9:8-10

Judas, Naomi, and Andrew sat on benches outside Naomi and Simon's house as they had every night since Judas' arrival in Capernaum. Andrew continually tried to assure Naomi that the missing fishermen were safe with Jesus. Judas, relaxed after a late afternoon swim, smiled when he heard Andrew's explanations. Each day since he arrived, Judas had grown more anxious to meet Jesus again.

At dusk, a man quietly walked through the shadows, unseen until he reached the courtyard entrance. Naomi and Andrew jumped to their feet when they saw him. "Jesus!" Andrew shouted.

"You're home," Naomi cried, looking over Jesus' shoulder. "Did you bring Simon?"

"He's behind me," Jesus replied. "And the Zebedee's are on the way to their homes." Jesus tried to embrace Naomi, but she pulled away.

When Simon arrived a few moments later, he chided Jesus for moving so fast.

"Maybe I wanted to see Naomi alone," Jesus teased.

Naomi grunted, "Don't try my patience." Then she turned on Simon, feet apart and arms folded. "You! Where, in the name of all that's sacred, have you been?"

Simon pointed to Jesus. "With him...at Caesarea Philippi."

"Really," she sneered. "What did you do there that you can't do here? Visit the pagan prostitutes?"

"Why don't we talk about it while we're eating?" Simon suggested. "I'll tell you everything then." Putting his arm around Naomi's waist, he asked, "Do you have any food for me?"

"Fish from the Salt Sea and rock hard bread," she shot back. "But don't even think about eating until I hear some answers."

"What would you like to know?" he asked, a look of innocence covering his face.

She looked at the sky as if she were counting the clouds racing over their heads. "You left me alone with the girl. What if you died? What if I died? What then?"

Simon pulled a bench next to the wall, seated himself, and sighed, "You ask too many questions."

"Is that all you can say?" She turned to Jesus with tears in her eyes. "You don't understand. You've preached to these men for as long as you have known them, yet when I ask where you went and why, their minds go blank. I don't know what you want from them, but whatever it is, you're working with the wrong men."

Simon noticed Judas before Jesus could reply to Naomi. "What are you doing here?" he asked.

Judas' enthusiasm about meeting Jesus again was dampened by Simon's disheveled appearance and Naomi's anger. "I came here to work with Andrew and Zebedee. We are…"

Simon stopped, crossed his arms, and looked at Judas. "I remember now. Your father Simon sent you here to make sure we are doing our jobs right." He chuckled. "Who is watching your father to make sure he isn't pulling dishonest tricks on us?" Simon put his hand over his mouth when Naomi poked him.

"He's the son of a respectable merchant," Naomi whispered.

Simon patted her rear. "I'm thirsty. Why don't you get me a cup of wine?" Raising his eyebrows, he added, "Mm, getting a little heavy, aren't we?"

Naomi swung at him. He ducked in mock terror and added, "Poor woman, not happy when I'm home, not happy when I'm gone. There's no pleasing you."

Naomi shook her head and replied softly, "I'll find some food." With that, she disappeared into the house.

Finding a break in the repartee between Simon and Naomi, Jesus talked to Judas. "I hope you came to do something more than listen to Simon talk," he said.

Judas nodded. "I fished a few times with Andrew but it didn't go very well for Andrew or me." He noticed Jesus' eyes, for a moment remembering how he felt the first time he saw Jesus.

Jesus glanced at Simon and Andrew. "Carpentry is a better trade than fishing. It's warmer, dryer, and safer," he said with a sly smile.

Later, while they ate supper, Naomi pressed Jesus and Simon for more details about their trip. "You were away for two weeks," she prodded. "What did you do in Caesarea Philippi?"

Simon looked at Jesus and said matter-of-factly, "We went to Mount Hermon where we prayed and meditated." He chewed a hard piece of bread into a soggy lump and washed it down with a deep swallow of wine. "You know, it took over a week just for travel."

"Excuse me," Naomi interjected, "I know better, Simon, son of Jonah. You've never prayed for an hour, much less two weeks." She waved her hand. "And meditate? Hah! The only thing you meditate on is wine and sex."

Andrew quickly changed the subject. "Then you spent a week at Mount Hermon. It's pretty cold there this time of year, especially if you camped in the mountains."

"It was too cold for me." Simon shook as he seemed to recall his nights of discomfort. "Jesus and the sons of Zebedee survived better than I. But there was that one time when..."

Simon paused when he saw Jesus raise his hand. "...we stayed in sheltered areas and built fires."

"I can't believe you went to Mount Hermon for a week," Naomi mumbled. "A bunch of supposedly grown men."

"I understand how you feel," Jesus replied. Then he looked at Andrew and added, "But it helped me decide what I have to do."

"You've decided to earn an honest living?" Naomi snapped. "Like a respectable man?"

Jesus smiled, "You sound like Zebedee."

"He's right," she retorted.

"He's right for who he is," Jesus replied. "Too often he measures people by what they do than by who they are."

"We can't eat if we don't do something...like work," Naomi countered.

"What decision did you make?" Andrew interrupted, trying to make sense out of the conversation.

"Decision?"

"Yes," Andrew replied. "You said you decided on what you're going to do."

"Oh--that, I'm going to Judea," Jesus replied. "I must leave Galilee to complete my mission."

Judas desperately wanted to ask Jesus what he meant by his statement, but chose to remain silent. The scene playing out in front of him was a complete surprise after his conversations with Andrew.

"I don't think the Judeans will listen to you," Andrew declared. "Why do you think you will succeed where so many have failed?"

Jesus looked at Andrew intently for a long moment, their faces chiseled into angles and shadows by the flickering oil light.

"What are you talking about?" Naomi asked, uncomfortable with the intense silence.

"You're a woman, you wouldn't understand," Simon muttered as he drained his cup and gestured for another. Simon looked at Andrew. "Did you teach Judas how to fish?"

Andrew answered, "Not yet, we thought we'd wait until you came back. You can teach him." A smile played around the corners of Andrew's mouth. "After all, you claim you're the best fisherman in the fleet."

"Claim?" Simon laughed. "I *am* the best fisherman, and I know old Zebedee misses those huge catches when I'm gone." Satisfied he'd made his point, Simon focused on Judas again. "I suppose Andrew told you he's the smarter brother." Simon waved his hand and continued, "He's right, but I'm a better fisherman." Simon handed his empty cup to Naomi and gestured to Judas. "How long are you staying in Galilee?"

"No more than a month. Then I'll go to Caesarea to work with my father's partner."

"Who is that?"

"Abiram."

"Abiram? Caesarea? Is he a Samaritan?"

"I believe so."

Simon raised his arms. "By all that is sacred, why do we trust our well being to a couple of Judeans and a Samaritan?" He waved his hands and added, "We can't win."

"Leave him alone," Naomi yelled.

Simon looked toward the Sea of Galilee, gently washing the shores of Capernaum, and then looked back at Naomi. "No one asked you." Then he put his arm around her waist. "But that's what I like about you; a quick tongue and a sour disposition." He looked in her eyes. "Did you really miss me?"

"Would I miss a scorpion?" She pulled herself away with more show than anger.

"Do you plan to fish tomorrow?" Andrew asked, gesturing to Simon with his cup.

Simon yawned. "I'd like to sleep, but Zebedee would have a fit if I did. I'll be there."

"Good," Andrew responded. "I want to hear all about your trip with Jesus." Then looking at Judas, he said, "I think we should go. I'm sure Simon and Naomi have things to talk about."

"Talk?" asked Simon with a smile.

Naomi shrugged and went into the house.

Judas wondered, as he walked back to the inn what it was about Jesus that was so special. Simon seemed to have a lot more intensity and Andrew showed wisdom he hadn't expected from a Galilean. At the same time, Judas couldn't remember a thing Jesus said while they were together.

CHAPTER ELEVEN

Now Herod the tetrarch heard about all that was going on. And he was perplexed because some were saying that John had been raised from the dead, others that Elijah had appeared, and still others that one of the prophets of long ago had come back to life.
But Herod said, "I beheaded John. Who, then, is this I hear such things about?" And he tried to see him.

Luke 9:7-9

Judas, now known to everyone in the Capernaum fishing community, treasured the times he spent at night around the fire next to the lake. Here he met Andrew and Simon's friends and fellow fishermen, including James and John bar Zebedee. Judas hoped someone would tell him more about the mysterious trip Jesus and the three men took to Mount Hermon, but they didn't talk about it. Even Naomi stopped asking questions.

One night, about three weeks after Judas arrived in Capernaum, John bar Zebedee sat next to him and pointed to the full moon. "Look at that," John said. "I think it's a man's face. My father says no, but does he really know? What do you think?"

Judas shook his head. "The Greeks say there is no man in the moon, only mountains."

"What do the Greeks know?" John snorted. He pointed to a grove of trees near the road. "Look how the shadows wave at us when the wind blows. They remind me of that man's fingers."

"That man?"

"Yes, the man whose face we see in the moon." John kept his face away from the light so Judas could not tell whether he was serious. Judas didn't know whether John liked him or just tolerated him.

Andrew came to the fire and stood stark still until everyone quieted. "John the Baptizer is dead," he announced, voice quivering.

The men started to murmur until someone asked from the darkness, "How do you know?"

Andrew sat next to the fire where Simon, the sons of Zebedee, and Judas warmed themselves. "Thomas returned from Judea this afternoon. He told Jesus."

"What happened?" Judas recognized James bar Zebedee's voice from across the fire.

"I don't know the details," Andrew replied. "Jesus said he'll bring Thomas to tell us."

"What do you think about John the Baptizer?" Judas asked John.

"I didn't know him as well as Andrew knew him," John replied. "But if Thomas' story is true, we should take revenge." He snapped a twig.

"Who is Thomas?" Judas asked.

"You ask too many questions."

"I'm new here," Judas pleaded.

"Thomas is Jesus' cousin--from Capernaum," John replied impatiently.

"Is there anyone in Capernaum not related to someone else?"

John threw the twigs in the fire. "The Gentiles. More than half the people in Capernaum are Gentiles."

"Can I ask one more question?"

"What now?"

"Why do they call Thomas the Twin?"

"You'll see," John muttered.

Later, three men walked toward the group sitting around the fire. Judas looked up when he heard Simon yell a greeting. He recognized Philip, Jesus, and for a moment, Jesus' twin. Judas poked John. "That's Thomas? He looks like Jesus in the dark."

John laughed. "He looks like him in the light as well." Touching Judas' arm, John added, "Be careful, Thomas is different from us."

"What do you mean?"

"He has strange ideas."

Judas' mind flashed with anticipation. Maybe now he would learn something important about this tiny group of fishermen and farmers who followed Jesus. "What ideas?"

John made a pile of dirt with his foot, and knocked it down. "You wouldn't understand," he replied.

Judas looked at John, younger than he, uneducated, and wondered what made him think he was so smart. Then he noticed that Philip and Thomas had come with Jesus.

Jesus signaled for quiet and said, "I want Thomas to tell you about John the Baptizer."

The man called Thomas stood and looked at the fire. "I heard about John's death from Herod's slave while I was in Perea. He told me that Herod had John's head cut off."

"Why?" Andrew asked, shocked at the words he heard.

"It started when Herod Antipas married his niece, Herodias. John the Baptizer accused them of adultery every place he went. Herod ignored him, but John the Baptizer frightened Herodias so she tried to force him out of Perea."

"I'm sure John resisted," Andrew interjected, still showing his anguish.

"He did, but Herod put him in prison at Machaerus."

"For what?" Andrew asked.

"He claimed John the Baptizer was trying to start an uprising."

"Then what?"

Thomas shook his robe and sat next to the fire. "I don't know how much of this story is true. The slave told me that Herod held a dinner for some Roman officials from Damascus. Her daughter..."

"Whose daughter?"

"Herodias--Herod's wife."

"Yes, go on."

"It was late in the evening and her daughter did some dances for Herod and his guests. One thing led to another. She started the last dance wearing several veils. She removed each one until she only had one or two veils left. Then she left the banquet room.

"Herod Antipas followed her and begged her to finish the dance, if you know what I mean." Thomas made a gesture with his hands and the others nodded. "Herodias heard them arguing and said she could finish the dance if Herod agreed to grant her a favor. Herod, half gone with wine and lust, agreed. So...she finished the dance. I guess the Romans loved it."

Kicking another pile of dirt, John hissed, "Herod Antipas is a filthy pig, just like his father."

John's interruption gave Thomas a chance to drink from the cup he held. Then he resumed, "Herodias came right back and demanded that Herod keep his promise, all the time winking at the Romans as if the party would never end. They goaded him to agree, and when he did, she told him to kill John... that night. He tried to ignore her, but she stood her ground. Finally, the Romans convinced him that the death of one trouble maker was a small price to pay for their entertainment. Herod asked for time but she insisted that it had to happen that night. So, he kept his promise and they cut John's head off." Thomas closed his eyes. "Then they brought his head on a platter to Herodias."

John bar Zebedee jumped up and screamed, "On a platter? Curse that bastard, Herod!" He raised his arms and continued, "Unclean bitch--that Herodias..." The words fell off as John started to sob.

Andrew tossed a heavy piece of wood into the fire. "I never thought of killing a man before, but I would do it to Herod Antipas if he were here now."

"You kill Herod," John retorted. "I'll kill his wife."

Jesus stood and gestured for quiet. "Do you know what you're saying? You talk as if you are one of them. Is that what you want?"

"Once!" John replied. "Once, so I can kill Herod Antipas."

"Then we place no more value on a life than they do," Jesus retorted.

The men looked at each other, confused and afraid to ask another question. Finally, Andrew asked, "What will you do now?"

Jesus stood and stretched. "I have no choice. I'm going to Judea as soon as we move the pauper's camp to Nazareth."

Simon stood and shook the dirt from his sandals. "Why do you want to go to Judea?"

"The people in Galilee have no faith in what I say. Perhaps the Judeans will be more open to my message."

"I don't understand," Simon argued. "They'll kill you the same..."

Jesus touched Simon's arm. "John died in Perea, under Herod. Judea is a Roman province." He pulled Simon aside. "Have you already forgotten our experience on Mount Hermon?"

Simon looked at the ground. Judas was close enough to hear their words and see their faces. He sensed a grave moment, as if something had come to a climax in Jesus' mind.

"You know I have to leave here," Jesus continued. "My time is ready."

Judas whispered to John bar Zebedee, "What's he talking about?"

John shook his head. "He's always turning normal talk into strange stories--parables he calls them."

Andrew jumped to his feet and said, "I'll follow you to the flames of Gehenna." He looked to the others for support, but they continued to stare at the fire.

"Think about it tonight," Jesus said. "I'll talk to each one of you tomorrow." Thomas and Jesus waved and started toward the merchant's square.

The men sat in silence. After a while, Simon looked at the others and shook his head. "What will he do in Judea? What can we do? We're fishermen, not preachers."

"We're near the end times," Andrew replied. "Soon the promises of the prophets will be fulfilled. It is time to prepare for the coming of the Messiah."

Simon raised his fist. "That's what your fanatics at the Salt Sea say. See what happens to those people? Already the water thrower is dead." He gestured toward the town. "The world will last forever. I don't know where you get these ideas about end times. Are you trying to scare us?"

Andrew smiled, "The Messiah will come during our lifetime."

Simon held Andrew by the shoulders. "Messiahs and end times are no concern of ours."

"But Jesus..."

"I don't care what you call him, but James and I have wives and children. We can't leave them alone because of Jesus. Besides, what will Zebedee say if we run off to Judea?"

Ignoring Simon, Andrew looked at James and John. "What about you?" he asked. "Will you go?"

Judas thought he saw fear on John's face, then he saw determination. "I'll go," he whispered. "I don't understand Messiahs and end times, but I believe in Jesus." He wiped a tear. "I have to follow him even though I can't explain why."

"So you'll leave with him?" Simon asked.

"Yes."

Simon looked at James. "What about you?"

James frowned. "Jesus is a problem for me, Simon. You and I saw things the others didn't see. Now I wish I hadn't." He looked into the fire. "I'm Zebedee's oldest son. He expects me to manage the fleet for him someday. He's already livid because we went to Caesarea Philippi. Not only that, Leah and I have young children." He looked at the other men and added, "Still, I'm a follower. I'll go with Jesus if the rest of you do."

Simon brushed his robe. "Don't worry, I'll see Jesus tomorrow and talk him out of his Judean dream." Andrew touched Simon's sleeve, but Simon pulled away. "You can go, Andrew. You believe in his strange ideas. I don't, and I have a right to tell him so."

"You say this after all you've seen and heard over the last two years?"

"What? A few people cured and a lot of talk. For God's sakes, Andrew, that's not what life is about. You, Thomas, and Jesus turn it into a circus with your talk about end times and kingdoms."

Andrew looked at the rest. "Well?" he asked.

"Jesus is my friend," Philip replied. "Tomorrow I'll go back to Bethsaida, settle accounts with my partner Gideon, and return back here as soon as I can."

Andrew clapped his hands. "It's settled; everyone except Simon will go to Nazareth and possibly go on to Judea with Jesus."

James raised his hand. "I'm not sure, I need to think."

Judas leaned next to John and whispered, "What happened on Mount Hermon?"

John brushed him aside. "I can't talk about it tonight; I have to find a way to tell my father I'm leaving."

"When will you tell me about Mount Hermon?"

"When the time is right," John answered abruptly as he pushed himself up.

Soon, each man started home, leaving Judas alone to ponder over the things he heard. Once they left, he listened to the gentle waves brushing against the shore and the creaking masts on the boats tied to the pier. For a moment, his mind flashed back to the first conversation he had about Galilee with his father in Kerioth. He smiled, thinking about how Judeans believed that these people were primitive. Uneducated, he thought, but not primitive. These strong men who worked the Sea of Galilee were people to be reckoned with.

CHAPTER TWELVE

The teachers of the law and the Pharisees brought in a woman caught in adultery. They made her stand before the group and said to Jesus, "Teacher, this woman was caught in the act of adultery. In the Law Moses commanded us to stone such women. Now what do you say?"
They were using this question as a trap, in order to have a basis for accusing him. But Jesus bent down and started to write on the ground with his finger.
When they kept on questioning him, he straightened up and said to them, "Let any one of you who is without sin be the first to throw a stone at her." Again he stooped down and wrote on the ground.
At this, those who heard began to go away one at a time, the older ones first, until only Jesus was left, with the woman still standing there.

John 8:3-9

Simon and Andrew stood on the edge of the Market waiting to meet Jesus and John. Silvery fish, still flopping in their baskets, arrived only moments before. The Market bustled with women hollering and jostling each other for the choice picks and the best prices. It seemed that life in Capernaum had settled down after the four men returned from Mount Hermon and since they heard the news about John the Baptist.

Judas had seen Markets in Judea, Perea and now Galilee. "Town Markets all looked alike," he thought. "The merchant's faces looked the same, the women were as skeptical, and the thieves as plentiful."

Andrew bought an orange from one of the stalls, cut it, and gave half to Judas. "You were very quiet on the boat today."

Judas shrugged.

"Is something wrong?"

Judas bit into his orange. "I'm confused. What is Jesus trying to do?"

Andrew nodded as they walked between rows of merchants selling jewelry and perfume on one side, and apples and live quail on the other. "Life is hard for most people. You saw how those people live at the Paupers Camp."

"It's a horrible place."

Andrew started to reply when they heard men yelling from the other side of the square. Judas shielded his eyes and looked in the direction of the noise.

"What's going on?" Judas asked.

"It looks like they're dragging someone from behind the jewelry stall. Probably a thief." Andrew held Judas back. "Stay here. I don't want to mix with that mob." Dust billowed behind the people who had stopped their activities and followed the crowd. Some picked up stones from the road as they ran.

To Judas' amazement, the disturbance stopped as suddenly as it started. When the dust settled and the edges of the crowd melted away, Judas saw only a few men standing around a figure lying on the ground.

The sounds of the crowd still hung in the air as a man in a gray robe knelt and wrote in the sand. After that, he stood and pointed to the person on the ground. Soon only the man in the gray robe and the person on the ground remained.

"Jesus!" Andrew gasped. He pulled Judas's arm and they ran to where Jesus stood. Judas whistled when he realized Jesus was standing over a woman. Her torn robe hung half off her shoulders and her face was distorted with terror. Jesus, in his clean gray robe stood in sharp contrast to her torn clothing, matted hair, and bruised skin. Before anyone spoke, he placed his robe over her shoulders.

"What happened?" Andrew asked.

Jesus looked at the woman, then at Andrew. "They accused her of adultery. They wanted to stone her."

Andrew glanced at her, then at Jesus. "Maybe they're..." He froze under the forbidding gaze of his friend.

"Maybe they're right?" Jesus asked his question for him.

"Perhaps...I'm not sure," Andrew mumbled.

"We have no right to judge others, much less kill them for the things they do." Jesus lifted his palms. "Who among us is perfect? Sure, not all of us commit adultery, but we do things that are wrong."

"Is that what you told them?"

"Not quite."

"What then?"

Jesus chuckled. "I asked to see the man who committed adultery with her. After all, justice for the woman should also be justice for the man." He put his arm on the woman's shoulder and asked, "Are you alright?"

She gave no reply.

"Do you have a home?"

Still no reply, only tears.

"What should we do with her?" Jesus asked Andrew.

"Take her to the Paupers Camp," Andrew replied.

"I can't do that, she needs someone to comfort her."

Eyes downcast, Andrew asked, "What about Naomi?"

Jesus smiled. "She may still be too angry at us to help, but it's worth a try." He looked at a group of men standing near the jeweler's booth. "Look, those vultures are waiting for us to leave. Let's take our chances with Naomi."

They left the Market area as fast as the woman's unsteady legs would allow. Judas kept his eyes on the Market square to see if the mob would follow.

Andrew suddenly stopped near Simon's house. "John! We forgot John." He gestured to Judas. "You stay with Jesus and I'll go back for John. We'll meet you at Simon's house."

Naomi met them at her gate with crossed arms. "What happened?" she asked as she scrutinized the woman. "Who is she?"

Jesus quickly told her about the events in the square. When he finished he asked, "Can you give her shelter?"

Naomi looked at him, eyes glowing like hot lava. "First you drag Simon to Caesarea Philippi, and now this. You want me to take a prostitute into my house." She stared at Jesus and pointed her finger at the ground. "You are standing on Simon's property. Take this woman to your camp with the rest of your shaggy friends."

The woman slouched in Jesus' arms. "She's fainting," Jesus pleaded. "Can't you at least clean her wounds and feed her?"

Naomi softened when she looked at the woman more closely. She pointed to a pail in the courtyard. "Judas, run down to the lake and fill this with water." Then she beckoned to Jesus. "Help me carry her in the house."

A short time later, Naomi came out of the house with her daughter, Jepthania in her arms. "How is the woman?" Jesus asked.

"She's asleep," Naomi replied. "And she's not a woman; she's a girl, maybe thirteen at the most. Her name is Sarah."

"Old enough to be a woman," Judas murmured.

"What do you know about girls and women?" Naomi snapped.

"Will you let her stay for the night?" Jesus asked.

"I suppose," she answered with a wave of her hand. "But take her away first thing tomorrow. I have enough trouble with Simon without bringing prostitutes in the house."

* * *

Judas and Jesus started the fire that night and waited for the others to join them. "You're lucky they didn't stone you in the square," Judas said.

"I suppose," Jesus replied.

"Why did you protect her?"

"I had to. I get angry when I see the strong oppress the weak. As I said earlier, we have no right to judge others."

Later, Andrew, John, and James joined them around the fire. "I saw Philip and Nathanael in town," John said. "They told me they'll be here soon." Then he looked at Jesus and added, "You upset the townspeople today. I was in the square shortly after you scattered the crowd and some men threatened me."

"Why is everyone so angry?" Judas asked.

"It's the times," Andrew answered. "People have lost hope."

"What can you do about it?" Judas continued.

"You looked at me when you asked that," Jesus noted.

Judas looked at the others then back to Jesus and said, "You are their leader."

Only the sea gulls wheeling and turning against the sky and the pounding waves made noise as Jesus poked the fire with a stick. "You say I am, yet..."

"What can you offer these people?" Judas persisted.

John shouted across the fire, "You don't understand..."

Jesus held his hand up. "Maybe he understands better than we do." He pointed toward the city. "Have we convinced anyone in Capernaum? How long has it been since Jericho? More than a year since I was with John the Baptizer on the Jordan."

John made depressions in the sand with his feet as he spoke. "They won't change. Yet they're frightened and uncertain the way they are." He looked at Jesus. "It's right for us to go to Judea. Maybe the leaders there will understand. After all, they know the prophets."

"Would we have to go there if they really believed the prophets?" Jesus queried.

Looking at Judas, John declared, "I know Jesus is a prophet."

"How do you know?" Judas asked.

John replied, "I saw Jesus in a dream one of the nights we stayed at Mount Hermon. I saw him dressed in a pure white robe and wearing a crown of gold." John stood and walked toward the water, then quickly turned to face Jesus. "But first I saw a different crown. The crown of a fool...sitting on the head of a man bleeding from his eyes...And that man was Jesus. I've thought about that dream ever since. It haunts me and makes me want to leave you." He stared at Judas. "There are days when I pray that everything will go back to the way they were...before Jesus came to Capernaum."

John stopped when he heard rustling in the bushes behind them. "That must be Phil..." A rock thrown from the bushes grazed his head before he finished.

Several men carrying clubs and rocks came toward them from the cover of the bushes. One of them shouted, "There he is!"

Andrew and Jesus stood between them and the fire. "What do you want?" Andrew asked.

"You took my sister," a man responded. "I want her back."

"Leave us alone!" John shouted.

"Give us the girl!" the man snarled.

"What girl?" Andrew asked. From the corner of his eye, he saw men circle behind John, Judas, and James.

"We won't hurt you if you give her to us," the leader continued. Now only he and one other man stood next to Jesus and Andrew.

"What do you want with her?" Jesus asked as he moved closer to the men. Instead of replying, the leader swung his club at Jesus. Then the other men jumped John, Judas, and James. Andrew and Jesus warded off repeated blows from the leader and his companion as they backed towards the fire.

John and James grabbed two men by their arms and slammed them together like dolls. John screamed--too late--when a third man hit James on the side of his head with a large rock. James dropped like a dead tree.

Judas and John soon lay on the ground, bloody and half conscious. Now the mob turned its attention to Andrew and Jesus and pummeled them to the ground.

Judas recovered enough to see some of the men heading towards Simon's house. He yelled at Andrew, and together they roused John and Jesus. Judas tried to wake James but he remained unconscious. The four men started after the assailants, shouting and screaming for them to stop. One of the assailants tripped, and John, running ahead of the others, caught him.

"What's going on here?" The words came from John in bursts.

The man started to cry.

John held him by the tunic and swung, but a huge hand grabbed his neck and threw him to the ground. Another man jumped Judas, but he wriggled free and kicked the man in the groin. He left him writhing on the ground while he went to help John.

Andrew caught another and screamed at Philip and Nathanael who just arrived on the scene. "Stop them!" He hit the man he held and gestured to those still running toward Simon's house.

Shuffling feet and men wrestling on the ground raised a curtain of dust that made it almost impossible to tell friend from foe. Judas, barely sensible, held

John's captive on the ground while the others fought. He choked a cry when a man came behind Jesus and hit him in the back of the head with a rock. Jesus fell as if killed on the spot. Now in a rage, Andrew lifted the assailant off the ground and threw him against a tree. The sight of Andrew lifting a man off the ground caused the other assailants to lose their taste for fighting. They threw a last barrage of rocks at Jesus' people and ran toward town.

After quickly surveying the area, Andrew hovered over John until he saw he was conscious. "Can you stand?" he asked.

John nodded and staggered to his feet. "I don't know what to rub first. Those pigs fight dirty."

Andrew went to where Philip leaned over Jesus. "Is he alive?" he asked.

"He's breathing," Philip replied.

Judas pulled his captive, a young boy, to his feet and led him to where the others stood.

By this time, Jesus regained consciousness. "Get some water on your head," Philip said. "That'll bring you back to life." Next Philip found James lying next to the fire. Leaning over and listening to his heart, he shouted to the others, "I think he's dead."

Jesus returned from the lake, hair dripping and water running off his beard, and knelt next to James. "He's alive," he said. "Throw some water on him."

Now they focused on the single captive Judas and John caught. John grabbed the boy's throat and yelled, "Who are you?"

The boy's eyes darted from John to Judas, then the others. "A…Asher."

"Asher what?" John demanded.

No reply.

John kicked dirt at him and raised his fist. "Talk to me before I turn your face into a..."

"John--stop!" Jesus yelled.

Asher looked at John, then Jesus and started to cry. Jesus held the boy's chin and looked into his eyes.

"They'll hurt me." the boy said.

"Who are they?" Jesus asked.

"They'll come back for me," he whimpered.

"Not any more," Jesus said in a soothing voice. "But tell me about these men and why you're with them."

"Their leader is a man named Mattatias," he replied. "They live by stealing and what money Sarah and I earn."

John gave Jesus a withering glance and pushed him aside. "You're too easy on him. I'll..."

Jesus took the collar of John's tunic and held it tight. "Leave him alone." Then turning back to the boy, he asked, "Earn money?"

"Sarah is Mattatias' sister. He sells her to other men."

"And you?"

"He sells me to both men and women."

Judas turned away, wondering if there was no end to the way people made other people suffer.

"Where do you live?" Jesus continued.

"In a camp north of Bethsaida." Asher looked at him anxiously. "But they'll move--you won't find them."

"He's lying!" John growled.

"Don't hit me," the boy pleaded.

"Wait a minute," Andrew interjected. "He says they'll come back for him. Why don't we wait for them to come to us?"

"What if he's lying?" John asked.

Philip signaled to Jesus and said, "James is awake."

Jesus' eyes brightened. "I'll get to him in a minute." Jesus turned back to the boy. "I've seen you before, at Cana. You're a servant from the house of Malech."

Asher looked at the ground. "I saw you...at the wedding."

Jesus rubbed the bump on his head. "You're less than thirteen years old. How did you get mixed up with those men?"

"I ran away from my master in Cana. I went to Bethsaida and met Mattatias and his people near the edge of town. He offered me a place to eat and sleep. Then after a while he started selling me in the area around Bethsaida."

Impatiently, Jesus asked, "Where will you go to avoid Mattatias and his friends?"

"I don't know, south maybe." He squirmed out of Jesus' grasp. "Let me go. I didn't do anything wrong...they made me come." He looked at John and shuddered. "Please let me go."

"For now I want you to stay with us," Jesus said. "We'll protect you from Mattatias and his gang. But promise you won't run away from us."

"What?" John shouted. This time Andrew stopped him. John glared at Andrew and walked away.

Jesus went to where James sat dazed and frightened. "Are you alright?" he asked.

James nodded.

"Can you do anything?" Andrew asked.

Jesus shook his head. "Not tonight. We have to wait." Then he motioned for the others to come together. He looked at each one sadly and said, "I'm going to leave this place before more trouble starts. I don't know what else to say." He drew circles in the ground with a stick. Judas noticed how calm Jesus seemed, even when he showed uncertainty.

Andrew moved toward him. "Where will you go?"

Jesus thought for a moment. "Simon's house."

"Simon is not home," Andrew said. "He went to Bethsaida this afternoon."

"I'll talk to Naomi."

"What about us?" John asked.

"I can't ask you to take the risks I'm taking after what happened tonight. You saw the hate in their eyes. We're lucky they didn't kill us."

"Will it make it easier for us if you go?" John asked.

Jesus quietly replied. "I don't know."

"You can't leave like this," John blurted.

Jesus sighed, "John...we need time to think about this."

He pointed to Asher. "I'll take Asher and the girl, Sarah, when I go to Nazareth." He put his arm around Asher. "Right now it looks like he doesn't have a friend in Galilee."

Jesus looked at his companions. "Take a few days to make sure you want to come." Then he said to Philip and Nathanael, "You stay at the Paupers Camp tonight and take the rest of the people to Nazareth tomorrow. After that you can come back here if you wish."

When Jesus went to Naomi's house to pick up Sarah, Naomi said, "The girl should rest in my house tonight. She'll be safe here."

"Did you talk to her?" Jesus asked.

Naomi's voice quivered, "Her brother used her and a young boy as prostitutes. He beat them when they didn't earn enough money."

Jesus took Naomi's hand. "Thank you for helping. I know this hasn't been an easy time for you." He kissed her forehead and added, "Take care of her, I'll take care of young Asher. Tonight we will sleep on your roof in case those men return."

CHAPTER THIRTEEN

Going on from there, he saw two other brothers, James son of Zebedee and his brother John. They were in a boat with their father Zebedee, preparing their nets. Jesus called them, and immediately they left the boat and their father and followed him.

Matthew 4:21-22

Early the next morning Judas, dressed in a warm robe, stood on shore with Andrew and James. Simon and Jesus were at Simon's boat talking and gesturing. Judas started toward the dock, but Andrew held his arm. "Wait," he whispered.

Off to the side, a man carrying a lamp went to each boat, leaving a flicker of light sitting next to the mast. Other shadowy figures followed him through the pre-dawn haze hanging over Capernaum and moved the lights to the masts. The fishermen threw their nets and supplies in their boats and slipped out of the harbor before the sun rose and the roosters woke the rest of the town. Only the lingering fish smell and the squawking gulls reminded Judas of boats and fishermen.

Simon called them over after he finished talking to Jesus and announced, "I'm not going out this morning."

"Why not?" Andrew asked.

"I'm going to Nazareth with Thomas," Simon answered coldly.

Andrew's jaw dropped. "Nazareth?"

Simon pointed to Jesus. "He asked Thomas to take a group of people from the Paupers' Camp to Nazareth and I said I'd help."

Andrew stroked his beard. "I thought you said..."

"I know, but that's all I'll do. I'm coming back after that. I have no interest in meddling in other people's lives."

"Then why are you going to Nazareth?"

"I don't know," Simon replied as Jesus walked over to where they were standing. "Ask Jesus why he wants me to do this." Gesturing at the boat, he added, "You can stay in shore today. I came to fix the rudder, but now you can do it."

"Are you leaving right now?" Andrew asked.

Simon shook his head. "First, I'm going to tell Naomi, then find Zebedee at daylight and tell him."

"He'll have a fit," Andrew said. "This may be more than..."

"Do you want to tell him?" Simon interrupted.

Raising his hands, Andrew replied, "I'll work on the boat."

Jesus held Simon's arm. "I'll go with you."

Simon straightened, turned and faced Jesus. His eyes spoke in a way he never could through his words. "Right now, you aren't popular with Naomi or Zebedee. I'll do better without you."

Judas asked, "What is the Paupers' Camp?"

"The Paupers' Camp is a place where poor people live south of Capernaum. It's a mixture of caves and shacks. To most people in Capernaum, the people living at the Paupers' Camp are unclean." Andrew cast a glance at Jesus, who clearly showed his disapproval of Andrew's explanation. Gesturing to Jesus, Andrew said, "Maybe he should explain the camp to you."

Jesus smiled at Andrew and said, "The people who live in the camp are outcasts. Some are sick, others crippled. There are diseased prostitutes, abused women and children; people who can't take care of themselves. They forage for their food. Sometimes they have to eat garbage from the town pit located near their camp."

Judas shook his head, indicating he heard all he wanted to know. Still, he persisted, "Why are Simon and Thomas taking them to Nazareth?"

"The people of Capernaum feel the camp has grown too large," answered Jesus. "They're afraid the people from the camp will make trouble in town." Casting a glance back at Andrew, he added. "I hope to help these people care for themselves in a friendlier place. In Nazareth, my family and friends will help these people build new lives. We already have a small camp on a hill across from the city."

Andrew leaned against his boat and looked at Jesus. "What did you say to Simon that made him change his mind?"

"Simon is a believer," Jesus replied. "He just needs someone to remind him."

"It isn't that simple. What did you say to him?"

"I asked him to help me move this camp to Nazareth," Jesus responded. "I told Simon that I'd leave him alone for a while if he helped."

"Will you?"

Jesus winked. "He didn't ask how long a while is."

Judas, Andrew, and Jesus walked back to Andrew's house in silence to eat breakfast. After breakfast, Andrew went back to his boat and Jesus invited Judas to go with him to the Paupers' Camp.

"How many people will Simon and Thomas take to Nazareth?" Judas asked as they walked along the road out of town.

"About ten or twelve," Jesus answered. "We'll take the rest when Philip returns from Bethsaida."

Jesus ran his hand through his hair. "They are rejected people who have no place in society. As I said before, many are crippled, some are blind..."

Judas raised his hand. "I heard you fixed people with those problems."

Jesus laughed. "It's not as easy as it sounds."

"Don't you do miracles?" Judas persisted.

"Did someone tell you that?" Jesus asked.

"I don't know."

Jesus put his hand on Judas's shoulder. "You'll have to see for yourself. Maybe you should stay with us in Nazareth."

"I only planned to stay in Capernaum for a month," Judas replied. "I've already stayed longer than I planned."

As they came to the top of a hill, they saw wild dogs fighting over the carcass of a small animal. The dogs stopped for a moment, cast malevolent glances at them, and then resumed their breakfast.

Jesus glanced at Judas. "Are you sure you want to see this place?"

Judas replied with a touch of exaggeration. "I've seen hardship."

* * *

When they reached the Paupers' Camp, Judas noticed the barefoot woman John told him about, still chasing crows and dogs away from the vegetables. Judas looked at the rubbish scattered throughout the camp and said, "I've never seen anything like this. It's hopeless!"

Simon and Thomas stopped their work and came over to greet Jesus and Judas.

"Did you find someone to help carry supplies to Nazareth?" Jesus asked.

Thomas gestured to a boy collecting wood for a fire. "He will help. His name is James bar Alphaeus. He lives in one of the caves with his mother."

Jesus smiled. "He doesn't look strong enough to carry a pack."

"He's stronger than he looks," replied Thomas.

"Who else?"

"Mary of Magdala, you remember her."

Jesus nodded and said, "We have to hurry if you're going to leave by mid day. Remember, go as far as Cana and look for Eli. He lives north of the city. He'll give you food and provide straw for bedding." Putting his hand on Simon's shoulder, Jesus warned, "Leave Cana early tomorrow morning." He looked toward the caves. "One more thing; stay away from Magdala. Mary's father might start trouble if he sees her with you."

Thomas pointed to a young man walking toward them. "That's the James I told you about...James bar Alphaeus. His mother, Mary, was the wife of Alphaeus. He died a few years ago in an uprising against Herod's soldiers"

"Forget them," Simon interrupted. "We have things to do. The sooner I leave, the sooner I'll get back." He looked at Jesus and muttered, "I don't know why I let you talk me into this."

"Because you're the only one who knows Eli."

"That's a poor reason," he retorted.

* * *

After Simon and Thomas left for Nazareth, Judas and Jesus returned to the city in time to see the boats coming in from morning fishing.

Jesus stuck his finger in the air when he saw the masts of the fleet peeking over the horizon. "Bad fishing today," he said, "it looks like rain is on the way."

Eager to escape the rain, the fishermen rushed to draw their sails and hang their nets. True to Jesus' prediction, there were few baskets of fish hauled to market that afternoon. Judas stayed behind while Jesus went toward James and John bar Zebedee's boat. The other fishermen stopped working on their boats when they saw Jesus and edged closer to listen.

"I know how your father feels," they heard Jesus say. "But you have to make a choice. I'm leaving in a few days, maybe tomorrow."

"What about Andrew and Simon?" James asked.

"Simon is on the way to Nazareth and Andrew is going with me," Jesus replied.

"He'll go with who?" Zebedee's voice boomed behind them.

All activity around the boats stopped when Jesus turned to face Zebedee and said, "I want John and James to come with me."

"Come with you?" Zebedee snarled. "You mean leave here?"

"Yes."

Zebedee smiled, "Well, I'm happy to see you go, but where do you think you'll take these boys?"

"To Judea."

Zebedee looked at the men gathered around them, then waved his finger at Jesus. "What in the name of the prophets will you do in Judea?"

"There's more to life than fishing," Jesus replied.

James caught his father's eye. "Jesus wants us to give up what we have, so..."

Zebedee's eyes flashed. "Give up? Give up what? What do you know about life? You're only thirty. John is not even twenty. His mother still has to wipe the snot from his nose." The onlookers backed away as Zebedee's anger escalated.

"What does age have to do with these things?" Jesus retorted. "Are people with white beards the only ones who understand God's word?"

"You insolent..."

"Stop!" Jesus brushed a few drops of water from his forehead. "I don't want to argue with you. I'm sorry that..."

"I suppose you're going to tell me that a voice inside you told you to do this," Zebedee yelled back. "You're willing to destroy my family and my business so you can act like a high priest in the market."

Jesus looked at John and James, then Zebedee. "You said they are fishermen. I want them to become fishers of men."

"That's crazy," Zebedee looked at the crowd for support. "What does that have to do with real fishing?"

"You're a self-righteous fool," Jesus snapped. He blushed as if he wished he could swallow his words. "Our spiritual life doesn't end at the synagogue door or with a few prayers at mealtime."

Zebedee waved his staff. "That's big talk for a drifter. The only thing you're good for is preaching." He pointed his staff toward the synagogue. "Preach in there and stay away from the places where people do real work." Zebedee looked around as the crowd murmured its assent.

James interrupted, "Father, we're..." He ducked Zebedee's staff and backed away. Judas saw the hurt in his eyes as he continued, "...not children. Have you been to the Paupers Camp? Do you care about those people?"

Zebedee waved his arms. "Who cares? What good will it do for you to stop working? You'll only end up as poor as them." Then Zebedee spun and asked Jesus, "What's going on here? These are men of the sea. What do they know about God and pauper's camps?" He looked back to his sons as swollen drops of rain fell into the still water.

Making sure he was at least a staff length away from Zebedee, Jesus answered, "To you, they are ordinary fishermen," he said in a soft voice. "To me, they are the heirs to God's Kingdom. It is not I who call them. It's the Father through me."

Judas, confused by Jesus' words, pulled Andrew's sleeve to ask a question just as Zebedee climbed into his sons' boat. Zebedee stared at James and John and said, "You have a choice! This boat, or that man and his dreams. I can't wait for you to grow up." He shook his staff with renewed intensity. "Now or never! Make your choice--now!"

John and James walked to where Jesus stood.

Zebedee pointed to them. "You are no longer my sons if you leave with this man." James and John stared at their father, who called them to their tradition and Jesus who called them to an uncertain destiny. "Decide now!" he repeated.

"Father..." Tears rolled down John's cheeks.

"NOW!" Zebedee flashed a withering gaze at Jesus.

"You won't listen," John cried. "You're so stubborn." Now Judas saw the Zebedean intensity in John's eyes. Son and father stared at each other as if the rage of Sodom and Gomorrah were passing between them.

Zebedee signaled to two men standing near the boat. "Push this boat away from the dock and get in. From now on, this will be your boat." The rain drenched everyone as Zebedee barked orders to the men who would now sail his sons' boat.

John and James stood at the shore watching their boat while most of the onlookers ran for cover. After a while, John walked away, then James and Jesus. Judas and Andrew returned to Andrew's house wondering what would happen next.

On the way back, Judas asked Andrew, "What did Jesus mean when he said he wanted them to become fishers of men?"

Andrew thought for a moment, then shook his head. "I don't have a good answer. He's asking us to leave our work, our families, and our homes to teach people about the Kingdom of God." Andrew paused, and then added with downcast eyes, "And he wants us to do it in Judea."

* * *

Nahum's Inn, located on the edge of the market in Capernaum, was a gathering and gossiping place for the men of the city. The inn had four small sleeping areas located on the far end of the courtyard, one of which was rented by Judas and a dining area on the market side. Travelers passing through Capernaum frequently stayed at Nahum's, bringing with them news from the outside world. Good news carriers were usually rewarded with a free meal in exchange for their information.

That evening, after the clash with Jesus at the pier, Zebedee and his partner, Aaron Yohaz, met at Nahum's Inn. Zebedee felt a chill even though the afternoon downpour had stopped after a few minutes. He sneezed and wrapped his robe tighter. “I’m going to disown my sons,” he rasped.

Aaron Yohaz sipped wine from his cup and watched Nahum listening in the background.

“I don’t want to do it, but that Jesus has twisted their minds. They don’t want to fish anymore,” Zebedee continued.

Aaron Yohaz tapped his fingers on the table. “Is there any chance that John and James will return?”

“They no longer fish for me.” Zebedee gestured thumbs down. “They decided they don’t have to work for a living.”

“If we lose them and Simon and Andrew...”

“We’ve lost nothing. We can replace them,” Zebedee replied sharply. “Besides, Simon will be back in a few days. He needs his wine.” He shook his finger. “And James will come back begging for work within a week. His wife, Leah will see to that.”

Aaron looked at the ground and said, “I...I don’t know, Zeb, these sons are as stubborn as their father.”

Zebedee’s eye caught Nahum listening. “What are you sneaking around for?” he yelled. “Gossip? Well, listen hard, innkeeper. We’ll still be the major supplier of fish long after those four...” He punctuated his words with another sneeze.

“Prodigal sons?” Nahum teased.

Zebedee stood and slammed his cup on the table. “Yes--yes, those prodigal sons! Those foolish boys who gave up their inheritance. For what?” He tilted his head back. “Fancy boys going out to preach. They don’t know scripture. They aren’t scribes. Help the poor?” He snickered, “If Jonah were alive he would beat some sense into Simon and Andrew.”

“He could handle your two sons as well,” Nahum mumbled.

Zebedee stood nose to chest with Nahum. “I can take care of my own boys. You’ll see.”

Aaron pulled them apart. “Easy, Zeb, you’ll have a fit if you keep this up.”

“What do you know about fits?”

“I know when I see one coming...and I see one now. Not only that, you have the makings of a bad cold.”

Let me get you some wine and warm bread,” Nahum whispered as he backed toward the kitchen.

Zebedee looked over Aaron’s shoulder and eye-walked Nahum into the kitchen. “If I catch a cold, it’ll be from arguing with that drifter in the rain. Here, let’s move closer to the fire.” Zebedee leaned against a post and scratched his head. “Why are they doing it?”

"That's the question I have," Aaron replied. "What did they tell you?"

"Nothing! This Jesus has been in and out of the city for a few years. They're always with him. They even took him fishing." Zebedee looked up when Nahum returned with fresh wine and a platter of food. "Sit down innkeeper. What do you have here? Ah, some fruit. And that bread, it is warm."

Nahum beamed. "It's free."

Zebedee tore off a piece of bread and washed it down with a cup of wine. "Where was I? Oh, yes, James lives in his own house, so most of what I hear comes from John. But John's young, less than twenty years old. He always wants to change things. He says our leaders treat people like they aren't human. So I say to John, tell me what we're doing wrong." Zebedee leaned closer to Aaron Yohaz and whispered, "And do you know what? He can't tell me, except that the rich live off the poor."

"That's the way it's been since the beginning of time," Nahum mused.

Zebedee ignored him. "So I say, give me one good reason why you want to waste your time with this man." Zebedee sneezed again. "John says he can't. But he says there's something about Jesus that makes people want to follow him." Zebedee shrugged. "He can't give me a reason, though. Does that make sense?"

"What's Jesus going to do?" Aaron asked. "Start a new religion?"

"What does religion have to do with peoples needs?" Nahum added.

Zebedee waved his hand. "John and James say that Jesus has new ideas about the Law. If you want my opinion, I think his head is full of pebbles."

"Ha, ha, what do they know? I'm twice their age and I don't understand everything I should about the Law." Aaron emptied his cup and beckoned for more, at the same time pointing to the platter, now left with only a few crumbs, and added, "This is the meaning of life."

Zebedee pointed to his friend's ample girth and laughed for the first time since they started talking. "Only if your spirit lives in your stomach. Another thing," Zebedee warned, "the men in this town have no interest in upstarts who take people away from their work. There will be trouble." He paused for effect; "there will be trouble."

CHAPTER FOURTEEN

As they were walking along the road, a man said to him, "I will follow you wherever you go."
Jesus replied, "Foxes have holes and birds have nests, but the Son of Man has no place to lay his head."
He said to another man, "Follow me."
But he replied, "Lord, first let me go and bury my father."
Jesus said to him, "Let the dead bury their own dead, but you go and proclaim the kingdom of God."
Still another said, "I will follow you, Lord; but first let me go back and say good-by to my family."
Jesus replied, "No one who puts a hand to the plow and looks back is fit for service in the kingdom of God."

Luke 9:57-62

By morning of the next day Simon, Thomas, and young James bar Alphaeus were on the road to Nazareth with the people from the Pauper's Camp. Philip, Nathanael, and Andrew would not leave Capernaum until the next morning when Philip returned from settling his affairs with his employer in Bethsaida. Meanwhile, John, Matthew and Jesus were well on their way to Nazareth with the boy and girl they rescued from Mattatias.

The slate grey clouds cloaked the ground and the chill that usually disappeared by the mid morning hung in every corner of Andrew's house. It was after a night of fitful sleep that Judas and James bar Zebedee sat staring into space while Andrew paced the floor.

James broke the silence. "I suppose that Simon and Thomas are near Nazareth by now."

"We need to talk to Simon," James said as he made piles of dirt on the floor with his feet. "You can leave at anytime because you have no families, but it's different for Simon and me."

Andrew said, “Maybe people will leave you alone. The real question is whether Zebedee will take you back.”

“He needs us,” James muttered.

“Yes, but he’s as stubborn as...” Andrew glanced at James.

James grimaced, “I know, as stubborn as his sons.”

Ignoring his comment, Andrew continued, “I am going to Nazareth tomorrow with Philip and Nathanael.”

“Are you still willing to follow Jesus?” Judas asked Andrew.

“For a while,” Andrew replied. “John the Baptizer made as much sense to me as Jesus.”

“Didn’t they teach the same ideas?”

“John wanted to purify Judaism,” Andrew answered. “Jesus wants to change the world.”

John bar Zebedee asked Judas, “Will you go with us to Nazareth?”

“I was planning on returning to Caesarea this week,” Judas replied.

James said, “I know I’m not as wise as some, but I believe Jesus is a prophet. What I mean is...” James’ eyes darted from man to man. “...We’ve been with him for a long time. We heard him preach, we heard him teach -- we talk to him almost every day. And you, Andrew, Do you doubt him?”

“My experience with him is like smoke,” Andrew replied. “I try to wrap my arms around it, and when I look there’s nothing there. I don’t understand kingdoms and spirits. Do you?”

“Yes,” James asserted.

“Then tell us what you know,” Judas interrupted.

Eyes downcast, James replied, “I understand, but I can’t explain.”

Before anyone could comment further, they heard a cough from the doorway. A man standing in the opening asked, “Is this Andrew bar Jonah’s house?”

“Yes, what do you want?” Andrew replied.

“I am Mordecai, and I’m looking for Jesus of Nazareth. I was told I could find him here”

Andrew looked at the man for a moment before he answered, “What do you want?”

Mordecai pointed toward the market square. “They sent me to warn you. The men of the town are meeting at the stall of Jonas, the poultry-man. They say your friend Jesus is a trouble maker.”

“Wrong! Jesus is a trouble identifier,” James growled.

“Where’s the prostitute he has been sleeping with?” Mordecai asked.

“He doesn’t sleep with prostitutes.”

Mordecai ignored James. “Jesus is not welcome in Capernaum.”

"Who told you to say that?" Andrew asked.

"The elders of the city," Mordecai answered. "He disobeyed Moses' Law by associating with prostitutes." Judas had trouble telling whether Mordecai was afraid or confident with his message. Continuing, Mordecai said, "Jesus has disturbed the town."

"Why are you telling us these things?" Matthew asked.

"They sent me to warn you."

"Who?"

"The Council. The Elders."

"That includes Zebedee and Aaron Yohaz," Andrew muttered to himself. "Tell them Jesus is gone." He gestured to the men in the room. "Some are gone; others will be leaving by tomorrow. Tell the elders I'll talk with them if they wish."

After Mordecai nodded nervously and ran from the house, Andrew paced the room with his hands clasped behind his back. "You better leave as soon as you can," he said in a calm voice. "I will leave tomorrow with Philip and Nathanael."

"This is short notice," James replied. "I didn't plan to leave so soon." He paused for a moment, then added, "But I'll go to Nazareth. Leah and the children are at her sister's house in Cana and I'll go there to tell her what happened here and pick up my son, Aaron." He looked at Judas. "Will you come? You can return with Simon if you wish."

Judas shrugged. "When will you leave?"

"As soon as we gather a sack full of clothes."

Judas brushed his hand through his hair. "Alright, I'll go." Then he raised a finger and added, "But I'm going back to Capernaum with Simon."

* * *

"There'll be more trouble," James told Judas on the way to his house. "There'll be trouble here, and in Nazareth when they see the people from the Paupers' Camp." He looked at the sky. "Hurry, it's starting to rain."

They arrived at James' house as the light rain turned to a wind driven downpour. James talked to himself as he threw clothes and provisions in a light canvas bag. "I'm glad I sent Leah and the children to Cana," James said as he threw some clothes at Judas. "Put these on and pack some fruit--we have to hurry if we're going to reach Cana before dark."

"James..."

"Yes?"

"Tell me why you're willing to risk everything to follow Jesus?" Judas pulled his robe tighter to block the chill in the air.

James sighed and leaned against the wall. "I'm only a fisherman. I don't know much about life. Yet...don't you think about where we came from and where we're going?"

"Yes, there are times when I think about those things. I even wonder why I was born."

"Or why you must die?"

Judas looked away. "I don't like to think about that."

"None of us want to, yet we do."

"What's your point?"

"Jesus says it's time for people like us to think for ourselves. The rabbis and scribes only tell us what they want us to know. They make the rules so they can control us." As James walked towards the door, he added, "Our father, Zebedee, thinks about these things, though he doesn't admit it. He once left his father to study with the school of Hillel. I heard that our grandfather tried to flog him when he returned, but Zebedee took the switch away and threatened to..."

"What happened to the commandment, obey your father?" Judas interrupted.

James laughed, "I don't think Zebedee worried about that until I was born." As he finished packing his bag, he asked, "Do you know who Hillel was?"

"No."

"Hillel lived about a hundred years ago. He was a teacher like Jesus, except I think he lived in Babylon." James smiled. "That reminds me: One night, John brought Jesus to a meal with our parents. Jesus and Zebedee argued about the meaning of scripture and the Law until Zebedee accused Jesus of heresy and told him to leave his house. My mother put an end to that conversation, but Zebedee has suspected Jesus ever since."

The rain dissolved into a soft mist as James bar Zebedee and Judas took a little used road out of town. Within a short time they found themselves on the road to Cana. They walked in silence for over an hour, Judas lost in his confusion over Jesus, and James thinking about what he would tell his wife Leah.

Judas broke the silence. "What do you really think about Jesus?" he asked.

James looked into the distance. "I've known for quite some time that he is special."

"What has this to do with fishing and raising families?"

"We're not separate from each other. When you hurt, I must hurt with you. That's Jesus' message. We need to live for each other."

"Do you think he has the only answer?"

"I don't know about answers. I only know a few questions. I heard about John the Baptizer, and I listen to Andrew and Thomas, the Twin. They all see the same things, but not the way Jesus does."

"How can you justify what you're doing?" Judas asked. "Like when you left your family and went with Jesus to Caesarea Philippi? Now after yesterday, your friends are gone and the town is ready to drive you away as well."

"We need to follow our dreams, Judas. What we are doing with Jesus is right for us."

"Sometimes I think you're crazy, like your father said," Judas muttered. Then he added, "I want you to do something for me if you will."

"What?"

"I want to talk to Jesus alone, and I want the whole story about Mount Hermon."

James brushed the bottom of his light beard with his fingers. "I will tell you about Mount Hermon when the time is right. Knowing Jesus, I'd say he'll talk to you anytime you want."

* * *

Judas and James came over a rise in time to see the sun setting behind Cana. Gesturing toward the town, James said, "Leah is staying with her sister, Ruth, and her husband, Jethro. We'll be surrounded by women and children when we reach Jethro's house." James smiled. "I hope you like children."

Judas nodded. He'd never given much thought to whether he liked children.

"I better warn you," James continued, "that my wife is no ordinary woman."

"What do you mean?" Judas asked.

"Leah is a strong willed woman, much the same as Simon's Naomi. Simon and I are convinced that they conspire against us when we're fishing on the Sea of Galilee."

The sun disappeared behind the hills to their west by the time Judas and James reached the deserted streets of Cana. Only a few candles and the mealtime odors drifting from the windows of homes near the road gave testimony to the life of the town. Judas glanced at the houses on either side of the narrow street, at the same time inhaling the friendly smells of soups and stews cooking over fires.

Judas noticed that Cana was smaller and much different than Capernaum. The booths and merchant's stalls in Cana had few fish and no pigs. The market square smelled of oranges, green vegetables and fresh bread. The whitewashed houses were clustered near the road, surrounded by fields patched with spring plantings and white blossomed olive trees. James noted that most of the people in Cana were Jews, while only half in Capernaum believed in Yahweh and Moses.

"Over there," said James, pointing to a group of houses hanging on the side of a hill. "Are you hungry?"

"Yes. And tired."

James steered Judas to a house on his left. "There it is. I hope Ruth has a warm supper ready for us."

"Do they know we're coming?"

"No, but a man can hope."

A young boy and two girls, followed by two women and a man, ran from the house to greet them. James hugged the boy and the two girls. "This is my son, Aaron, and my daughters, Anna and Rachel," he said proudly. Then James introduced his wife, Leah, her sister, Ruth, and her brother-in-law, Jethro. Jethro invited them into the house where Ruth quickly prepared a meal of cold fish, fruit and barley bread.

James looked at the food. "I was hoping for hot stew."

"Send a messenger the next time, and you might get a hot meal," Leah replied. "After all, we're not prophets like Jesus and John."

Smiling James asked, "Now, is that any way to treat your husband?"

Leah glanced at Judas. "Why did you come with him?"

"I'm not..."

She turned to James. "You did come to take us home."

James blushed. "I came for Aaron."

"And?"

"Judas and I are going to Nazareth to help Jesus." James tried to sound authoritative, but gave himself away by flinching slightly as he talked.

A dark shadow crossed Leah's eyes. "What's going on here? Are you a fisherman or a drifter?"

"I don't want to talk about it, I'm tired and hungry."

"Well, it seems to me..."

"If I wanted your opinion, I'd ask for it," James said, pointing to a bench. "Sit down and I'll tell you what I can."

Judas marveled at the exchange between Leah and James. She was attractive, especially for a woman who was at least thirty years old. And she had fire; a woman who could match a son of Zebedee in intensity.

James continued, "I'll follow Jesus to Judea if he asks."

"What will I do in the meantime?" Leah shouted as her sister and brother-in-law shrank toward the corners of the room.

"Come to Nazareth, stay here, or go home to Capernaum."

"What will I use for food?"

A wicked smile played around his lips. "One thing for sure, they're trying to kill prostitutes in Capernaum. You better not..." He ducked in time to miss a well aimed plate. It hit the wall and fell to the floor in pieces.

Judas suddenly regretted his decision to follow James to Nazareth.

James held his arm in the air to deflect any flying objects that might follow the plate. "You can come with us or..."

Leah's eyes narrowed to a slit. "You're crazy, James bar Zebedee. You, your father, your brother, and now our son." She waved her arms. "The whole family is mad." She looked around the room. "Where's John? Why isn't he here to make the insanity complete?"

"John is on his way to Nazareth with Matthew," James answered cautiously.

Leah laughed sarcastically. "I see. All the fools will be in Nazareth."

"Very funny..."

Judas raised his hand. "Will you please...?"

"Stay out of this." Leah snapped.

Judas liked her passion.

James yawned as a ploy to end the argument. "We can talk about this in the morning."

"I'm not done yet," Leah shot back. "The best thing you can do is go home, repair your nets, and get back to fishing."

"True," James replied impatiently. "But it isn't going to happen this week."

Ruth stepped between the quarreling couple and offered them cups of nectar. James took one, drained it, and slammed the cup on the table. Ruth quickly refilled the cup, giving it to James before he could say another word. Judas noticed that the nectar was sweet--a welcome change from the conversation between James and Leah. He wondered where people got their information about Galilee, and whether the historians of the past had ever witnessed such exchanges between a husband and wife.

* * *

It was agreed that Judas and James would sleep that night on the roof with Aaron. Judas reasoned that James wanted to stay as far away from Leah as he could until her temperament improved. Judas woke the next morning when James nudged him before he went down the ladder. Within minutes, he heard Leah and James picking up where they left off the evening before. Judas heard James mumble something about sleep, but the tone of Leah's voice said there would be no more rest.

"I talked to Ruth last night after you went to sleep," she declared. Judas peeked over the edge and saw her standing with her hands on her hips. "She'll watch our girls while we take your holiday in Nazareth." Glancing at the roof, Leah caught Judas trying to duck out of sight. "What's wrong, afraid to come down?" she chided, "Not that you don't have reason to fear."

Judas looked over the edge and waved to her.

Unimpressed, she waved back. "Hurry, we need to eat before we leave."

Leah, James, and Judas sat on benches around a small table filled with bread and fruit. Ruth served a warm barley cereal in clay containers while James cut apples and pears into small pieces over the bowls.

Leah caught Judas' eye. "What made you decide to go to Nazareth?" she asked. "A fever? Maybe a brain fever?"

"James promised..."

She laughed. "Don't ever believe his promises."

Judas didn't know how to answer.

"I'll tell you why I'm going," she continued. "I'm going to see Jesus. He's done enough harm to our family." She played with a piece of bread as she talked. "Maybe his mother and I can talk some sense into him." Her eyes narrowed. "Yes, Jesus' mother will talk sense to him and that bunch of dreamers chasing after him." Despite her harsh talk, she seemed a little softer than the previous evening.

They ate the rest of the meal in silence, a quiet Judas welcomed almost as much as the food. They prepared for their journey immediately after breakfast and, after an exchange of goodbyes, left Cana before mid morning.

* * *

Later that morning, on the road to Nazareth, James pointed to a valley where green fields rich with vegetables stretched from hill to hill. "Jesus said we can work in the fields when we go to Judea. He says the harvest will be ready and the farmers will be looking for workers."

Later, as they walked past a field full of sun burnt crops, they saw a small structure standing in the middle of the field. It was a crude shelter made from branches and covered with a piece of goatskin. A man slept under the canvas instead of working his field. Leah tugged James by the arm and pointed to the scene. "That looks like the type of field work you and your friends are capable of doing."

James paused in his stride, attempted to look insulted, and replied, "Mind yourself, woman." Judas sensed that the rebuke had fallen far short of its target.

In the meantime, young Aaron provided a constant stream of conversation, asking questions and giving answers before anyone replied. After a few hours of Aaron's banter, Judas longed for some quiet companionship. Finally, James gestured for Aaron to walk with his mother. "I don't know who that boy takes after," he mumbled.

"He's a Zebedee!" Leah shot back. "He talks all the time and he knows everything."

"You're jealous because you aren't as smart as the Zebedee's," James retorted.

She tossed her head back. "You call yourselves smart? If you're so smart..."

"Why did I marry you?"

"You're lucky you did," she countered.

By mid afternoon they saw the hills of Nazareth in the distance. "This trip didn't take long," James declared. "As you see, we're not far from Capernaum and only a short walk from Cana."

Leah pointed to a cloud of dust heading toward them.

"It's either soldiers or a small caravan," James said as he watched it move closer. "It has to be soldiers, the dust is moving too fast for a caravan." He ran toward the side of the road and called for the others to do the same.

Within minutes four soldiers rode up to them and one pointed to James. "Who are you?" he asked in a broken Greek dialect.

"James bar Zebedee," James replied in an equally poor Greek dialect.

"From where?"

"Capernaum."

The soldier gestured at the others. "Who are they?"

"She's my wife, the young boy is my son, and the young man is a friend."

The soldier dismounted and walked over to Judas. "Where are you from?"

"Kerioth," Judas answered cautiously.

"Kerioth?"

"Judea..."

"I know where it is," the soldier countered.

He walked around Judas and asked, "When was the last time you were in Caesarea?"

"What?"

The soldier shoved him. "You heard me, when were you last in Caesarea?"

"Two months ago."

The leader shook his head and turned to James. "Why are you on this road?"

"We're visiting relatives in Nazareth. Is something wrong?"

"Where did you say you lived?"

"Capernaum."

The soldier looked closely at Judas and mounted his horse. "You can go." The soldiers spurred their horses and continued down the road.

"What was that about?" Judas asked.

"I don't know." James rubbed his forehead with his sleeve. "Soldiers control people with fear. You're lucky Herod's soldiers didn't interrupt your fight with those men two nights ago. Someone usually dies when they stop fights."

Leah put her arm in Judas's. "There's more trouble around here than we know about. We need to work together so I can bring these boys home before it is too late."

"Too late for what?" James asked as they approached the last hill before Nazareth. In the distance, people worked in the fields harvesting winter grain and pulling weeds.

"I think your father will take you back in the fleet if you apologize to him."

James wrinkled his nose. "I think he'd make us wait."

* * *

They met James bar Joseph, the brother of Jesus, walking on the road shortly before they reached Nazareth. Leah ran to him and took his arm. "Where are you going?" she cooed.

James pulled his arm away. "I might ask you the same question."

"Don't answer my question with a question," she scolded.

James bar Zebedee interrupted. "We came to see the Nazareth Camp."

"And then we're going back to Capernaum," Leah added.

James bar Joseph seemed pleased by her remark. Looking at Judas he asked, "Who are you?"

"Judas from Kerioth."

"I am Jesus' brother," James bar Joseph said, ending their short exchange

"Where are you going?" Leah asked James bar Joseph.

James pointed to a field of trees behind them. "My partner and I own that orchard and I'm going there to prune some trees. We had a late frost this spring. We lost a few trees and several branches." Suddenly he turned to Leah, eyeing her sadly, and said, "Anything you can do to take these people from Nazareth will help us. Jesus and Thomas are already dividing the town after arriving here yesterday."

"What did they do?"

"They are setting up a camp on a hill south of town. The camp has no water or facilities. It's like a dirty squatter's town." James waved his arms. "How are we going to care for the people they bring there? Prostitutes, beggars, thieves. My friends blame me for what Jesus does." Sighing, he continued, "I want to prune trees, not worry about beggars." He looked at James bar Zebedee. "Your brother John and someone named Matthew are in this with Jesus and Thomas. I thought you knew better. Go home, go back to the sea."

"That's what I want as well," Leah mumbled.

"Good, I'll help you wherever I can," James bar Joseph said.

Putting his hand on Aaron's shoulder, James bar Zebedee commented, "At least now I know who's on my side,"

"He's too young to know any better," James bar Joseph retorted.

James bar Zebedee smiled. "Have you forgotten the time when Jesus talked with the elders in the Temple? He was Aaron's age at the time."

James bar Joseph rubbed his forehead and looked at the sky. "Jesus fools people into thinking he knows more than he does. Besides, what does temple talk have to do with common sense?"

Leah locked arms with James bar Joseph. "Now here's a man I understand. I think I married the wrong James." This time, James didn't pull his arm away. After a few more words, they parted, James bar Joseph to his orchard, and James bar Zebedee to Nazareth. Judas wondered, as he watched James bar Joseph walking away, how Jesus could convince his friends to follow him but not his own brother.

CHAPTER FIFTEEN

Jesus went through all the towns and villages, teaching in their synagogues, proclaiming the good news of the kingdom and healing every disease and sickness. When he saw the crowds, he had compassion on them, because they were harassed and helpless, like sheep without a shepherd. Then he said to his disciples, "The harvest is plentiful but the workers are few. Ask the Lord of the harvest, therefore, to send out workers into his harvest field."

Matthew 9:35-38

James bar Zebedee and Judas reached Nazareth long after Simon and Thomas arrived with the people from the Capernaum camp. Early evening shadows lengthened in front of them as they swung southeast of Nazareth toward the low hills separating the town from the Paupers' Camp. Judas counted at least five small tents, two large ones, and a small cluster of crude shacks. Coming closer, he heard the sounds of children playing and smelled the enticing aroma of fresh baked bread from the cooking tent.

Looking over his shoulder at the town, Judas noticed that the houses looked like steps rising from the fields separating the town from the camp. He wondered if he could reach the synagogue on the hill from the roofs of the houses. He snapped back to the moment when James pulled his arm toward Andrew, who had arrived earlier with John and was waiting for them next to a large fire.

Judas' mood changed when he saw the people at the camp. Some crippled, others old and decrepit, and more young children than he expected. Soon, other aromas reached his senses; those of garbage, human waste, and people who hadn't bathed for too long a time.

Andrew greeted James and Judas and took them to a clearing. "Praise God that you're safe, that's the important thing." Then he looked at James. "What took you so long?"

"I picked up Leah and Aaron in Cana."

Judas gestured toward the tents. "Why do you keep these people away from the towns? Is it because they are unclean?"

Andrew nodded as he led them through the camp. "This is a temporary settlement," he said. "We need to provide a water supply and drainage for waste."

Judas scanned the area. "There are people in Kerioth who think all Galileans live this way."

Andrew ignored his comment, preferring to wink at the children as they ran by.

"Will we stay here tonight?" Judas asked.

"Yes. We'll put some tents where we can find a level piece of ground."

"Where the wind blows away from us?"

"Good idea," Andrew replied as he signaled for John to join them. The four men circled the camp and found a site upwind from the other tents. Judas stopped to watch a group of children playing near the spot they selected. Four children held hands and danced in a circle, while a fifth stood in the middle. After a while, Judas realized the child in the middle, a girl about six years old, was blind. The others called her name, teasing her to tell where they stood. A young boy, maybe ten, stood off to the side. Judas noticed a stump where the boy's hand used to be.

"Is something wrong?" Andrew asked.

Judas looked at him with moist eyes and said, "I don't understand. Why am I here--in this place?" Shrugging, he added, "Why are you and John here?"

John overheard Judas and answered, "It confuses me as well. I've seen enough in my nearly twenty years to make me ask whether God cares, or only just uses us for amusement." John's face reddened as he talked. "And what do our priests and rabbis worry about?" He looked into Judas's eyes. "Themselves! They holler about the purity of their texts and the correct interpretation of ritual, then line their purses with gold and lay at night with loose women." Spitting on the ground, John added, "Then they condemn others for doing the same. If I had the power, I would drive them into the sea."

"Along with the Romans?" Andrew asked.

"Yes, the Romans," John agreed. "Idol worshipping pigs. We will see the day when the Messiah will destroy those evil people." Eyes narrowing to slits, he continued, "I see legions of God's soldiers on horseback with a great warrior in gold armor leading them. He'll ride a pure white stallion and I see his fiery sword cutting a swath through his enemies."

Judas wiped his forehead. "Where did you see these things?"

John raised his chin. "I see them in my dreams," he answered.

"Dreams?"

"Yes, and I heard them from the followers of John the Baptizer. They say the time is right for a holy war--a war that will change the world." John bar Zebedee looked at the camp from the corner of his eye and drew the men closer. "There are times," he whispered, "when I wonder why I followed Jesus instead of John the Baptizer. He was a man of action." John shrugged. "But now he's dead. Perhaps Jesus will see the light and fight the Romans and their sandal licking friends in Jerusalem."

Andrew stroked his beard as he pointed to two women washing clothes. "Why are we here--with them? They'd make a poor army."

John looked at Andrew and sighed, "I don't know. Sometimes I think Jesus...well; I'm convinced he can lead people. Look at us. Who else could lead us to a place like this?"

"That's fine for now," replied Judas. "But you only see Galilee. The Romans have three thousand soldiers in Samaria and Judea. They keep more than a legion each in Alexandria and Damascus. They can bring fifteen thousand soldiers to Galilee within three weeks. I don't know much about war, but there's no one here who can raise an army that size or furnish it with weapons."

John stared at Judas. "What do you know about war?"

"It's common knowledge in Judea."

John muttered, "I forgot, you're a Judean. Judeans know everything. No wonder you don't understand."

Judas retorted, "We have to live with the Romans. You don't. Show me men in gold armor riding white horses, and what was it? Flaming swords? Show me that and I'll believe anything you say."

Andrew enjoyed their discussion from the side until he sensed John was reaching his breaking point. "Let's set the tents before dark," he said. "We can worry about armies tomorrow."

* * *

The same day, Jesus went to his home in Nazareth to visit his mother. His eyes moistened as he approached the house. Built on a short hill, the lower half still served as a carpenter's shop, while the upper section was used for living quarters. Jesus had been a reluctant apprentice to his father, Joseph. He remembered the heavy leather apron his father wore when he worked in the shop, and the adz and chisel used to smooth the wood. They would still be in the shop along with the other tools his father used. Now, his brothers, James and Jude, had developed the same love of wood his father had. Perhaps there would still be a carpenter in the family after all.

Mary concentrating on milking a nervous goat didn't notice Jesus coming around the corner of the house until a rooster gave him a full throated scolding. She jumped and quickly waved her finger at him. "You frightened me," she scolded.

Jesus said nothing, choosing instead to reach down and embrace her.

Later, Jesus took her to the Paupers' Camp, then to a wooded area where they could talk in private. There they sat; one on a large stone, the other on a fallen tree, and talked.

"Your brother James and your sisters are unhappy with me," Mary said, twisting her linen belt cord around her finger. "But it will pass." Eyes averted, she added, "People think you're a zealot."

"I'm not a zealot in the way they think," he replied.

"I know; that's the way people are. I remember when the men from Nazareth rejected you at the synagogue. Now they're angry about the camp." She shrugged. "Nazareth isn't like Capernaum. Little problems become big issues here." Mary looked into his eyes and added, "But you're not here to listen to my problems. Tell me what you want."

Jesus stood and wiped his hands on his hips. "I wasn't sure what I wanted until a short time ago." He paused for a minute. "I'm going to Jerusalem."

"You've been there before."

"John the Baptizer is dead..." He stopped, unsure how to continue.

"What happened?" she asked.

"Herod killed him."

"Will Herod try to kill you as well?"

"Not as long as I'm in Judea. He has no authority there. And I'm sure he'd want me out of Galilee the same as everyone else."

"Can you blame them?"

"Yes I can," Jesus replied with a hint of bitterness. "I didn't do anything to challenge their control or take away their money."

"What about your preaching? This business of setting up tent cities full of..."

"It's within our tradition--well, at least within the tradition of our people." Jesus stood in front of Mary and bent slightly so he could look into her eyes. "Mother--the world is full of pain and suffering. Is that what God wants? I think not. I think God wants us to live in peace and with dignity." He raised his hands. "Why do we do the things we do?"

"Do you know the will of God?" she asked quietly.

"Ask me if I think a person needs to enter the Holy of Holies in the Temple to know the will of God."

"What does that have to do with you?"

“We can all know the will of God if we listen with our hearts. God speaks to me just as he spoke to the prophets and...”

“Are you a prophet?”

“Perhaps not, perhaps I am. Is it prideful to call myself a prophet?” He leaned closer to her. “I hear voices--commands. That means either I’m insane or God talks to me.”

“What does God say?”

“Leave Galilee, go to Judea,” Jesus replied slowly, powerfully. He closed his eyes and paced between the tree and rock. “I failed in Galilee.”

She followed him. “Things didn’t work the way you planned, but that doesn’t make you a failure.” She paused for a moment and asked, “Now, what will we do here? You can’t take those poor people on the hill to Judea with you.”

“Not now, there’s no place to put them.”

“I heard you talk about healing. Why don’t you go up the hill and heal them?”

He looked at her sadly. “You too?”

“I’m sorry. This is a difficult time for me.” Mary turned a ring on her finger and walked away from Jesus. “Oh, how I wish Joseph was still alive. I want to hear what he would say. All I hear now is chatter behind my back and scolding from James and the girls.” She turned and looked at him with shining eyes. “I believe in you. Maybe it’s a mother’s foolishness, but I believe. It’s just that you make it hard for us.”

“I know, but we’re dealing with stiff-necked people, as Moses did.” Jesus sat back on the rock and looked up at his mother. “I need your help.”

“I can’t do it alone.”

“Your friend, Portia, will help. I’ll leave Philip and Nathanael here. Maybe James will stay and his son, Aaron as well.” Jesus gazed into the distance. “I have to meet with Andrew and Philip. We need to plan our trip to the market in the morning.”

They walked together toward Mary’s house as evening surrounded them. She took his hand in hers and squeezed it. “Life with you is an adventure.”

“You mean, never a dull season?”

“Never a dull season.” Mary put his hand to her cheek.

CHAPTER SIXTEEN

After this, Jesus traveled about from one town and village to another, proclaiming the good news of the kingdom of God. The Twelve were with him, and also some women who had been cured of evil spirits and diseases: Mary (called Magdalene) from whom seven demons had come out. Joanna the wife of Chuza, the manager of Herod's household; Susanna; and many others. These women were helping to support them out of their own means.

Luke 8:1-3

The next day Jesus called his followers together, including his mother, Mary, and Leah, the wife of James bar Zebedee. Jesus waited until everyone seated themselves, then he sat on a large rock. "I know most of you wonder why I brought you to Nazareth," he said. "You might also wonder why you agreed to come. I'll try to give you some answers this morning." The questioning looks from the people confirmed Jesus' thoughts.

Looking at each person, he said, "Rich and powerful men have their comfort and satisfaction on this earth. But poor people like yourselves must wait while the strong use you for their own purposes." Suddenly Jesus stopped and waved his hand, asking, "How many here believe in God?" Everything went silent; it seemed the birds stopped singing and the insects stopped buzzing and chirping.

Jesus continued, "Do you think God wants us to live in poverty?"

Some shook their heads. Others remained still.

"Do you think God wants his people to go hungry?"

"No," Andrew answered. "Yet, there are more people who suffer than those who live in comfort. How do you explain that?"

"It happens because we allow it to happen," Jesus replied. "Look, my friends tell me I should stop before my enemies destroy me. If I stop, I've given in to them, conceded to their power." He looked at a man standing nearby. "Do you think God wants me to do that?"

"What makes you think God wants you to do anything?" The man asked. "Where do you get your information about God?"

"I get my information from the same place you do," Jesus answered, pointing to his chest. "I listen with my heart." Jesus cleared his throat. "Our leaders have nothing to gain by making our lives better. We have to do that for ourselves."

"There are two ways we can improve our lives," he continued. "The first is to start a rebellion like the Maccabees did against the Greeks." John raised his fist but Jesus ignored him. "The other is to serve the people around us."

Jesus went to the blind girl and took her hand. "What's wrong with this girl?" he asked.

"She's blind," someone shouted.

Jesus looked at his mother, Mary. "What do you think is wrong with her?"

"Nothing."

"That is correct," Jesus said. "Her blindness prevents her from seeing what we see. Does that make her less of a person?"

"She can't work," a man muttered. His statement caused the crowd to murmur and whisper among themselves.

Jesus pointed to the man. "Stand up," he ordered.

The man rose.

"Do you work now?"

"No," the man answered with downcast eyes.

"Why?"

"No one will hire me."

"Why?" Jesus persisted.

"There's no work for me."

"What's wrong with you?"

"Nothing," the man replied indignantly.

"You said there was something wrong with this girl because she's blind; because she can't work?"

The man's face reddened. "You're twisting my words."

Jesus waited until he had everyone's attention. "Our leaders define our roles in life. We accept those roles and, in doing so, we give them power over us."

Thomas whispered to Jesus, "They don't understand."

Jesus nodded. "I see it in their eyes. Why should they care about roles and power if they don't have enough food?"

"Maybe they should, but they don't," Jude replied.

Jesus nodded his agreement and continued, "We need places where people who can work will help those who cannot. Those with eyes and ears will see and hear for those who cannot. Those who have food and shelter will share with those who have none."

John bar Zebedee interrupted, "You said you'll leave Galilee soon. Where do you intend to do these things?" Stifling a laugh he added, "Certainly not Jerusalem?"

"For now, we'll care for these people in Nazareth. Philip and Nathanael will be in charge of this camp. I hope to add another camp in Samaria and one near Jericho..."

"Samaria!" John gasped. "Why Samaria?"

Jesus shrugged. "Well, maybe outside Samaria. After all, the Samaritans are our brothers," he added with a playful grin.

"Why not Rome?" John asked sarcastically.

"Why not Rome?" Jesus retorted.

* * *

Jesus' mother came to him after the others returned to their tents. "I agree with you, but we have no power to change things." She quickly covered her mouth when she saw the look in his eyes. "Oh, I said the wrong thing."

Jesus laughed. "No--you may be right, but I have to try."

"I know," she said in a low voice. "These people will be safe for now. I talked to Leah this morning. She said she'll stay for a while--until the camp is established."

"What about my brother, James bar Joseph?" Jesus asked.

"I asked him to meet us here," Mary replied. "Maybe he'll help if we both talk to him."

Nodding, Jesus asked, "How did you convince Leah?"

"Where do you think you learned how to influence people?"

"From you, I suppose."

"Yes, and don't forget it. Sometimes the soft persuasion of a woman is more effective than God talk and yelling."

He tossed an offended look at her. "I don't yell."

"Hah! You boys are all alike. You stand over people until you wear them out. Then you wonder why they're angry with you."

"Maybe James..."

"Yes, and James says, maybe Jesus, but I tell him the truth. You are both Joseph's sons and sometimes you are as hard-headed as he was."

"What did we inherit from you?"

Mary smiled. "Good looks, wisdom, and a sense of humor."

"I'm ready for lunch," Jesus said, changing the subject.

"Will you wait for James bar Joseph?" Mary asked as Jesus started down the slope.

"James is stubborn, as you say, and will have more interest in making his point than eating lunch. Besides, he wouldn't want to eat with these people."

"You boys! You're so sure you know what the other one thinks." She gestured toward the tents. "No matter. Leah made porridge and I brought some bread. I saw someone cutting cucumbers, so there should be enough food for all of us. Unless you want to..." Mary chuckled.

"Don't," he warned. "I know what you're going to say."

"Well, it's an interesting idea. Some people believed it happened."

"It did happen, but not the way you think."

Philip happened to overhear the exchange between Mary and Jesus. "Are you talking about..." his words trailed off when he saw the look on Jesus' face.

Mary touched Jesus' arm. "The time you fed those people."

Philip nodded. "The bread and fish. It was the first time Nathanael heard Jesus preach. He became a believer after that." "Don't forget I lived with you and Nathanael in Bethsaida," Jesus countered. "I hope I had some influence on him then."

* * *

After lunch, Jesus met with Andrew, James, John, and Thomas to discuss their plans. They cleared an area on the ground near a small date grove and knelt over the crude maps Thomas brought from Judea. Jesus and Thomas outlined the areas under the control of Herod Antipas and the parts under the direct control of the Roman procurator, Pontius Pilate.

Jesus made a rough line on the largest map with a piece of limestone. "This is the route I want to take. See here, the road bends between Galilee and Samaria until it reaches the Jordan Valley. Then we'll travel south along the Jordan River until we reach Beth-Shan." He pointed to another line. "After that, we can always use this road to go to Jerusalem."

Andrew circled the maps for a moment and said, "Your plan follows a well traveled trade route." He pointed to a spot on the map near the Sea of Galilee. "But I suggest we go through Tiberias, it's safer."

"Tiberias is northeast of Nazareth," Jesus protested. "We want to travel southeast."

"I know," Andrew replied. "But it's safer to travel south from Tiberias than from Nazareth. We'll add less than a day to our trip." He looked at Jesus. "What do you think?"

"I don't want to stay in Tiberias--it's unclean," Jesus answered. "We can travel south from here." He looked at the map again. "I don't see any threat to a group our size."

"Where will we camp?" John asked.

Jesus looked at John and winked. "Here, near the borders of Samaria and Galilee. We can stay near a town on the Harod River called Beth-Shan."

"Scythopolis," Andrew corrected.

Jesus looked at him. "Yes, Scy...that's the name the Greeks gave it."

"Why there?" John asked.

"You ask too many questions," Jesus replied, putting him off.

"Will the people there act any different toward us?" James asked.

"I don't know." Jesus sat back on his haunches and looked at each man. "I don't know."

* * *

When it became obvious that Jesus' brother James was not coming to the camp, Jesus looked for Judas and found him sewing a tent. Tapping Judas on the shoulder, he said, "Matthew said you wanted to talk to me."

Judas looked up. "Yes I do."

Jesus pointed to a path leading to the top of the hill. "Let's walk up there where we can talk alone."

Judas nodded and they started up the hill.

"I heard what you said about the camps," Judas said when they reached a secluded spot.

"What do you think?"

"I don't know. It's a nice idea, but..."

"Why don't you come with us?"

"I plan to go back to Capernaum with Simon, pick up my belongings and return home before the weather changes."

"Simon will leave shortly." Jesus touched him on his shoulder. "Stay with us and you will be able to join a caravan on the Jordan Road. You will get home just as fast that way."

"I have to tell Zebedee and my father that I'm traveling with you."

Jesus laughed. "I am sure Zebedee will be overjoyed to hear that. I will make sure that a message reaches both men."

"You pull people toward you." Judas observed as he brushed a fly away. "But I don't understand it; why do men and women leave their homes, their families, and their work? What do you say to them?"

"The same things I said to the people this morning."

Judas raised his hands. “That’s not enough; I want to know the real reason why they follow you.”

“Everyone has a different reason. John dreams about the Messiah. Andrew thinks the end times are near. Thomas is certain he knows the mind of God.” Jesus sighed, “I’m not sure why some of the others follow me.”

“What?” Judas heard his own voice echo in the stillness surrounding them.

“Does that surprise you? You could ask why I chose them to follow me.”

“I meant to ask that question.”

“Or why did I choose these people to help me? They have no power, most can’t read or write, and some are still children in many ways.”

Judas rubbed his hands. “We Judeans think that the Galileans are a primitive people who believe anything they hear.”

“Maybe we are. I often choose people who are weak in the eyes of others. What about you--why are you here?”

Judas picked up a stone and threw it at an anthill. “I’m here because James brought me here.” He stopped, then blurted, “Do you know what I really want?”

Smiling, Jesus asked, “What?”

“I want to be a merchant like my father and marry a girl in Jerusalem.”

“That’s good.”

“Is that all you can say?”

“You can do that, same as John is free to fish in the Sea of Galilee or follow me to Judea.”

“He’ll choose to fish,” Judas replied.

“He’ll fish, but not on the Sea of Galilee.”

“Where? The Mediterranean Sea?”

Jesus chuckled, “No, the sea of mankind. We’ll fill our nets with men and women.” He gestured toward the camp. “And someday you will do the same thing.” He looked into Judas’ eyes, and suddenly Judas no longer heard the noises from the camp or the birds singing in the trees. “Judas, you are chosen. God placed you in Galilee and chose you to be his messenger. Everything that’s happened to you until this day has been preparation for your life’s work.”

“Is that what you tell the others, the ignorant and illiterate?” Judas surprised himself with his comments. “Would it surprise you if I said I don’t believe you?”

“No it wouldn’t. Belief is a journey. But you do believe in something, otherwise you wouldn’t be here.” Jesus found two large rocks and gestured for Judas to sit.

“You talk as if you know me better than I know myself.”

"Maybe I do," Jesus said. "Are you ready for my story?"

"That's why I'm here."

"Alright," said Jesus as he shifted to find the most comfortable spot on his rock. "Did anyone tell you about the time Andrew and I met John the Baptizer at the Jordan River near Jericho?"

"Andrew told me, but not the whole story."

"That experience changed my life. I left Andrew after that evening with John the Baptizer to return to the monastery at Qumran. Instead, something led me to the desert, like Moses and the Israelites. I decided to live off the land and, before I realized, a few days led to a week, then a month." Jesus chuckled, "Living off the land is not easy for a man trained as a carpenter. Luckily, I found a cave near a pool of water and ate berries, herbs, and roots. Andrew told me later I could have poisoned myself." Jesus waved his hand. "No matter, I emptied myself of my worldly possessions, or at least my need for them. But it was hard, and after a while I started to question what I was doing."

"I don't understand," Judas interrupted, shifting uneasily on his rock.

"Well, why would a man willingly live in the desert?"

"I can think of some reasons. There are times when it's nice to be alone, although you did say you were there longer than a month. That's a long time."

"Yes, and after a while, my mind played tricks on me. I dreamt about Satan and God pulling me in opposite directions." Jesus looked at the sky. "I remember one day when I walked from the cave to the pool and the rocks seemed to come alive. A voice told me to eat the rocks, that they were bread."

Judas stiffened. "A voice? What do you mean?"

Jesus smiled in a way that told Judas he was thinking about things far away. "The voice came from inside me."

"Then it was you."

"No, not all the voices I hear are mine."

Judas shook his head. "I'm more confused than ever."

Jesus caught Judas' eyes in his gaze. "Remember what I said before. We hear with our heart, not our mind."

"What about the rocks?"

"What I thought about was that God fed manna to Moses and the Israelites in the desert, so why not me. Maybe the stones would turn to bread if I looked at them long enough."

"Another time, I saw myself on the roof of the temple in Jerusalem. I thought about how hard it is to teach people about the Kingdom of God. Then I remembered that the psalmist said the angels would protect God's messenger from danger."

"Do you believe you're God's messenger?"

"More than that; I wanted to jump--to prove that God would rescue me... then I woke up. I was sweating and too dizzy to stand. But I felt peace. I realized then what I have to do."

Judas stood and stretched. "What do you mean?" he asked.

Jesus ignored his question. "A week later, I went to a mountain about a half day's walk from my cave. I stood on top of the mountain and looked over the Salt Sea and the towns around it. I saw almost as far as the Olive Mount outside Jerusalem." Jesus looked into Judas' eyes. "At some point we need to believe in the Spirit of God."

Judas looked back without comprehension.

"I heard a clear message. The Spirit of God talked to me and I knew I would do more than teach others about the Kingdom of God. My dream about the Temple was real." Jesus' eyes narrowed. "But! Another voice--Satan's voice, so real I felt his physical presence." Jesus paused for a moment, then added, "He showed me the world and said I only had to say the word and it would be mine."

Judas jumped. "Yours? The world?"

"Yes. Don't you see? There isn't much a rabbi from Galilee can do to change the world. But a chief priest, a king, or an emperor can do many things to affect how people live and think."

Judas frowned and ran his hand across his forehead. "That makes sense to me."

"Maybe so, but that isn't what God wants me to do. The voice--Satan--offered me the easy path. He promised I would succeed, that Jerusalem and all the other cities would fall at my feet. People would believe that I am the Son of God."

Judas sat on the rock again and looked at Jesus. "Isn't that what you want?"

"That's what I thought when I went into the desert. I desperately want to succeed because I believe in what I'm doing." Jesus looked at Judas, trying to draw understanding from him. "But don't you see this world really belongs to Satan...to our corrupt side?"

"I don't see things that way."

Jesus laughed. "I suppose not. I see things as evil or good. Sometimes I feel hindered like the prophets that came before us."

"What do you think you should do?"

"I am a person, a spirit, a man. That time in the desert taught me to measure myself by who I am, not what I do. The things people do disappear overnight, but the memory of the person lives beyond their lifetime. Moses was great, not for what he did, but for who he was...and still is to us."

Judas shook his head. "I don't understand." Pointing to the people on the hill below them, he added, "They don't understand."

"Some do."

"Who?"

"My mother, Andrew, and maybe John. Thomas thinks he understands, but he needs to learn more. He reasons with his mind instead of his heart."

Judas looked at the ground. "I've learned not to trust my heart. People who think with their heart become slaves to others."

Smiling, Jesus replied, "Ah, like Thomas, you will learn."

Judas tried to understand Jesus' words as they sat looking across the valley to Nazareth. He broke small twigs in his hands and sifted them into a pile next to his feet while Jesus watched a man run up the hill toward them. The man whispered something to Jesus, who nodded and sent the man back to the camp.

"How many people live in Nazareth?" Judas asked, ignoring the exchange between Jesus and the man.

"A few hundred."

"Leah told me the people from Nazareth rejected you."

Jesus nodded.

"Then what makes you think you can go to Judea or somewhere else and convince those people to believe you?"

"I'm not sure I can."

"Then why do it?" Judas asked impatiently.

Jesus looked toward the makeshift camp below him. "I can't answer that. Those who come with me will decide for themselves. I can't decide for you or anyone else. But I'll tell you this, God does not speak through the mouths of the High Priests, the Herods, or the Romans."

"Who does he speak through?"

"People who understand pain and loneliness. People like that blind girl understand life." He gestured toward the tents. "Those people--God speaks to us through them." Jesus looked back at Judas and clapped his hands. "Will you come with me to Beth-Shan?"

"I don't know."

Jesus stood and gazed at the valley below him. "That means yes. Did you bring your personal belongings?"

"Only what I have in my bag."

"We'll travel light," Jesus said. "We will provide warm clothes for you. It is the time of year when things cool down."

Jesus held Judas' arm as they walked down the hill. "Don't tell the people in the camp about our conversation. I haven't told them about my desert experiences yet."

"Why did you tell me?"

"So you can report to your father in Kerioth."

"That's all?"

"For now," Jesus replied as he spied Andrew walking toward the cooking tent. "Andrew," he called, "that man you sent had a message from Chuza."

"The manager of Herod's household?" Andrew asked as he approached Jesus and Judas.

"Yes," Jesus said, "his wife, Joanna, is sick again."

"What's wrong?"

"She has painful headaches. I told his servant I would go to Tiberias to help her. I'll take a few men with me early in the morning. You can follow with the rest when you're ready," Jesus raised his hands, palms up. "It looks like we'll travel south from Tiberias after all."

"Are you going into the city?" Andrew asked.

"I'll go as far as I have to help her. In and out...I'll go in and out and we'll camp outside the city tomorrow night."

"For now, I want to meet with my brother James," Jesus declared.

Mary caught his arm and asked, "Do you want me to go with?"

"I'll talk to him alone. I need to know how he feels."

"I told you..."

"Yes, but I want him to look in my eyes and say it to me."

"You'll be back before supper?" Mary asked.

"Yes." He held her arm for a moment and said, "I'm going to Tiberias early tomorrow morning." With that, he started down the path to Nazareth.

Judas, still baffled by his conversation with Jesus, went to Andrew and said, "I'm going to Beth-Shan with you and Jesus."

"What made you change your mind?" Andrew asked.

"Something Jesus said."

"What?"

"I don't know."

Andrew laughed. "Say, you're the one who keeps asking me why I follow Jesus. Now you can't give me your reasons." He stroked his beard. "I'll send you to Tiberias with Jesus. Get ready tonight; he'll want to leave before dawn."

* * *

Jesus found his brother James in his vineyard, located on the northeast edge of Nazareth. It was a beautiful place, surrounded by sweet smelling orchards and gardens. Jesus savored the smells as he thought about ways to pacify James. The idea of a series of camps dedicated to helping people grew stronger in Jesus' mind everyday and he knew James was a better carpenter than he, and a better organizer. James loved to plan for the future.

James saw Jesus coming and waved to him from the edge of the field. "What brings you here?" he asked Jesus when they came close enough to hear each other.

"You," Jesus answered.

James pointed to the package Jesus carried under his arm. "Did you bring a gift for your long suffering brother?"

Smiling, Jesus replied, "I brought some food for us to share."

James' eyes lit. "Good, I'm hungry."

"You look like you haven't eaten in a month," Jesus said.

"I'm fasting," James replied. "Rosh Hashanah is only a short time from now."

"And you want to start early," Jesus said, shielding his eyes from the sun.

"Yes," James chided. "And judging from the size of your robe I think it would help if you did the same thing."

Jesus thought he saw a smile creep around his brother's lips, a possible opening. He looked at his waist and laughed. "It's a loose belt."

"What did you bring?" asked James as he reached for the bag.

"Pears, grapes, some barley bread, and honey from our mother."

James gestured to a place where the squat wall was clear of vines. "Let's eat there," he said, looking at Jesus from the corner of his eyes. "I hope you're here to tell me you're taking those people on the hill away from Nazareth."

Jesus offered him a pear. "I did come to talk to you about the people on the hill," he said.

James washed the bread down with a cup of apple juice he brought from his shelter. "I'm sorry, but those people are the first thing I think of when I see you."

"I know you disapprove of them. Why?"

James shook his head. "The townspeople blame me for bringing those people here..."

"But you didn't," Jesus interrupted.

"I know that, but you aren't here and they won't talk to our mother about it." James bit into a pear. "Besides, those people on the hill should work for a living like I do. We can care for crippled people or people too old to work, but there are healthy people up there who are too lazy to work."

Jesus sighed, "Maybe some are too lazy. But we have to give them a chance, offer them hope."

"Hope for what?"

Jesus stood and turned in a circle, digging a depression in the ground with his sandal. “There’s more to life than poverty and suffering. There’s a difference between the way we treat people in Israel and the way they’re treated in other countries.”

James spat a mouthful of seeds on the ground. “Gentiles--Pagans. Why should we do things their way?”

“Not only Gentiles” Jesus argued. “What about the Diaspora Jews?”

“Converted Gentiles,” James replied with a dismissive wave of his hand.

“Let me finish,” Jesus continued. “The Diaspora Jews educate everyone, rich or poor, male or female. They provide food and clothing for the needy without judging whether they can work. Even the physicians in the Diaspora care for people without regard for their ability to pay.”

James snickered, “It sounds like you would rather live in the Diaspora.” He pointed toward the hill. “Don’t forget to take that pack of beggars with you.”

“I’m sorry you feel that way,” Jesus replied sadly. “Does our God stop at the doorways of the poor?”

James’ face reddened. “That’s not a fair question. I worship Yahweh--I pray more than any man in Nazareth. I follow the Law and I pay my Temple taxes.”

“And?”

“And what?”

“What does Yahweh command you to do?”

“Follow the Law, observe the feast days, and...”

Jesus touched his lower lip, saying, “Is it in the scriptures? Deuteronomy, I think says, love your brother.”

“I do,” James eye twitched when he replied. “I wouldn’t talk to you if I didn’t love you. What do you want me to do, give everything away so I can live on the hill with them?”

“You might think about that,” Jesus replied with a smile.

A wall of silence hung between them for a long moment. Then James stood and stretched. “Loving you is struggle enough. Tell me now; what are you going to do about those people?”

“I’ll find a place for them to live and work. It might be in Galilee or somewhere in Judea.” Scratching his cheek, Jesus added, “Judea might be the best place. Galilee seems too poor to support what I want to do.”

“Are you trying to undo what Moses started?” James asked.

“No, I want to finish what Moses started.”

“He gave us the Law and he led us to the Promised Land,” James continued. “Is there a new law or a new promised land?”

"Maybe both, I'm not sure."

"Then..."

Jesus put his hand on James' shoulder. "I need your help. Give me a few months to resettle the people on the hill. I promise I'll find a place for them by next Passover. In the meantime, help our mother when you can."

"I'll help her even though I disagree with what you're doing," James replied. "You know you make life hard for all of us."

"I know," Jesus replied as he embraced James. As he started toward the road, he said, "This will work, and some day, you'll be glad we helped those people."

James nodded half-heartedly, and whispered, "I'll pray for you."

* * *

Jesus, John, and Judas left for Tiberias early the next morning with the messenger from Chuza. Jesus told Judas and John that he would meet Chuza's wife in Tiberias, then join Andrew and the people from Nazareth in a village south of Tiberias.

"If we hurry," Jesus said, "we'll reach Tiberias by late morning. That way, we won't be traveling during the hottest part of the day."

"Why are you willing to take so much time and trouble to help a woman in Tiberias?" John asked.

"Chuza and Joanna are friends of mine," Jesus said. "They helped me once when no one else would. Unfortunately, Joanna has terrible headaches. Sometimes the pain is enough to make her insane."

Jesus gave John and Judas a sly glance. "Who knows? Maybe someday we'll get to that fox, Herod Antipas, through people who work for him like Chuza and Joanna."

"What can you do?" Judas asked. "You're not a physician."

"People's problems aren't always physical. I'm no physician, but I know when a person needs healing instead of a cure."

"I thought curing and healing were the same," Judas said.

"They can be," Jesus replied. "To me, a physician cures. He takes care of a physical problem. But all of us have the power to heal, that is, we can help people cure themselves." Jesus glanced at John. "Do you remember that woman in Capernaum? The one who touched my robe?"

John nodded.

"She told me that physicians treated her for twelve years without a cure. That day she touched my robe and her bleeding stopped. How do you explain that?"

John shrugged. “It was an accident of nature.”

“Maybe. But it’s possible she cured herself, or even more possible that she and I cured her together.”

“I don’t understand.”

“I told her that her faith saved her. I should have said her faith healed her. She believed she would be cured if she touched my robe, and it happened.” Jesus punched his fist in the air. “It could happen more often if more people had true faith.” He looked at Judas and John. “Don’t forget--there is power in prayer. I’ve seen prayerful people do powerful things. Prayer can move mountains.”

“I heard you say that faith can move mountains,” John said.

“That too,” Jesus replied.

* * *

Jesus waited near the Sea of Galilee while the messenger went to tell Chuza and Joanna that Jesus was waiting for Joanna along the shore just south of Herod’s palace. At the same time, he sent John and Judas away so he could talk to Joanna in private.

“Did you cure...that is, heal her?” John asked afterwards when Jesus found them lying on the beach.

“Joanna will be healthy in time,” Jesus said with a smile. “Her distress is not physical but she didn’t admit that until today.”

“Joanna,” Judas mumbled.

“What?” Jesus asked.

Judas looked at him. “I don’t...”

“You said, Joanna.”

Judas nodded. “Joanna is a woman I met in Jerusalem.”

“Is she the one you want to mother your sons?” Jesus queried.

Judas looked away, red faced.

“Stay away from women,” John cautioned. “They will cause you more than headaches.”

Jesus looked at John. “Are you speaking from experience?”

Now John’s face reddened.

Before he could answer, Jesus pointed to the market square. “Let’s buy some food while we’re here. We’ll need supplies for tonight and tomorrow.”

CHAPTER SEVENTEEN

When the Israelites along the valley and those across the Jordan saw that the Israelite army had fled and that Saul and his sons had died, they abandoned their towns and fled. And the Philistines came and occupied them. The next day, when the Philistines came to strip the dead, they found Saul and his three sons fallen on Mount Gilboa. They cut off his head and stripped off his armor, and they sent messengers throughout the land of the Philistines to proclaim the news in the temple of their idols and among their people. They put his armor in the temple of the Ashtoreths and fastened his body to the wall of Beth Shan.

When the people of Jabesh Gilead heard what the Philistines had done to Saul, all their valiant men marched through the night to Beth Shan. They took down the bodies of Saul and his sons from the wall of Beth Shan and went to Jabesh, where they burned them. Then they took their bones and buried them under a tamarisk tree at Jabesh, and they fasted seven days.

1Samuel 31:8-13

Jesus, John and Judas arrived at Beth-Shan, on the second day after leaving Tiberias. Beth-Shan, now known by its Greek name, Scythopolis, sits in a small valley where the Harod and Jordan Rivers converge. Andrew, Matthew and Thomas had already set up camp next to the Harod River near the foot of Mount Gilboa, within eyesight of Scythopolis.

The small community followed the purification ceremony to make the grounds ritually clean. Afterwards, they erected a tent near a clearing to store food and supplies. As night fell, they quickly threw up temporary shelters.

While sitting next to the community fire that night with John and Andrew, Jesus told a story about Mount Gilboa. "This is where King Saul fought his last battle," Jesus declared. "The Philistines defeated Saul and killed most of his men near this mountain. Saul retreated toward Jabesh-gilead to recruit more soldiers, but when he heard the Philistines killed his sons, he killed himself with his own sword."

"When did that happen?" Matthew asked.

"About a thousand years ago," Jesus replied. "The Philistines took Saul's body and the bodies of his sons to Beth-Shan. There they cut off Saul's head, stripped his armor, and nailed his body to the wall of the city. That frightened the Israelites east of the Jordan and they abandoned their towns."

John threw a stick into the fire and added, "It's the same today. Only it's the Romans who hang Israelites from the walls of our cities." He shook his head. "An unclean death--bodies rotting on a Gentile's wall until they..."

"No," Jesus interrupted. "Certain men from Jabesh-gilead heard about Saul. They went to Beth-Shan during the night and brought the bodies of Saul and his sons to their town for burial. Later, King David defeated the Philistines and united Israel."

John pointed to Jesus. "You're a leader like David. You could raise an army and fight the Romans if you wished. Judas said the Romans only have three thousand soldiers in Israel. People would follow you--I know they would."

"Maybe so, but that's not the will of my father," Jesus said. "I'm a man of peace, not a warrior like Saul. I want to bring people together rather than separate them."

Matthew spoke up. "I once heard you say you didn't come to bring peace, but a sword. You said that you would set sons against their fathers and daughters against their mothers."

"Sometimes we cause division when we wish to make peace," Jesus replied. "Look at John and his father, Zebedee. They no longer talk to each other."

"Is that what you want?" Matthew asked.

"No, but there are times when we must sacrifice parts of our lives to become children of the Kingdom. Someday Zebedee will understand that God wants John to fish for men instead of musht." Jesus noticed that Matthew was making notes on a tablet and asked what he was writing.

"I started keeping notes about us while I was in Nazareth. It gave me something to do during the slow times."

"What are you writing about?"

"The things that have happened to us since you invited me to join your group."

"I would like to read these notes someday," Jesus said.

Matthew's face reddened. "Then I should be extra careful about what I write."

"Just tell the truth." Jesus yawned. "It's late and tomorrow we will visit, ah, what do they call it now?"

"Scythopolis."

"Yes, Scythopolis. Greek names are hard to pronounce."

Later some of the men wondered, as they stared through the top of their tents, whether they would end up hanging from the walls of a city like Saul and his sons.

* * *

After a week of moving boulders, digging sanitary ditches, and hauling water, the workers at Scythopolis had turned the rough countryside into a small village. Each day, Matthew woke to the sound of squawking birds and noisy exchanges among the campers; except for the morning Simon came to the camp. That morning, Matthew had ignored the signs of activity to sleep off his fatigue, keeping his eyes closed against the bright light that filled his tent. He slept until he felt Andrew prodding him awake.

"Jesus, Judas, and John left for town and you're still sleeping," Andrew chided. "Are we working you too hard?"

Matthew squinted at Andrew. "Where did they go?"

"Scythopolis for supplies." Andrew opened the flap to Matthew's tent and pointed to a plume of dust in the distance. "Look, there's a caravan coming from the north. Maybe we'll have some visitors."

Matthew threw his tunic over his arm and rushed to the river with Andrew. He washed his face and hair, then said to Andrew, "Before I went to sleep last night, I realized John underestimated the size of the Roman Army."

Andrew stared at the caravan. "What do you mean?"

"I heard that the Romans have at least one legion in Alexandria and two more between Antioch and Damascus."

"I forgot--how many men in a legion?"

"Six thousand plus support."

Andrew whistled. "Would they use those legions in Israel?"

"I'm sure their legates would make them available. The procurator, Pontius Pilate, only has to ask."

"That's interesting," Andrew replied. "Despite John's boasting, I don't want to challenge Rome." Andrew gathered the cool river water in his cupped hands and splashed it across his face. "I know Jesus feels the same way. We have no grudge against the Romans. We would like to see them leave Israel, but Jesus' message has little to do with whether the Romans are here or not. *Our* leaders are the problem. Actually it's the Sadducees--they're the ones." Andrew shook the water from his hair and asked, "How do you know so much about the Roman army?"

"Did you forget that I was a tax collector before I joined your group?"

"So you actually worked for Rome."

"Well…yes and no. I did learn a lot about how Rome rules its provinces."

Matthew and Andrew watched as several people left the caravan before it veered toward Scythopolis. Matthew recognized Simon, James bar Zebedee, with his son, Aaron. There was also a small group of pilgrims heading toward the camp. The people in the camp gathered around the newcomers as soon as they arrived, all talking at once.

Simon walked over to where Andrew and Matthew stood. "Where is Jesus?" he asked.

"In town," Andrew replied.

"Supplies?"

Andrew nodded.

"How is it going?"

"We only arrived a week ago and some of our men already found work in the fields."

Simon rubbed his eyes. "I talked to Zebedee before I left."

Eyebrows arched, Andrew asked, "What did he say?"

"He'll take us back if we ask."

"Do you want us to go back?"

"I want to talk to Jesus first," Simon replied. "I will say..." Glancing at Matthew, he said, "Ah, the Tax Collector. Would you mind finding some more water for me? My mouth is dryer than the Judean desert." Then he added, "I only came here because James asked me to come with him."

Later that morning, Matthew saw James resting against a tree. James looked up when he heard Matthew coming and said, "It's good to see you again. Do you know how many people came from Nazareth?"

"About fifteen," Matthew answered. Then he looked over his shoulder at the people still talking to Simon and whispered, "What happened to Simon?"

"What do you mean?"

"His eyes are puffy and his face looks like red cabbage."

"We had a bad trip. Simon drank wine from the time we left Capernaum until last night."

"All the time?"

James shook his head. "Simon only drinks at night. He's not the type to drink when there's work to be done."

James and Matthew watched the birds chasing insects around the flowers. "Birds enjoy a nice life," James muttered. "All they need to do is catch insects." He pointed to the valley. "It's tougher for us. We have to work in the fields *and* catch fish for our food."

* * *

That night, as Jesus' followers sat around the fire, Simon called for silence and raised his cup. "It's good to be back with my friends," he shouted. "James will tell you I was an unpleasant traveling companion--I didn't want to come." He refilled his cup and offered the wineskin to Jesus.

Jesus half filled his cup and looked at Simon. "You are my friend," he said. "When I look at you, I think of..."

"A clown?" John shouted.

Simon shot an angry glance at John. "You're a..."

Jesus raised his hand. "No, Simon is a pillar, a rock."

"Are you talking about his head?" John asked.

"Let me finish," Jesus countered. "What is the Greek or Roman word for rock?"

"The Greek is Cephas...the Latin would be Peter," Matthew answered.

Jesus looked into the fire. "That's it, then. Let's call him Cephas or Peter. How does Simon-Peter sound?"

Simon's face flushed. "Do you think this is funny? What gives you the right to change my name?"

"I'm sorry. I meant to show my love and respect for you," Jesus replied.

"What do you mean--love?"

Jesus tried to brush him off. "We'll talk about it later."

"No, I want to talk now." Simon's face turned crimson.

"You had a long trip and it's late," Jesus said turning away.

Simon grabbed his tunic. "Who do you think you are?"

"Who do you think I am?" Jesus asked.

Simon glared at him for a minute, then emptied his cup in the fire and walked toward the river. Jesus followed and they walked along the river bank, talking and gesturing.

* * *

The next morning the men Jesus selected as his leaders met near the river. Matthew listed the names of the men in his journal; brothers John and James bar Zebedee, Simon-Peter and Andrew, Judas from Kerioth, Philip, Thomas and Matthew. Younger members included young Jude (also known as Thaddeus), James, son of Alphaeus, Nathanael, and Simon bar Zelotes. After a while, Jesus and his chosen disciples called an assembly of the people in camp.

Jesus sat on a low boulder and signaled for silence. "Simon," he said, "is going back to Capernaum. He says that Zebedee will take back anyone who wants to return to his fleet." Then Jesus gestured to Simon.

Simon continued, "I don't want you to think you have to come back with me. Make your own decision." He looked at Jesus and asked, "Will you tell them what you told me last night?"

"No," Jesus answered.

"Why not?" Simon asked. His eyes reflected his frustration with Jesus.

Jesus remained silent.

"Why not?" Simon repeated. Andrew put his hand on Simon's shoulder, but he shook it off.

"I'm not ready," Jesus said.

A bright color rose from Simon's neck until it flooded across his face. "I think you should."

Finally Jesus answered, "I can tell the others but they won't understand."

Simon sneered, "That's the trouble with people like you and Thomas. You think you're smarter than the rest of us."

"I'm sorry you feel that way," Jesus retorted.

"You won't tell them what you told me last night?"

"I'll let you tell them someday."

"I'll tell them now!" Simon spread his arms and signaled for quiet. "He told me that he..."

"That I will go to Jerusalem to talk to the high priests and teachers of the Law," Jesus interrupted. "They use the Law to enslave our people instead of helping them to be free as Moses intended."

"They'll throw you out of the Temple," Simon rasped. He pulled Jesus away from the others. "Did you drag these people from their homes and work so you could go argue with a few priests in Jerusalem?"

Jesus pushed Simon. "Simon, get away from me. Go back to Capernaum. You still think like you did before we met. You don't understand that God wants us..."

Simon raised his hands in the air. "How do you know which thoughts are God's and which are yours? Does God talk to you and no one else?"

Jesus glared at Simon. "That's enough, Simon!" he declared. "Maybe God talks directly to me and Satan talks directly to you."

Simon stood on the balls of his feet. "Satan? Are you calling me Satan?"

"No, you're a man like the rest of us." Jesus made a conciliatory gesture.

Simon brushed him away. "I can't believe I followed you in the first place."

"Simon, Simon--have you forgotten Mount Hermon so soon?"

Simon looked at him, eyes bulging. "Tricks, just tricks to fool stupid fishermen like me."

Andrew started to speak but Simon turned his back and growled, "Don't say anything, brother. You started this with your friends from..."

"Qumran?"

"Those people think they're smarter than God. Essenes!" Simon spat on the ground and left the camp.

The people watched in silence as Simon walked away from them. Not a word was spoken until he disappeared over a distant hill. Finally, James stood next to Jesus and asked, "Should we bring him back?"

Jesus thought for a moment, and then answered, "No, Simon must learn in his own way. He will come back in time to lead my sheep."

Upon hearing Jesus' comment the people in the camp began to murmur and question what Jesus meant by his words. Matthew recorded the events he witnessed.

Matthew often went to the weathered shack used to store camp supplies to write in his journal. He jammed a board between the makeshift shelves and found a piece of a tree trunk the right height and width to serve as a stool. From there, he wrote in his journal during afternoons while waiting for the men to return from the vineyards.

CHAPTER EIGHTEEN

When a Samaritan woman came to draw water, Jesus said to her, "Will you give me a drink?" (His disciples had gone into the town to buy food.)

The Samaritan woman said to him, "You are a Jew and I am a Samaritan woman. How can you ask me for a drink?" (For Jews do not associate with Samaritans.)

Jesus answered her, "If you knew the gift of God and who it is that asks you for a drink, you would have asked him and he would have given you living water."

John 4:7-10

The next week Jesus went to Scythopolis with Judas, Andrew, John, and James. Jesus and Andrew met with the Jewish leaders in the city while the other men went to the market square.

Judas started haggling with the vendors for food and supplies as soon as he reached their booths. It was clear that he learned from his father and uncle how to handle money and deal with wily merchants. John, however, was less than enthusiastic about Judas. Zebedee's family knew that all merchants were crooked, conniving thieves.

They found a merchant named Abdel who was willing to transport their supplies to the camp, and started toward the city gate with him to make sure he delivered all they bought. They stopped halfway through the city when a group of Samaritans stood in their path. The Samaritans looked at the merchant, then the three Jews. "Made some new friends Abdel?" one man asked.

Abdel's face paled as he searched for a reply. "They paid for these supplies, Elah. I agreed to help them."

Elah frowned. "You are helping Jews?"

"They paid for the food and my services."

Elah eyed the food and supplies, and then looked at Abdel. "Why don't we take the supplies and give them to the poor as long as the Jews paid for them?" His companions laughed.

John noticed that the Samaritans carried clubs. He gestured to James, who at the same time felt a hand on his shoulder. James yelped and groped for his knife, startling everyone including the Samaritans. He breathed a sigh of relief when he turned and saw Andrew and Jesus behind him.

"What's going on here?" Andrew asked.

Elah glared at him, saying, "We're helping your friends carry their food. Stay out of the way if you don't want to get hurt."

Jesus started to answer but Andrew cut him off. "Are you looking for a sore head?" He said, turning to face Elah.

Jesus sighed. "Andrew," he said, "you remind me of Simon. We don't want trouble." He eyed the Samaritans. "We're Galileans, not Judeans. We have no quarrel with you."

"You're a Jew," Elah snickered. "I have a quarrel with all Jews. We're going to punish your people and this cowardly merchant."

Fingering his short Roman sword, Andrew moved toward the Samaritans, but Jesus held his arm. Looking at Elah, he said, "We're here as friends." Jesus released Andrew's arm and walked past James. Elah lunged, but Jesus stepped aside, caught him by the shoulder and pushed him toward his friends.

The Samaritans yelled epithets and made threatening gestures until they saw a centurion and several soldiers running toward them. Appraising the situation, the centurion looked at Abdel. "Are these people molesting you?"

Jesus tapped the centurion on the shoulder before Abdel could reply. The centurion turned and hit Jesus across the forehead with the back of his hand. Andrew reached for his sword again, but this time John held his arm.

Abdel pointed to John, Judas, and James. "These men bought supplies and hired me to deliver them to their camp." Then he turned to the Samaritans. "These men thought I was in trouble and came to help."

"Help what?" the centurion asked.

"They're Jews," Elah snarled.

The centurion looked at the group with Jesus, then the group with Elah and shook his head. "I can't tell the difference between Samaritans and Jews. I don't understand why you people fight each other." Then he stared at both groups and said, "Fight in Palestine if you want, but not here. You," he said to Andrew and Jesus, "go back to your camp. And you," he said to Elah, "go home. I don't want trouble from you and your friends." Then he addressed Abdel, "Unload your cart. Let them carry their own supplies."

The soldiers waited until the merchant and the Samaritans left, then walked the Jews toward the city gate. The centurion asked Andrew, "Who is your leader?"

Andrew pointed to Jesus. "He is."

The centurion beckoned to Jesus. "What are you doing here?" he asked.

"We established a camp outside the city. We came here to work in the fields and the town."

"Scythopolis isn't a rich city. Why did you camp here?"

"This is our second camp. We also plan to set a camp in Judea." Jesus searched for words that would satisfy the centurion. "We also want to use this as a base to visit our Samaritan brothers."

The centurion shook his head. "Wait a minute, first you fight with them in the streets, and then you say you want to be friends. Which do you want?"

"We're going to send people from our camp to Samaria to heal the sick, feed the poor, and bring peace to their houses."

The centurion gave Jesus a look of disbelief. "Every time I have a problem, it's with one of your types. This god of yours is strange. You preach against each other. When that doesn't work, you try to kill each other, all in the name of your god."

"Our God is no stranger than yours," John snapped. "At least we don't worship a deranged emperor."

The centurion shot an angry look at John. "Look here Jew, I'd think hard before I criticized the way Romans worship. Our gods help our armies win wars. When was the last time your god won a war?" He smiled, satisfied with his wisdom.

John and Andrew stiffened when they heard the centurion's words. Jesus, sensing their tension, waved them off. Then he said to the centurion, "I can't argue with your logic."

When they reached the city gate, Jesus thanked the centurion for his help and apologized for the fracas in the city.

John grabbed Jesus' sleeve as soon as they passed the gate. "Their armies win wars," he hissed, "not their gods!"

"I know," replied Jesus, "but what good would it do to provoke him?"

CHAPTER NINETEEN

For my Father's will is that everyone who looks to the Son and believes in him shall have eternal life, and I will raise them up at the last day."

John 6:40

Several weeks after Jesus and his followers set up camp at Scythopolis, Matthew watched a young man dressed in merchant's robes come into the camp. After some hesitation he walked to Andrew's tent, where he introduced himself and sat down. Andrew and Thomas talked with him for a while, then Andrew took him to the tent shared by Jesus and John. Jesus saw Matthew watching and gestured for him to come over.

"Matthew," Jesus said, "this young man is called Isaac..."

"Ben Lazarus," the man interjected.

Jesus continued, "Isaac came to talk to us. I thought you would like to join the conversation."

Matthew nodded and exchanged greetings with Isaac while Jesus handed Isaac a cup of wine.

Isaac took the cup and drank it in one gulp. "Oh," he said, "I was thirstier than I thought."

"I understand," Jesus said as he handed the cup to John for a refill. "Now tell me...are you hungry?"

"I wasn't until I smelled your food."

Jesus asked John to bring some food from the cooking tent, and then offered Isaac a seat next to him. "I see from your clothing and the refinement of your voice that you are not a farmer or laborer," Jesus remarked.

Isaac nodded. "My father is a merchant in Jerusalem. I travel to Galilee four times a year to visit his customers."

"Ah, the same as Judas."

"Judas?"

"Judas from Kerioth."

John returned with a platter of bread and cheese. Jesus tried to coax a smile from John, but he simply handed the food to Isaac and walked away.

Isaac pointed to John. "Did I make him angry?"

"John and his family don't take kindly to merchants." After a few minutes Jesus asked, "Who told you about us?"

"Some people in Scythopolis told me you are a teacher, a healer, and a man of God."

Eyebrows raised, Jesus replied, "Sometimes people amaze me by what they say. But why are you here?"

"I want to find out how I can gain eternal life?"

Matthew gasped, "Can you repeat that?"

"Eternal life," Isaac repeated. "I'm sorry, do you understand Aramaic?"

"Yes, it's just that your question startled me."

"You want to know about eternal life?" Jesus asked.

"Yes," Isaac replied. "What happens to us after we die?" Isaac handed his plate to Matthew. "I've studied the Greek philosophers, and they claim there is a life after death..."

"So have I," added Matthew over his shoulder as he put the plate inside the tent.

Isaac continued, "I want to learn more. Is there such a thing as eternal life and if so, where is it and how do I get there?"

Jesus took a deep breath and released it slowly as he contemplated his answer. "Those are deep questions for a young man. You're right, there is eternal life. The Kingdom of God is eternal life." He looked into Isaac's eyes. "What do you have to do to earn eternal life, you ask? The priests at the temple teach that you must honor the Law and obey the commandments. You know the commandments; don't murder people, don't commit adultery. Don't steal or lie."

"I obey those Laws," Isaac replied. "What else?"

Jesus took Isaac's arm and led him through the camp. "These people, the poor--the sick, will lead you to riches in heaven." He looked into Isaac's eyes. "Do this; Return home and tell your father that you intend to follow me. Ask for your inheritance and bring the money here so we can give it to the poor."

Isaac paled. "What?" he gasped.

"You heard me," Jesus replied, smiling. "Give your inheritance to the poor and then come with us."

Isaac looked at Jesus with disbelief. "You ask for more than I can give. My father will never grant my inheritance for this purpose."

"Then forget your inheritance and come with us. Tell your father he can do what he wishes with your property."

"You're making fun of me," Isaac moaned. "I came here with serious questions and you give me cryptic answers." He looked toward the setting sun. "I think I still have time to find a place to sleep in Scythopolis."

"You're welcome to stay with us," Jesus said softly.

Isaac frowned. "I'd feel safer at the inn."

"I understand."

"Do you?"

Jesus looked at the ground. "I've asked myself the same questions you asked, and I'm not sure my answers always make sense. Yet we must do what feels right for us." He glanced at Isaac. "Maybe we'll meet again someday."

"Maybe," Isaac said quietly.

"Do you want us to walk with you to town?"

Isaac cautiously scanned the camp. "I'll go by myself."

That night, at the fire, Andrew asked about Isaac.

Jesus said, "A nice man, but not ready for what we ask."

John snickered, "His type will never be ready. Can you see him working in the fields or pulling fish nets? His hands would fall off."

Jesus replied, "We can't measure people by the dirt under their fingernails. Isaac is a rich young man and it's very hard for a rich person to enter the Kingdom of God." The people gathered around him waited for him to say more, but he only stared at the fire.

"Why is it hard for a rich person?" Matthew persisted.

Jesus' eyes lit again. "It is much harder for a rich person; ah...it's like trying to pass a camel through the Eye of the Needle."

John smiled. "I believe that. Rich people..."

"No John," Jesus interrupted. "Not for the reasons you think. Money is no more harmful to us than food. The problem is that rich people worry more about money than they worry about other people. They worship wealth, not Yahweh."

Jesus jumped when a loud voice behind him said, "Some people worry about their pride."

"Simon!" Jesus yelled as he rose to embrace his friend.

"Call me Peter," Simon said as he waved to the others.

"You came back." Jesus shouted.

"Yes, I needed to come back--at least for a while." He added, "This time I left everything I have to return here."

Jesus, visibly moved by the return of Simon replied, "You will receive a hundred times more than you gave up. Simon, you have the Spirit of God within you."

“I don’t know about spirits, but you can call me Simon-Peter if you wish. I like the sound of that name--rock--that’s me.”

Judas, still bothered by Jesus’ comments about rich people, interrupted, “I still don’t understand...”

“That’s because you’re one of them,” John shot back.

“One of who?” Simon asked, suddenly aware of a heated discussion in the making.

“A merchant from Judea,” John shot back. “Judeans come to Galilee, take our money, and slink back to their fancy houses and loose women.”

Judas glared at John. “You’re a bigoted, ignorant fisherman who thinks he knows everything. I know a lot of rich people who know the law better than you.”

John laughed, “Typical Judean insult. You have worms in your body. Someday they’ll eat through your skin and show people what you’re like.”

Thomas signaled to John and Judas for quiet. John hollered at Thomas, “You belong in Judas’ tent. You think you’re better because you know how to read.”

This time Jesus signaled for them to stop arguing. “John, you are truly a voice of thunder.” Then he asked Matthew, “Who is the god of the Greeks with the lightening in his hands?”

“Zeus?”

“John, if you were a god, you would be Zeus with the thunder bolts.” Jesus slapped a mosquito on his arm. “Here they come; I’m going back to my tent.” He took Simon’s arm. “Come on, Simon-Peter, we have a lot to talk about.”

John sulked as he walked away from the fire, but Judas smiled at the idea that he almost won an argument with John.

CHAPTER TWENTY

The king of Assyria brought people from Babylon, Kuthah, Avva, Hamath and Sepharvaim and settled them in the towns of Samaria to replace the Israelites. They took over Samaria and lived in its towns. When they first lived there, they did not worship the LORD; so he sent lions among them and they killed some of the people. It was reported to the king of Assyria: "The people you deported and resettled in the towns of Samaria do not know what the god of that country requires. He has sent lions among them, which are killing them off, because the people do not know what he requires."

Then the king of Assyria gave this order: "Have one of the priests you took captive from Samaria go back to live there and teach the people what the god of the land requires." So one of the priests who had been exiled from Samaria came to live in Bethel and taught them how to worship the LORD.

Nevertheless, each national group made its own gods in the several towns where they settled, and set them up in the shrines the people of Samaria had made at the high places. The people from Babylon made Sukkoth Benoth, those from Kuthah made Nergal, and those from Hamath made Ashima; the Avvites made Nibhaz and Tartak, and the Sepharvites burned their children in the fire as sacrifices to Adrammelek and Anammelek, the gods of Sepharvaim. They worshiped the LORD, but they also appointed all sorts of their own people to officiate for them as priests in the shrines at the high places. They worshiped the LORD, but they also served their own gods in accordance with the customs of the nations from which they had been brought.

To this day they persist in their former practices. They neither worship the LORD nor adhere to the decrees and regulations, the laws and commands that the LORD gave the descendants of Jacob, whom he named Israel. When the LORD made a covenant with the Israelites, he commanded them: "Do not worship any other gods or bow down to them, serve them or sacrifice to them. But the LORD, who brought you up out of Egypt with mighty power and outstretched arm, is the one you must worship. To him you shall bow down and to him offer sacrifices. You must always be careful to keep the decrees and regulations, the laws and commands he wrote for you. Do not worship other gods. Do not forget the covenant I have made with you, and do not worship other gods. Rather, worship the LORD your God; it is he who will deliver you from the hand of all your enemies."

They would not listen, however, but persisted in their former practices. Even while these people were worshiping the LORD, they were serving their idols. To this day their children and grandchildren continue to do as their ancestors did.

2Ki 17:24-41

It was late fall and cool winds brushed the valley to remind people that cold weather would be upon them soon. Andrew, Matthew, and Judas were putting the finishing touches on a drainage ditch that would take garbage and waste away from the camp. Shaking the dirt from his hands, Judas asked Andrew, "How long will we stay in Scythopolis? I thought we would be moving toward Jericho by now."

"Jesus wants to send some of our people to Samaria first," Andrew answered.

Pacing in a circle, Judas continued to question Andrew. "Why Samaritans? There are times when I fail to understand anything Jesus does. What's the purpose of all this?"

"Look around you," Andrew said. "There are more people coming to our camp each day." He pointed to the hill across from where they stood. "Last week there were no tents on that hill. Now look--a small town grew up overnight."

"They came for the free food," Judas argued.

Andrew laughed. "That's one thing you and John agree on. Yes, some of them want food. But most of them want a chance in life. Look at that young man sitting next to that tree. I remember when he was at the docks in Capernaum looking for waste food when we came in from fishing. Other times I saw him in the fields around the city eating leafs and roots."

"He eats well at this camp," countered Judas.

Andrew ignored Judas and continued, "He's almost blind in one eye and he has a lame leg. I remember when he hurt his leg."

"What happened?" Matthew asked.

"He was on the dock in Capernaum when some older boys pushed him aside. He caught his leg between a boat and the dock and the boat almost crushed him."

Judas mumbled, "Do you have any happy stories?"

Andrew laughed, "Someday he will help us. He knows which leafs and roots are edible and finds fruit where no one else sees it."

Andrew looked at Judas. "Jesus wants us to leave for Samaria in a few days. You can join one of the caravans heading to Jerusalem if you wish to leave."

Judas shook his head. "I'll stay with Jesus for now."

* * *

Late that afternoon, Jesus assembled his leaders in a small hollow, near a clump of acacia trees. The trees provided shade, making it pleasantly cool, and the grass offered a comfortable place to sit. When they seated themselves, Jesus sat on a rock near the brim of the hollow and talked to them about his plan to send them among the Samaritans.

After the evening meal, Judas, John, and Matthew walked by the river to sort out what they heard. Suddenly they found Jesus walking next to them.

Jesus looked at Judas and said, "I am happy that you agreed to stay with us a while longer."

"I had not heard that news," Matthew said. "What made you decide to stay?"

"I think that what Jesus is doing is right. I believe that he is a true prophet."

Matthew nodded and asked Jesus, "What will you have Judas do?"

Jesus replied. "I'm putting him in charge of our purse."

John shook his head in disgust.

Surprised, Matthew asked, "So soon?"

"Judas learned how to handle money from his father and I trust him," Jesus replied. He walked with his hands clasped behind his back, inhaling the crisp night air. After a while he asked Matthew, "Do you intend to continue your journal telling about what we are doing?"

"Yes, if you don't mind."

"There's not much to write about; a few months of fishing and some arguments around a campfire."

"I don't always understand why we should care about the things you talk about." said John.

"What things?" Jesus asked.

"Why you want to send our people to Samaritan towns."

"Like us, Samaritans believe in the Law."

John interjected, "The Samaritans have disobeyed the Law."

"Were not the people we call Samaritans once part of David's kingdom?" Jesus queried.

John looked toward the river and shrugged.

"Then why can't they be part of God's Kingdom?" Jesus continued.

"Samaritans are like Gentiles," John replied. "Why should we have an interest in Gentiles?"

"Are not Samaritans and Gentiles creatures of God?" Jesus asked stiffly.

John snickered, "You tell us."

Jesus' face reddened. "Even the Romans are creatures of God." He looked into John's eyes. "Your father has Gentile business partners. Are Gentiles only valuable when they send you money?"

John grunted, "That's different."

Pounding his fist into his hand, Jesus said, "I came here," he pointed at the ground, "to declare the Kingdom of God on earth! It's here--it's now! Forget the things that bind you to your old lives. Forget earthly things and your differences with other people." For the first time, Judas saw Jesus' face harden. "Tomorrow you'll go like lambs among the wolves when you visit the cities of Samaria. That will prepare you for the time when people will torture you and kill you because you believe in me. These Samaritans will help you prepare for your future journey."

John said nothing in reply, preferring to keep his anger inside. He left Matthew, Judas, and Jesus walking along the river bank but later he told his brother James that, for the first time, he believed Jesus had enough intensity to raise an army.

After John left, Jesus said to Judas, "You are a true believer. What do you know about our idea of a single God--the `One God' the Greeks talk about?"

"I haven't thought about the idea," said Judas.

"I think God called the Jewish people to show himself to all nations. Our God is not only in the Temple in Jerusalem. God is in all of us--in our hearts."

Nodding, Judas said, "Help me understand one thing."

"Yes..."

"Your people are confused about who you are and what you want to do. The things you talk about seem vague, uncertain. Even you express doubts."

Jesus stopped and leaned against a tree. "I have doubts," he said. "I've had doubts ever since that time in the desert. In a sense, doubt is my temptation. I want certainty that I'll succeed. My followers want the same certainty. But I can't have certainty and still follow God's path." Jesus gazed into Judas's eyes with a look that penetrated his deepest being. "To doubt, Judas, is to be human. Faith as we know it is the overcoming of our doubts and fears." Jesus waved his hand in the direction of the camp. "They will learn that true faith is not the absence of doubt, it's a crucible of pain and uncertainty."

By this time, Judas found a stump. He sat, all the time looking at Jesus. "I asked you," he said, "to help me understand. Now I'm more confused than ever."

Jesus smiled. "I'm sorry, but I don't know any other way to say it. You will learn, along with Simon-Peter and Thomas, as you open yourselves to the spirit."

Judas smiled. "I have to learn to ask simple questions, and then demand simple answers."

Laughing, Jesus replied, "What you need is a little more certainty in your life." Before Judas had a chance to reply, Jesus added, "Pray that God will open your heart and your mind to his will."

Judas looked at Jesus and said, "I need to pray that my father will accept this path that I have chosen. I don't want to hurt him."

CHAPTER TWENTY-ONE

He was in the world, and though the world was made through him, the world did not recognize him.

John 1:10

The community at Scythopolis finished working the summer harvest just before the annual celebration of Rosh Ha Shana. For the first time since Jesus came to Scythopolis, a group of Jewish believers from the city celebrated with the people in the camp.

Following the celebration, Jesus and Judas took advantage of the interval to travel to Jerusalem. Jesus wished to visit friends in Bethany before going on to the temple to observe the Day of Atonement (Yom Kippur), while Judas planned a short visit to the home of Joseph of Arimathea in Jerusalem, then his father in Kerioth.

Upon arriving in Jerusalem, Judas went to the house of Joseph of Arimathea. Joseph's son, Reuben, greeted him at the gate and invited him into the courtyard. Quickly appraising Judas, he said, "You look healthy." Reuben snapped his fingers and a servant approached. "Take his belongings and bring us some wine," Reuben instructed as he led Judas to the main living area. There Reuben pulled Judas to a bench beside a table. "Tell me everything that happened since I last saw you. Let's see, that was at Pesach." He shook his head, "Too bad so many people were hurt in the rioting that occurred that week. The Romans have tightened security even more since then."

Judas turned the thick stem of his cup with his fingers as he collected his thoughts. Then he told Reuben the story of meeting Jesus and his people. After talking for an hour without stopping he took a break and signaled that his cup was empty. The servant materialized out of the shadows with a decanter full of wine.

"Who is this Jesus person? Your father is worried that you've joined a group of pagans."

"I'll tell you about Jesus later, when your father is with us," Judas replied. "I will tell you now that I've been living with Jesus' people and I handle the purse for his camp."

Reuben laughed, "That's no surprise. Your family has a way of falling off walls and landing near money."

Judas acknowledged Reuben's comment with a smile and drained his cup before he continued. "Some of our people work for the merchants in Scythopolis; others work in the vineyards and farms." Judas lifted his hands. "We earn enough money and supplies to take care of our camp as well as a camp in Nazareth. We send food and supplies to the Nazareth camp every week. Our married workers support their families the same way."

Rubbing his chin, Reuben answered, "That surprises me. All I hear are stories about poverty and disease in Galilee. In fact, most Judeans won't travel to Galilee because of the stories they've heard."

"Like what?"

"I heard the rich and the poor fight in the streets and there are bandits everywhere." Reuben snickered, "I hear it isn't safe to walk the roads of Galilee after dark." Suddenly Reuben's eyes lit. "Say, you said you didn't want anything to do with the Galileans."

"I know," Judas replied, "but the people I met are different than I thought they would be. I will say this; Galileans have the same low opinion of Judeans that we have of them."

Reuben shook his head. "Yet they put you in charge of their money?"

"Yes, but there are some people who don't trust me. They watch every move I make."

"My father says that your father can sweep money off the table faster than anyone he knows. It sounds like you're following in his sandals."

Judas frowned. "I'm not in this for the money."

Grinning, Reuben asked, "What else is there?"

Judas looked around the courtyard. "I'd rather take a bath and talk about it when your father is here."

Reuben, sensing Judas' resolve, signaled to the servant to take Judas to his room.

* * *

At supper Judas repeated his stories about meeting Jesus. Joseph of Arimathea listened with interest until he noticed Reuben yawning.

"Do these stories tire you, son?" he asked.

"No," Reuben answered, "but I heard them earlier. I'm waiting for the good part--the stories he wouldn't tell until you came."

"What's more interesting than what you have already told us?" Joseph asked with raised eyebrows. "After all, few people meet a person as remarkable as this Jesus you talk about. Come," he added, "it's a pleasant evening. I'm anxious to sit in our new porch. The carpenters finished it just last week."

"You have an interesting home," said Judas as they reclined on cushions scattered around the perimeter of the porch.

"I'm not sure what you mean," answered Joseph. "Most of my friends find it plain, but it is a house that expresses my life-style and philosophy." Joseph took a handful of nuts from a dish sitting on a low table next to him. "You have to understand I was born in Arimathea, not Jerusalem. My father was a farmer as was his father before him. We lived moderately well, but never on the lavish standard that I now enjoy." Joseph paused as he sipped a warm concoction made of milk and honey from his simple clay cup. Then he continued, "The father of my wife was a wealthy merchant, in fact a person of exceptional wealth. When his only son died, we inherited her father's property. I live in a house fit for a king, but I still have the heart of a farmer."

Pulling his cushion closer to Judas, Joseph said, "Now, tell me about this Jesus and the people who follow him."

"The people who follow Jesus are ordinary," Judas quickly answered. "But he's different."

"In what way?" Joseph asked.

Judas sighed, "He heals people..."

"What..."

"...and he talks about things I never heard of before."

"I've seen healers before," Joseph responded. "They use trickery to fool the crowds. You know, they plant accomplices in the crowd who pretend they're sick or crippled."

"Jesus doesn't do those things," Judas retorted as he grabbed another cushion and put it behind his back. "I saw him cure people."

Joseph shrugged. "How do you know whether these people were sick?"

"You're talking like the people who argued with him in Galilee."

"Which people?"

"The priests, the scribes...and the Pharisees."

Joseph laughed. "I am a Pharisee, my friend."

"There you are; you're just like them. You have to see things to believe them. Jesus said people won't believe what they can't see."

Reuben raised his hand. "I believe, tell me more."

Judas cast a sideways glance at Reuben. "Jesus is a...prophet, maybe even the Anointed One."

Joseph put his cup on the table and looked into Judas' eyes. "What makes you think...how do you know Jesus is the Anointed One? You only met him a little over a year ago."

Judas' voice faltered for a moment. "I know it sounds strange, but there's not much more to tell." After a long silence, Judas looked at Joseph. "Listen, he's in Bethany tonight, and tomorrow he will observe the Day of Atonement at the temple. Would you like to meet him?"

"Yes, if you can arrange it, I want to meet him," Joseph quietly replied. He looked past the courtyard wall, lost in thought. It seemed that he wanted to ask more questions, but thought the better of it.

Ending the conversation, Judas said, "I'll leave a message at a friend's house. Would you like to meet with him tomorrow night?"

"Not tomorrow night," said Joseph. "Ask him to meet us after sundown the following night."

CHAPTER TWENTY-TWO

As Jesus and his disciples were on their way, he came to a village where a woman named Martha opened her home to him. She had a sister called Mary, who sat at the Lord's feet listening to what he said. But Martha was distracted by all the preparations that had to be made. She came to him and asked, "Lord, don't you care that my sister has left me to do the work by myself? Tell her to help me!"

"Martha, Martha," the Lord answered, "you are worried and upset about many things, but few things are needed—or indeed only one. Mary has chosen what is better, and it will not be taken away from her."

Luke 10:38-42

When he reached Bethany, Jesus stopped at the crest of a rock strewn hill and looked at the flat roofed houses located on either side of the road. The town had grown since the first time he saw it, stretching almost to the foot of the Mount of Olives to the west. At first, he watched two men and a boy walking amid a flock of sheep in the meadow on one side of town, then spied several women working on small patches of land on the other side. Listening to the laughter of children playing near the houses and scolding birds flying over the roofs, he walked to the field where the women worked. They looked up as he came toward them. Finally one gave a sign of recognition.

He waved and hurried toward her. "Mary bas Lemuel," he said as he embraced her. "You're the exact person I came to see."

Pushing him away, she muttered, "Really?"

"I know, it's been a long time," Jesus said. Then he saw the other women watching them and added, "Let's talk somewhere else."

Mary pointed toward a stand of trees located on the edge of the field. "We can sit over there." She picked up a goatskin and handed it to him, asking, "Would you like some fresh juice?"

Jesus nodded and glanced at her from the corner of his eye as they walked toward the woods. Her black hair, cut shorter than most women's, framed her tan face and accented her high cheekbones. He reflected on how she had grown more beautiful every time he saw her since they first met five years earlier.

"Did you see my brother, Lazarus?" she asked.

"I looked for him, but only saw a few shepherds in the fields."

She glanced over her shoulder. "He went to the orchard-the one you probably passed this morning. I thought he might return by now." After a few moments she asked, "Will you stay for supper?"

"Am I invited?"

Her face reddened. "Always."

He squeezed her hand and pointed to a pile of flat rocks. "Let's sit here."

"I miss you when you're away so long," she whispered. "Did you miss me?"

"Very much." She blushed and looked at the ground. He touched her chin, turning her face toward him. He looked into her moist eyes for a moment, then to her warm lips and kissed her. A faint aroma of freshness touched his senses even though she perspired from working in the field. The scent reminded him of the attar she spilled over him years earlier.

He wiped his forehead. "It seems warmer than when I came."

"You're wearing a wool robe," she said.

"That must be the reason," he replied.

* * *

The house of Lazarus stood apart from the main row of houses, amid other more costly homes. A modest wall surrounded the courtyard, barely large enough for a few benches and some large mulberry bushes planted for shade and privacy. Jesus put his bag next to the ladder leading to the roof and followed Mary into the house. They drew a deep breath when they entered the house and felt the cool inside air.

Mary gave Jesus a kettle and pointed to a well near the road. "Change your clothes, then fill this with water." Looking through the window, she added, "Martha will be home soon."

Jesus waited at the door for Martha while Mary prepared a light lunch of bread, fruit, and cheese. When Martha arrived, she greeted Jesus with a broad smile. "Are you that happy to see me?" he asked.

"Didn't Mary tell you?" she replied, still grinning from cheek to cheek.

Mary shouted, "Eli the tailor asked Martha to marry him next spring...after Passover. I forgot to tell you."

Jesus raised a cup of water and said, “Blessed be God.”

Martha nodded and poked Jesus in the ribs. “That’s what Lazarus said. Now my younger sister is free to marry.”

He looked away for a moment. “You caught me by surprise. I...I don’t know what to say.”

Martha wiggled her finger. “I’ll tell you what...”

Mary slammed her cup on the table. “Martha! Please!” she hollered.

“Do I know Eli?” Jesus asked.

“You met him a few years ago.” Martha replied, jabbing him on the arm. “Of course, you only come here once a year.”

“I was here a few months ago. Where were you then?”

Martha thought for a moment. “Jerusalem. Yes, I was in Jerusalem. You always come when I’m not around.”

* * *

Lazarus invited Eli the tailor to supper with his sisters and Jesus that night. “I wanted an excuse to celebrate ever since...”

“Be careful,” Martha warned.

“...the last time you left,” Lazarus said as he embraced Jesus. “How long are you staying?”

“I came to observe the Day of Atonement at the temple,” he answered. “I’m leaving after that to join my friends to start a new camp near the Jordan River.”

Lazarus coughed deeply and leaned against the wall.

“What’s wrong with him?” Jesus asked Martha.

Martha shrugged. “He’s had a cough for three months.”

Lazarus waved his hand. “Nothing,” he gasped, “it’s a late summer cold.”

“Summer colds don’t last three months,” Martha retorted.

Jesus took his arm. “I didn’t notice you coughing the last time I was here. Let me listen to your chest.”

“Are you a physician now?”

“No, but I know a sick person when I see one.”

Lazarus waved his hand. “I’ll be fine if you give me a cup of wine and leave me alone for a few minutes.” Lazarus quickly drank the cup and, true to his word, he quickly recovered.

They ate supper, drank wine, and laughed until the moon took its place among the stars. Later, Jesus and Mary walked up a small hill and looked at the sky, brilliant with the millions of stars Yahweh showed to Abraham two thousand years before. Jesus pointed to the Mount of Olives, less than a mile away. "The Mount blocks your view of Jerusalem. I often thought if a person lived on that mountain, they could see the sun reflect off the temple every morning."

"Except on cloudy mornings."

Jesus laughed. "Except on cloudy mornings." He looked into Mary's eyes and thought he saw a reflection of the moon. "What are you thinking about?" he asked.

"You--and how much I miss you."

He remained quiet for a moment, savoring the faint tease of her perfume. "Sometimes I forget how untroubled I feel when I'm with you," he whispered.

"You do miss me?" she teased.

"Every day. Knowing you is like a sting from a wasp that breaks its needle in you. The wasp leaves but her memory stays." He stood and stretched. "Sometimes I forget about the important people in my life. So much has happened in the last year."

"Lazarus asked me what I'm waiting for now that Martha is marrying Eli." She stood and looked into his eyes. "Lazarus is your friend."

Jesus nodded.

"But he asks why you never married..." She covered her mouth. "Oh, I said too much."

Jesus put his arms around her. "You never say the wrong thing. Lazarus is right, I'm over thirty, but people in my family are slow to marry. James is not married. Mariel married two years ago but she was already seventeen. And Jude...I don't know if he'll ever marry."

"Are you coming back after tomorrow?" she asked.

"I hope to stay in Jerusalem tomorrow night--with a friend--well a friend's mother." Jesus seemed uncomfortable telling Mary that he intended to visit Mark's mother. "I hope to return the next day, stay with you overnight, and leave for Jericho the following morning."

She took his hand. "One of these days I'll leave with you. You won't be able to leave me--ever."

He squeezed her hand. "I like that idea. I have things to do right now, but after that...maybe."

They sat in silence, bathed by the pale light of the moon, still looking at the stars too numerous to count, until the evening chill drove them back to the house of Lazarus.

CHAPTER TWENTY-THREE

You levy a straw tax on the poor and impose a tax on their grain. Therefore, though you have built stone mansions, you will not live in them; though you have planted lush vineyards, you will not drink their wine.

For I know how many are your offenses and how great your sins. There are those who oppress the innocent and take bribes and deprive the poor of justice in the courts. Therefore the prudent keep quiet in such times, for the times are evil.

Amos 5:11-13

Jesus went to the Temple early the next morning; arriving at the same time the merchants came to unload their wares underneath the Temple platform. When he entered the Court of the Gentiles, he noticed fresh dew clinging to the booths and floors and a light fog that gave the entire scene an ethereal air. After lingering for a moment to watch the birds dashing about, Jesus went to the Court of the Israelites and rested on a marble bench next to an old man wearing a skull cap. The man gestured to a crowd gathered around a preacher, and said, "Do you listen to them?"

Jesus nodded.

"Well I don't think it's right," the man said.

"Why?" Jesus asked.

"They tell people anything they want to. Most of them talk to hear their own voice."

"We can ignore them," Jesus replied.

"Most people don't have the sense to walk away from a fool when he's talking," the man groused.

"At least they provide entertainment," Jesus noted, trying to find a positive side to the conversation.

"We come here for worship, not entertainment."

Jesus looked at him. "You're making it difficult for me."

The man's eyes widened. "What do you mean?"

"I intend to speak after he finishes," Jesus answered.

The man slapped his knee. "Another fool!"

"Perhaps, but I'm serious about what I say."

Another man overheard them and asked, "What will you talk about?"

"The Kingdom of God," Jesus replied.

"What about it?"

"It's here--now," Jesus answered.

Both men looked around the Court. The man on the bench raised his hands in a helpless gesture. "Where? I don't see it."

"That's because you look with your eyes instead of your heart," Jesus declared. "We're all part of The Kingdom, but we choose not to see it because of the way we live."

As more men gathered around Jesus, the man asked, "How do you know how I live? You don't know me."

Jesus looked into his eyes. "Do you obey the Law of Moses?"

"Yes."

"And do you observe the feast days?"

"I'm here, aren't I?" the man replied scornfully.

"Do you give food and clothing to the poor?"

The man hesitated, and then laughed. "Do you think I'm rich?"

"Judging from the quality of your robe and the width of your belt, you're not a poor man," Jesus replied.

"I'm not as poor as the people who live outside the city, if that's what you mean."

"You will find God among those people," Jesus said.

The man sneered, "My teachers told me I will find God here at the Temple." He pointed to the sanctuary. "In there. God is in there." Then he added, "Who are you to tell us where God is? Judging from the quality of your robe and your accent, you're from Galilee or Ituraea."

"I'm from Nazareth, in Galilee."

Laughing even more, the man shouted, "A Galilean. Is that where you learned about God?" Passersby, sensing an exchange, paused in their walk and added to the crowd circling Jesus.

"A man learns about God with his heart, not in a province," Jesus retorted.

A newcomer said, "I can tell you're either a Pharisee or an Essene by the way you talk. You want to destroy the Temple. You want to turn us into Greeks and Romans."

Jesus looked at him. "I see by your robe that you're a priest." Pointing to a small platform, he said, "Come here and we'll talk to these men together."

The circle of men opened a path for Jesus and the priest. When they reached the platform, the priest asked, "What are you telling these men?"

"That faith is more than coming to the Temple on holidays."

"I agree," the priest replied. "But we must remember that the Temple is the only authentic place to worship God." He looked at Jesus. "You are synagogue trained, aren't you?"

"Yes."

The priest clapped his hands. "That explains it; you want to destroy the Temple and what it means to us." He turned away as if there were nothing more to discuss.

Calling him back, Jesus said, "That's not true. Tell me; what about the people outside the Sheep Gate? Have you seen them?"

"Of course," the priest replied.

"Some are blind and lame, others paralyzed. Some can't think or talk. All of them are poor and hungry, and will be all their lives."

"I understand," the priest replied. "I pray for those people everyday."

Jesus touched the priest's robe. "Did you ever think of giving them one of your fine robes?" The priest blushed when some of the men laughed. The laughter drew more onlookers, until Jesus and the priest were totally surrounded.

The priest frowned at the crowd and replied, "We'll always have people who are blind and stupid. We send them alms, but not too much. If we send too much, people will believe that begging is better than working and we'll have beggars everywhere."

Jesus smiled. "We have blind and stupid people here in the Temple. We don't have to go to the Sheep Gate to find them."

"Watch out, Galilean, that you don't over-step your limits," warned the priest. "We have enough problems with your kind in Jerusalem."

"I only want to teach people about the Kingdom of God."

Eyes narrowing, the priest added another warning. "I don't care what you talk about as long as you don't start trouble." He hesitated for a moment and added, "And I'll make sure you don't. I'll have a Temple guard watch you."

"Don't worry about me," Jesus said.

"What should I worry about?"

"You destroy people's hope with your neglect. Then you make rules that turn them into slaves. Worry about the day when you are called to account for what you've done."

The priest shook his head. "I lead a good life and I follow the Law of Moses. You should do the same. Go back to Galilee and do whatever Galileans do. We don't need your voice in Judea." He scanned the crowd. "However, you are welcome to preach on these steps. Eventually your listeners will discover your stupidity and blindness."

The priest stood on his toes and signaled to a guard who rushed to his side. The priest gave instructions to the guard, all the while gesturing toward Jesus. Then he walked to a circle of men on the other side of the Court. Meanwhile, the crowd slowly drifted away until only one man remained.

"Why did they leave?" Jesus asked.

The man shuffled his feet and replied, "I'm from Athens and I understand what you said. We care for our poor in Athens. We teach our people how to read and write rather than condemn them because they're ignorant." He pointed toward the Sheep Gate and added, "We would never allow our people to starve outside the gates of our city."

"You do understand," Jesus replied. "The Temple is not land and stone." He thrust his thumb in the direction of the priest. "They're rich and they depend on the Romans for protection. There would be no Sanhedrin if it weren't for the Romans. But there are members of the Sanhedrin who will listen and change their ways." Jesus put his hand on the man's shoulder. "Thank you for staying with me."

Jesus left the Court of the Israelites under the watchful eye of the guard, eventually losing himself in the large crowd gathered in the Court of the Gentiles. From there, he quickly left the Temple grounds for the Upper City and a possible reunion with an old friend.

CHAPTER TWENTY-FOUR

Finally the temple guards went back to the chief priests and the Pharisees, who asked them, "Why didn't you bring him in?"
"No one ever spoke the way this man does," the guards replied.
"You mean he has deceived you also?" the Pharisees retorted.
"Have any of the rulers or of the Pharisees believed in him?
No! But this mob that knows nothing of the law—there is a curse on them."
Nicodemus, who had gone to Jesus earlier and who was one of their own number, asked,
"Does our law condemn a man without first hearing him to find out what he has been doing?"
They replied, "Are you from Galilee, too? Look into it, and you will find that a prophet does not come out of Galilee."

John 7:45-52

Jesus left the temple through the gate leading to the Upper City and, within moments, came to the house of Nicodemus. He knocked on the gate and whistled an old folk song while he waited for a response. Soon, he heard rustling on the other side, followed by an old man's voice.

"Who is it?" the man asked.

"I am Jesus of Nazareth. Is this the house of Nicodemus?"

The man looked through the lock hole. "Yes--what do you want?" "Who are you?"

"I am the chief servant."

"Then let me in..."

Another voice called from the courtyard, "Who is it?"

"Jesus from Nazareth," the servant answered.

"Is he alone?"

"I think so."

"Well then, let him in."

The servant opened the gate and Jesus walked through, coming chin to chin with Nicodemus. "Remember me?" Jesus said with a smile.

Nicodemus hesitated, "You...you're the one I talked to..."

"Jesus bar Joseph from Nazareth. We met a few years ago."

"Of course...Jesus." Nicodemus led him into the courtyard. "Excuse my reaction, but I was talking about you only this morning." Nicodemus led Jesus to a softly lit room where the scented oil burning in the braziers gave the space a glow that appealed to the sense of smell as well as sight.

"You talked about me?" asked Jesus.

"Yes, do you know a man named Judas?"

"I do," Jesus said as he lowered himself into a couch. "He's been living at our camp outside Beth-Shan."

Nicodemus smiled, "Then you are the same man. I assume you know Judas is in Jerusalem, staying at the house of Joseph of Arimathea." Nicodemus flashed a sign to his servant and continued, "Judas really believes in you, and he certainly impressed Joseph with his stories about your camps."

Jesus rubbed his hands. "I keep telling my people not to spread stories about me. They still don't understand what I'm trying to do."

"Neither do I." Nicodemus said, stroking his slightly graying beard. "I remember when you and I talked a few years ago. I told my wife about our discourse, and I almost told Joseph a few times, but I lost my courage. I never told anyone else."

"Did you believe what I said the first time we met?"

Nicodemus seated himself on a bench across from Jesus. "I believed more than I understood. The idea of rebirth confused me, but there was something about you I couldn't forget. No matter; what brings you here today?"

"I came to talk to you and perhaps Joseph of Arimathea if he is interested and anyone else who will listen."

"That probably means you don't want to talk to the Sadducees?"

Jesus grinned, "First I'd like to talk to you and Joseph."

"This is a busy week for us." Nicodemus looked up when the servant came in the room with a tray of assorted nuts and fruits, two cups, and a jug of wine. The servant offered the tray first to Nicodemus, then to Jesus. Nicodemus shook his head after the servant left the room. "I tell him to serve guests first, but he forgets as soon as I turn my head."

"Perhaps," Nicodemus said, "we can arrange a dinner with Joseph of Arimathea." He paused for a moment then continued. "Maybe after sundown tomorrow."

Jesus started to reply, but Nicodemus interrupted, "How long do you plan to stay in Jerusalem?"

"Tomorrow I want to observe the Day of Atonement at the temple. I would like to meet with you and Joseph tomorrow night. That way, I'll be free to leave for the Jordan Valley the following morning."

"You can stay at my house while you're in Jerusalem," Nicodemus said.

"I appreciate your offer," Jesus answered with a smile, "but I have a friend who rents sleeping rooms in the city. I had planned to stay at her house."

"As you wish," Nicodemus replied. "I have to return to the Temple soon, is there anything you want to talk about before I leave?"

"We can talk when we meet with Joseph. That way you won't hear my story twice." Jesus took a pear from the dish in front of him. "There is one thing: The people at the temple seemed tense when I was there today. There were more guards than I've ever seen before."

"The Sadducee Party, and particularly Annas, sees enemies everywhere" Nicodemus replied. "They fear the Essenes, the Pharisees, and people like you." He looked at Jesus. "Do you know the real reason we first met?"

"I assumed you were interested in spiritual matters."

"You might remember that you were preaching at the temple at that time. Some people complained to the priests. They wanted to know who you were. The Sanhedrin sent me to discover what you were talking about."

"They wanted you to spy on me."

"Yes." Nicodemus shrugged. "I didn't tell the priests everything I heard. When they asked who you were, I told them a half true story to end their questions. "I told them not to worry. Then you disappeared. Today is the first time I've seen you since that night we met."

Picking his striped wool robe from the bench where he originally put it, Nicodemus said, "The things you told me that night are still hard to understand. As I told you earlier, I didn't even tell my best friend, Joseph, about our conversation."

"Was what I told you so unbelievable?"

"Not really." Suddenly, Nicodemus shook his head and waved his hands. "Yes it was unbelievable."

"You mean the part about needing to be born again?"

Nicodemus nodded.

As they walked to the gate, Jesus asked, "Do you think the authorities would remember me from before?"

Nicodemus laughed. "To them, you're another face in the crowd. You know how many people preach at the Temple. Many preachers say more threatening things than you. The priests only remember the ones who attract large followings and promise to make war with Rome."

Passing through the gate, Jesus noted, "You're not a Sadducee. Why were you chosen for the Sanhedrin?"

"The Sadducees want people to think the Sanhedrin represents everyone. But they don't invite us to their important meetings." Nicodemus chuckled, "There's even an Essene on the Council. They don't invite him to any of their meetings."

"You said we are at war, tell me more."

"We're at war for the heart of Judaism." Nicodemus answered with a wave of his hand. "And that's a long story--for another time." He stood and extended his hand to Jesus. "I must return to the temple before sundown, please excuse me." As he walked away, he looked over his shoulder at Jesus, saying, "One of the reasons I dismissed our talk was that I didn't think you were important--or a threat to the Sanhedrin."

"What do you think now?"

"I still don't see you as a threat, and I don't know you well enough to make any other judgment."

* * *

Jesus went to the temple the next day, this time being careful not to draw attention to himself. He prayed alone and with the other worshippers, often pulling his shawl over his head and reciting the traditional prayers for the Day of Atonement.

He left the temple shortly before sundown and reached the house of Nicodemus, tired and hungry from his day of fasting and praying. Judas arrived a short time later with Joseph of Arimathea. Judas, for his part, had a look of satisfaction on his face. The man he discovered in Galilee would now break bread with his important friend from the Sanhedrin.

Joseph of Arimathea wore a skull cap, a light scarf over his shoulders, and a long white robe. He walked directly to Jesus and embraced him. "I thank you for protecting the son of my friend, Simon of Kerioth." His short white beard moved up and down in precise rhythm to his words.

After Joseph finished exchanging greetings with Jesus, Nicodemus led the three men into a room he used as a guest room. He took a gold decanter from a table and filled four cups with wine, handing one cup to each man.

"Will your family be here for the evening meal?" Jesus asked Nicodemus.

Nicodemus replied, "My wife is the only member of my family living in Jerusalem and she's visiting friends. We have a son living in Jamnia and a daughter visiting relatives in Greece." He bowed his head. "Unfortunately my son prefers not to come to Jerusalem for the holidays, so we'll dine alone with Joseph and Judas."

Jesus sighed, "So many young people are either discouraged or uninterested. Why?"

Nicodemus replied, "I wish I knew. I'm a member of the Sanhedrin and my own son refuses to follow the Law of Moses."

"Children today have their own ideas," Jesus mused. "Perhaps they'll teach us something before we're done."

Nicodemus excused himself for a moment and left the room. Joseph took the opportunity to ask Jesus during the lull in the conversation, "Were you at the Temple yesterday?"

Surprised by Joseph's question, Jesus gave a wary answer. "Yes, why?"

"Did you preach in the Court of the Israelites?"

"I talked with several people," Jesus replied.

"I heard about it," Joseph said, stroking his beard. "I talked to the priest you argued with. He told me that a radical Pharisee was talking stupid in the Court of the Israelites."

"He must be the one who threatened me."

Joseph chortled. "He made it sound like you threatened him."

Jesus tapped the rim of his cup. "What's really happening in Jerusalem?"

"We're at war," Nicodemus answered as he reentered the room. "Remember I mentioned that before we parted yesterday morning?"

"With Rome?"

"With ourselves. The Romans give us a government and a police force. We could live in peace with them if we wished."

"Then who is at war?" Jesus asked.

Joseph shook his head. "We...Jews are warring for the souls of our people, just as the Romans are fighting to save their republic."

The elderly servant came to where Nicodemus was standing and whispered to him. Nicodemus waved at the three men. "Our repast is ready," he announced. "Please join me in the dining area."

At the table, lavishly decorated with flowers and fine dishes, Jesus, Joseph, Nicodemus, and Judas offered salutes to each other with cups of dry white wine. Spinning his wine in his cup, Nicodemus prayed, "May we enjoy our respite from the day with this beautiful gift of the earth. Bless the Lord. Blessed art Thou, O Lord our God, King of creation, who brings forth bread from the earth."

Joseph raised his cup and added, "Bless this wine, harsh and dry like the land it came from." They laughed as they raised their cups to Joseph's salute.

A servant brought a broth gently spiced with pepper and a hint of garlic. Joseph smelled the savory mist, looked at Nicodemus, and gestured toward the kitchen. "As usual, your meal is unsurpassed."

Nicodemus replied, "Your only weakness, my friend, is your enjoyment of other people's food. Don't forget I've eaten at your house. Your wife, Miriam, prepares meals that are beyond comparison." Secretly, however, Nicodemus was pleased. Joseph of Arimathea was known as a man of discernment in all things.

Jesus and Judas finished their broth and watched as the others let theirs turn cold. A servant took the four bowls, two full and two empty, back to the kitchen. Two servants entered the dining area with platters of fish, beans, small cuts of melon and squash covered with melted goat's cheese. Joseph's eyes sparkled. "The fish, I smell musht from Galilee."

"Enough," Nicodemus shouted. "Our guests will think we carry an evil spirit within us." He gestured at Joseph. "Neither of us likes broth, so we find excuses not to eat it until they serve the main meal." He leaned over and smelled the fish, waving the odor toward him with his hand. "See, they seasoned the fish with pepper and dill weed, only enough to tickle our senses without masking the fish taste."

"My suggestion," Nicodemus added, "is that we enjoy our meal with light conversation and save our serious discussion for dessert in the courtyard."

Joseph nodded his agreement and they proceeded to eat and tell stories with equal gusto. Their loud talk and laughter penetrated the night air and wafted over the city like a fresh blanket of dew.

After dinner, they went to the courtyard and sat near a lightly scented wood fire. Nicodemus gave each of them a small plate and gestured to a table containing two platters laden with fruit and sweet breads. Joseph took a handful of berries and figs and sat on a couch. "Jesus--Judas told me interesting things about you," he said, popping a fig in his mouth. "He says the deaf hear, the blind see, and the lame walk after they meet you. Is that so?" Joseph asked his question in a friendly way, but it lent a sense of tension to the atmosphere.

Jesus tapped the rim of his cup. "These things have happened, although, I am more concerned about people's spiritual healing." Jesus slowly turned his cup in his hand. "That's why I asked to meet you. I sense that there are people in Jerusalem who feel as I feel... that we've lost our way. We're no longer faithful to our traditions."

Joseph looked at Nicodemus and said to Jesus, "I think we agree, but tell us more."

"To begin with, we call ourselves the chosen people of God."

"And so we are," Joseph asserted.

"What," Jesus asked, "do we mean by that? What does the term `chosen people' mean to you?"

Judas was the first to venture an answer. "God led us out of Egypt and made a covenant with Moses, that we would be his people."

Jesus smiled. "Yet are we any different from the Greeks and Romans, or the tribes north of us? Our priests and wealthy people live in luxury while people starve outside our city gates and in the hills."

Nicodemus, red faced, looked around his courtyard and asked, "Do you include Joseph and me in your condemnation?"

Jesus suddenly had a sense he was on trial with Nicodemus and Joseph, and made a mental note to be careful about what he said. "Perhaps, but we fail as a society as well as individually," he answered quietly. "People live in caves in Galilee because they have no place to live." Raising a finger, he added, "They lost their homes because of unpaid taxes or debts, not because they're primitive--as so many people think."

Nicodemus stood and stretched. "The same is true in Judea." He broke a walnut shell as he continued, "But don't condemn us for the actions of our leaders."

"But you are the leaders," Jesus countered. Suddenly, Judas wondered if it was such a good idea to introduce Jesus to Joseph.

"What has this to do with the stories Judas told me about healings and camps of workers?" Joseph asked.

Jesus sipped his wine, seemingly lost in thought as they silently waited for his answer. Then he said, "There is healing, but what is healing after all? We have power within to cure ourselves as we have the power to make ourselves sick. Yes, the blind see, the deaf hear, and the lame walk, but only after they choose to do so."

Jesus stood and stretched, and leaned against a pillar. "There's a man in our camp named Abner who lost a hand when he was a child. He caught it in a carriage wheel. His parents couldn't provide for him so they left him in the hills to survive on his own. They were sure he would die from starvation, or perhaps the animals would kill him. But Abner survived and one day returned, full of hatred, to his parent's home to kill them."

Jesus took a deep breath and continued, "But they no longer lived at their old house. A creditor had evicted them. After a long search, Abner found his family starving in a cave near the town. He passed by without them knowing who he was. He forgot them after that, satisfied that they suffered the fate they condemned him to."

Nicodemus refilled Jesus' cup. "It sounds as if they received their fair reward."

Jesus shot a disagreeing glance at Nicodemus. "People in the town avoided Abner because his face carried a threatening stare. They saw the filthy cloth wrapped around his arm and turned away because he was not like them. Finally, soldiers caught him stealing and flogged him. My people found him, bloody and dying, in a field near the town."

Jesus put his cup on the table. "We took Abner to our camp, and after a while he recovered. More important, he forgave those who tormented him. He learned that God didn't condemn him in the first instance, so how could he condemn others?" Jesus looked into Joseph's eyes. "Even a man with one hand can plow a field if he wishes."

"Last month he sent food and clothing to his family and now he wants to bring them to our camp." Jesus looked at the three men. "Now I ask you, suppose by some miracle we restored his hand. Is that a greater miracle than restoring his heart?"

Only a small turtledove singing in its cage broke the silence. Finally Joseph asked, "How old is the boy now?"

"I don't know--twelve or thirteen. Does it matter?"

"No, I guess not," Joseph replied. "What does this mean to us, or to the Sanhedrin?"

Jesus felt uncomfortable, as if he really was on trial before Joseph and Nicodemus. "You most of all should care," he said to Joseph. "These are the things our Pharisee rabbis teach." The servant had brought another bowl of fruit to the courtyard, placing it within easy reach of Jesus. Jesus took the bowl and offered it to each man in turn.

"I know," Joseph replied irritably, "but the Sanhedrin has no interest in our teachings."

Nicodemus interrupted, "They also believe if we, as leaders, focus on rules, we can make the people think we're always right. We control the common people by controlling the explanation of the Law. Do you agree?"

Before Jesus could answer, Joseph broke in, "If we control people through spiritual manipulation, they won't question our social performance. They never think to ask us about our responsibility to them."

Jesus clapped his hands. "Exactly!" he declared. "That's the point I'm making. Our leaders, whether they are Jewish or Roman, place a burden on our people that take their hope away. I want to change that." Jesus circled behind the men seated in front of the fire. "If there is one thing I see clearly, it is the relationship between being the chosen people of God and hope. I am here to bring that hope to our people."

Joseph laughed. "You? One man? You don't have a chance. Great teachers of the past are still seen as a threat by the Sanhedrin, even though they've been dead for years."

"You should hear them talk about Philo of Alexandria," Nicodemus added. "Annas flies into a rage whenever he hears his name."

Joseph sighed and reached for a handful of roasted pistachio nuts. "The Sanhedrin consists of seventy men. The priests, most of the scribes, and many elders are Sadducees. They make the decisions in the Sanhedrin." He popped a few nuts in his mouth and washed them down with a swallow of wine. "They expect us to lend legitimacy to their acts." Signaling that he'd finished talking; Joseph went to the table for a new supply of nuts and wine.

"There are many reasons they feel threatened," Nicodemus added. "Most important, they depend on the Roman Procurator for support. He supplies the army, builds roads and aqueducts, and appoints the high priest. The Romans will support the Sanhedrin as long as Israel remains stable."

Following a short pause in the conversation, Joseph glanced at Jesus. "I've been meaning to ask; are you an Essene?"

"No," Jesus replied. "The Essene way of life is too other-worldly for me."

"The Essenes have vowed to take the Temple from the Sadducees," Joseph noted. "They claim the Sadducees defile the Temple." Again he looked at Jesus. "Do you know any Essenes?"

Jesus nodded. "I knew the man Herod Antipas executed." Tapping his cup Jesus added, "The Pharisees challenge the Sadducees as well. We question the existence of temple as the only legitimate place for Jews to worship God."

"The Temple means everything to them," Nicodemus said.

"Everything," Joseph echoed.

Jesus continued, "Yet we can no longer claim that Jerusalem is the only place to worship--the only place to fulfill our obligations under the Law."

Nicodemus warned Jesus, "Caiaphas will send the Temple guards after you if he sees you as a threat."

"Why would he see me as a threat?" Jesus asked.

"Do you remember the time you led a large crowd of people into the hills near the Sea of Galilee?" Nicodemus asked.

Jesus' eyes grew with disbelief. "How did you find out?"

"Some of Herod's people were in that crowd," Nicodemus continued. "They reported the incident to him, and he casually mentioned it to Pontius Pilate."

"But how did you find out?" Jesus repeated.

"Pilate told Caiaphas and he told the Sanhedrin. After listening to you tonight, I guessed it was you."

"It was I," Jesus replied.

"How many people went with you that day?" Nicodemus queried.

"I don't know, maybe five hundred."

"Caiaphas said that between four and five thousand people followed you."

Jesus grinned. "I'm not that good, but what's your point?"

"Suppose there were five thousand people," Nicodemus speculated. "That's almost double the number of Roman soldiers in Judea and Samaria. I don't know how many soldiers Herod Antipas has in Galilee, but I assume he has fewer than twenty five hundred."

"So you're saying they could see me as a military threat."

"Not Pilate, he viewed it as Herod's problem."

"Then they know who I am," Jesus muttered.

Nicodemus rose from his bench and put his hand on Jesus' shoulder. "They thought they did, but that was a few years ago. I don't think they'll connect you with that group in Galilee. Apparently Herod never learned who you were." Nicodemus raised his hands, palms up. "But! If you come to Jerusalem with five thousand, or even five hundred people, the Sanhedrin will take notice."

Glancing at Joseph, Jesus said, "I've preached in the temple before and argued with the priests." Jesus paused as the implications of his words hung in the cool night air.

"Don't worry about that," Joseph replied. "People preach in the Temple every day."

Nicodemus stifled a yawn, then said, "Be careful, they will react if you remind them of Hillel or Philo of Alexandria."

Jesus, pointing to a sleeping Judas propped against a pile of pillows, said, "I've overused your hospitality. Tomorrow, I intend to return to the Jordan River." He looked at each man. "But, I'll return to Jerusalem for the Festival of Lights this year. Can we meet then? I need to know more about you--what you think, and whether you're willing to help me once we move to Judea."

Joseph rose and tossed a pillow at Judas. Then he said to Jesus, "We understand. We've talked about many things tonight. We need time to absorb what you've said."

"And I need your assurance that our conversation will stay within these walls," Jesus retorted.

"Done," replied Nicodemus. After Joseph and Nicodemus indicated their agreement, they helped Judas to his feet. Jesus exchanged long, warm goodbyes, with Joseph, Nicodemus, and Judas and left the house.

* * *

When Jesus left the house of Nicodemus, Joseph of Arimathea and Nicodemus returned to the fire to discuss the events of the evening while Judas fell back on his pile of cushions. Nicodemus dismissed his servant after he refilled the wine decanter and gestured for Joseph to sit near the fire.

"What do you think of Jesus?" Nicodemus asked.

Eyes locked on the fire, Joseph thought for a moment, trying to recall the things they talked about during the evening. Then looking up, he said, "Jesus seems wise enough. Yet, he may find himself in trouble if he starts too many arguments or steps on too many sandals."

"Do you think he's impetuous?"

Joseph shook his head. "No, I think he's an intense individual with a deep sense of justice."

Smiling broadly, Nicodemus said, "That attitude would be viewed as a threat by our leaders."

"I agree."

"Then where would he fit in our struggle with the Sadducees?"

Joseph drank half his cup of wine and threw the rest into the fire. "Jesus has a following among the poor. We do not. I think we should support him until he proves unreliable or threatens to put us in danger."

Nicodemus flashed a knowing nod to his friend. "That makes sense to me."

With that, Joseph rose, re-woke Judas, and wished Nicodemus a pleasant evening. Taking Judas by the arm, he left for his own house. Judas, for his part, wondered about the snatches of conversation he heard while dozing on the cushions.

* * *

Within minutes after leaving Joseph's house, Jesus reached through the latch-hole and quietly opened the gate leading to Mary Marcia's courtyard. Closing the gate as quietly as he opened it, he started across the courtyard toward the living quarters. Halfway there, he realized it was too dark to find his room, so he decided to sleep on a bench in the courtyard.

"It's you." A whisper not more than five feet away startled him. "I thought the high priests put you in prison."

"Mary Marcia?"

"I worried about you," came her soft reply.

"I can't see in the dark," Jesus whispered.

"The wine and food dulled your senses?"

"That's not why I'm late. I think I found some people in Jerusalem--in the Sanhedrin who see things the way I do."

"I'm sure they do," she whispered. "Now, do you want to go to your room?" Without waiting for an answer, she said, "Stay here until I find a lamp." A moment later she returned with an oil lamp.

"I'm sorry I kept you up so late," he said.

"I waited because I want to talk with you before you leave."

Jesus looked at Mary Marcia, her face made mysterious by the light of the flickering lamp. "We can talk now if you wish."

She put her finger to her lips. "Talk quietly or people will hear us." She led him to a table nestled amid several benches. Placing the lamp on the table served as an invitation for him to sit. "It's about Mark. I know he's happy in Alexandria but I would like him to live with us here in Jerusalem. Does that make sense?"

"You're a typical mother. Look at me, I'm over thirty and my mother still worries about me."

"You--Why?"

"I'm not married. She wonders about that."

"That is unusual these days, especially for a person as captivating as you." She trembled. "I know this is personal--ah, you don't have to answer..."

"I have a friend who lives in Bethany." He touched her arm, adding, "Her name is Mary--Mary bas Lemuel."

"Mary is a common name in Israel."

"Yes, I know several Mary's."

Mary Marcia looked away. "I saw your eyes shine when you mentioned Mary from Bethany. Is she a special...?"

"All Mary's are special. I don't..."

Mary Marcia rolled her eyes. "A typical man. It wouldn't hurt you to admit you love a woman."

"Well yes, I do love her. To me, she's very desirable."

"Have you told her how you feel?"

"Not as often as I should." Sighing, he looked at the black sky drenched with the same stars he saw in Bethany. "Maybe I'm afraid."

"You men--you pretend you're so strong, but you can't talk to a woman."

"It's not that; I don't fear rejection. My fear is for her. I have a mission, a calling if you wish."

Jesus' right hand was lying on the table. Mary reached over and took his hand in both her hands. "What's wrong with that?" she asked.

"I lead a strange life. There are times when I have no place to sleep and other times I go for days without food. Besides, there's risk. People get so angry at me they drive me from their towns. How can I ask a woman to live a life like that?"

Even by the dim light Jesus saw Mary's eyes flash. "You declare concern for this woman," she snapped. "Yet you're willing to deny her the fulfillment of sharing your pain as well as your joy." She released his hand. "Look at me; I lost everything when I married Veturius Marcius. I went through even more pain when he died. I still grieve over those memories." She moved closer to him and whispered, "But I would not trade a day of my life with Veturius to free myself from that pain!"

Jesus shifted uneasily on the bench. "Not now, I can't do anything now." Mary Marcia started to reply but he stopped her, saying, "I told Mary that I need to wait until after the next Passover." The tone of his voice implied that he said all he wanted about his relationship with Mary of Bethany.

They said nothing for a few minutes. Then, looking into her eyes, he said, "You wanted to talk about Mark. What do you want from me?"

"Advice--help--anything."

Jesus grinned. "You love him; that's enough. Do you write letters to him?"

"Of course," she replied.

"Good, ask him if the people at the library trust his work. I want to know what they think." Raising a finger, he added, "Also tell him he's welcome to spend time with us whenever he wishes."

The lamp flickered, hiding the tears forming in Mary's eyes. "I'll do that," she said quietly. "I'll show you to your room before this lamp runs out of oil." Feeling the warmth of his presence, she realized how easy it would be to fall in love with him and, for a brief moment, she envied Mary of Bethany.

CHAPTER TWENTY-FIVE

On a Sabbath Jesus was teaching in one of the synagogues, and a woman was there who had been crippled by a spirit for eighteen years. She was bent over and could not straighten up at all.
When Jesus saw her, he called her forward and said to her, "Woman, you are set free from your infirmity." Then he put his hands on her, and immediately she straightened up and praised God.
Indignant because Jesus had healed on the Sabbath, the synagogue leader said to the people, "There are six days for work. So come and be healed on those days, not on the Sabbath."
The Lord answered him, "You hypocrites! Doesn't each of you on the Sabbath untie your ox or donkey from the stall and lead it out to give it water?
Then should not this woman, a daughter of Abraham, whom Satan has kept bound for eighteen long years, be set free on the Sabbath day from what bound her?"
When he said this, all his opponents were humiliated, but the people were delighted with all the wonderful things he was doing.

Luke 13:10-17

Following the late olive harvest at Scythopolis, Andrew and Thomas led the workers and their families to a new camp along the Jordan River, near a town called Phasaelis. They chose Phasaelis because the slope running to the river from the Judean Hills was gentler than most other places along the Jordan highway. Andrew quickly found an area large enough for more than ten tents and organized his people to set up family tents, cooking and storage tents, and a primitive system for handling human waste and garbage.

John came to the camp from Galilee a week later and reported that Simon-Peter and James would rejoin the band within a month. He also told Andrew that Zebedee was still upset over Jesus' leading his fishermen away from the fleet. The fact that Simon-Peter and James returned to Capernaum for a month did nothing to discharge his anger.

Jesus returned, full of enthusiasm from his trip to Jerusalem. He told Andrew, John, and Thomas about his meetings with Nicodemus and Joseph of Arimathea. John reacted with suspicion, but Thomas asked questions about Nicodemus and Joseph of Arimathea.

Andrew shrugged and suggested they devote their attention to finding work for the men in the camp. "We've been here for more than two weeks," he said. "But there are no crops to harvest and little need for day labor in the town."

"There is activity south of here," Jesus replied as he wrapped a light shawl around his shoulders to protect against the late afternoon dampness. "The date palm plantations and orchards around Jericho need workers. Also, the Romans are building an aqueduct from the Saddle of Benjamin to Jericho." Jesus' eyes darkened as he continued, "Sadly, the Romans are hesitant to hire Galileans for their building projects after the problems they had with the Jerusalem aqueduct."

Andrew said nothing in reply as he handed Jesus a goatskin filled with water. Jesus tasted it and signaled his approval. "This water tastes good; certainly it's not water from the Jordan."

Andrew pointed toward the town, its walls barely visible over the rise separating the town from the camp. "We're getting water from the town on the other side of that hill."

"Has anyone from Galilee come to our camp since I left?" Jesus asked after he returned the skin to Andrew.

"There are a few new people in the camp, but none from Galilee," Andrew replied.

Thomas added, "Many of the new people are unable to work or hunt. Andrew, and John killed enough animals so far, but we don't have enough grain or vegetables to last more than another week." He gave Jesus a sad look. "What will we do for food then?"

Instead of answering Thomas, Jesus looked to the east. The Jordan River was visible from where they stood, twisting through the Ghor Plain. The landscape, filled with marls and marked by arid, tumbling badlands, only carried water seasonally.

When Jesus looked over the camp, he saw people milling about as if they had no sense of direction. They reminded him of sheep waiting for the order of a shepherd. "There are more tents here than I expected," he said to Andrew. "And more children."

"The children seem to find us by instinct," Andrew replied as they walked toward the tents. "They know they're safe in our camp. Trouble is they can be a burden. More mouths to feed, more clothing, but fewer workers." He shook his head. "Most of them came to us wearing filthy rags. We usually burn their clothes before we let them stay with us."

Jesus looked at Andrew. "Let the children come. The Kingdom of God belongs to them. I tell you, unless you see life through the eyes of a child, you will not enter God's Kingdom."

John grunted, "That doesn't make sense to me."

Jesus glanced at John. "We need to find the Kingdom of God in our hearts, not our heads. Children know that."

Jesus picked a straw from a bale stored near the supply tent and stuck it between his teeth. "Where are their parents?" he asked.

"We don't know," Andrew replied. Grabbing Jesus' sleeve, he pointed to a tent near the edge of the camp. "See that boy next to the tent?" he added, changing the subject slightly.

Jesus saw a thin, dark skinned boy sitting by himself, rocking from side to side.

"Bandits killed his parents," Andrew said. "The boy saw them kill his father, then rape his mother and kill her."

"Why didn't the bandits kill him?" Jesus asked as they walked between the people milling through the camp.

"He hid in a clump of bushes until they left," Andrew answered. "Now he rocks from side to side, staring into space. He doesn't talk, eats very little, and stays apart from the other children."

"How did you learn about his parents?"

Andrew pointed to a girl sewing cloth, sitting a short distance from the boy. "That's his sister. She was at another farm a short distance away. She found him after the bandits left."

"They didn't see her?"

"No, they left before she came."

Wiping a tear from his eye, Jesus asked, "How is she?"

Shrugging, Andrew replied, "They'll never recover."

Jesus approached the tent and put his hand on the boy's head. "I disagree; we can help them recover with love."

"I wonder," Andrew retorted.

"We underestimate the power of love in healing," Jesus said. "What about Mary of Magdala; has she talked to them?" Sensing the boy's fear, Jesus lifted his hand and walked toward the center of the camp.

"She said she won't talk to people about these things," Andrew replied. "She remembers her own pain too well."

Jesus glanced at Andrew from the corner of his eye and said, "That may be, but she also understands their pain better than you and I."

Later, when Jesus saw Mary of Magdala carrying water with two other women, he hurried to her side to help her with the jugs. Andrew watched as

Mary first reacted to Jesus' words with anger, then shook her head vigorously. When Jesus came back to Andrew's tent, he shrugged. "As you say, she won't talk right now, but I know she'll help them when she's ready."

Jesus slept that night in Andrew's tent. The next morning, Jesus, John, and Thomas went to Phasaelis to buy supplies while Andrew led a small hunting party to the dense underbrush near the Jordan. The women in the camp spent the day cleaning and tanning the hides of animals the men hunted the week before.

* * *

Phasaelis, built by Herod the Great in memory of his brother, was surrounded by date palm plantations and orchards rich with pears and pomegranates. The original occupants located the city away from the Jordan River to take advantage of the natural wall provided by the Judean foothills. They also dug several deep wells, giving the city a reputation for the cleanest, most refreshing water north of Jericho.

"I know this place well," Thomas said as they approached the single gate leading into the city. "I occasionally stay here overnight on my trips to Arabia and Judea."

John asked, "Does that mean we have friends here?"

Thomas shrugged. "We'll find out. The people of Phasaelis are strict about the Law and may object to who we are and what we do."

"Why should that matter?" Jesus asked.

Laughing, Thomas replied, "You tend to upset people who are strict about the Law,"

"Perhaps I do. I upset them because they worry too much about the Law and too little about other people." After thinking for a minute, Jesus added, "They don't like it when I tell them that."

"People are sometimes blind to reality," John commented.

"Exactly," Jesus replied as they reached the town gate. "Blindness is the issue for all of us. We worship the form of our faith and ignore the content. We forget God punished Cain because he denied he was his brother's keeper."

John raised a finger in protest. "God punished Cain because he killed his brother."

Jesus shielded his eyes as the wind blew dead weeds and dust past them. "We'll talk more on the way back to camp. Right now we have a chance to make some new friends."

Once past the labyrinth of streets and buildings inside the gate, the town combined the best of Roman architecture with a physical setting commanding spectacular views of the mountains on the east and the river on the west. The facades of the shops and offices surrounding the small forum were made from white marble, with the most important buildings fronted with ornate Doric columns. Thomas showed them one of the shops where the stones fit together without mortar. They were so closely matched that one could not slip a thin knife blade between any stones in the building.

Jesus was also pleased to find friendly people in Phasaelis, for the natives greeted the three men more warmly than any city since they left Galilee. Passing from a fruit stall to a place where men sold grain, they met a man called Jochanan ben Phabi. He knew Thomas from Thomas' previous visits and invited Jesus, John, and Thomas to a Sabbath meal the following day.

* * *

Jochanan greeted the three men when they arrived and led them to a sheltered area in his courtyard that held a table and several benches. Jochanan's home was small by Jerusalem standards, but easily one of the largest and best decorated houses in Phasaelis. Pouring a cup of nectar for each man, Jochanan thanked them for coming. Then he looked at Thomas, adding, "I hope you will stay overnight and teach at the synagogue tomorrow."

Thomas' face turned crimson when the nectar seemed to catch in his throat. "Don't ask me to preach," he croaked. "This man...Jesus, is the one you should ask."

Jochanan shifted his gaze to Jesus. "Are you an experienced teacher?" he asked.

"I am," Jesus replied, "but my friends say I make my listeners uncomfortable."

"We are a minority in this town and only a small assembly," Jochanan said. "We welcome other voices, even when they disagree with us."

"Do you practice Pharisee traditions?" Jesus asked.

"We do, but the men in the town watch us. They treat us like heretics."

"Well, most Sadducees consider..."

"Not Sadducees--Essenes," Jochanan interrupted. "Most of the men in this town follow the Essene ways."

"What about the women?"

"Few men in our town care what women think," he responded.

"I'll teach tomorrow if you promise something in return."

"What would you like?"

Smiling, Jesus answered, "Don't stone me if I offend you."

Jochanan laughed, "We wouldn't do a thing like that."

Andrew interjected, "He's right, Jesus, we all know that devoted Jews refuse to work on the Sabbath."

Missing Andrew's humor, Jochanan continued, "I'll show you to your quarters, then we'll come back to the courtyard for our meal. There's a chill in the air," he said, pulling his robe tighter. "My servant will build a fire for us before sundown."

* * *

The next morning, as Jesus entered the synagogue, he saw several men milling around the large open area in the center of the building. The synagogue was alive with the smell of incense, candles, and freshly picked flowers. Jesus frowned when he spied the platforms to the rear where the women stood behind screens. A bell rang and the men opened a path to allow Jesus to walk up the steps to the pulpit. He waited a few minutes, and then gestured for the women to move to the main area. The women remained behind the screens, however, when a few men cast warning glances at them.

After the service, a woman dressed in a tattered black robe and bent with pain approached Jesus. Pointing to John, she muttered, "That man said you heal people. Are you a physician?"

Jesus looked over her head and saw John wiggle his fingers and smile weakly. "I'm a teacher, not a physician," he answered. "Sometimes I'm able to help a person with faith. Do you have faith?"

She nodded.

"How long have you been sick?"

"Eighteen years," she rasped.

Jesus looked at her, middle-aged, weary of life, face lined with signs of pain and struggle. Short black whiskers grew out of her chin and her teeth had taken a sickly yellow color. He glimpsed at John's sour expression, realizing that John, and many other men around him were repelled by her appearance.

Jesus took the woman to a quiet corner where they prayed together. After a while, he stood, put his hand on her head, and declared, "You're free from your disability."

She looked at him with unbelieving eyes until she felt her body straighten. Then she cried, "How did you know?"

John thought he saw a look of amusement on Jesus' face when he said to the woman, "I didn't. What happened?"

"I lived in Jericho when I was younger," she said. "My husband owned the largest vineyard in Jericho along with several orchards. We had a beautiful house with gardens that rivaled any in Judea. We had two sons; one worked in the orchards and the other remained at home. One night a fire burned our house and, as I tried to escape, the door lintel fell on me and knocked me unconscious. I woke the next day to find that my younger son and husband died in the fire."

She showed Jesus her badly scarred arms and neck. "I couldn't move my arms and legs for several weeks. Then when I finally was able to leave my bed, I couldn't stand straight." Tears came to her eyes as she continued, "My husband's partner used the occasion to take the vineyard and orchards from us. He left me with no house and no money. My son and I fled the city rather than risk being sold as slaves to settle our debts." She looked into Jesus' eyes. "I hated God for causing me that pain. I carried that hate with me until today, when I heard you speak."

Several men from the synagogue approached Jesus and the woman. One stood out from the others and said, "Why did you heal her today?"

Jesus noticed the man's ink stained hands and knew he was dealing with a local scribe, perhaps the local legal expert. Jesus smiled at him and asked, "Assuming I healed her, why do you object?"

"Today is the Sabbath," the man replied. "Our Law forbids such activities on the Sabbath."

Jesus shrugged. "Come now, aren't you a little deceitful? Do you feed your animals on the Sabbath? Do you untie your ox or donkey from the stall and lead it to water on the Sabbath?" Without waiting for an answer he added, "This woman, a daughter of Abraham, was bound for eighteen years by her hatred and pain. Why should she wait until the day after the Sabbath for healing?"

The men looked around, each waiting for the other to answer. Finally one of them pointed to the synagogue. "You invited the women to come from behind the screen. Why?"

"Women are equal to men in the sight of God."

The men fell into a hush. For a moment, it seemed the city had stopped living. No animals, no carts, no people arguing at the market. Finally, the man Jesus identified as a scribe, shouted, "You're demented! Where do you get your information?"

"The prophets..."

"What do you know of the prophets?"

"I know," said Jesus, drawing closer to the group of men, "that they spoke for all our people, including our women and children. What do the words 'chosen people' mean to you? Do they refer to a chosen few?" Jesus waited for an answer, but the men remained silent. "No--they spoke to *all* our people, even the demented ones like me."

Jesus signaled to John and Thomas to follow him to Jochanan's house. As he walked away from the men gathered near the synagogue, he looked over his shoulder and said, "Stop wasting your lives worrying whether your women stand behind screens." Then he stopped, turned, and faced them. "Go in peace my friends."

Later Jochanan looked at the three men seated in his courtyard and shook his head. "You caused trouble for yourself and maybe for me," he said sadly.

"I'm sorry for you," Jesus replied. "I only told them what I believe."

"True, but understand that we are a small community in a town filled with Essenes and Sadducees. They watch us to make sure we observe the Law of Moses as well as they do."

"Do you?" Jesus asked.

"Do you?" Jochanan retorted.

"I asked first," Jesus answered with a smile.

"We observe the Law and teach it in our synagogue, but to many that's not enough."

"Will anything happen to you because of me?"

"They are angry with me," Jochanan said. "And I'm sure they'll refuse to give you water."

John slapped his hands. "Those pigs!"

Jesus touched John's arm. "This is their town. They let us use their well and shop in their market." He looked at Jochanan and asked, "Will they allow us to draw water for a few days?"

"Yes, as long as they know you'll move on."

Jesus nodded and stretched. "We'll stay at your house until sundown, and then return to our camp."

"Please forgive my neighbors," Jochanan said sadly. "These are hard times for all of us."

Jesus sighed, "I guess it's time for us to move to Jericho."

John went to a corner of the courtyard and meditated. He wondered where this journey would end. Jesus was no longer welcome in Capernaum, Nazareth, and Phasaelis. How long, John wondered, would it take the people of Jerusalem to reject Jesus?

Jesus, apparently sharing the same thoughts, decided to celebrate the next Passover with the people he had selected as his disciples.

CHAPTER TWENTY-SIX

(Passover - Following Year)

I crossed this floor in spoken friendship, as I would speak to Arrius. But when I go up those stairs I become the hand of Caesar, ready to crush all those who challenge his authority. There are too many small men of envy and ambition who try to disrupt the government of Rome.

BEN-HUR by Lew Wallace (1880)

Pontius Pilate had come to Jerusalem to observe conditions in the week prior to Passover, intending to avoid the problems experienced during the previous year's Passover riots. The Roman sentries, also mindful of the approaching Passover week, watched the open square outside the gates of the Antonia Fortress. At the same time, men dressed in light tunics and turbans worked on the roof of the adjacent temple, preparing the cages that would lower them into the Holy of Holies for maintenance work.

Suddenly the men on the roof stopped their work and stared in the direction of the Fish Gate. The crowd outside the North Wall had burst through the Fish Gate, running through the streets leading to the fortress. The workers saw them, but the dusty haze covered the mob, preventing the guards from seeing them until they spilled into the square.

A few men dashed into the square ahead of the crowd and threw rocks at the guards. The guards responded by holding their shields in the air and calling for help. Within minutes, reinforcements poured through the gate and ran at the mob, which by now numbered more than fifty men.

They screamed ordinary insults and epithets at first, then chanted, "DEATH TO ROME!" The tribune in charge, Vehilius Gratus, met his centurion on the steps. They talked for a moment, then looked up to the southwest tower of the fortress. A bald, stocky man watched from the window as the mob continued to yell insults and throw rocks at the soldiers. He beckoned to the tribune who nodded and ran back in the fortress.

Noticing the narrow street next to the Temple wall, the centurion called to a guard, "Take some men to patrol that passage. They may be coming from that side as well."

In the meantime, the tribune returned to the square at the head of a cluster of soldiers carrying leather shields. The crowd surged and repeated their yell, "DEATH TO ROME! DEATH TO ROME!" The mob's intensity escalated when someone saw Pontius Pilate standing in the window. A man with a heavy black beard came to the front of the mob and screamed, "MAY THE BLOOD OF OUR PEOPLE CURSE ROME FOR SEVEN GENERATIONS!"

Rioters continued to break through the line of soldiers defending the square, but reinforcements stopped them short of the fortress gate. Soon several men lay on the ground, some wounded, some dead.

The soldiers formed a phalanx using their long leather shields around the perimeter and small metal shields over their heads. Foreheads glistened with sweat when the mob pushed the soldiers back into the square.

The soldiers grabbed people closest to them to serve as human shields, but those in the rear continued to throw stones and hurl insults with equal impunity. Pontius Pilate pounded his fist in his hand and disappeared from the window. Within minutes, more soldiers raced from the fortress to support the men blocking the streets.

Vehilius Gratus hollered instructions to the soldiers but the crowd noise drowned his words. "DEATH TO ROME," they screamed, "YOU MURDERERS! CURSE YOU! CURSE CAESAR--CURSE CAESAR!" Suddenly the mob changed their chant. The words, "DESTROY ROME!" resonated through the square.

The midday sun poured heat into the square, making the crowd angrier and the soldiers more impatient. Rocks bounced against shields, off buildings, and into the square.

A swarthy man, apparently lying unconscious in the square blinked his eyes and squinted at the sun shining in his face. Without moving his head, he looked to his side and saw Vehilius Gratus standing a short distance from him. At the same time, he heard the centurion ordering the men watching the street next to the Temple to help the soldiers in the square. The swarthy man remained motionless, closing his eyes whenever a soldier came near. No one saw him move until Pontius Pilate, still standing at the window, saw the glint of his knife blade.

"Sicarus!" Pilate shouted to Vehilius Gratus. He realized his shout was a helpless gesture as he watched every detail of the man's movement as if the incident occurred in suspended motion. Vehilius Gratus never heard Pilate's warning, nor saw the man as he jumped at the tribune and drove the knife in his throat. A stream of blood spurted from Vehilius Gratus' neck when the man withdrew his knife, then fanned to a crimson spray. For a moment, the soldiers stood paralyzed as the tribune staggered toward them, his eyes bulging with terror and his armor glistening red from the blood spreading across his chest.

The crowd gasped and retreated when the tribune fell to the ground. The murderer hesitated for a moment, escaped down the unguarded street next to the Temple wall. Soldiers ran after shouting, "Stop him! Stop him!" The only image remaining in Pilate's head was the knife in the assassin's right hand and a left hand that had only two fingers.

Almost two hundred soldiers, now driven by anger and frustration, herded the mob into the narrow streets leading to the Fish Gate. A few stayed in the square to guard Vehilius Gratus, who now lay dead in an expanding pool of his own blood.

Pontius Pilate turned away from the window and pulled a cord hanging from the ceiling. His room seemed silent, almost tomb-like compared to the uproar in the square.

His aide came to the door and presented himself.

Pilate waved him into the room. "I suspect we lost another good officer," he mumbled. "Although perhaps a foolish one, to those fanatics. Find the centurion and send him to me."

"Yes sir." The aide started to leave.

"Wait, Is Herod Antipas in Jerusalem?"

"I'll send someone to check at the Hasmonean Palace."

"Fine, let me know as soon as possible."

"Yes sir." The man bowed and left the room.

Pontius Pilate sat at his desk and wrote a note on a piece of parchment. He thought for a moment, then rose and went to the tree where his armor hung. He carefully removed a leather riding crop and held it in his hand. This one, especially made for him, had good balance and flexibility. He stroked it fondly and flicked his wrist and the crop whistled through the air as the tip arced to catch the handle. He slapped it on his thigh and went back to his desk.

He returned to the window when a scuffle to the left of the square caught his attention. He watched the soldiers dragging a man through the dirt toward the military compound. The man squirmed and fought until a soldier hit him across his face with a baton, then he fell limp and they dragged him away. Pilate smiled when he saw the man's left hand scraping the ground. It had only two fingers.

Soon it would be peaceful in Jerusalem again; like nothing happened. Only the stains from the blood of a Roman tribune would linger as a reminder. Pontius Pilate rubbed his forehead and thought about ways he could teach obedience to these obstinate Jews.

CHAPTER TWENTY-SEVEN

The Roman army under Augustus consisted of 25 legions. Each legion consisted of about 6000 men and a large number of auxiliaries. A legatus, supported by 6 military tribunes, led a legion, composed of 10 cohorts. 6 centuries made a cohort. By the time of Augustus, a century had 80 men. The leader of the century was called a centurion.

about.com[3]

Pontius Pilate heard a discreet rap on his door, followed by the entry of his aide, Adrien. "The centurion is waiting in your outer chamber."

"Tell him I'll see him in a minute."

"Yes sir." Adrien walked a few steps and turned around. "Sir, will you wear your uniform this afternoon?"

"Not now," Pilate replied as he waved Adrien out of the room. He threw his riding crop on his bed, pulled a cloak over his tunic, and tied it with a silk cord. Then he went to a small cupboard, poured a cup of wine and drank it in one swallow. Returning the cup and decanter to the cupboard, he squared his shoulders and walked toward the door.

The centurion fidgeted as he waited, but stiffened and saluted as soon as Pilate entered the chamber. Pilate returned the salute and gestured to a bench next to a small table. The centurion sat while Pilate paced across the room.

"What is your name?" Pilate asked.

The centurion replied nervously, "Zoran."

Pilate looked into the distance and said, "Tell me about the problem in the square."

"There's not much to tell, my lord," Zoran said. "It's the same people who started the trouble the other night—Zealots, I think. They tried to trap our soldiers in the square."

"Yes--yes, I saw that. What started the trouble?"

---

3 http://ancienthistory.about.com/od/romeweapons/p/RomanArmy.htm

"The mob started on the hill outside the North Wall and came through the Fish Gate. They were protesting the crucifixions."

Pilate clapped his hands. "When will they learn they can't stop Rome with talk and rocks? What else?"

"Well, they killed..."

"Yes, I saw the man kill Tribune Vehilius Gratus Lucullus as well. You caught a man. Is he the one?"

"We're not sure."

"How many fingers does he have?"

"What?"

"Never mind; have you questioned him?"

"He's still groggy--we're waiting until he regains his senses."

Pilate slammed his fist on the table. "What is this; a seaside retreat? Since when do we wait for THEM to come to their senses?" Pilate spun and faced the centurion. "Where is he?"

"The dungeon. He's in the dungeon."

"Bring him to the courtyard."

The soldier hesitated for a moment.

"NOW!" Pilate screamed, veins protruding from his neck.

Zoran jumped off the bench and ran out of the room without looking back. Pilate returned to his apartment and pulled the cord. Adrien appeared at the doorway in an instant, as if he were standing right outside the door.

"What is his name?" Pilate asked impatiently.

"Zoran of Ebla."

"He looks young for a centurion."

"About twenty five years old."

"A Syrian?"

"Yes."

Pilate rubbed his chin. "Did Pacuvius send him here to spy on me?"

"I doubt it. I think Zoran is loyal to the Jerusalem Cohort."

"Fine." Pilate pointed to his armor. "I changed my mind. Help me dress. I have work to do." Pilate watched his reflection in a mirror and patted his stomach. "I'm gaining weight. Pretty soon I'll be fat like Caesar." He chuckled at his humor, at the same time flashing a warning glance to Adrien. "Don't tell anyone I said that."

Adrien pretended he hadn't heard Pilate's comment as he continued to gird Pilate with his uniform and armor. He buffed Pilate's breastplate with his sleeve until it glistened. Pilate held Adrien by the arm for a moment and looked into his eyes, then he pushed him away and went out the door. They passed halfway through the next room when Pilate snapped his fingers and turned.

"My crop. I forgot my crop. Bring it here."

"Yes sir." Adrien ran back to the apartment and returned with Pilate's riding crop.

The slap of their heavy sandals, resounding with military precision, echoed off the stone walls and paved walkway as they marched toward the courtyard.

As he snapped his crop against his thigh, Pilate asked, "Tell me, Adrien, what do you know about these rioters?"

"Most of the trouble-makers are people from outside the city. Some are zealots, others political opportunists, and a few fight for religious reason. The Sicarii, dagger bearers, are more organized and they usually direct their violence towards the upper class Jews." Adrien tugged at his belt. "I wonder why they do those things."

"So do I," Pilate interjected. "I've done everything I can to keep these people happy. We build an aqueduct to provide water to Jerusalem and people riot. We provide military and civil protection to the Jews and people hate us." He slapped his crop against a pillar for emphasis. "We start out trying to make friends and the next thing you know, we make more enemies."

"I doubt whether any of the trouble makers have an interest in the people they say they represent," Adrien observed. "I think most are after power or out to prove their manhood."

"There are less dangerous ways to exercise power."

"The incident in the square is a good example of what they like to do," Adrien continued. "You saw the man who stabbed Vehilius?"

"Yes."

"That's a Sicarii trademark. They ambush our soldiers and terrorize their own people. The Jews fear them more than we do."

"I wonder," Pilate mumbled.

"Wonder?"

"Yes, I yelled the word `Sicarus' at Vehilius Gratus when the man attacked. It slipped out of my mouth."

"Then you know about them."

"They're nothing more than common thugs, yet they must be on my mind." Pilate held his hand up as they approached the door leading to the courtyard. "Stay here," he warned. "I know how violence makes you sick, and I want you to feel well for supper tonight."

"As you wish."

Pilate entered the courtyard to the sound of hands slapping chests and heels striking together. The bright sun, in contrast to the dark passageway, momentarily blinded him. He returned their salute and stood next to the

Centurion, Zoran. A young man stood at the near end of the courtyard, hands and feet tied, and held by two soldiers.

Pilate surveyed the prisoner from a distance before he walked over to him. The prisoner's hair hung in greasy strands over his face and he alternately stared at the floor and the sky. Pilate looked at the man's blood splattered tunic and pointed his crop to the black eye and red welt running from his forehead across his nose and cheek.

Finally, he walked behind the prisoner and checked his hands. His left hand had only two fingers. Then he turned to Zoran and asked, "Can he speak Greek or Latin?"

The centurion shook his head.

Pilate glared at Zoran and roared, "Fine, does anyone here speak his language?" He looked at no one in particular. "You know, when I watch our soldiers in action, I wonder how we ever win a war."

A soldier stepped forward and presented himself to Pilate. "I speak Aramaic."

"Good! Progress! Ask him some questions--like who is he, and what was he doing out there killing Roman soldiers." Pilate nervously flicked the riding crop on his thigh while he waited for a translation and answer.

The interpreter asked a question but the prisoner remained silent. He asked another question. Silence. Pilate felt himself losing patience. "The man does have a tongue?"

Zoran nodded.

"Then what in the name of Jupiter is wrong with him?" Pilate pushed the soldiers aside. "Who...?"

The prisoner spat in his face.

Pilate swung his riding crop across the man's face and cut a welt parallel to the one he received earlier. Then he whipped it in the opposite direction and opened a welt perpendicular to the other two. The prisoner showed no emotion as Pilate whipped the crop across his face and neck. Finally Pilate grimaced and drove the handle of the crop into the prisoner's groin. He moaned and doubled over. Then Pilate lashed the man's neck and ears until they bled.

When he finished, he held Zoran by the shoulders and said, "Flog him." He shook the centurion. "Forty times at least. Tomorrow morning, put a stake on the place where Tribune Vehilius Gratus died. Tie this pig to the stake." Pilate's eyes narrowed to a slit. "Then cut his body so his blood drips on the ground--slowly. I summoned Annas and Caiaphas for a meeting here tomorrow. Make sure he lives until they arrive. I'll grant you and your men a bonus if you keep him alive until sundown tomorrow." He released the centurion and turned away. Before he reached the door he stopped and shouted, "Do what you must to make him talk and tell me exactly what he says."

Pilate shot a sideways glance at Adrien as he walked through the door. "I think you could have handled this one. Listen, I want more information on these--what do you call them?"

"Dagger bearers?"

"No, no, the other name."

"Oh, the Sicarii."

"Yes." Pilate absently flicked the riding crop on his thigh. "Find out if they have a leader. Find someone who will talk. Bribe them if you have to." Then he mumbled to himself, "I'd like to know what Annas and Caiaphas have to say about these terrorists when we meet."

"That reminds me, sir. The High Priests, Annas and Caiaphas, sent a message confirming your meeting. The messengers will remain in the outer chamber until you call for them."

"Good." Pilate put his hand on Adrien's shoulder. "Draw a bath and lay out my official garments. I want to look my best tonight."

"You always look good, sir."

"What do the messengers look like?"

"One is dark skinned and full, while the other is a little thin, but has silky red hair and a willing way."

"Are you speaking from observation or experience?"

"They arrived just before we went to the courtyard."

"Observation, I guess." Pilate shifted his crop from hand to hand. "Are they Jews?" he asked.

Adrien showing some discomfort at Pilate's question, replied, "No... Idumeans, I think."

"You act surprised that I would ask?"

"Yes, the Jews would never use their own women as prostitutes."

Snickering, Pilate muttered, "At least as far as we know." He waved his crop, signaling a new subject. "Do we have anyone who can replace Vehilius Gratus?"

"We have four centurions assigned to Judea. Zoran is the most experienced."

"How old did you say..."

"About twenty five," Adrien interrupted.

Pilate shook his head. "He's too young, besides he handled that incident in the square poorly. Who else?" Pilate asked with a sigh.

"There's the head of your praetorian guard, Marcus Rutilius."

Pilate shook his head again. "I need him in Caesarea." He shifted his crop. "What about Lucius Tullius Cotta?"

Adrien nodded. "He's responsible for three centuries in Jericho. Most people think he is a full tribune."

"He was a tribune once," Pilate replied impassively.

"I didn't know that."

"His father is or was a senator," Pilate replied. "Lucius Tullius led a cohort in Hispania at a young age, but something went wrong--something with his father."

"Perhaps he crossed Tiberius or made some other political mistake."

Pilate snapped his fingers. "Exactly; I don't know what it was, but his father--I think his name is Julius--fell into disfavor." Pilate smiled. "Maybe he's a republican." Pilate gave a helpless gesture. "You know Tiberius...he still hasn't forgotten the incident with the banners. He never forgets."

"Maybe Lucius needs a new assignment," Adrien suggested.

Pilate ignored Adrien's comment and stopped abruptly. Looking into Adrien's eyes, he said, "Perhaps Lucius Tullius and his father are involved in the some sort of conspiracy."

"Then Tiberius would have them killed."

Pilate nodded. "You're right. I suppose I could bring Lucius Tullius to Jerusalem on temporary assignment until I learn how the wind blows in Rome." Pilate slapped his crop against a pillar. "That leaves me without a decent officer in Jericho. Damn it, Adrien, a person can't win. There aren't enough good officers to go around."

Pilate started to walk into his quarters but turned for one more question. "The tribune they killed--what do you know about his family?"

"He was originally from Greece. His father was a Roman army officer, his mother was Greek. He has two children, boys, and his wife is also Greek. That's all I know."

Pilate rubbed his chin. "That's right; she lives here in the fortress."

"Yes."

"Make arrangements to send her back to Greece. We need the tribune's quarters for his replacement. Oh yes, tell her I regret that her husband died." Pilate disappeared into his quarters, rubbing his forehead and mumbling about foolish men.

CHAPTER TWENTY-EIGHT

Caiaphas was appointed High-Priest of the Jews by the Roman procurator Valerius Gratus, the predecessor of Pontius Pilate, about 18 C.E. He was removed from that office in 36 C.E. by the procurator Vitellius shortly after he took charge of affairs in Palestine. During this period Annas, father-in-law of Caiaphas, who had been high-priest from 6 to 15 C.E., continued to exercise a controlling influence over Jewish affairs, as he did when his own sons held the position.

Pontius Pilate looked forward to the meeting between himself, Annas, and Caiaphas, the High Priests of the temple. He also invited Herod Antipas, Tetrarch of Galilee and Perea. Pilate needed to find a solution to the increasing unrest in Judea and Galilee, a task which required the priests' and Herod's cooperation. Trouble with bandits, zealots, and other outlaws migrating from Galilee to Samaria and Judea had caused Pilate many sleepless nights. Now he was determined to bring those problems under control before his superiors in Rome decided he needed help.

The meeting was held in a tastefully decorated room away from Pilate's living quarters in the Antonia Fortress. The Chief Priest, Caiaphas, and his father-in-law, Annas arrived first, ushered by a guard to the meeting chamber located in the northwest tower of the citadel. They walked around the room, inspected the furniture, and exchanged wary glances while they waited. Annas had been Chief Priest until the previous Judean procurator deposed him and appointed his son-in-law, Caiaphas, in his place. However, most orthodox Jews still looked to Annas as the true leader of the Jewish religious and political establishment.

There were small tables in each of the corners. One had a platter with fresh fruit; another, a vase with flowers. A third held the oil lamps they would use if the meeting lasted past sundown. The fourth table was empty. The room was as nice as any in Jerusalem, yet the priests felt ill at ease in this Gentile building.

To them, the building was unclean, and no amount of physical embellishments would change that.

They stiffened when they heard the tread of heavy sandals in the passageway leading to the room. The door flew open and two soldiers stood against the door and slapped their hands against their chests. Pontius Pilate walked past them, making a half gesture in return. The guards quickly closed the door and remained outside.

After greeting the priests, Pilate looked around the room. "It seems we're missing a guest," he commented.

The high priests raised their palms as if to show that they were not their brother's keeper.

Pilate noticed that the priests dressed in garments that symbolized their high office. Joseph Caiaphas wore an ornamental breastplate that held twelve precious stones, one for each of the twelve tribes of Israel. Beneath that, he wore a simple blue robe fringed with cords woven from gold thread. Annas wore the simpler and more comfortable dress of a Levite. It consisted of a white flowing garment with a gold braided belt around his waist. His sleeves tapered to a woven braid above the wrist. His one concession to adornment was a thick gold bracelet on his left wrist which he continually twisted with his right hand. Both men wore plain turbans on their heads.

Pilate gestured to a cluster of chairs arranged near the middle of the room, inviting his guests to be seated. Then he walked to the window and looked at the young man tied to the stake; the man who had killed his tribune the previous day. Now the guards had another rebel, caught this very morning, tied to a stake next to him. Pilate made a slight hand gesture and a guard began flogging the new arrival. His screams echoed off the courtyard walls and rose toward the window, increasing rather than decreasing in volume as they reached the window.

Pilate turned to his guests and smiled. "Another rebel. It's interesting how their bravery turns to fear when we reverse roles." He looked out the window again. "Ah, look at the crowd. Maybe they'll learn a lesson from this." The priests looked at the floor as Pilate continued, "Soon the flies and ants will feast on his open wounds, and when he's too weak to resist, the birds will pick at his flesh. I hope he shows as much courage as he had when he strutted around the city with his dagger." Pilate looked at the men, sitting uneasily in their chairs, and added, "I'm sorry. Does this offend you?"

Annas looked up when Pilate snapped his riding crop against his thigh. "You must dispense justice as you see fit," he said quietly.

They looked toward the door when they heard a loud noise from the hallway. Soon, the door swung open, revealing the smiling face of Herod

Antipas. Waving him into the room, Pilate said, "Good morning, Excellency. I hope you had a pleasant trip to Jerusalem."

"The trip from Jericho to Jerusalem was fine," Herod replied, "But I almost died going from Machaerus to Jericho."

Pilate smiled. "We know there are plenty of Herods, but hardly one who could replace you if you die." Pilate looked at the priests, then back to Herod. "You're late, did something detain you?"

Herod Antipas grimaced at Pilate. "Your soldiers are busy torturing another victim in the square," he replied. "The crowds blocked my way."

Herod, dressed in a white robe cinched at the waist, and a dark blue cape secured at his right shoulder with a copper medallion, greeted Annas and Caiaphas. Herod always dressed like a king when he met with other leaders. Pilate had dressed in his toga so as not to irritate the priests, but he cursed himself for not wearing his military uniform. It seemed that even though Herod and he were of equal rank, he looked plebian while Herod reflected his royal blood.

"I assume the man is a criminal," Herod continued.

"This window has an excellent view of the proceedings in the square," Pilate responded sarcastically. "I found it interesting yesterday, when that young man killed Vehilius Gratus. The mob challenged our soldiers with stones and curses."

"I wondered," Pilate continued, "when I first came here, why there were so many stones on the ground. Now I know; Jews throw stones as a form of recreation." Pilate looked out the window. "Ah, the new rebel already hangs limp. Look at his body twitch. Come look, Antipas, I'm sure you have a stronger stomach than the priests."

Herod declined with a shake of his head.

Pilate smiled, "Don't tell me you've suddenly learned compassion. Or do messy things upset you?"

Herod was about to respond when Adrien entered the room carrying a gold tray with a gold decanter and four cups. Pilate gestured to the empty table in the corner. Adrien put the tray on the floor, brought the table to where the men sat, and then placed the tray on the table. Pilate gave him his riding crop as he left the room.

Adrien returned moments later with a stylus in his hand and a writing pad under his arm. "Adrien will take notes from this meeting," Pilate announced. "I need to send a report to the legate in Damascus and Rome about affairs in Judea and Samaria." He pointed to the table and added, "Help yourself to some wine."

Annas poured the first cup, smelled the bouquet, wrinkled his nose and sipped. Caiaphas did likewise. Herod Antipas poured a cup and drank it straight down.

Pontius Pilate stood by the window and watched his guests. "There's some fruit on that table in the corner, but don't eat too much; I planned dinner in my private dining room after this meeting."

Adrien handed Pilate the writing pad. He studied it for a minute then turned to the others. "You recently celebrated your feast known as Passover."

The priests nodded.

"It seems that more people come for this feast than the other celebrations."

Annas replied, "That is true."

"It gives troublemakers an opportunity to come to Jerusalem and mix with the crowds," Pilate added stiffly.

"Perhaps," replied Annas thoughtfully. "Perhaps."

Pilate looked at the pad again. "Let's see. Seventeen soldiers injured, three killed. Six Jews executed, not counting the two in the square. Several more Jews injured during the riots on the third and fifth days. Three major fires. Damage to the aqueduct. Widespread destruction of property--mostly public property. And the countryside--my men tell me that the pilgrims left so much litter, we have a problem with rodents and predatory animals."

Herod's eyes brightened. "Perhaps the predators will eat the rodents and solve half your problem."

Pilate shot an angry glance at Herod. "Please save your humor, such as it is, for our dinner. I might appreciate it then." Herod responded by pouring another cup of wine.

Rubbing his forehead, Pilate looked at the priests. "Who caused these problems--Judeans or outsiders?"

Annas cleared his throat and replied, "Probably both."

Pilate looked at the pad. "Zealots?"

"Not as many as you might think."

"Essenes?"

"A few."

"Pharisees?"

"I don't think so," Caiaphas answered. Looking at Herod Antipas, he added, "People from Galilee and the northern tribes." Then he looked back to Pilate before Herod could respond. "To be truthful, the construction workers are causing more problems than anyone. They sit outside the walls at night and drink until they can't walk, then they try to enter the city and cause problems."

"That problem will go away," Pilate responded. "We're scheduled to finish our current construction projects within forty-five days." He looked at Herod

Antipas, who so far enjoyed the discomfort of the high priests. "What about the Galileans and Pereans?"

Herod snapped to attention. "I know you've had problems with the Galileans before now."

Pilate nodded. "There are always a few trouble makers. I remember we terminated two Galileans the last time I was in Jerusalem."

Herod clapped. "Terminated. Is that a new word the Romans use to describe torture and crucifixion?"

"How do you like decapitation?" Pilate snapped. Herod turned red but Pilate continued before he could respond. "We have a dilemma. Your terrorists murder our soldiers, bandits freely roam the countryside between Judea and Galilee, and religious zealots spread hatred. We need to deal with these problems."

Making eye contact with each of the men, he continued, "We all have enemies. Mine live in Rome. Herod Antipas has enemies in Palestine and in Rome." He noticed a look of disagreement on Herod's face. "Yes, my prince, there are people in Rome who don't love you."

Pilate pointed to the priests. "As for you, I know you have enemies in Palestine."

"Israel," Annas mumbled.

"Israel?" Pilate echoed.

"Yes, we live in Israel, not Palestine."

Pilate waved his hand. "No matter, the point is these mobs feed on events like the Jerusalem riots and assassinations in the countryside. My couriers tell me that people from Rome no longer wish to travel to Israel because they fear for their safety." He slammed his fist into his hand. "In a word, there is a widespread impression that we can't control our territories. I intend to change that impression." He paused and looked at the others. "Now, let's figure out what we're going to do about it?"

They sat in silence, trying to sort out Pilate's words. Pilate quickly grew impatient. "WELL?"

Annas jumped up. "Yes-yes. We have serious problems. It's no secret there are divisions within our leadership. You know we share power in the Sanhedrin with the Pharisees."

Pilate rubbed his forehead. "I can't keep all your parties and factions straight, but doesn't your Sadducee party still control the Sanhedrin?"

"Yes."

Pilate looked at Caiaphas. "Are there powerful people in Jerusalem who oppose our latest building projects?"

Caiaphas fingered his breastplate. "People were upset over the chaos caused by the construction. And you know, procurator, that over the years too many men have died in the process." Caiaphas looked into the distance.

"Never mind," Pilate said, dismissing the subject. "What about the Essenes?"

Herod raised his hands in the air. "My god, we have enemies everywhere!"

"Yes," Pilate replied, "and our task is to keep our enemies from becoming Rome's enemies. Now Caiaphas, tell me about the problem you're having with the Essenes."

Caiaphas sighed, "The Essenes are committed to purifying the Temple. They say the Temple has been defiled since the days of Pompeii. They live in Qumran, near the Salt Sea, south of Jericho."

"Sadly, they were once one of us," Annas added.

"One of whom?" Pilate asked.

"Sadducees, our beliefs go back to a common tradition."

Pilate looked at Caiaphas. "Go on."

"They also have small communities of believers in several cities in Israel and the Diaspora," Caiaphas added.

"Oh, you mean the people who live in the real world," Pilate replied sarcastically.

Caiaphas ignored his comment and continued, "The Essenes are radicals like the zealots. It wouldn't surprise me if they were behind the trouble in Jerusalem. They want to embarrass us."

Pilate waved his arm. "Why don't we just go out to this Qumran place and level it? Get rid of the fanatics?"

Annas gasped, "We can't do that. Our ancient scriptures are stored there. They copy them for us."

"Who cares?" Pilate asked. "They're not on your side."

Annas looked into Pilate's eyes. "How sad it is that you don't understand us. We may disagree, but we believe in the same God--Yahweh. Our differences deal with how we worship God and who should lead our people." He tapped his chest. "The Sadducees will prevail in time. There are threats to our leadership, but we can absorb them. We have a sacred trust to preserve our ancient documents and the community at Qumran is doing that for us."

Annas inched toward the window and glanced at the courtyard from the corner of his eye. "First, we must protect the integrity of the Temple. Then we can coexist with Rome if our people remain obedient to the laws of the Temple..."

"And the laws of Rome," Pilate interjected.

"...Jews have no interest in challenging Rome."

"He's right," Herod affirmed. "There are hotheads who will challenge any authority. Most of the people in my provinces want peace and security. They have no interest in affairs of state." Herod held his cup upside down to signal that the wine decanter was empty. Pilate shook his head.

"What about the Sicarii?" Pilate continued. "They've been a thistle in your groin for a while now. Someone tell me what you know about them and how you intend to deal with them." He went to the corner table and pulled a pear from the dish.

Annas broke the long silence that followed Pilate's question. "The Sicarii, as you call them, are very few in number...mostly young men--zealots."

"But we can't ignore them," Pilate insisted. "They're revolutionaries and we need to deal with them."

Caiaphas raised his hand. "Let's organize our thinking. There are reasons for terrorism. Our people have grievances against Rome and against us. We cooperate with Rome and they think that's wrong." He fingered his breastplate. "Besides, your taxes are too oppressive."

Pilate ignored his comment. "I don't care why these people make trouble. I want to know how we can stop them." He instinctively flicked his wrist. "Do I make myself clear? I don't want a repeat of this year's incidents. I have to report these things to Rome," he softly added. "After all, Tiberius doesn't send tribunes to Judea to be murdered."

Pilate stood by the window looking at the men in the square. "I will, if necessary, cancel celebrations of your holy days if these incidents occur again," he said coldly.

The priests gasped. Annas' eyes flashed as he addressed Pilate, "You can't do that. Tiberius will..."

"Don't tell me what Tiberius will do!" Pilate shouted. "I'm here to administer Roman territory. Herod--say something before I kill these bastards! What is your opinion? No wait!" He sneered at Caiaphas. "If the tax burden is too high, lower your temple taxes. Certainly the taxes from Rome are fair."

Annas rose to his feet. "Then stay away from the temple treasury. Raise your own const..." Annas stopped when he noticed the rage in Pilate's eyes.

"That's our secret!" Pilate sputtered. "You promised!"

"We did nothing," Annas shot back. "You..." Suddenly Annas clutched his chest and fell back into the chair. "Now look what you did," he said to Pilate. "You made me short of breath."

Herod watched the scene with a scornful look, then signaled for quiet before anyone could react. "We won't solve our problems by yelling at each other," he declared. Snapping his fingers, he added, "I have an idea. I suggest each of us take some time to think about these problems. Perhaps we can meet in a few months and discuss this subject with less passion."

Pilate patted Herod on the shoulder. "That's a good thought. I knew your devious mind would come up with a solution."

Annas interrupted, "We can meet here in a month."

Pilate shook his head. "We'll meet in Caesarea...in two months. I'll return to Jerusalem in a month; I can finalize arrangements with you then."

Annas frowned. Herod smiled.

Pilate looked at the high priests. "Don't worry about the trip. I'll send an escort to take you from Joppa to Caesarea so you won't have to cross Samaritan territory."

"Good, we settled that," Herod exclaimed. "Let's eat."

Pilate asked the priests, "Will you eat with us tonight?"

"Our law forbids us to eat in the house of a Gentile," Caiaphas replied.

"Does that mean no?" Pilate asked.

"That's right," Caiaphas answered sadly.

"Is there a way we can eat together and not break your law?"

"Only in a building separate from your living quarters," Annas replied.

Caiaphas rubbed his breastplate. "Besides, our people are waiting for us to report on this meeting. Please accept our apologies."

After Pontius Pilate and Herod Antipas escorted the priests from the tower, Herod turned to Pilate and asked, "What's this talk about the Temple treasury?"

"Nothing you'd be interested in."

Herod Antipas scratched his chin. "I just figured it out. You're financing building projects with temple funds." He smiled broadly. "How did you ever get them to agree to that?"

Pilate fingered his dagger. "I threatened to cut their penises off." Then he added, "This is between the high priests and myself. I don't want anyone else to know."

"You can trust me," Herod replied.

"I have to," Pilate said. "We have a common enemy."

"Those men that just left the room?"

"Right."

As they turned the corner to Pilate's private quarters, Herod asked. "Do you plan any entertainment with supper?"

"I thought you lost your appetite for entertainment after your birthday party."

"Only when Herodias is around."

Pontius Pilate and Herod Antipas headed to the baths, ready to replace affairs of state with purely physical pleasure.

CHAPTER TWENTY-NINE

The high priest, the one among his brothers who has had the anointing oil poured on his head and who has been ordained to wear the priestly garments, must not let his hair become unkempt or tear his clothes.
He must not enter a place where there is a dead body. He must not make himself unclean, even for his father or mother, nor leave the sanctuary of his God or desecrate it, because he has been dedicated by the anointing oil of his God. I am the LORD.

Lev 21:10-12

Judas was called back to Jerusalem shortly after Jesus and his followers set camp at Phasaelis. Abiram's agent in Jerusalem claimed that the last two shipments of fish from Capernaum were improperly preserved. Abiram wanted someone familiar with these shipments to go to Jerusalem to mediate the problem, or at least determine if there was a problem. Judas was chosen because he was familiar with the proper methods for preserving fish and he was available. He checked the most recent shipment and found that there indeed was a problem and sent messages to Abiram and Zebedee outlining his recommendations. He had to wait in Jerusalem an extra day to join a group of merchants traveling north so he contacted Joseph of Arimathea to see if Joseph would fulfill his promise to take him to the Temple. He agreed but warned Judas that things at the Temple were unsettled because of the murder of Vehilius Gratis.

Judas and Joseph went to the Temple the day after Pontius Pilate met with the high priests and Herod Antipas. Judas looked forward to spending a day with the Temple leaders. He was certain that if he listened carefully, these men would reveal their secrets of success to him.

Judas pointed to the sentinels visible in the towers of the Antonia Fortress as he and Joseph entered the Temple grounds. "How can you worship and conduct Temple business with the Romans watching everything you do?"

"We learned how to survive domination by other people a long time ago," Joseph replied. "You forget we started in Egypt thirteen hundred years ago making bricks for the pyramids."

"Did the Egyptians torture and crucify our people the way the Romans do?"

"Our scriptures tell us the Egyptians were very cruel to the Hebrews."

Judas persisted, "You told me there were several men hanging on crosses the last time I came to Jerusalem. What do you say to that?"

Joseph glanced upward to collect his thoughts. "People from the provinces come to Jerusalem thinking they can push the Romans around. They come to Jerusalem, start fights with the Romans, and the next thing you know, they're hanging from crosses."

"You certainly have a casual attitude about Jews hanging from Roman crosses," Judas commented.

"Never! I can't accept that," Joseph replied angrily. Waving a finger at Judas, he said, "Don't confuse patience with consent."

Judas started to reply but Joseph interrupted, "Let me finish. The zealots--we call them zealots--are no more than bandits and terrorists. Our people fear them because they place a low value on human life. That man they hung in the Antonia Fortress, next to the Temple? He killed a Roman officer. What can we do?"

"What about the aqueduct? What do you think of that?"

Joseph led Judas to a marble bench just inside the Court of the Israelites and they sat down. "For the first time in history," Joseph said, "Jerusalem has enough water. That means we can build a sewage system to keep our city clean. The aqueduct is not an issue to the average Jew." Joseph waved to a man hurrying past their bench and continued, "I don't want to see our people die. But this isn't the first time. Jews are survivors. After the Egyptians, there were Syrians, Babylonians, and Greeks. They're gone and we're still here. Some day the Romans will leave and we'll still be here." He looked into the distance. "We won't gain anything by rashly challenging their power. Too often, young men get their courage from a wine jug rather than their heart. Wine increases our rashness, not our resources."

A man interrupted Joseph, "Why do you have such a serious look on your face?"

Joseph looked up and greeted the man and introduced him to Judas. "Judas, this is Caiaphas, the Chief Priest of the Temple." Then to Caiaphas he said, "I was explaining to young Judas that living under Roman rule is no worse than other times in our past."

Caiaphas raised his eyebrows. "You mean times like the Babylonian captivity?"

"That's one," Joseph replied.

"That's another subject," Caiaphas stated. "The Romans will tell you we brought them here to keep the peace. They say we can't govern ourselves."

Caiaphas signaled to a priest across the courtyard. "I have to hurry," he said. "I'm sure you know that Annas and I met with Pontius Pilate yesterday."

"How did it go?" Joseph asked.

"It's a long story. Listen, I invited some people for a mid-day meal at my house today to tell them about the meeting. You can either meet us there or wait for a full meeting of the Sanhedrin."

Caiaphas followed Joseph's eyes to Judas.

"Bring...Judas with if you wish."

Joseph nodded. "Sixth hour?"

"Seventh. I'll see you then." Caiaphas turned and hurried toward a group of men standing near the Nicanor Gate (the Temple gate separating The Court of the Priests from the rest of the Temple).

Joseph stood and put his hand on Judas' shoulder. "I have some things to do before we eat lunch. Would you mind waiting here until I finish?"

Judas nodded and watched as Joseph entered the Court of the Women. He chose to remain on the bench tracing the outline of a star on one of the ornate tiles with his sandal. He remembered the times as a boy, when he knelt on the same floor of the Temple and traced the multicolored circles, stars and hexagons with his fingers. His father said some of the tiles had an extra star within the smallest circle but he never found one that did.

* * *

Caiaphas lived in one of the largest houses in the Upper City. A high stucco wall punctuated with three entrance gates surrounded the house. Judas and Joseph entered a large, partially shaded courtyard where Joseph introduced Judas to some of his friends, most of whom were leading merchants and lawyers from the city.

The only names that stuck with Judas were those of Rabbi Helcias and a man named Nicodemus. From his name and accent, Judas guessed Nicodemus was of Greek descent. Nicodemus and Caiaphas seemed younger than most of the other men of the group. Their youth set them apart from the bald and gray-bearded elders of the Temple.

As Judas sauntered around the courtyard, he noticed that the colonnaded portico surrounding the main living quarters resembled the Royal Portico at the Temple. He wondered if that was a coincidence. Later, he sipped a cup of wine and watched men talking in small groups. He rolled each sip around his mouth to enjoy the quality of what he sensed was an excellent vintage. Eventually, he stood next to a circle of men talking with Caiaphas but moved away when he noticed their disapproving gazes.

He strained to hear what they were talking about. Caiaphas ignored him and turned his attention to the others. "As you know," he said, "we met with Pontius Pilate yesterday."

A merchant asked, "What do you think of him?"

This was information Judas wanted to hear, so he burrowed closer to the group.

Caiaphas frowned at Judas and moved closer to the other men. "I don't like him, but I must cooperate with him so he will leave us alone."

"What did he say about the riots?" the merchant asked.

"He said we need to manage our own affairs."

The man persisted. "Why then, are the Roman soldiers hanging Jews?" The group fell silent. Any answer might be considered treacherous if misinterpreted.

"We know the Romans will execute insurgents and murderers," Caiaphas answered. "We gave them that responsibility when we abolished capital punishment."

"Does that give them the right to rape Jewish women?" someone asked.

"The soldiers do that on their own," Caiaphas replied.

* * *

At lunch Judas sat between a merchant whose name he immediately forgot and the man named Nicodemus. He listened to the conversations around the table for a while then looked at Nicodemus. "I always thought important people only talked about important things."

Nicodemus laughed. "Important people, as you call them, talk about food, trips to the sea, and servant girls like everyone else. They're like you, except they live in better houses and spend more money."

After they finished their meal, Caiaphas signaled for quiet. "It's time for the business at hand," he said. "I want to tell you about our meeting with Pontius Pilate and Herod Antipas." Caiaphas fingered his breastplate while he waited for their attention. "Pilate is in a rage over recent problems in Jerusalem," he announced after he made sure everyone was listening. "Pilate says he will put an end to civil unrest if we fail to do so. The problem is that we can't end it easily. What control do we have over fifty thousand pilgrims and a thousand construction workers?"

The men at the table gave each other questioning looks. Finally a man raised his hand, asking, "What's Pilate's plan?"

"He has the same answer as always, torture and execution," Caiaphas responded. "Only this time he's added another twist."

"What's that?" Joseph asked.

"He said he'll close the Temple during our holidays if the situation doesn't improve." Suddenly, the room erupted with astonished looks and frantic conversation. Caiaphas waited until the room quieted. "I don't have to tell you what that would mean."

Joseph asked, "Do you think he means it?"

"I don't want to find out," Caiaphas replied. "We need to find who the troublemakers are before they reach Jerusalem and keep them out during our feast days."

"That won't be easy," a man commented.

"We can't let Pontius Pilate obstruct our worship," Rabbi Helcias declared.

Caiaphas signaled for quiet. "I talked to Pilate privately this morning. He had a terrible headache and was hung over from too much wine. He was much more malleable than yesterday afternoon. He told me that if he had his way, he would never kill a Jew. He'd rather live in peace with us." Caiaphas sighed, "I think he's telling the truth."

"Tell him to leave Judea if he wants peace," a scornful voice shouted from across the room.

Caiaphas ignored the man and continued, "Herod Antipas was at the meeting as well. Pilate told Herod to do a better job of keeping the Galileans under control."

"It's about time," Jacob declared. "How did Herod look?"

"A little fatter than the last time I saw him. A little smarter, if you know what I mean." Caiaphas frowned. "I don't like him. He's a weasel."

* * *

"These Galileans...They're a funny people," Joseph muttered to Judas on the way home from the house of Caiaphas. "Most are illiterate and poor. They're always talking about messiahs and end times. They think differently than we do." He looked at Judas. "Be careful."

CHAPTER THIRTY

Now upon his observation of a place near the sea, which was very proper for containing a city, and was before called Strato's Tower, he set about getting a plan for a magnificent city there, and erected many edifices with great diligence all over it, and this of white stone. He also adorned it with most sumptuous palaces and large edifices for containing the people; and what was the greatest and most laborious work of all, he adorned it with a haven, that was always free from the waves of the sea. Its largeness was not less than the Pyrmum [at Athens], and had towards the city a double station for the ships. It was of excellent workmanship; and this was the more remarkable for its being built in a place that of itself was not suitable to such noble structures, but was to be brought to perfection by materials from other places, and at very great expenses.

Josephus Flavius (Antiquities - Book XV, 9, 6)

Herod the Great built the harbor and the city of Caesarea Maritima in honor of Caesar Augustus. Prior to that, he rebuilt the Temple in Jerusalem, his winter palace in Jericho, and the lofty Salt Sea citadel of Masada. Herod the Great built Caesarea to rival Alexandria in opulence and magnificence, and crowned his achievement by naming it after the most powerful man alive.

Now, some forty-five years later Herod Antipas and his wife, Herodias, walked the marble stairway of the palace built by his father. As Herod Antipas looked over the grounds, he remembered the times he swam in the large bathing pool and played in the tropical gardens. That happened over twenty years earlier, when his brother, Herod Archelaus, lived in Caesarea, ruling as Tetrarch of Samaria, Judea and Idumaea. Now Pontius Pilate, the Roman Procurator ruled those provinces from Herod's palace.

Herodias tugged at Herod's sleeve when she saw Pontius Pilate at the top of the steps. "This house belongs to the Herods, not a Roman lackey."

"Be quiet, we've discussed this to its death," Herod hissed. "It's not our fault my brother Archelaus was a fool." Herod Antipas pulled his arm free and began the process of responding to Pilate's greeting.

Pilate descended a few steps and, smiling broadly, he took Herodias' hand in his. "I'm pleased you agreed to join us." He cast a sideways glance at Herod. "Your presence clearly offsets the tedium of conducting state business." Pilate savored the sweet scent of her perfume before placing a light kiss on the back of her hand.

Herod forced a smile. "We've been looking forward to this visit."

"Yes, we'll make this a festal event," Pilate replied as he led them up the last few steps. "My wife, Procula, will join us in the courtyard as soon as you refresh yourselves."

"Who needs refreshing?" Herod responded. "The servants can take our belongings and..."

Herodias shut him off with an abrupt glance. "I prefer to bathe and rest before we meet with the Procurator and his wife."

Pilate ignored their sniping. "I chose the rooms overlooking the harbor for you." He pointed to an upper porch where columns framed the sea below them.

"Good." Herod Antipas muttered as he looked for familiar sights. "We'll enjoy the cool breeze from the sea." He asked Pilate, "Have the High Priests arrived?"

"They'll come tomorrow. I sent a guard to Joppa to provide an escort. I hear they brought their wives as well," Pilate added. "It looks as if your idea for a holiday caught on."

Herod waited until Herodias left the atrium before replying. "I'm sure you heard the news about old Annas. His wife died last year and after an acceptable period of mourning he married a young woman that..." Herod used his hands to illustrate his description. "...will make every woman in the place jealous."

"Are you still interested in passion after what happened at Machaerus?" Pilate needled. Then he put his hand over his mouth. "I'm sorry, there's no excuse for saying that. Would you like some wine before you take a bath?" Herod nodded. "One thing we have in common, procurator, is the sharpness of our tongues."

Pilate snapped his fingers. "Did you know I invited your...what do you call them?"

"Them?"

"Yes...Philip...is he your cousin? Or half brother?"

"I hope you mean Philip from Ituraea." Herod declared.

"Yes."

Herod sighed. "Good, I try to avoid the other Herod Philip since I married Herodias."

Pilate shook his head. "Do I know that Herod Philip?"

"He is my half-brother, the son of Mariamme." Herod Antipas leaned against a pillar. "Philip of Ituraea is the son of Cleopatra of Jerusalem."

"No relative of the famous Cleopatra?"

"Hardly. You remember Archelaus?"

Pilate nodded.

"He and I are the sons of Malthace."

"Ah yes, Archelaus," Pilate croaked. "He was too cruel even for Roman tastes. Where did he go after he was deposed."

"Still in exile--Greece, I think. I heard his health is failing."

"I don't know how you measure your family." Pilate used his fingers to number the events. "First your father married several women, and then gave his sons and daughters the same names. How many Philips are there?"

"I'm not sure," Herod stammered.

"What about Herodias, your wife?"

"What do you mean?"

"How is she related to you?"

"Ah, she's the daughter of my half brother Alexander."

"Your niece?"

"She is," Herod replied stiffly. She married Herod Philip but lost interest in him because he spent more time in Rome than Palestine."

"So she divorced him and married you."

"Yes. Actually Herod Philip is dull and...you know." Herod Antipas waved his hand.

Pilate nodded. "At least I invited the right Philip."

"Yes."

"I'll never understand your family."

"Maybe I can draw a family sketch for you someday. My problem is that I don't know all my half brothers and sisters, much less cousins and in-laws."

* * *

Later that day, a sharp starboard tack carried the small but comfortable ship between six massive stone statues rising from the end of the jetties protecting the harbor at Caesarea. Annas and his new wife Athalia, along with his daughter Marian, the wife of Joseph Caiaphas stood against the ship's railing. Caiaphas remained in his cabin where he had stayed since the boat left Joppa. As the boat weaved its way through a forest of masts, Annas shielded his eyes and said to Marian, "It's time to revive your husband. I think we'll enjoy safe passage from this point."

Marcus Rutilius, the Prefect of the Praetorian Guard, saluted as they came down the gangway. “My men will escort you to your living quarters in the Jewish section of the city,” he announced. When Annas signaled his approval, Marcus Rutilius gestured to the honor guard. They blew a trumpet fanfare for the passengers, while Marcus Rutilius escorted them ashore. Annas wondered why Pilate failed to welcome him personally, but chose to ignore his snub.

That night Pontius Pilate held a reception in the gardens of the Herodian Palace. He wanted to stage a banquet, but Jewish law prevented the orthodox Jews from eating meals in a Gentile house. Furthermore, to the chagrin of Herodias, the women watched the festivities from a balcony overlooking the gardens. She viewed this as another insult caused by a silly Jewish law. She developed a pounding headache early in the evening and retired to her quarters before Marian and Athalia arrived.

Pilate stood next to a pillar watching his guests while he swished thick red wine around his cup. The Herod half-brothers circulated among the Roman officials visiting from Damascus, listening for gossip that would benefit their political position. The high priests concerned themselves with the local Jewish officials, ignoring Herod and the Romans. Pilate circulated near the Jews, heard their whispers, and cursed himself for not learning Aramaic or Hebrew when he came to Palestine.

Sauntering near the Herods, Pilate heard Philip ask Herod Antipas, “Where is Herodias?”

“Headache,” Herod mumbled.

Philip scanned the balcony. “Did you bring her daughter?”

Herod Antipas shook his head.

“Too bad,” Philip mused. “I was looking forward to seeing her.”

Pilate left the Herods when he noticed a Roman officer entering the gardens. He quickly escorted the soldier to an isolated corner and talked to him for a few minutes. Then he took the man to where the high priests, Annas and Caiaphas, stood.

“This is Tribune Manius Decius,” Pilate said. “He arrived today from Rome.” The priests acknowledged his presence as Pilate pushed the tribune between them, adding, “He will remain at the Antonia Fortress until your feast of Pesach ends. He’s a temporary replacement for Vehilius Gratus, the tribune killed during the riots in Jerusalem.”

The priests nodded, and then turned to resume their conversation with the other Jewish leaders as if Pilate and Manius Decius were not there. Raising his eyes, Caiaphas noticed Pilate’s irritation and pulled him aside. “I apologize for not including you in our conversation,” he said. “But you do not speak our language.”

Smiling, Pilate replied, "Perhaps I should consider a decree that commands you to conduct your conversations in Latin or Greek at these events."

Caiaphas frowned, "We would object to such a decree."

"You object to most ideas that come from Rome."

"We like the aqueduct."

Pilate looked at Manius Decius. "I'm sure you heard that we built an aqueduct from Bethlehem to Jerusalem. Jerusalem has more water now than at any time in its history. This will enable us to build a better sanitation system for the city." He looked at Caiaphas. "The Jews thanked us with a riot because we borrowed temple funds to help finance the project."

"You used the Corban, you..." Caiaphas started to perspire.

"And the Jerusalem cohort," Pilate interrupted.

"You used the Corban and shed Jewish blood," Caiaphas countered.

"The Jews shed their own blood when they rioted," Pilate shot back.

"What is a Corban?" Manius Decius asked.

"The Temple treasury," Pilate replied.

"The *Sacred* Temple Treasury," Caiaphas corrected.

Pilate slapped his hand on his hip. "We can argue about these things tomorrow." He looked at the balcony and smiled. "Tell me about this wife of Annas, she's the talk of Caesarea."

Caiaphas was about to speak when he saw Annas walking toward them. He looked at Pilate and said, "I'll tell you later."

Later, Pilate caught a full glimpse of Annas' wife, Athalia, before she left the palace. He made sure Procula was out of sight, then tugged at the sleeve of Manius Decius. "Did you see her?" he asked.

The tribune whistled softly.

Pilate said under his breath, "It would be worth a circumcision if all the Jewish women looked like her." He smiled broadly and added, "But she'll kill Annas before long...If you know what I mean."

* * *

Herod returned to his quarters after the reception and found an angry Herodias waiting for him. "Is your headache gone?" he asked with a smile.

Glaring at his every move, she reached for a vase, then pulled her hand back. "I'd throw this at you, but we may live in this palace someday and this vase is too valuable to waste on your head."

"Since when does the value of a vase stand in the way of revenge?" Herod asked acidly. "Did you really have a headache?"

"I would've if I had to spend the night with those harpies from Jerusalem." She wrinkled her brow. "Procula is so pretentious."

Herod Antipas snickered, "Procula is lucky to be alive. Do you remember when Pilate first went to Jerusalem and she entered the forbidden Inner Court of the Temple? Think of it; a Gentile and a woman."

Herodias looked up. "I do remember, and so do the High Priests. She started Pontius Pilate's days in Israel like a dead donkey."

Herod poured a cup of wine for Herodias and himself. "Sometimes I wonder whether it's worth it."

"What do you mean?"

"I hate kissing Roman sandals, acting as if I like them."

"I thought you liked Pilate."

"He's a tyrant and a fool."

She nodded. "We should be the ones ruling Judea and Samaria." She sipped her wine. "Maybe we will someday."

Herod Antipas tossed an apple in the air. "There might be a time when a Herod rules Israel again." He cut the apple and handed half to Herodias. "But it's too late for me."

"We still might have a chance if Pilate stumbles."

"They'll send another thick headed soldier to replace him."

Herodias went to the window and looked at the moonlight reflecting off the soft waves breaking against the jetty. "At least the Romans treat their women like people," she muttered. "I don't understand why women have to sit like statues while the men have all the fun."

"Fun? What fun?"

"You tell dirty stories, gossip, and plot against each other and cover your schemes with a smile. I saw it from the balcony. People pulling each other aside to whisper in their ears." She rolled her eyes. "And that new Tribune... what's his name?"

"Manius Decius."

"What a man!" she exclaimed. "He looked at me like I was a goddess when he first arrived."

"So?"

"Don't ask," she giggled. "You must have noticed the difference between your soft belly and his Roman muscles." She sighed, "I'll bet he wrestles naked with his slaves."

Herod waved his cup. "You missed Annas' wife Athalia."

"I heard about her."

"And?"

Herodias laughed. "I heard she's a woman men dream about."

"Where did you hear that?"

"From the same person that told me how you cornered that servant girl near the swimming pool." She wiggled her finger at him. "Naughty Herod, when will you learn to take me seriously?"

* * *

Pontius Pilate greeted each leader the next morning as they entered the large meeting room located to the left of the atrium. Adrien led the men to a table surrounded by curule styled chairs. Adrien, considering himself to be a historian of sorts, kept notes on how each participant wore their uniform of office to show their importance. Pilate wore a toga praetexta with a purple border while Tribune Manius Decius wore his full dress officer's uniform without armor.

Adrien was unfamiliar with Jewish customs, so only noted that Annas and Caiaphas wore the traditional dress of a Jewish high priest. Caiaphas wore the twelve jeweled breastplate signifying his position as Chief Priest, while Annas' plain robe carried several stains from his hastily eaten breakfast.

The Herods, on the other hand, were resplendent in their long robes, fringed at the borders with purple decorations and gold thread. Herod Antipas added a gold belt, a small scabbard and a knife with a jewel encrusted hilt.

Pilate opened the meeting by introducing Adrien, then gestured to the tables laden with fruits and breads. He looked at Annas and asked, "Can you nibble in the palace of a Gentile or is that forbidden as well?"

"Strictly forbidden," Annas replied stiffly.

A smile crept around Pilate's lips. "Yes, well that's the way you are, strict."

"Maybe my son-in-law will grant dispensation," Annas mused.

"I didn't know there was such a thing," Pilate countered.

Annas gave Pilate a wry look. "You have much to learn about our traditions and laws."

"Life is too short to accomplish such a task." Pilate said.

Clearing his throat, Herod Antipas interjected, "Did we come here to play out a Greek comedy or conduct business?"

Pilate nodded. "I'm sorry; this man keeps tangling me in his web of confusion."

Annas' eyes twinkled with satisfaction.

Walking behind the chairs, Pilate said, "We're here to discuss our plans to keep peace during your holidays." He looked at Caiaphas. "I hope you came with some ideas."

Herod raised his hand. "I see little problem from our standpoint--that is between my brother and I. We have no jurisdiction over Jerusalem. Now if you were to..."

Pilate cut him off. "You have enough to do in the provinces you already control." He slapped his hand on his hip. "Tribune Decius recommended that we bring additional troops to the city during the holidays." Again he looked at Caiaphas. "Are you willing to pay the extra cost?"

"Of course not," Annas snapped. "If I had my way, there would be no Roman soldiers in Jerusalem."

Pilate glared at him. "You miss the point of history, Annas. Your people originally asked Rome to send soldiers to protect you from yourselves."

"That was over ninety years ago," Annas protested.

"Palestine is more secure now than anytime since Solomon," Pilate responded. "All we ask is that you bear part of the expense and control those who want to destroy the Roman Peace."

"Perhaps my brother Philip can send soldiers from his provinces to help during the holidays," Herod suggested.

Pilate dismissed Herod's idea with a wave of his hand. "I'll order soldiers from Syria and Egypt in an emergency. If things go well, we will only need a few centuries, and we can take them from Galilee or Perea."

Herod Antipas nodded. "I'm planning to visit Jerusalem during the Passover celebration next year. I can keep my soldiers at the palace."

Pilate arched his eyebrow. "Your father's palace?"

Herod shrugged.

Pilate continued, "I want soldiers loyal to me at Herod's Palace. However, you are free to billet your soldiers at the Hasmonean Palace."

Annas slammed his fist on the table. "Why all this talk about soldiers? You're over-reacting to the problems of the past. Our holidays are events of worship and celebration, not war games. The presence of so many soldiers in Jerusalem will distract our people."

"Our soldiers will stay inside Herod's Palace and the Antonia Fortress as long as the city remains calm," Pilate stated. "The presence of three or four hundred soldiers is hardly noticeable in the crowds you draw to the city." Pilate reached for a pear. "Here, take some of this fruit before it spoils." He looked at the others, but only Philip and Tribune Manius Decius followed his suggestion.

Pilate resumed his monologue, "Now, I want to make this clear to you. I'm more tolerant than my superiors in Rome. Unfortunately, people send reports to Rome along with their personal analysis so they can enhance their position." Pilate bit into the pear. "Rome keeps asking me why I let Jews kill Roman soldiers. They want to know why your people burn buildings and disrupt caravans. They want me to explain why your people riot when we construct improvements in your cities." Pilate bit into the pear again and sprayed bits of pulp as he talked.

Herod Antipas, enjoying Pilate's outburst and the priest's discomfort, chose that moment to interrupt. "Dear procurator," he said smoothly, "even after six years in Israel you fail to understand the mind of these Semitic people. They repay kindness with a bite on the hand of the provider." Herod laughed. "The more vicious the bite, the better. Why, they even kill the prophets God sends to them." Herod looked at Caiaphas. "Isn't that true, my friend?"

Before Caiaphas could reply, Pilate shouted, "Rome authorized me to bring soldiers from Syria if I see a need." Raising his fist, he added, "Listen to me! I intend to keep peace in Jerusalem! I'll close the gates to the city if trouble starts again. Do you understand?"

Annas, red faced and shaking, jumped to his feet. "You can't do that! It would cause more..."

Pilate threw the core from the pear at a bowl and turned his back to Annas. "I can and will do what I must to keep peace in Judea." Then he spun and glared at Annas. "You didn't hear me! My superiors in Rome expect me to maintain order. Understand?"

Suddenly calm, Pilate sat across from Annas and Caiaphas. "You criticize us," he said quietly, "for using force to keep peace in Jerusalem. You're angry because Jews hang from crosses outside the city gates. I don't like it any better than you do. But it's up to you to restore the peace and make the city safe for everyone."

Caiaphas replied, "We have an agreement with Rome, that they will protect us."

"We will protect you from the Parthians and the tribes to the east, but we can't protect you from yourselves. You ask us to keep order, then you tell us not to use brutal force, don't kill troublemakers, and don't let your men consort with our women." Suddenly Pilate's mood swung and he slammed his fist on the table. "Dammit! Damn You! You can't have it both ways. Unless you do the work of policing your own people, you'll have to endure our methods. Is that clear?"

Herod Antipas beckoned for calm. "What are we arguing about?" he asked. "Let's deal with these problems before they start." He looked at the high priests and added, "For once I agree with Pontius Pilate. Jerusalem is a cauldron of anger and unrest." He waved his finger at Annas. "And the people are angry at you as well as the Romans."

"Are you suddenly a man of the people?" croaked Annas.

"Hardly," added Caiaphas.

"The people of Israel are restless," Herod continued.

Pilate beckoned to his aide. "I asked Adrien to list the reasons why people feel the way they do."

Adrien rose and read from a scroll. "People resent the Roman occupation of Palestine..."

Annas interrupted, "I agree, but please stop calling our country, Palestine. The provinces of Galilee, Samaria, and Judea are part of Israel. The Philistines no longer exist."

Pilate shifted in his chair. "Annas, you're a bigger pain in the ass than I thought." He nodded to Adrien to continue.

"The people are indignant over the taxes paid to Rome and the Temple."

"That's because you robbed the Corban," Caiaphas muttered.

"Damn you, Caiaphas!" Pilate hands shook as he strained to keep his composure. "You know as well as I that you agreed to use the Temple Treasury to build the aqueduct. That riot occurred because you lied to your people."

"There are Jewish factions that wish to start a war with Rome," Adrien droned.

Pilate grabbed the scroll and pointed to an item. "This one. Religious fanatics who pretend to be--what--kings?"

"Messiahs," Caiaphas responded in a calm voice. "It's the Essenes. They stir people up with their talk about divine warriors and Sons of Light."

Pilate, also more subdued, asked, "Are those the people in Jericho that we talked about last time?"

"Qumran, near Jericho. They are also active in most large cities in Israel. There are Essenes in Caesarea."

Pilate sat with his hands clasped. "It looks as if we have more problems than solutions." He looked at Annas and Caiaphas. "We must put our differences aside for a while. Understand that Rome will do what she must to retain the provinces of Palestine, excuse me, Israel under her control. These provinces are our last defense against the tribes to the east. To your benefit, we also defend your people against their invasions."

Caiaphas sighed and leaned against his chair. "What do you want us to do?"

"I want you and Herod Antipas to do a better job of policing your people in Judea and Galilee."

"Why do you include me?" Herod asked.

"Because your Galileans keep coming to Judea to cause trouble during the holidays. Every revolutionary and criminal in the world seems to gravitate to Judea. I want you to take care of them in your own province. Hang a few criminals if you have to." Pilate waved his hands. "Maybe hang some every week so people get the idea we intend to keep the peace."

"That's barbaric," Herod Antipas responded.

"It's no worse than the things you do in the province of Perea."

This time Caiaphas signaled for order. "Yes--yes, we all have our embarrassments. That's in the past. For now, we need to cooperate with each other." He gestured to Pilate. "What do you want us to do?"

"First, stop using the Romans as dupes. Most important, stop the troublemakers before they start. You control your preachers and any uprisings by the peasants. We'll keep our soldiers in the Fortress, but will make them available to you in case of trouble." Pilate looked at each man. "Use your spies for something other than politics for a change. You don't have to kill the troublemakers. Just hide them in caves until the danger passes." Pilate sighed, "I don't know of any other city in the world where thousands of people come to celebrate their holidays and end up killing each other."

Annas' bushy eyebrows rose. "There is no other city in the world where God is present as he is in Jerusalem."

Pilate snickered, "Your god is truly strange if he lives in Jerusalem."

"That isn't what I said."

"I don't care what you said. People create Gods in their own image. A god created by a Jew is truly one to worry about. It appears that your god has six minds, an infinite memory, and an unlimited capacity for confusion. On the hand of Jupiter, I rejoice that Rome has no such gods."

* * *

It took several more hours before the men who controlled the destiny of so many people came to an agreement. In the end, the Jewish leaders agreed to provide security during their important holidays. The Romans would remain out of sight, available only as reinforcements for the Jewish guards. Herod Antipas agreed to crack down on insurgency in Galilee and Perea. "Stop trouble before it starts," he said proudly.

On the crucial point of administering civil justice and executing condemned criminals, Pilate agreed that the Roman tribunal would continue to operate as it had in the past. Rome would try civil cases, decide punishment if necessary, and carry out the decision of the tribunal.

After that, the men only had to agree on a place where they could eat their evening meal without violating someone's law, tradition, or palate. Adrien kept no record of their decision.

CHAPTER THIRTY-ONE

"My people are fools; they do not know me. They are senseless children; they have no understanding. They are skilled in doing evil; they know not how to do good."

Jeremiah 4:22

Philip, the Tetrarch of Ituraea, returned to Tiberias with Herod Antipas and Herodias after their meeting with Pontius Pilate at Caesarea. As he viewed the lush gardens of Herod's manor, Philip grunted, "It looks like you inherited our father's gift for building monuments."

"You saw them before," Herod replied, leading Philip past a pond surrounded by yellow iris imported from Egypt.

"I know, but it always takes my breath away." Gesturing toward the grounds Philip added, "This palace doesn't match the one our father built at Caesarea, but it is beautiful."

"Our father had more money and labor available for Caesarea than I did for Tiberias," Herod Antipas responded.

Philip took a deep breath. "What type of flowers are they?"

Herodias walked ahead of them and described the flowers and bushes. "Some of the smells come from the herbs we grow," she said. "For example, the leaves of these sage plants produce a musty flavor and smell. On the other hand, this cumin only produces a strong smell when the fruit appears." She pointed to a tall shrub with grayish-green leaves. "Of course the henna has a more distinctive odor." She stepped carefully to avoid a network of vines crossing the path. "Over here we have roses, although some of them have a fragrance too faint to smell on dry days like today."

Herod Antipas pointed toward a series of embankments near the wall. "I prefer small shrubs and palm trees. They're hardier." He glanced at Philip. "Isn't that exciting? I could listen to Herodias talk about flowers all day. The longer I live with her the more she reminds me of her first husband."

Philip stifled a laugh. “You better send me to my quarters before Herodias buries us in this garden.”

Herod Antipas signaled for a servant, who escorted Philip to a suite of rooms in the north side of the palace, overlooking the Sea of Galilee.

* * *

Herod’s chief aide, Manaen, ate supper with them that night. They discussed their meetings with Pilate and the High Priests over a salad prepared with cucumbers, beans, and covered with a light cheese sauce.

Herodias smiled at Philip when the servants brought the main course. “I thought you might like fowl after all that fish we ate in Caesarea. Do you like partridge?” Ignoring Philip’s attempt to answer, she continued, “Ah yes, smell the gentle seasoning on the vegetables. I especially like the mustard sauce on the cucumbers and onions.”

Herod Antipas wrinkled his nose. “Why do you always try these new variations? No one uses mustard sauce on cucumbers.”

“Stop complaining,” she replied. “It’s a delicate mustard sauce, just enough to tempt your palate.”

Herod waved a drumstick in the air. “Enough of this! That’s why the Jews make their women eat in another room. Women would rather talk about mustard sauce than affairs of state.”

“There are times when you act like a pompous pig,” Herodias replied, voice quivering. “You think you’re the only one who thinks important thoughts...”

“Shut up!” Herod hollered. “I can see why your last husband still lives in Rome...”

Her face crimson with anger, Herodias stammered, “Why you...”

“You’re like most women,” Herod continued. “You think you are smarter than me and you think you should be tetrarch.”

“Now that you said it...”

“Don’t...”

She looked at Herod and Philip with rage in her eyes. “At least I’d stand up to Pontius Pilate better than you two reeds. He must croak with laughter after he deals with the Herods. All of you--a bunch of greedy sex maniacs with no backbone.”

Philip snorted, “What are you if we’re sex maniacs? You’re a Herod--once removed.” With that Herod Antipas and Philip broke into uncontrolled laughter.

Herodias stood and looked at the half-brothers. Then her eyes caught Manaen trying to shrink out of sight. “See lackey, the type of men you worship.” She pulled her stola off her shoulders and stood bare breasted in front of the three men. Pointing to her breasts, she yelled, "See! These are the only things you're interested in. The only affairs of state you care about are which servant girl you can take to bed. You hear stories about the fun people are having in Rome and you wish you were a part of them." She turned to a red-faced Herod Antipas. "And you're not so smart. Pilate treats you like garbage from his table."

Herod looked at her from the corner of his eye. "Pull that thing back up and sit down. You've had too much wine."

"I've had too much Antipas."

"No woman can have too much Antipas," Herod roared as he eyed the other two men. To his surprise, Herodias cracked a faint smile as well. "Now, what were we talking about?"

"Pontius Pilate," Philip answered.

"Oh yes, he's dull...like Herodias' last..." Herod Antipas watched a crimson hue wrap itself around Herodias' neck. "Enough of this; Philip and I need to discuss our own problems tonight."

Philip shrugged. "My province is calm, even where we touch Galilee and parts of the Parthian territories. It helps to have the Roman legions in Syria."

"How many are there now?" Manaen asked.

"Close to three," Philip replied. Raising a finger, he added, "but they have a large territory to defend."

Herod signaled for another serving of wine. He looked at Herodias pouting at the other end of the table. "These cucumbers aren't bad. I might learn to like your mustard sauce."

She ignored his glance.

Herod looked back to Philip. "Things are normal here. The peasants cause trouble but our soldiers handle it well." He raised the decanter. "Here, have some more wine."

Later, Herod Antipas, Philip, and Manaen retreated to the comfortable surroundings of the garden while Herodias went to bed complaining of a headache. Herod gestured toward her room and said, "She worries too much. She thinks the Romans will get the best of us, maybe kill us." He looked at Manaen. "What do you think?"

"I agree; she worries too much."

Herod Antipas looked at the sky. "No, you fool. What about the Romans?"

Feeling the effect of too little food and too much wine, Manaen stumbled on a rock and almost fell. "Excuse me," he said, "I'll be fine in a moment." Then he added, "I talked to the prefect of the Praetorian Guard while we were in Caesarea. Pilate has enough grief with Judea. He has no interest in our territories right now."

Herod twisted his ruby ring around his finger. "The thing that bothers me is that Pilate keeps dragging us into his Judean problems. You know, like the meeting in Jerusalem after the Passover riots. We have nothing to do with Judea or Jerusalem." Herod waved a hand. "He makes up stories about Galileans causing trouble in Judea to make us look bad."

"What about your spies?" Philip asked Herod. "You interfere in Judean affairs when you think it benefits you."

Herod laughed. "That's my job. It helps keep the procurator on his feet." Herod looked at the flowers, illuminated by the pale moon. "But there is more to this than we think. I'll watch myself in the future. I don't want to involve our people with Jerusalem problems and give Rome an excuse to put another Roman sandal licker in charge of Galilee and Perea."

"Not to mention my territory," Philip added.

"Even so, we need to keep a closer watch on people who might cause trouble" Manaen observed. "Pilate is right about not letting them go to Jerusalem during the holidays."

"How can we find out who the troublemakers are?" Herod asked.

"I have spies planted in most of the larger towns in Galilee," Manaen replied. "Also, there are people in Galilee and even Judea who favor the Herods over the Romans."

Herod's eyes brightened. "The Herodians."

"Yes, we can use them as spies as well."

Herod stretched his arms. "Yes! Maybe we can even spy on our beloved procurator. Then we can learn some secrets we'll use to our advantage."

Philip heard leaves rustle outside the garden and signaled the other two. He whispered in Herod's ear, "Speaking of spies, someone is listening to us."

Herod whispered back, "It's probably Herodias. She can't stand to miss these discussions." He looked toward the edge of the garden and shouted, "Who's there?"

No reply.

He called again, "Who's there? I'll call the guards if you don't answer." After a while, he poked Philip in the side and whispered, "Let's sneak over and catch her."

Philip, not wishing to earn more of Herodias' wrath, held Herod's arm.

"Alright, I'll do it myself," Herod hissed. But before he moved, the daughter of Herodias presented herself at the end of the path and beckoned to Philip.

Given enough light, Manaen might have seen the amused look on the face of Herod Antipas.

CHAPTER THIRTY-TWO

But Zacchaeus stood up and said to the Lord, "Look, Lord! Here and now I give half of my possessions to the poor, and if I have cheated anybody out of anything, I will pay back four times the amount."

Luke 19:8

After the uproar in Phasaelis, Jesus and his followers moved further south, to a new camp across the Jordan River from Jericho. They chose a campsite near a Perean town called Bethabara on one of the few level and open areas next to the Jordan River. The site was located halfway between Jericho and Bethabara, so the workers could work in the almond and pear orchards west of Jericho and the vineyards and farms around Bethabara. Also, their proximity to the Jordan assured them of adequate water for bathing and washing clothes.

The community of workers and families, originally camped at Scythopolis and Phasaelis, had more than doubled since they traveled to Scythopolis from Nazareth a year earlier. The caravan that plodded south from Phasaelis on the Jordan Road now consisted of two carts laden with tents and supplies, three sleds, several animals, and forty seven people. Of Jesus' close disciples, Andrew, John, Thomas, and Judas stayed at the camp. Simon-Peter and James were expected to return within the month, while Philip and Nathanael still remained with the Nazareth camp.

* * *

Once encamped near Bethabara, Jesus, Andrew, and two young boys hitched a donkey to a cart and went into Jericho to buy supplies. Before they left, Jesus instructed them to stay with him or Andrew, for Jericho had a reputation for dangers such as theft, kidnapping, and prostitution. The boys, who had never before set foot in a large city, nodded with every warning, silently looking forward to the temptations and delights of such a dangerous place,

They passed through the Jericho's east gate and headed directly to the Roman style forum and market located in the center of the city.

The young men suddenly found themselves immersed in the largest market they had ever seen. They passed booths jammed with sweet smelling saffron, daisies, tulips, and roses. Next to them, stalls loaded with pears, apricots, and pomegranates. They shook their heads when they passed merchants selling several varieties of beans from clay pots filled to the rim. Further on, bakers screamed the benefits of their breads and cakes to anyone within earshot. Butchers selling recently slaughtered animals and live birds competed for space in an area to the rear of the bakeries, away from the central market.

Another part of the market accommodated merchants whose wares were suited for wearing rather than eating. Their shops and booths crouched nearly below ground level, covered with large canopies stretching from one stall to another. Protected from the elements, these merchants operated out of the natural light, day and night, rain and shine. Booths filled with jewelry, clothes, religious trinkets, and ready cooked food sat in such close proximity to each other that only a few people could pass between them at any one time.

Jesus and Andrew kept a close watch over their young companions, knowing full well that this was an area full of danger and temptation. It didn't take the boys long to realize the same thing when two women leaving a thick trail of jasmine and dressed in tight fitting tunics brushed against them. Andrew frowned. "This place is unclean and dangerous."

"If I avoided a city because of danger, I'd never leave Nazareth," Jesus answered. He hardly finished speaking when he heard a commotion at a booth they had just passed. When he and Andrew turned, they saw an angry merchant holding one boy's arm with one hand and the second boy's tunic with the other hand. Jesus and Andrew ran to the stall where the red faced merchant was yelling at the boys in three languages.

The merchant looked at Andrew and Jesus and asked in fluent Aramaic, "Are they yours?"

"Yes," Andrew replied.

"Accomplices?"

"I don't understand," Andrew said.

The merchant's face looked like the ripe apples in the stand they had passed only moments before. "You're a bunch of thieves," he yelled.

Andrew tried to pacify him, saying, "I'm sure they were only looking."

The merchant's swarthy face went to a deeper shade of crimson. "You're a Galilean. I can tell by your clothing and accent. Also you have a strange sense of humor if you think these boys were only looking."

"All that after a few words," Jesus retorted with raised eyebrows. "You are a perceptive man."

"Shut up!" the man shouted. "Who'll pay for the jewels these men touched?"

By this time, Andrew's patience had run its course. "Listen, you filthy Pagan. Either you release those boys or I'll cut a permanent smile in your face!" Jesus put his hand over his mouth to keep from laughing. Andrew and his brother always seemed to find the right words to frighten their enemies.

The merchant's face softened, "Get them out of here. I never want to see their faces again." Satisfied he had dealt firmly with the Galilean transients, he returned to the rear of his booth.

Jesus scrutinized the merchant for a few minutes, and then said to Andrew, "Take the boys back to the food market. I want to visit that synagogue across the square." As he left, he called over his shoulder, "Don't forget the beans. Buy two or three varieties so the women don't complain when we return to the camp."

Andrew replied, "Next time I'll bring one of the women. I don't know anything about beans."

Jesus exited the market past stands of fruit and pastry and deftly side-stepping vendors hawking birds and articles of clothing as he walked to the synagogue. Once there, he stood next to a pillar and listened to a group of men standing in a circle. After a while, one of the men noticed him and called him over.

Looking at Jesus, the man said, "I assume from the blue fringe on your robe that you are a rabbi."

"I am," Jesus replied.

"Then will you help us settle a question?"

"I'll try."

"Tell us; is it lawful for a man to divorce his wife?"

Jesus rubbed his chin. "What are you really asking?"

"What does the Law say about divorce?"

Jesus, standing in the center of the circle of men, said, "We know that in the beginning the Creator made us male and female, and said, `For this reason a man will leave his father and mother and be united to his wife, and the two will become one flesh.'" Jesus shrugged. "So they no longer will be two, but one. I say we should not take apart what God joins together."

A second man licked his lips and replied, "But Moses allowed a man to divorce his wife and send her away."

"Ah yes, Moses did so because the men of his time demanded it. That's not the way it was in the beginning. If a man divorces his wife for a reason other than adultery and marries another, he is guilty of adultery." Jesus moved around the men and sat on the upper step. "Do you mind if I sit?" he asked. A few men grunted their assent and he continued, "Worse yet, the wife often has little choice than to become an adulteress."

The first man caught his eye. "What is adultery?" he asked.

Jesus laughed. "You know that answer. I think you're asking these questions so you can have some fun with a Galilean rabbi." Jesus' friendly manner relieved the earlier tension between himself and the men. A few men chose to sit on a step near Jesus as he continued. "We know that a divorced woman has no rights, no protection, and no place in our community. Often, her only option is to become someone's lover. Is that adultery?"

"Maybe so," the man replied. Then changing the subject, he asked, "Tell me, why are you in Jericho?"

"Some friends and I brought a group of workers from Galilee," Jesus said, rolling his sleeves up to his elbow. "We have a camp across the river."

"Why did you bring Galilean workers to Jericho?"

"There's more work for them in Judea than in Galilee. Many of our people would starve if we didn't bring them here."

Another man tugged at his beard with ink stained hands. "Your Galileans will take jobs away from our people. That will cause trouble." The group moved closer to Jesus when a small company of soldiers passed by. When they were alone again, Jesus said, "Our people will do work no one else wants. That way we live in peace with our neighbors."

"How many people came with you?"

"All together? About fifty."

The second man whistled. "That's a small army."

"Hardly," was Jesus' smiling reply. "Half are women and children."

"Why are you, a rabbi, doing this? There must be enough work for you in the Galilean synagogues."

"I leave the synagogues to other rabbis and teachers. My synagogue is on the road sides and in caves." He looked at the men. "Do you understand?"

"That's a nice idea," a man dressed in merchants' garb said. "But what are you trying to tell us?"

Jesus quickly looked across the square to make sure he hadn't lost sight of Andrew and his companions, then continued. "My purpose is to talk about justice. You see, God calls us his chosen people, and gave us special knowledge about himself through Moses and the Prophets." Jesus looked at each man. "Yet we ignore their teaching. Do any of you remember we are a people born out of poverty and suffering? We came from Egypt and survived as poor people for forty years in the desert." Looking the merchant in the eyes, he continued, "Now we're too rich to remember our own poor."

The men looked at him with a sense of dejection. One of them, the one with ink stained hands, asked, "If I hear you right, God, as you see him, will punish us for ignoring poor people?"

"I believe he will."

"What makes you think you're right?" the man continued.

Jesus waited until a group of noisy children passed by before continuing, "God is the master of his house, and the people of Israel knock on his door and ask to be let in. But he answers, `I don't know where you came from!' Israel replies, `We ate and drank with you; you taught in our towns, you blessed our children.'"

"But God says, `I don't know where you came from. Get away from me, you wicked people.'" Concern filled Jesus' eyes as he looked at the men. "Will God condemn my Jewish mother because of you?" He pointed to the crowd in the marketplace. "Will God condemn those people because our priests and scribes ignore his covenant? People will come from east and west, from north and south, to sit at the feast in the Kingdom of God. That's where those who are last will be first, and those who are first will be last."

One of the men stood and faced Jesus. "Sir, you speak in riddles," he said stiffly. "I tithe and observe the Sabbath. I go up to Jerusalem for our feast days. I didn't create the poor, the lame, and the blind. What am I to do? Become poor? Cut my leg off?" Looking to his friends for support, the man added, "And what about the so called starving people who are too lazy to work? Yet you say that we find no favor in the sight of God." The men nodded and looked to Jesus for an answer.

"Either we share our plenty with people who are less fortunate, or God will pass by us and select other people for his work."

The combination of the hot sun, the nearness of the midday meal, and their growing frustration with Jesus' answers made the men restless. Finally one of them stood and said, "Enough of this. I've got to tend to my business." He turned to Jesus and added, "Much of what you say is true. But I blame the Sadducees and the Sanhedrin for this sorry condition. I think you're wrong when you blame people like us."

"I'm sorry if I made you feel uncomfortable," Jesus replied.

"You heap your ashes of contempt on the wrong heads," the man with the ink stained hands said over his shoulder as he walked across the square to the market.

Jesus caught Andrew's gaze as the men separated. He crossed the square and looked for the young men. "The boys are alright," Andrew assured him. "I left them at a stall where they serve warm meals. The proprietor won't let boys leave until I pay for their food." He gestured toward the synagogue. "What did you say to those men?"

"The usual."

Andrew laughed. "In other words, you ruined their day." As they walked toward the stall where the boys were eating, he added, "There are times when I wonder about you. Then there are times when I understand everything you say. Right now I feel you're more than a rabbi or prophet."

"I *am* more than a rabbi or prophet."

Rubbing his forehead, Andrew said, "A few weeks ago, when we moved the camp from Scythopolis to Phasaelis, I thought you were a fool. But right now, I could easily believe that you are the Messiah."

Jesus laughed as he pushed Andrew toward the market. "I wonder if there's any real difference between the two."

* * *

After they finished their mid day meal, Andrew, Jesus, and the two young men purchased the food and supplies they needed and started toward the city gate. Halfway there, Jesus noticed a disturbance near a large sycamore tree. Suddenly the people surrounding the tree turned and headed toward Jesus. Feeling for his sword, Andrew signaled to Jesus and the two young men. The tension eased slightly when a heavy set man ran to Jesus and greeted him, saying, "Are you the one who spoke at the synagogue this morning?"

"Yes I am," Jesus answered, warily remembering the incident at the market in Scythopolis. "Why do you ask?"

The man pointed to the sycamore tree. "Do you see that man sitting in the tree?"

Jesus and Andrew squinted in the direction of the tree but saw nothing but leaves. "Is this a trap?" Andrew asked. Pulling Jesus to side, he whispered, "Be careful."

The man ignored Andrew's discomfort. "There is someone in that tree who wants to talk to you," he stated. "Will you come with me?"

Jesus agreed and, as they walked toward the tree, he saw a man sitting on one of the branches. Andrew gestured to the man and asked, "Why are you in that tree?"

"You would see, if I were standing on the ground, that I am a very short person," the man responded. "I heard about this rabbi and decided I wanted to meet him before he left Jericho. So I waited in this tree next to the road. Sooner or later, I thought, he will pass by." He added with a twinkle in his eyes, "That was a very good idea, wasn't it?"

Jesus looked up at him and asked, "What is your name, and what do you want from me?"

"I am Zacchaeus, the local tax collector. I want to invite you to my house for supper with my friends," he pointed to his chest, "and me. Will you come?"

"When?"

"Tonight."

"How did you learn about me?"

"I'm a prophet," Zacchaeus replied, almost falling off the branch from laughter. He waved his hand. "It would surprise you to find out that many people in Jericho heard about you. Here, help me down," he added. "This branch is uncomfortable."

Zacchaeus brushed his tunic when he landed on his feet. "I heard what you said to those men," he continued. "I want to know what you will say when you meet my friends at supper."

Jesus looked at him. "Is this one of Herod's traps?"

Zacchaeus slapped his stomach. "No," he replied, barely able to contain his glee. "I am genuinely interested in what you will say to us."

Jesus looked at Andrew, who shrugged.

"Bring your friends if it will help you feel safer," Zacchaeus prodded.

"I'll come later today," Jesus replied. "And I'll stay at your house this evening."

Zacchaeus, smiling broadly, signaled his friends to let Jesus and his band pass through to the city gate. "I'll see you later." Holding a young man by his sleeve, he added, "My servant here will wait for you at the gate to show you the way to my house."

* * *

Jesus arrived at the house of Zacchaeus that night with John and Judas, who had recently returned to the camp from his trip to Jerusalem and Kerioth. Andrew stayed at the camp, not wanting to mix with the likes of this tax collector and his friends. Zacchaeus for his part invited several people. By the time Jesus arrived, his dining area and atrium were filled with men and women eating, drinking, and talking.

As they walked through the courtyard, Judas tugged Jesus' sleeve. "This is not an orthodox house," he commented. "Look how the women mix freely with the men."

Before Jesus could reply, Zacchaeus greeted them again with a twinkle in his eyes. He took Jesus by the arm and introduced him to his friends, several of whom worked in the commercial trades of transport and shop-keeping. During a short lull, John pulled Jesus aside and whispered, "These are tax collectors, butchers, camel owners, and money lenders. What are we doing here?"

Jesus replied, "I think Zacchaeus is testing us."

"Why?"

Suddenly, Zacchaeus had Jesus' arm again. "Do these people offend you?" he asked.

"John seems outraged and Judas is disgraced," Jesus countered. "Should they feel that way?"

"Of course they should," Zacchaeus replied, barely able to control his laughter. "My friends are outcasts in the opinion of those in Jericho who call themselves holy."

Jesus looked into his eyes. "Why did you invite these people? Do you want to trap me or cause trouble for my friends?"

"If you are the man you claim to be, you will have no trouble," Zacchaeus replied with a smile.

"Who do you think I am?"

"You are a man who understands that God loves his children." Zacchaeus gestured toward his guests. "These are God's children--as much as those men you talked to at the synagogue." He blushed and added, "Being small has its advantages. I stood behind a pillar at the synagogue while you talked. Now, I want you to tell my friends what you told those men."

"I'll try," Jesus replied. A buzzing from a group of people standing near the edge of the dining area caught Jesus' attention. Two very attractive women had just entered the room. One, dressed in a lavender robe with a gold cord around her waist, stopped near a table laden with fruits and sweetbreads. The other woman, dressed in a white robe and a red sash walked directly to Zacchaeus.

She took his hand and kissed him on the forehead. Then she reached for Jesus' hand. "You must be the teacher Zacchaeus told me about." Smiling broadly, she added, "I can tell you're not one of his worker friends by your honest face and clean fingernails."

Jesus almost lost his breath when he sniffed her warm, sensuous perfume. "I suspect you are one of the guests of honor," he declared.

She looked at Zacchaeus and laughed. "People call me a lot of things, but never a guest of honor." Then she leaned close to Jesus and whispered, "I was a prostitute at one time." Pointing to her companion, she added, "And, people say the woman who came here with me is an adulteress." She moved away, leaving the fragrance of her delicate rose perfume in Jesus' nostrils.

John gulped when he overheard the conversation between Jesus and the woman. Jesus, noticing his discomfort, observed, "John--are you well? Your face is as white as bleached cloth."

John looked at Zacchaeus and the woman and gave Jesus an angry stare. "What are we doing here?" he asked.

Jesus smiled, "Look on this as an adventure. By the way, where is Judas?"

"I don't know," John replied in a tone that indicated he wasn't Judas' keeper. "I haven't seen him since we arrived."

Jesus scanned the room until he spied Judas standing next to a table. "There he is--talking to that woman. Oh-oh."

"What's wrong?" John asked.

"I can see him hiccup."

"Again?"

"Does he hiccup often?"

"Judas and Simon-Peter have one thing in common," John replied. "They can drink a skin of wine in an evening. Then they spend the rest of the night belching." John flashed another look at the table. "I'd better slow him down."

Jesus turned to Zacchaeus and the woman and smiled. "See, my people aren't perfect either."

Later, during the formal meal, Jesus sat next to Zacchaeus. "Tell me about your friends," he said. "What about the woman accused of adultery? People usually stone women caught in adultery."

Waving a chicken leg in her direction, Zacchaeus replied, "She's a Gentile."

"Ah," Jesus mumbled as he cast quick glances at Judas to see if he was still stable. Turning back to Zacchaeus, he asked, "What about the woman I met first?"

Zacchaeus wiped his mouth with a cloth. "I found her outside the city gate one night," he replied. "As she said, she was a prostitute. That night, I convinced her to change her ways and now she helps me in my business."

"Now she's a tax collector?" Jesus asked, almost laughing.

"Yes."

"She's a tax collector and a prostitute?"

"She *was* a prostitute and now she's a tax collector. Does the idea offend you?"

Jesus finished chewing a mouthful of salad before he replied. "Zacchaeus, you amaze me. You're one of the few people who can out do me in mystery." He snapped his fingers. "I know why..." A loud noise outside the house stopped him in mid sentence.

Zacchaeus' face lost its color as he jumped from his couch and ran to the courtyard. By the time Jesus reached the courtyard, a crowd of angry men had gathered outside the walls and pushed the gate open. A man standing in front of the crowd pointed a finger at Jesus and screamed, "There he is! This holy man eats meals with prostitutes and tax collectors! Unclean! Unclean!" Soon other people outside the gate picked up the chant, "UNCLEAN! UNCLEAN!"

Jesus grabbed Zacchaeus by the collar and asked, "Is this your doing? Did you invite us here to trap me?"

Zacchaeus shook with fear. "No Rabbi," he gasped. "I had no idea. Please..."

Jesus released him and walked to the gate. "What do you want?" he hollered.

"You eat with tax collectors and prostitutes!" the man who appeared to be their leader yelled.

"What of it?" For a moment, Jesus wished he had Andrew at his side with his sword.

"How can you eat with these people after preaching to us at the synagogue? You're a hypocrite! Unclean!"

Jesus answered, "These people seek the Kingdom of God as you do. But you treat them like outcasts." His face hardened as he continued, "You're so sure of yourselves! I tell you these people will be safe in the Kingdom of God long before you escape the fires of Gehenna."

A man from the rear shouted, "They are sinners!"

Jesus walked through the gate into the crowd. "You better watch out for your own lives. You came here in the night like hypocrites to prove you're blameless in the sight of God." He pointed to the house. "Sick people need a physician, but those who are healthy do not. Believe that I didn't come to call self righteous people to the Kingdom of God." Dismissing them with a wave, he concluded, "Go home and leave us alone." With that, the crowd melted away as quickly as it appeared.

Zacchaeus shrank into a corner when he returned to the courtyard while John prodded Jesus. "Let's leave this place," he hissed.

Jesus shook his head. "We have no reason to leave here. I meant what I said to those men." Leaving John next to the gate, Jesus went to where Zacchaeus was cowering. "Come," he said, "We have a meal to finish."

Later, Jesus returned to the atrium, found a comfortable pile of cushions and talked to each person in the house. One by one, the torches in the city went dark, and the merchants retreated to the safety of their homes. Soon, the only activities they heard outside the walls of Zacchaeus' house were the footsteps of the Roman patrols.

Later, Jesus told the butcher he was clean even if his work involved contact with blood. He added that pigeon trainers and herdsmen, the ignoble people of Judean society, reminded him of the fisherman and farmers of Galilee.

Zacchaeus was still sitting next to Jesus when the first light of dawn peeked over the east wall of the city. "We took advantage of you tonight," he said. "We snatched your sleep away."

Jesus stretched as if every muscle in his body ached, then pointed to Judas and John. "They slept half the night," he said. "Perhaps I'll be able to steal some sleep from them." His eyes showed his weariness as he looked at Zacchaeus. "First, I would like a cup of hot tea, then we'll return to Bethabara. I'd like to leave early to avoid the people who came to your gate last night."

Eyes downcast, Zacchaeus replied, "I apologize for them."

Jesus touched Zacchaeus' arm. "Meeting with your friends more than made up for it."

Zacchaeus nodded. "I can tell that my friends believe they have value in God's eyes after talking with you. I wish you could stay here forever."

"I can't--but you're here," Jesus replied. "You can give them hope. Challenge the authorities and ignore the self-righteous. God will see your work and look on you with pride."

* * *

Jesus scrutinized the expression on John's face as they walked toward the city gate. For his part, John shuffled along, staring at the ground, without saying a word. On Jesus' other side, Judas carried a frown and continuously wiped his hands on his tunic. Finally Jesus asked, "Are you two angry, or tired?"

"What do you mean?" Judas asked.

"You both disapprove of what I did."

"I wonder why I came to Judea," John snapped. "My father begged me to stay in Capernaum." He thrust his thumb toward the house. "Soon we'll be outcasts like them."

Judas spit on the ground and added, "Or else we'll be stoned in a public square. I should've stayed with my father in Kerioth."

The men turned when they heard a group of people running behind them, waving their arms and shouting. At first they feared it was the mob from outside Zacchaeus' gate. Then, as the people came closer, Jesus said, "It's Zacchaeus and his friends."

John wiped his forehead. "Good, now the rest of Jericho will know we consort with those people."

Judas quickened his pace. "Hurry or they'll catch us."

Jesus held their arms until the people caught them. Zacchaeus came from behind the people, breathing heavily and smiling broadly. Acting as spokesperson, he handed a package to Jesus. "We want to give you this gift for the people in your camp." He paused to catch his breath. "Also, we want to walk with you to the city gate."

Jesus looked at John and Judas. "That's a good idea."

As they neared the gate, a blind beggar sitting next to the road seized the robe of a woman walking with Jesus and asked who it was that just went by.

"Jesus of Nazareth," she replied.

The beggar screamed, "Jesus of Nazareth, Son of David! Have mercy on me!"

John tried to pull Jesus ahead, but Jesus stopped when he heard the man call his name. "What did that man say?" he asked.

The beggar repeated his cry, "Jesus of Nazareth, Son of David, have mercy on me!"

"Bring him here," Jesus ordered.

A man ran to the beggar and said, "Cheer up, he called for you!"

The beggar threw his cloak on the ground and stumbled toward Jesus.

Jesus held the man's arms and asked, "Who are you?"

Looking at Jesus' face with unseeing eyes, the man replied, "Hazael bar Timaeus, from Jericho."

"What do you want from me?"

"I want to see again."

"Did you have sight at one time?"

"Until I was sixteen; when a fever caused my blindness."

"How did you know my name?"

"A woman told me?"

"How did you know my ancestor?"

"I heard about you at the Jordan when you were with John the Baptizer. My friends had taken me to him to see if he would cure me." Tears filled Timaeus' eyes. "You were at the Jordan on the same day. Then you disappeared." Wiping his face with his sleeve, Timaeus continued, "I felt your presence that day, and I've waited at this gate ever since for your return."

Jesus looked at him and embraced him. "Your faith has made you well," he whispered.

Suddenly Timaeus screamed and fell to the ground, sobbing. The people jumped back, thinking he had a fit. Then John touched him on the shoulder. Timaeus looked at him with teary eyes. "I--I can see. The bright light--it hurts. But I can see." He grabbed John by the tunic and pulled his face close to him. "You are a handsome man. God bless you."

Zacchaeus helped bar Timaeus steady himself. "What will you do now?" he asked.

Timaeus looked at Jesus. “I want to follow you.”

Jesus smiled. “What’s your trade before you went blind?” he asked.

“I was a carpenter.”

Jesus laughed. “We can always use an extra carpenter.”

Hazael bar Timaeus picked up his cloak and a small bag that held all his personal belongings and followed Jesus, Judas, and John through the east gate. Zacchaeus and his friends watched at the gate until the four men blended into the hill separating Jericho from the Jordan River.

Jesus opened his gift when they returned to the camp at Bethabara. Tears came to his eyes when he found a small pouch containing several pieces of silver.

CHAPTER THIRTY-THREE

Jesus said, "If those who lead you say to you, 'See, the Kingdom is in the sky,' then the birds of the sky will precede you. If they say to you,' It is in the sea,' then the fish will precede you. Rather the Kingdom is inside of you, and it is outside of you. When you come to know yourselves, then you will become known, and you will realize that it is you who are the sons of the living Father."

The Gospel of Thomas (3)

Simon-Peter, James, and his son, Aaron, arrived at the Bethabara camp after Jesus' meeting with Zacchaeus. By this time, the farmers near Bethabara had started sowing their winter grains and the orchards in Jericho were yielding the last of their summer fruit. The workers in the camp still had enough work because these tasks needed to be completed before the first rains of winter turned the fields into a quagmire.

The most important news Simon-Peter and James brought from Capernaum was that Zebedee had softened his attitude toward the men who left his fleet to follow Jesus. He said he would forgive the men if they returned to Galilee in time for the spring fishing season. Jesus said nothing when he heard the news, preferring to let the men make their own decisions about returning to Galilee.

Judas noticed that Jesus seemed increasingly preoccupied with events outside the camp since his last trip to Jerusalem. Now he wondered what Jesus intended to do about the increasing number of women, children and cripples coming to the camp. To Judas, Jesus' mission lacked direction. Judas needed to know where they were going and why. He tried to talk to Andrew and the other disciples about his feelings, but they shook him off. At night, around the fire, there was talk of Jerusalem and high priests, of forgiveness, and hints of a new order, but no plans.

When Jesus told Judas he wanted to meet with Joseph of Arimathea during the Festival of Lights, Judas eagerly jumped at the opportunity to accompany him. A trip to Jerusalem would give him the chance to learn what Jesus was really up to. Judas' joy abated, however, when he learned that John had invited himself along. Judas did not look forward to enduring John's hostile comments on the way.

It was mid-day on the road from Jericho to Jerusalem when Jesus and Judas sat on their sacks at the side of the road watching John massage an injured heel. They used the opportunity to eat a few grapes, drink water from a skin, and rest their own tired legs and feet.

Jesus wiped his lips and asked John, "Why did your father change his mind about you and James? It sounds as if he's ready to forgive and forget."

John winced as he rubbed his heel. "He needs us in the fleet. We're the best fishermen on the lake."

Then Jesus asked Judas, "What does your father think of us?"

Judas shrugged. "He begged me to stay with him in Kerioth when I saw him after we met with Joseph of Arimathea."

"But you came back." Jesus said.

"I believe in you more than anyone I've ever met. Even more than my father," Judas replied self-consciously.

Jesus took another drink of water. "But you have doubts about what we're doing."

"I think everyone does." Judas stood and watched a lizard wiggle from one rock to another, realizing this was the opportunity he had wished for. As he answered Jesus, he noticed from the corner of his eye that John had stopped rubbing his foot. "I have doubts about your people, not you. Why should we care for people who don't care for themselves? Look at the money we could earn if..."

"If you worked harder," John interrupted.

Jesus raised his hand and gazed into John's eyes. "I assume from your comments that you also have a problem with what we're doing. Do you doubt me?"

John looked at his sandal, still lying on the ground. "Once in a while," he replied. "Then I remember the story Andrew told about that day in the Jordan with John the Baptizer. Something happened there. Later--on Mount Hermon--it happened again." He shook his head. "I can't ignore what I heard and saw. During the time I've known you, I've seen the lame walk, the deaf hear, and sight restored to the blind."

Hearing John's words, Judas sighed and said, "I'm a true believer even though I don't see those things."

"I wonder if it matters." He shook his head. "I don't understand what it is that attracts me to a group of Galileans who have nothing in common with me except you." He half smiled. "I wanted to go to Athens and Rome, not Nazareth and Bethany."

"Maybe you wanted to be with people who are smarter than you," John interjected.

Judas flashed an angry glance at John. "That's what I mean," Judas snapped. "What can I learn from a bunch of uneducated fishermen and farmers?"

Jesus watched the two men quarrel for a while, then said, "Wisdom was not born in the mines of Solomon, but in the mind of Solomon."

Judas let Jesus' statement pass for a moment and shook his head, asking, "What did you say?"

"Words, Judas, words. The children of Galilee are sometimes wiser than the High Priests of Judea."

Judas flinched when he heard the sound of horses behind them. He quickly pulled Jesus to the side when he spied a group of men riding toward them at full gallop.

Jesus shielded his eyes with his hand. "Soldiers," he warned, "Let's wait until they pass."

When the soldiers reached them, one dismounted and walked toward Jesus. "What are you doing on this road?" he asked, his hand gripping the handle of his sword.

Looking toward the southwest, Jesus replied, "We're going to Jerusalem."

"Do you have weapons?"

"Enough to defend ourselves against bandits."

The soldier extended his hand. "Let me see."

Each of the men unveiled the weapons they were carrying.

It looked as if John wanted to say something, but the officer stared him down. "Where do you live?" he asked Jesus as he inspected John's dagger.

"We're camped near Jericho on the other side of the Jordan."

The officer inspected Judas' sword and returned it to him. Then he said to Jesus, "Last night robbers attacked a small settlement near here."

"Did they hurt anyone?" Judas asked.

"Hurt anyone?" the Roman grunted. "They killed two men, three women, burned their tents, and made off with two young girls."

"I hope you find them," Jesus said as he sheathed his dagger.

"We did-the girls that is."

"Are they alright?"

The officer spat on the ground. "We found them dead--raped and murdered. Bless Caesar, they were Jews."

John tightened his grip on his dagger. "What do you mean by that?" he snapped.

The officer snickered, "There are enough Jews as it is." He gestured when he saw the anger on the men's faces. "Oh, it was bad for the girls." He looked at Jesus. "Where did you say you were going?"

"Jerusalem. Are we in danger?"

"The people from the settlement told me there were at least five or six armed men. Probably a group of zealots more interested in starting a war with Rome then harassing travelers to Jerusalem." He snickered. "I hope they find us." With that, he mounted his horse, shouted to his men, and led them toward the Jordan River. A cloud of dust followed the soldiers to the top of the hill, and then disappeared.

Jesus ran his sleeve across his eyes and pointed to John's belt. "Are you ready to use that sword?" he asked.

"Yes."

"Good."

Judas stood with his hands at his waist. "I thought you hated violence."

"I do," Jesus replied. "But I'm not stupid. I'll use a sword to protect another person or defend myself." He put his hand on Judas' shoulder as they resumed their walk to Jerusalem. "Remember, however, that those who live by the sword risk death by the sword."

The Roman patrol came back, riding next to Jesus, Judas, and John shortly before they reached the Mount of Olives. The officer who spoke to them earlier gestured over his shoulder to a pallet carrying four bodies. "We caught four of them," he said proudly.

John and Judas looked behind the soldiers to where the officer pointed.

"They're dead," the officer said. "They chose to fight…too bad." He took a pouch from his belt and dipped his finger in it. "Still, death by the sword is easier than crucifixion." He raised his finger to his nose and sniffed.

"Did the others escape?" Jesus asked.

The officer pointed to the barren valley to the north. "They're out there somewhere. One of these men told us about their hideout before he died. At least I think he's dead," the officer added with a cruel grin.

* * *

Jesus, Judas, and John passed through Jerusalem's North Gate shortly before sundown. John had promised his brother that he would stay at his uncle's house in Jerusalem, so he separated from Jesus and Judas at the gate with a promise to meet them at the Temple the next morning. After waving goodbye, both men pulled their shawls over their heads to rebuff the evening chill as they strode past servants lighting torches hung from the outside walls of homes in the Upper City.

Once inside Mary Marcia's gate, Jesus shouted with delight when he saw Mark coming to the courtyard.

"I came back to Israel to find you," Mark declared. "And here you are."

"Did you come to gather more stories for your African teachers?" Jesus asked.

"I did, and you saved me the trouble of finding you. Am I still welcome at your camp?"

"Always," Jesus responded. "We're going back to Jericho the day after tomorrow. You can come with us then if you wish." Casting a sideways glance at Mary Marcia, he added, "That is, if your mother approves."

Mark's temper almost rose to the surface, but he quickly calmed when he recognized Jesus' tease.

Judas waited until they finished their greetings before he talked to Mark. Pulling Mark aside, he squeezed his hand and said, "I'm glad you came back to Israel. There are days when I feel there isn't a single person in Jesus' camp I can call a friend."

"They still don't accept you?" Mark asked.

Judas shrugged. "They tolerate me. Jesus wants me to handle the money for the camp, but some of his followers watch every move I make." Looking into Mark's eyes, Judas asked, "Do I look like a thief?"

"I don't think so," Mark replied. Then responding to Mary Marcia's glance, he added, "I better take you to our room. My mother just indicated that our evening meal will soon be ready."

* * *

During the long evening meal, the people staying at Mary Marcia's house talked of recent events, upcoming plans, and the weather, which would soon be cold enough to freeze water at night. Following the meal, Rebecca went to her room on the first level, while Mark and Judas retired to Mark's upstairs room located at the rear of the house. Jesus remained in the courtyard alone with Mary Marcia.

Before he sat down to talk to Mary Marcia, Jesus sent a servant to Nicodemus and Joseph of Arimathea with a note asking for a meeting. When the servant bowed and left the courtyard, Jesus sighed and sank into a pile of cushions lying near the fire burning in the middle of the courtyard.

Mary Marcia handed Jesus a cup of red wine and wiggled a finger at him. "You look tired."

"I am tired," he replied, gesturing toward the house. "I try to teach men like Judas and John, but they hear other voices." He added, shaking his head, "Judas is right about one thing; we have little sense of direction."

Jesus rested against the cushions, holding his hands out from time to time to catch the heat of the fire. "They look at *me* when I ask them to see the One who sent me. They believe in *me* when I ask them to believe in the One who sent me. They don't understand that I am the messenger, not the message."

"If you are the messenger, who sent you?" Mary asked.

Jesus raised his arms. "The Lord." Gazing into Mary's eyes, he added, "I see this vision in my dreams. The priests will drive me from the Temple, but the people are still following me. That troubles me, so I ask the Father to let me do something else." Jesus looked toward the house for a moment. "And do you know what I hear back?"

Mary shook her head.

"This is why I'm here, the reason my Father sent me."

"Who said that?"

Again, Jesus raised his hands in the air. "God? Moses? Satan? I don't know."

"You always seem so sure of yourself," Mary whispered.

Jesus nodded. "I am sure of myself. I know why I'm here. The problem is that I have little control over events or people. The people who follow me go where they choose. Some stay for a while, then leave. Others talk about me behind my back. I learn the same lesson every day; Let go, don't try to control things."

Mary Marcia fetched some blankets from a cabinet as she listened to Jesus' answer. Dropping a blanket on his knees, she said, "You look cold as well as tired." Changing the subject, she asked, "Can you tell me what you'll do with Mark?"

Jesus smiled as he wrapped the blanket around his legs. "I'll send Mark back in time to help you prepare for the Passover celebration. Can you live without him until then?"

"I see little of him as it is," she replied. "That's fine--I believe he's in good company, whether with you or Abraham." She looked toward the hills outside the city. "Will you see Mary of Bethany during this trip?" she asked.

"I intend to stop at her house on the way back to Jericho," he replied without emotion.

"Have you done anything--you know what we talked about?"

"Ah--no. I suppose I should marry her when I pass through Bethany this time."

Mary slapped him on the arm. "That isn't what I meant."

"I know," he replied. "As I told you last time, I'll do something next spring. Her sister, Martha, promised to marry Eli the tailor after the next Passover."

"That leaves a clear field for you."

"I'm sure you'll remind me of that whenever you have a chance," he replied. After a few moments, he asked, "What is it in women's minds that turn them into matchmakers?"

"Our motherly instinct?"

"My friends would tell you that your explanations are no better than mine." He rubbed his hands together. "There was something I wanted to ask you before I...Oh yes, do you still do things with medicine?"

"Medicine? For what?"

"Mark told me you use medicines made from plants and herbs from Africa. I want to visit my friend, Lazarus, on the way back to Bethabara. He's sick--a terrible cough."

Mary rubbed her chin. "I'll give you some medicine, but he should see a physician." She looked at him out of the corner of her eye. "Has he?"

Jesus chuckled. "If he is a typical stubborn man..."

"Of course not," Mary chided. "I'll prepare some medicine before you leave."

Mary had barely finished speaking when her servant returned to the courtyard. "Joseph of Arimathea has invited you and whoever you wish to bring to supper at his house tomorrow," he told Jesus.

"What time?"

"I'm sorry," the servant replied with a blush. "Sundown." Having delivered his message, the servant disappeared into the house.

Jesus and Mary Marcia talked for a few more minutes, and then rose to go to their rooms. On the way, she clutched his sleeve. "Be careful," she whispered. "Mary of Bethany and I want to see you in Jerusalem during Passover."

* * *

Jesus and Judas met John at the Temple the next morning. Except for a few people milling around the Court of the Israelites, the area was quiet and serene. The three men stood, shawls over their heads, facing the Court of Priests and prayed. Soon others joined them and watched as the priests began their ritual sacrifice of animals and birds.

By mid-day, several hundred men crowded the area near the sanctuary. Small groups of men prayed, studied scripture from carefully preserved scrolls, and talked. Jesus had ambled over to Solomon's Porch to protect himself from the cold desert wind and stayed there to teach and answer people's questions.

A man approached him, saying, "You teach as if you know all the answers. You act as if you're the Anointed One?"

"What do you mean?" Jesus asked.

"What I said. Do you think you're the Anointed One--the Messiah?"

Jesus replied, "The things I do and say are done in Yahweh's name. Perhaps you don't believe in me because you are not one of my sheep. My sheep listen to my voice; I know them and they follow me."

John took Jesus' arm while the men muttered among themselves. "You better be careful, they look angry."

The man turned to Jesus and asked another question. "We don't understand your talk about sheep. It sounds like you should return to wherever you came from and hire yourself out as a shepherd."

Another man spoke, "On the other hand, if you said what I think you said, we should stone you to death."

"I teach the Law and the words of our Prophets," Jesus retorted. "What have I said to make you want to stone me?"

"We don't want to stone you for your good deeds, whatever they may be," the man answered. "But we heard you say you are acting in God's name." Raising his fist, he added, "That's blasphemy! You are only a man, yet you claim to be God's agent?"

Jesus shrugged. "I say that God is my Father." Backing away from the men, he raised his arms. "Is it not written in our Law; 'You are gods?'" He stared at them for a moment. "We know that scripture is true forever. God called those people gods, the people to whom his message was given. As for me, the Father called me and sent me into the world. How can you say that I blaspheme when I answer my Father's call?"

Jesus paused until the crowd settled. Then he continued, "Don't believe me if I'm not doing the things my Father wants me to do. But if I do those things, you should at least believe my deeds so you will know once and for all that the Father is in me and I am in the Father."

The man looked at him with fear in his eyes. "You are possessed...by a demon."

Jesus stepped toward him in an effort to calm him, but the man waved his hands and stepped backwards. Jesus continued, "I am not possessed by a demon. The truth is that I honor my Father. I don't seek glory for myself; but there is one who seeks it, and he judges me. I tell you, whoever obeys my teaching will never die." He looked at John and Judas who stood on the edge of the crowd. Their eyes darted from Jesus to the crowd, then to the Court of Priests.

Another man stepped forward. "Now I know you're possessed by a demon. Abraham and the prophets died, yet you say that if a man keeps your word, he will never die." He looked at the others for support. "Are you immortal?"

Jesus replied, “Your father, Abraham, rejoiced that he was to see the time of my coming; he saw it and was glad.”

The men questioning Jesus gasped while John stood behind the crowd gesturing with his hand across his throat. Then the man who was questioning Jesus said, “You aren’t fifty years old--and you’re telling us you saw Abraham?”

Jesus looked at each person and said, “I tell you the truth;” his eyes flashed, “before Abraham was born, I am!”

The man closest to him stared in amazement and laughed. He walked away, but another man came up to Jesus and said, “If I had the power, I would kill you at this instant for blasphemy. Only an agent of Satan would stand before the Holy of Holies and declare that he is God.” He shook his fist at Jesus. “The day will come when lightening will come down from heaven and split your head like a melon.”

Jesus glared at him and asserted, “I tell you that same lightening will strike the Temple and reduce it to ashes, but I’ll restore it in three days.”

The man sneered, “You’re insane!” He looked at the small crowd still standing in Solomon’s Portico. “I have a mind to throw you off the Temple wall.”

Jesus put his hand on the man’s shoulder, walked past him, and left through the gate leading to the Women’s Court.

Judas tugged at Jesus’ sleeve as they strode away, feeling sweat over his body even though it was cold enough for a woolen robe. “Why did you say those things?” he asked. “Those men were ready to kill you.”

“Is it wrong to tell the truth?” Jesus asked.

“How do you know you’re telling the truth?” John retorted.

“Listen more closely next time and you’ll find out.”

Changing the subject, Jesus asked John, “Will you come with me to Joseph’s house tonight?”

“I can’t,” answered John. “My uncle invited every relative in Jerusalem to eat an evening meal with me tonight.”

“You’re going to dine with a bunch of Judeans?” Jesus asked with a hint of mockery in his voice.

“Transplanted Galileans,” John snapped. “You’re the one eating with Judeans.”

“Enjoy your celebration,” Jesus said as he and Judas headed toward Joseph of Arimathea’s house.

John grunted and started in the opposite direction.

Judas smiled. He enjoyed watching someone else rib John.

* * *

Nicodemus and Joseph were warming themselves next to a lively fire in Joseph's courtyard when Jesus and Judas arrived for the evening meal. Joseph invited Jesus and Judas to refresh themselves in his private quarters before they joined him in the courtyard.

Joseph ushered Jesus to a comfortable couch next to the fire when he returned to the courtyard as his servant brought a platter of mixed fruit and vegetables and set it on a table near the men. Then he brought a beaker of wine and four cups, filled a cup for each man, and placed the beaker on the table next to the platter.

After each man sampled the platter, Joseph said to Jesus, "I saw you in the Temple this morning."

Jesus replied, "I didn't see you."

"You were talking to some men. I wanted to listen, but someone distracted me. By the time I turned around, I saw you, Judas, and another man leaving in a rush."

"We had to leave in a hurry," Judas muttered.

"So I heard," Joseph replied. "Exactly what was it you said that made the men so angry?"

"I talked about my beliefs."

Judas rolled his eyes. "They say he blasphemed. They threatened to kill him."

Joseph's eyes widened. "Is that true?"

"I didn't blaspheme," Jesus replied calmly. "I only repeated some sayings from the prophets."

"Like what?" Nicodemus asked.

"That the Spirit of God is within all of us. Does that sound like blasphemy?"

"Not the way you say it here," replied Judas. "But at the Temple you said the Father and you are one."

Jesus touched his chest. "The Spirit of God is within me."

"No," Judas replied waving his arms. "You said God is your Father!"

"You know what I meant."

"What about the other thing?" Judas asked.

Jesus' eyebrows rose. "What other thing?"

"What you said about destroying the Temple and rebuilding it in three days."

"I said restore, not rebuild."

Judas scratched his head. "What's the difference? Besides, where did you get an idea like that?"

"Our real Temple is spiritual--within us. It's pointless to say that we can only worship God in one place. The Sadducees have no concern for those who worship at the Temple. The Temple exists for their benefit, and they serve God and his people only after they fill their plate."

He looked at Judas. "Where did I get the idea? It came into my head as we were talking. However, it is..."

"You can't say everything that comes into your head," Joseph interrupted. "Why, you'll be dead within a year if you do that."

"I'm not the only one that talks that way," Jesus replied to Joseph. "You know that some Pharisees teach that we can fulfill the requirements of the law in the synagogue as well as the Temple."

"What about the other thing?" Joseph asked.

"What thing?"

"That you called yourself a god, and that you're older than Moses." Joseph grinned at Jesus. "People sometimes accuse me of being older than Moses--but you?"

Judas interrupted, "That isn't what he said..."

Jesus held Judas' sleeve. "Wait--we can talk about this later." Then to Joseph, he said, "Your servant is trying to attract your attention."

Joseph looked toward the atrium and signaled his assent. "Our meal is ready," he announced. "Please follow me to the dining area."

* * *

"You upset some important people at the Temple today," Joseph said as he put his broth aside. Nicodemus nodded his agreement.

"Who?" Jesus asked.

"The priest you argued with the last time you were at the Temple saw you and reported to Caiaphas. His name is Isaac ben Jonah."

"What's wrong with that?" Jesus asked as he sipped his broth. "Maybe Caiaphas will learn something."

Nicodemus smiled. "Caiaphas already knows everything he wants to about God and religion."

"I'm not talking about religion," Jesus declared. "The high priests use religion as a substitute for faith."

"These things aren't as simple as you think," Nicodemus replied. He looked around the room and leaned toward Jesus. "Right now, eating supper with you could put us at risk. The tension at the Temple is thicker than porridge. To make matters worse, Philo Judaeus is in Jerusalem."

"Why are they worried about him?" Jesus asked.

"He's a powerful leader in the Diaspora," Nicodemus replied as he pushed his broth aside. "Annas says he's a Gnostic."

Joseph gestured at the steaming platters of meat and vegetables. "Let's eat while the food is hot. We can talk about Philo later." Glancing at Jesus, he added, "Besides, there are matters we need to discuss with you."

"About what happened at the Temple today?"

"I have that on my mind among other things."

"Maybe I'm pushing too much too fast," Jesus replied as he dipped his bread into a warm cheese sauce. "But you know how I feel. We're no longer faithful to the Covenant of Moses."

Joseph's eyes widened. "That's the last thing I expected to hear you say. We follow the Law more closely today than at any time in our history. There may be differences in interpretation between Pharisees, Sadducees, and Essenes, but we are faithful to the Covenant."

Jesus smiled and replied, "There is a difference between the Covenant and the Law. The Law is only one part of the Covenant. Besides, that isn't the point I'm trying to make."

"What is your point?" Nicodemus asked.

"The Law is useless for people without food or those who are blind or crippled." He looked at the men assembled around the table. "Do you believe in eternal life? Do you think there is such a thing as heaven or the Kingdom of God?"

They stopped eating and mumbled between themselves. After a few moments Joseph replied, "We believe, but how can we be sure? What proof do we have?"

"I am here to tell you there is a Kingdom of God--the very thing you would call heaven."

"Why is it hidden from us?"

"It's not hidden."

"Now I know why you make the priests so angry," Joseph muttered. "You confuse people. How can you say that heaven is not hidden from us?"

"We are blind to it," Jesus replied. "The Kingdom of God is here--now." He tapped his cup with his finger. "The problem for the Temple people is spiritual blindness."

"But you are not?" Joseph retorted.

"I am not," Jesus replied. "That's why I came back to Jerusalem. The Temple people concentrate on the Law instead of God's command to love each other."

Joseph stood and stretched. "Now look what you did. My meal is cold and I've lost my appetite." He put his hand on Jesus' shoulder. "Let's take time to clear the dust from our minds and relieve ourselves. I feel we're in for a long evening."

After they returned to the courtyard, Joseph looked up to the sky, dotted with stars and a bright moon and said, “It’ll be cool again tonight.” Pointing to a cabinet just inside the atrium, he added, “I have extra shawls and robes for those who need them. Feel free to take what you want.”

Joseph took a handful of walnuts from a dish the servant had placed on the table and sat on a cushion. “We need to talk about the situation in Jerusalem. Pontius Pilate warned Annas and Caiaphas that he would take drastic measures if the recent problems in Jerusalem resurface.”

“You mean the Passover riots?” Jesus asked.

“Yes and the murder of Roman soldiers.”

“What does that have to do with us?” Jesus queried.

“Our leaders see everyone who attracts a crowd or disagrees with them as a threat. Our leaders include both the Romans and the Sanhedrin.”

Jesus waved his arms. “I can’t ignore God’s call. I feel the power of the Spirit even as I speak to you.” Pointing to the wall, he continued, “I want to stand on your wall and scream to everyone about God’s Kingdom.”

“You wouldn’t do that...would you?” Joseph asked nervously.

“Not here, but somewhere I will stand on high to proclaim God’s Kingdom.”

“Why?” Nicodemus asked. He jumped from his couch and paced around the fire. “What makes you do these things?”

“Do you remember the time we met a few years ago?”

“I’ll never forget it.”

“I told you then that we must be reborn--born of water and the Spirit. That is the way we enter the Kingdom of God.”

“That’s what you said.”

“What difference did it make in your life?”

Nicodemus felt heat rise up his neck. “I should throw away everything I know because of one conversation with you?”

Jesus smiled. “You would if you understood who I am.”

Joseph rose from his bench and gestured for the group to move to the atrium. As he walked behind Jesus, he eyed every thread on his robe and seemed to count every hair on his head. When they sat in the atrium Joseph said, “Nicodemus has changed in the last few years.” He paused for a minute, then asked Jesus. “What do you mean--born again? Is Judas born again?”

Jesus put his finger to his lips. “We must be born of the Spirit--the spirit of truth. The world will not accept the Spirit because it neither sees nor knows her.” He pointed to Joseph. “But you--you know her, for she lives within you.” Jesus paused for a moment, then rose from his couch and stood next to the fire. The flames cast odd shadows on his face as he proceeded, “Someday you will realize who I am. For now, you must be content with what you see.”

Joseph reflected on what Jesus said. "You are not an ordinary man," he said quietly. "I've studied the prophets and the writings of learned men and they seem to have one thing in common with you." Joseph stretched his arms. "You have a connection with a higher power, perhaps you are a higher power."

"Like God?" Judas gasped.

"I'm not a higher power," Jesus said firmly. "But you are right about the connection. I know the way, the truth, and the light. You can come to the Father through me as our ancestors did with Moses." With that, Jesus looked at the sky and gestured to Judas. "Come friend," he said. "I suppose that Mary Marcia will be waiting for us to return to her house."

"We don't want you to go yet," Joseph protested. "We've asked all the questions tonight. Don't you want to question us in return?"

"I don't have to," Jesus replied. "I know what's in your heart."

Joseph cast a worried glance at Nicodemus and asked Jesus, "What do you see in our hearts?"

"You want to make life better for the people around you," Jesus replied. As he headed for the gate, he turned and looked into Joseph's eyes. "I want to add one more thing," he said as his gaze shifted from Joseph to Nicodemus and back again. "We know God asks us to love him but, as you said, we can't see him. How then can we satisfy his wish?"

Joseph shrugged.

Jesus spread his hands and said, "Love one another. You see, we are all Sons of God."

* * *

Nicodemus and Joseph poured themselves another cup of wine and sat next to the fire after Jesus and Judas left.

Joseph shook his head. "I wonder about Jesus. I'm drawn to him, yet he frightens me. Why should I care about what he says?"

"You claimed you saw me change after I met him two years ago," Nicodemus responded. "I realize now that I did change."

"That may be true, but we could put ourselves in danger by associating with him."

"Perhaps," Nicodemus said, "we can help him financially, but keep him at arms length." He put his cup down. "Certainly we have a common interest with him. We both want to get out from under the Sadducee yoke."

Joseph thought about what Nicodemus had just said, then nodded. "What you said makes sense, but I wonder if he would openly challenge the Sadducees without our visible participation."

Nicodemus rose from his couch and stretched. "It's late--time for me to go home. Let's think about it some more and, if it makes sense, we can contact him at his camp."

At they walked to the gate, Joseph grasped Nicodemus' sleeve. "Remember," he whispered, "we need stability these days, not confusion."

Nicodemus sighed, "I agree. I wonder if Jesus is an agent of God, of change, or stability. I don't understand everything he says and does." With that, Nicodemus bade his friend goodnight and walked out of the courtyard into the deserted street.

* * *

Jesus, along with John, Judas, and Mark arrived at Bethany the next morning to find Lazarus sick in bed. After visiting with Lazarus, Jesus left the medicine Mary Marcia gave him and went outside with Mary and Martha. "What did the physician say?" he asked Martha.

She shrugged. "He said it's a disease of the lungs, but he doesn't see any signs of cancer."

Jesus rubbed his chin for a moment, then said, "Contact Mark's mother in Jerusalem if he doesn't show improvement. She has a gift for healing. Contact me if you need to. My camp is located east of the Jordan, near Jericho." He thought for a moment. "That's no good. I'll send someone to Bethany in a few weeks to make sure Lazarus is mending."

Jesus glanced at his companions, already at the top of the hill overlooking Bethany. "I have to hurry," he said to Martha and Mary. Looking into Martha's eyes, he continued, "Soon you will marry Eli. I look forward to that day. And for now, don't worry about Lazarus; it's not his time--or my time for that matter."

CHAPTER THIRTY-FOUR

To the Jews who had believed him, Jesus said, "If you hold to my teaching, you are really my disciples.
Then you will know the truth, and the truth will set you free."

John 8:31-32

Mark, Jesus, Judas, and John left Bethany early in the morning and arrived at the Bethabara camp after sunset the same day. Mark stopped when they reached the small rise overlooking the camp. From there, he saw in one glimpse, the tents stretched from the Bethabara road to the low hills north and east of the camp. The light rain that followed them from north of Jericho pelted the green and brown striped tents held taut by ropes stretching to heavy wood stakes driven in the soft earth. After the rain, the same ropes would hold a variety of robes, tunics, and towels hung out to dry. A wood shack used for food and clothing, and a black tent made from goatskins used for storing weapons and tools stood in the center of the camp. A sizeable ring filled with burning thistle and wood gathered from the sparse Jordan Plain served as the camp's social center. Finally, near the hills to the east, the west wind carried the smoke from a smoldering pile of waste toward Bethabara.

The men and women from the camp welcomed the tired travelers, quickly leading them to the fire. Jesus smiled when he saw Zacchaeus hobbling toward him, for it was Zacchaeus' size rather than his face Jesus first recognized in the dusk. Zacchaeus greeted Jesus then embraced him, his head barely reaching Jesus' chest. "Who collects the taxes while you're gone?" Jesus asked after they separated.

"The people who work for me," Zacchaeus replied.

John grunted, "How do you know you can trust them?"

"I can't," Zacchaeus replied. "But I've devised ways to prevent them from cheating me while I'm gone."

"What are your ways?" John asked, his manner a little friendlier than the last time he met Zacchaeus.

Zacchaeus raised his hand. "That's my secret. If I tell you too much, you'll want to take my place."

John frowned and went over to the tent he shared with his brother, James.

Rubbing his hands over the fire, Jesus asked, "Is it safe for me to return to Jericho these days?"

"That depends on who you talk to," Zacchaeus answered. "The Romans don't know you and the prostitutes and butchers are very receptive. You only have to worry about the religious people."

Jesus suddenly realized that Mark had not met Zacchaeus. He introduced Mark, then explained to Mark how he came to know Zacchaeus. Winking at Zacchaeus, he asked, "Will you ever invite me to your house again?"

"Anytime you wish." Zacchaeus replied, rubbing his chin. "I wonder," he mused, "how would you like to meet the Roman tribune in charge of the Jericho garrison?"

"Why would I want to do that?" Jesus asked.

"Well, eating at the house of a Gentile would offend the people at the synagogue you missed the last time you were in Jericho," Zacchaeus replied.

Jesus laughed. "You like to cause trouble--especially for me."

Zacchaeus crossed his arms. "I like to bring people together, people who have no chance of otherwise meeting."

"Zacchaeus, I think you have a good idea," Jesus said as he put his hand on Mark's shoulder. "I can take my Roman translator with me. Yes, I'll meet your tribune if you wish."

As they approached the tents Mark would share with Judas, Mark said to Jesus, "I'm only half Roman."

* * *

The following evening, Simon-Peter and Jesus sat alone next to the fire after the others went to their tents. Simon-Peter rubbed his hands together, inched closer to the fire, and gave Jesus a questioning look.

"What's wrong?" Jesus asked as he picked up a branch.

Simon-Peter looked at the sky and mumbled, "I wonder how long I'll stay here."

"That's a question I can't answer."

"I still have doubts about you and what you're doing."

"But you came back. Why?"

Simon-Peter yawned. "Like James and John, I remember that day on Mount Hermon. The things I saw there changed the way I think."

Staring into the fire, Jesus shifted the branch from hand to hand. "Then why do you doubt?"

Simon-Peter flashed an angry glance at Jesus. "Because I still act the same as I did before then..." Pausing for a moment, Simon-Peter threw a piece of wood on the fire. "...and I don't understand what you're doing. I don't understand about God and the other things you talk about." Slamming his fist into his hand, Simon-Peter grunted, "I'm a fisherman, that's all I am!"

They remained silent after that. Jesus saw Simon-Peter's eyes glisten but pretended not to notice. Later, Jesus said, "I know it seems strange to talk to people about God in these small towns. They already have enough on their minds."

"Naomi says you meddle with men's minds."

"That's why I'm here," Jesus declared.

"To meddle with our minds?"

"I want to help you think about who you are and what you're doing."

Simon-Peter leaned toward him and replied, "We're only fishermen and farmers. We don't understand the Law. What can you do with us? After all, there are plenty of priests and scribes who know these things."

Jesus poked at the fire with the branch. "I called you to help because the scholars and priests don't want to do the things I'm asking you to do."

"I don't understand."

Jesus smiled. "Someday the Spirit will touch you, and you'll be like these coals--full of fire and heat." He put his hand on Simon-Peter's knee. "I wish I could show you what I see, then you would understand everything. It kills me when I realize I can't."

After another long silence, Simon-Peter sighed. "There's something you should know," he said in a low voice.

"What's that?"

"James and I promised Zebedee we would return to Capernaum after Passover--no later. He said he'll take us back if we ask."

"Is that what you want?"

Gazing into the fire, Simon-Peter replied, "I need to. I have no money."

"What about the money we sent from the camp?"

"Gone."

"What do you mean?"

"I used it."

"What did you use the money for?"

"You must know by now," Simon-Peter mumbled.

"I want you to tell me."

"Damn you!" Simon-Peter hissed, and then looked around to see if anyone was near them. "I spent it on prostitutes and wine! What do you care?"

Jesus poked the stick until it flared. "I care."

"I'm no good for you," Simon-Peter muttered. "I drink too much and I do things--you know..."

"You're impulsive."

"Yes. I'll make you look bad if I stay with you."

"I don't agree."

Simon-Peter leaned closer and whispered, "I'm a weak man, always giving into my craving for wine. Everybody knows that." Seizing Jesus' sleeve, he added, "Everybody but you."

"I've known for a long time."

"Sure, you know everything. People talk about you. You like to hang around with drunks, prostitutes, and tax collectors. Why don't you stay with normal people?"

Jesus smiled. "The people you named are normal people, and so are you. You are the ones I came to serve."

"Serve?" Simon-Peter's eyes narrowed. "What do you mean by that?"

Jesus waved his hand. "That's another subject." He took Simon-Peter's hand. "For now, I'm happy that you will stay with us until Passover. Maybe Naomi and Jepthania will meet us in Jerusalem."

"Maybe," Simon-Peter muttered as he stood and stretched. "One more thing."

"Yes."

"We're sending workers to an irrigation project on the other side of Jericho. I want to continue working there for the time being."

Jesus shrugged. "Andrew will have to make that decision."

"I'll talk to him in the morning," Simon-Peter replied as he headed toward his tent. Suddenly he stopped, almost knocking Jesus aside. "One last thing... thank you for believing in me."

* * *

It was an unusually warm day for early winter when Jesus, Mark, and Zacchaeus went to the Roman garrison in Jericho to eat their evening meal with Lucius Tullius. Upon arriving, they stood in the immense courtyard with dust swirling around their ankles, observing the evidence of a Roman presence in every corner of the garrison. There seemed to be soldiers everywhere; brushing horses, shining the brass rails on chariots, and testing their bows for accuracy. Leaning toward Jesus, Zacchaeus whispered, "This is what's left of the palace built by Herod the Great about fifty years ago." He gestured to what appeared to be an open field. "Rebels burned much of the palace. You can still see part of the wall." He made a sweeping gesture at the rest of the complex. "Now the Romans use what's left as a garrison."

A young man escorted them to the atrium where Zacchaeus introduced Jesus and Mark to tribune Lucius Tullius. Lucius Tullius looked at Mark for a moment and raised his eyebrows. "Mark--is that your birth name?"

"Marcius..."

"Marcius, that's a family name I recognize," Lucius said.

"My full name is Jonah Marcius Africanus," Mark replied proudly. "I'm originally from Cyrene." Mark felt a certain pride in being a Roman. At the same time, he realized he had to be careful whenever he talked to another Roman.

"I knew a man named Gnaeus Marcius Caldus," Lucius replied, rubbing his chin. "We were boyhood friends. I think his younger brother once served in Palestine."

Mark beamed. "Gnaeus Marcius is my uncle. My father lived in Jerusalem until he married my mother."

Lucius looked at Zacchaeus and Jesus. "Forgive me for ignoring you. Zacchaeus didn't tell me he was bringing a Roman to our meal."

"Only half Roman," Mark said.

"Ah...and the other half?" Lucius asked.

"Jewish."

"A volatile combination," Lucius commented as he led his guests to the atrium. Couches and cushions surrounded a sizeable pool filled with rose tinted water. Once they seated themselves, Lucius beckoned to his servants who brought platters filled with nuts, fruit, and bread followed by several decanters of wine made from grapes grown in the valleys west of Jericho.

Pointing to Jesus, Zacchaeus said, "I first met Jesus this summer, but I feel I've known him my whole life."

Turning to Jesus, Lucius remarked, "Zacchaeus told me that some of the people from your camp are working on the irrigation project west of Jericho."

"Yes," Jesus replied.

"Where are your people from?" Lucius asked.

Jesus took a swallow of wine before he answered, "Galilee, and a few from Samaria and Decapolis."

"And Cyrene." Lucius noted, looking at Mark.

"I live in Alexandria now," Mark replied. "I came here to write about Jesus and his people for my teachers at the Library."

"Wouldn't you wonder why people in Alexandria would want to know about an itinerant preacher and his followers?" Jesus asked Lucius.

Lucius smiled. "Perhaps they feel you're doing something important." He took a handful of nuts and popped them in his mouth, one at a time. "Actually I'm not sure what you're doing or why. Living conditions are no better here than in Galilee."

Zacchaeus went to the edge of the pool and looked at his reflection in the water. "That's not all," he interjected. "Jesus challenges the way we think."

"Zacchaeus told me this would be an interesting dinner," noted Lucius. "What do we have here? A tax collector, a religious reformer doubling as a provider of day labor, and a Roman-Jewish scribe." He slapped his knee. "That's an interesting combination. Zacchaeus was right." He looked at Jesus. "I want to hear your ideas about your deity--what do you call him?"

"Yahweh."

"Yes, Yahweh. Your leaders won't talk about your Yahweh when I'm with them. They tell me I'm unclean." Lucius looked at his arms as if they were dirty. "I don't know what they're talking about." Then he turned to Mark. "Who do you believe in? Jupiter, Tiberius, this Yahweh--or is there some Egyptian deity for you?"

Mark felt blood rushing to his face as he stammered, "I...I..." He sighed with relief when servants entered the atrium with platters of steaming lamb, light green beans, and squash garnished with sage and artichoke leaves.

Lucius looked at Mark. "Saved by the lamb. We'll wait until later to learn about your God." Then gesturing to the others, he said, "Enjoy the food. I believe we prepared it according to your Law." His eyes narrowed as he looked at Jesus. "I hope you're not too rigid about following the exact letter of your dietary mandates."

Smiling, Jesus replied, "You're the equal of the scribes at the synagogue who wish to trap me. Many of our leaders forbid us to eat in the house of a Gentile. I observe that rule for the benefit of people who do not understand." He wiped his mouth with a towel. "There are more important things to worry about."

"Like what?" Lucius asked.

"Like the kingdom of God," Jesus replied as he scooped a mouthful of squash using the dried shell of a gourd.

"Here we are," Lucius joked. "I wanted to relax during dinner and talk philosophy afterward. Can we wait?"

Jesus nodded, apparently more interested in eating while the food was still warm. He nodded approvingly when he realized the red wine the servants had just placed before him was also warm.

Turning his attention to Mark, Lucius Tullius said, "Now Mark, tell me about your uncle Gnaeus. Have you seen or heard from him lately?"

"I haven't seen him since the last time I went to Rome with my father, almost six years ago. He does write to me on occasion, however."

"Are things going well for him?"

Eyes downcast, Mark replied, "I'm sure they are."

"Mm," Lucius mumbled as he drained his cup. "You didn't answer my question with much conviction. Is there a problem?"

"I don't know."

"Well, at least your father is safe in Cyrene."

Mark looked away. "My father is dead." He felt trapped by Lucius Tullius' questions.

"I'm sorry."

"He died at sea," Jesus interjected. "Pirates."

Lucius winced. "On the way to Rome?"

"Antioch," Mark answered.

Lucius Tullius rubbed his chin and looked at a shield hanging on the wall opposite them. "Was your father in trouble?"

The question shocked Mark. He had noticed a subtle mood change in Lucius with each question. Mark wondered what Lucius knew about his father and a conspiracy to restore the Roman Republic. "I'd rather not talk about it," Mark replied, trying to deflect further questions.

"Now you live in Alexandria," Lucius persisted.

"Yes sir."

Lucius shook his head. "We live in difficult times. My father is a retired senator and chooses to live as far from Rome as he can. My superiors offered me better posts than this one, but I feel safe in Jericho." Eyes narrowing, Lucius added, "No officer wants to live here. The only thing I worry about is whether the troubles in Jerusalem will spill over to Jericho."

"Jericho has fewer Jews than Jerusalem," Zacchaeus observed.

"Yes," Lucius replied. "Only half the people are Jewish and that helps." He looked at his guests and blushed. "I'm sorry, I made an unkind statement."

Jesus ran his finger around the edge of his cup. "There are serious problems among the Jews, and between the Jews and Romans. I understand why you feel the way you do."

Lucius drank the last of the wine from his cup. "What would you do about those problems if you were in charge?" Lucius asked Jesus.

"I would try to bring people together, perhaps help them see their similarities rather than their differences."

Nodding, Lucius continued, "There's a settlement a few miles from here at a place called Qumran. I sometimes suspect those people want to assemble an army. They're much disciplined and they could make trouble for us."

"One of our leaders lived in Qumran for a while," Jesus replied. "He told me that the only people they want to fight are the ones in charge of the Temple in Jerusalem."

"What do you call those people?" Lucius asked.

"The men in charge of the temple?" Jesus asked as he finished the last of his beans.

"No, at Qumran."

"Essenes," said Zacchaeus.

"Yes, Essenes," Lucius remarked. "I heard the Essenes are sending their men into every town from here to Rome."

Raising his eyebrows, Jesus commented, "You know more about us Jews than you profess."

"Information is necessary for survival," Lucius replied as he stood and stretched. He looked at each man to make sure he had finished his meal, then said, "Let's go to the courtyard. There's a nice fire out there that'll keep us warm while we talk. There, you can fulfill Zacchaeus' promise that you would tell me everything I want to know about your God."

"Zacchaeus overstates my ability," Jesus replied.

Lucius turned to Mark after they settled in the courtyard. "Now--you've had an entire meal to think about my question. Which gods do you worship?"

Mark looked at Jesus. "I attend the synagogue in Alexandria."

"Your temple?"

"Synagogue."

"What's the difference?" Lucius asked.

Zacchaeus interrupted, "Sir, we only have one Temple--in Jerusalem. The Jews in Jericho worship in a building we call a synagogue."

Lucius pressed on, "Mark, you attend services at the tem...excuse me, synagogue. Does that mean you worship your Jewish God?"

"I guess so." Again, Mark felt uncomfortable with Lucius' questions.

"You guess so? Does *guess* mean you believe in your God?" Lucius' eyes darted between his three guests. "After all, I salute Tiberius Caesar and light candles in honor of the Divine Augustus. But," his voice reduced to a whisper, "does that say I believe?"

Quickly, Mark asked, "Do you?"

Lucius waved his finger at Mark. "I asked you first."

"I don't believe Augustus is a god," Mark replied.

Lucius and Jesus burst out laughing. "He's a true scribe," Lucius said. "He answers questions with questions and changes the subject when we corner him. In the end he believes in nothing but the power of his papyrus and pen."

Mark stiffened. "Just as soldiers believe in nothing but the power of the sword."

Lucius handed a plate of figs and apricots to Mark. "Well put, young scribe," he said. "We Romans need to hear more about the power that guides the world. We hear too much nonsense from our leaders."

"Romans have no monopoly on that," replied Jesus.

Instead of replying to Jesus, Lucius signaled to a servant standing near the edge of the courtyard. The servant came over to the group with a pot and four cups and proceeded to pour hot tea made from chamomile leaves.

"Thank you for the meal," Jesus said after they settled themselves in cushions placed around the fire. "I have to be careful; I've eaten too many good meals during the last month."

"Careful of what?" Lucius asked.

Jesus laughed and pointed to his sash. "The last time I saw my brother, he told me I look like I'm eating too well."

Changing the subject, Lucius asked Jesus, "You mentioned a kingdom during our meal. What were you talking about--Herod's kingdom?"

Jesus shook his head. "God's." He shifted his weight so he could face Lucius directly. "Look at it this way: A rich tax collector," Jesus quickly glanced at Zacchaeus from the corner of his eye, "a man like our friend here died and was mourned with a lavish funeral." Now Jesus looked at Mark. "A poor scholar also died, but no one attended his funeral. When an explanation was demanded, it was said that although the tax collector had not lived a pious life, he did do one good deed before his death. He arranged a banquet for the town leaders, but they did not come, each one giving his excuse. So," Jesus proceeded, "the tax collector gave orders that the poor should come and eat his banquet so his food would not be wasted. That is how the kingdom of God works. Often the pious are rejected in favor of the poor."

Lucius clapped his hands. "Well told, preacher. But...if I heard you right, you told me how your kingdom works, not what it is."

"The kingdom of God *is*," Jesus replied. "It's here and it's now. God's kingdom welcomes everyone, asking them only to forgive and love as a price of admission." Jesus slowly rose from his cushion and stretched. "It also represents a challenge to us, Lucius. It changes our lives and moves us to a moral regeneration."

"Would you accept a Roman tribune as a citizen of this kingdom?" Lucius asked.

Jesus smiled as he replied, "The kingdom is already within you and I." Then he pointed to Mark and Zacchaeus. "As it is in them. We need to learn how to release it and put it to good use."

The four men talked until there were only a few lights visible from the homes in the city. Noticing that Mark and Zacchaeus were falling asleep, Jesus said to Lucius, "I think we better take our leave. My friends and I thank you for your excellent meal and our time together."

"It is I who should give thanks," replied Lucius. "Thanks to Zacchaeus for bringing us together and thanks to you for sharing your ideas. I do want to talk with you again." With that, Lucius ordered an escort to take Jesus and his friends back to the house of Zacchaeus, where they were to spend the night.

Mark walked alongside Jesus until they came close to the house of Zacchaeus. Suddenly, he snapped his fingers. He realized that the kingdom Jesus talked about was like a huge mosaic. This night, Jesus laid several valuable tiles--ideas that would spring to Mark's mind often over the next several years.

* * *

Jesus and Mark returned to the Bethabara camp the next morning, arriving shortly after the workers left for the irrigation project. Jesus talked with John and Judas for a while, then walked out of the camp toward the low hills to the north.

When Mark asked John where Jesus went, John answered, "Jesus told me he wanted to be alone. I don't know why, but he said he needs time to prepare by fasting and praying."

"What is he preparing for?"

John shrugged. "I told you--I don't know."

"I'll disappoint my teachers in Alexandria," Mark said with a sigh. "What will I tell them? That this man leads a group of people into the desert then runs off to fast and pray. What would happen to his followers and these camps if a wild animal killed him?"

"I don't know," John said as they walked toward the river. "We all wonder what we would do if something happened to Jesus. Who's capable of taking charge?" Pointing to himself, he added, "I don't know what Jesus wants to do."

"But you follow him. Why?"

"That question throbs in my head every day." John replied, looking at the sky. "James and I knew Jesus long before John the Baptizer baptized him." John paused for a moment, watching a colony of ants file in and out of a line of anthills next to his feet. "Then we went to Mount Hermon. After that, I never questioned him. One thing I know for sure..." He waited until Mark looked at him. "...he's not one of us. He is different. I can't explain why, but I know he is different."

As they walked closer to the water, John held Mark's sleeve. "I don't see everything he sees, but I see things other people do not see. There are things he says that only I understand--from my visions."

"You have visions?"

"Yes, and they drive me crazy."

Mark saw an intensity in John he had not seen in Jesus' other disciples. John reminded him of Philo Judaeus. Not in size or looks, for John was smaller and thinner and his thick reddish hair contrasted sharply with the ring of black curls crowning Philo's head. Curiously, it also occurred to Mark that both John and Philo were left-handed. Then another idea occurred to Mark. "You're like Jesus in some ways," Mark said. "But he's calmer, more serene."

"Of course," John snapped. "He's calm because he has us in constant turmoil. The pressure is on us, not him."

"Do you really talk about who would take over if something happened to Jesus?"

"We talked about it--just talked."

Mark walked in small circles, hands clasped behind his back. "That's funny," he muttered.

"What?"

Mark gestured toward the camp. "This all happened after you went to Mount Hermon. That was a year and a half ago?"

"About that."

"How could so many things happen in eighteen months?"

"We knew him before that," John replied.

"Yes, but now you have two camps, one here and one in Galilee. I hear stories of healing, yet people chase you from their towns." He gazed into John's eyes. "There are mornings when I wake up thinking all this has been a dream."

John laughed, "You think you're in a dream. What about us? People think we're crazy, and there are times when I agree." He gestured toward the desert. "What are we doing here? We're like Moses and the Israelites wandering forty years in the desert."

Mark raised a finger. "Ah, but it's only been a year or so since you left Capernaum."

John grabbed Mark's tunic and pulled him closer. "I think Jesus is right, but he chooses too many followers who are wrong."

"What do you mean?"

"You know--people like Judas and that runty Zacchaeus. I don't trust those people."

"Because they're short?"

"No," John replied impatiently. "Because they're dishonest." He gave Mark a light thrust as he let go of his tunic and started back to the camp, leaving Mark standing near the river.

Mark watched John disappear in the brush between the camp and the river, then sat on a flat rock a short distance from the bridge and thought about the previous night and the men who represented his universe. He saw the power of Rome in the person of Lucius Tullius. But what did he see in the person of Jesus? Jesus was like his uncle Abraham or his mother--that's all. Did someone slap you? Turn the other cheek. Did someone threaten to kill you with their sword? Bare your neck. Is your brother hungry? Feed him. Mark snickered at the idea that people would respond if treated decently.

A snapping twig alerted him to danger. He drew his knife from his belt and listened. Holding his breath, he heard birds flutter away as if chased by an unseen hand. He looked out the corner of his eye but saw no one. Nothing! He waited, ready to jump. He heard a grunt. It startled him, making his palms sweat even more.

He exhaled and quietly stood with his back to a tree, knife drawn and ready for a fight. Another twig snapped to his right and he turned, eyes burning with fear. When he jumped from behind the tree and yelled, his stalker screamed and slumped to the ground face first on top of a pile of clothes.

Mark quickly looked to see if anyone else was near, then turned the woman on her back. He whistled softly when he saw it was Mary of Magdala. He ran to the river and took some water in his hands, but it drained away by the time he reached her. Then he grabbed a shawl, plunged it in the water, and put it on her forehead. He tried to pull her out of the sun, but felt almost as faint as she. Then he sat with his legs crossed, cradling her head on his lap.

He studied her face and saw signs of aging, even though she was only a few years older than he. Her face, arms, and legs carried scars as if she had been cut or burned. After a few minutes, she woke, eyes filled with terror. She gasped and wriggled free from Mark.

She stood over him with her hands on her hips. "What did you do to me?" she shouted.

"Nothing," Mark replied, trying to back away. "I jumped from behind this tree--you fainted--that's all."

Her dark eyes surveyed him from head to toe. "What did you do to me when I..."

"I told you--nothing!" he hollered. Then he put his hand over his mouth. "I'm sorry," he added in a more moderate tone. "I didn't mean to shout. Why are you so upset?"

She felt her breasts through her tunic, then muttered, "Nothing." She looked at the ground. "Why are you here?"

"I came here with John and decided to rest for a while. Did I do something wrong?"

"You waited for me with that knife." Her eyes shifted to his waist. "Where is the knife you had?"

He saw it lying on the ground near the tree and picked it up. "I dropped it when you fainted. I meant no harm; it's just that I feel a need to protect myself."

"You're not a woman. Why do you need protection?"

He gazed into her eyes and asked, "Why were you so frightened?"

She stood close to him and pointed to her face. "You see these scars. Did you also notice I have a crooked nose?"

He nodded.

"Things happened to me in the past. It wouldn't interest you." She started to pick up the clothes.

"Maybe we have some common experiences," he said as he bent to help her.

"I doubt it," came her curt reply.

"Then I'll forget it. Can I help you wash the clothes?"

"Why don't you stand guard with your knife? You probably could scare half an army with it."

Mark felt his face flush. "You're making fun of me."

She walked past him toward the river. "What do you want me to do? Thank you for scaring me to death?"

She washed the clothes and laid them on rocks to dry. After a while she said, "Turn around, I want to wash my tunic."

Mark felt his face redden. "You mean take it off and..."

"No, I thought this would be a good time to drown myself. Stop asking stupid questions and turn around."

"Maybe you want to wash mine too."

"Are you trying to start something?"

"Ah..."

"Well forget it. Just stand guard until I put a dry tunic on." After a few minutes she said, "Now you can turn around."

He turned to see her dressed in a damp white tunic. It hung on the curves of her body like silk and stretched over the soft mound of her breasts. He gawked at her until he realized his tunic revealed his own passion, and then looked away.

She walked up the short hill to where he stood and touched him on the shoulder. “I wasn’t nice to you.” Her voice trailed off to a whisper, “I thought you were like the rest.”

Mark took her hands in his and held them for a moment. Then he pulled her to him and put his arms around her. She cried, her hot tears soaking into his tunic. After a while, he held her shoulders and looked into her eyes made soft by her tears and said, “I don’t know what to say.”

She looked at him for a moment and smiled. “Don’t...” She turned away and threw her head back. “Leave me alone.”

“What did I do?”

“Nothing,” she gasped as she ran toward the camp.

Mark waited until the clothes dried, then collected them and returned to the camp. On the way back, he wondered about the people in his life and what, if anything, they had to do with Roman garrisons and the kingdom of God.

CHAPTER THIRTY-FIVE

Then James and John, the sons of Zebedee, came to him. "Teacher," they said, "we want you to do for us whatever we ask."
"What do you want me to do for you?" he asked.
They replied, "Let one of us sit at your right and the other at your left in your glory."
"You don't know what you are asking," Jesus said. "Can you drink the cup I drink or be baptized with the baptism I am baptized with?"
"We can," they answered. Jesus said to them, "You will drink the cup I drink and be baptized with the baptism I am baptized with, but to sit at my right or left is not for me to grant. These places belong to those for whom they have been prepared."
When the ten heard about this, they became indignant with James and John.
Jesus called them together and said, "You know that those who are regarded as rulers of the Gentiles lord it over them, and their high officials exercise authority over them. Not so with you. Instead, whoever wants to become great among you must be your servant, and whoever wants to be first must be slave of all. For even the Son of Man did not come to be served, but to serve, and to give his life as a ransom for many."
Mark10:35-45

It had been almost a week since Jesus went to the hills north of the Bethabara camp. Each night, as they huddled around the fire, the followers of Jesus talked about searching the hills if he didn't return the next day. Judas, watching the light from the fire dancing off their eyes, sensed their fear that Jesus might be dead. It seemed that, in less than a week, the fabric of the camp was unraveling. After only a few days, Simon-Peter, Andrew, and John renewed their argument about who would run the camp in Jesus' absence, yet Judas wondered if there would even be a camp if Jesus disappeared. The pressure of caring for their families, responding to Zebedee's entreaties, and the danger of attack from bandits might easily convince them to abandon Jesus' dream.

It was a cold night when James bar Zebedee, wrapped tightly in his heavy wool robe, sat on a crude bench at the edge of the camp. The icy looking moon hung in the sky, barely casting enough light for him to whittle a piece of wood without cutting his fingers. Turning the wood in his hand, examined it for several minutes, then cut a notch in the middle and shaved small slivers off the end. At the same time, he constantly watched the trees outside the camp and the short hills beyond for signs of life. Once, when he looked up from his carving, James thought he saw a tree moving, like it was walking toward him. The next time he looked, he saw nothing. Later, a single figure emerged through a grove of trees about two hundred yards from the camp. James squinted, wondering if the figure was a man or his imagination. He jumped to his feet when he recognized Jesus slowly walking toward him.

Eyes filled with tears, James ran to greet Jesus. When they met between the camp and the trees, he took Jesus' hand. "You look tired and hungry," he said, peering at Jesus by the pallid rays of the moon. "When was the last time you ate?"

"I ate my last regular meal before I went into the hills," Jesus replied. "And I haven't been warm since the last time I sat next to our campfire."

"No food?" gasped James.

Wiping his lips with his sleeve, Jesus answered, "Oh, I found some berries and a few fruit trees where I stayed. That was enough."

James pulled his cloak off and threw it over Jesus' shoulders. "We were worried about you," he said quietly.

"Better you worry about yourself, my friend. My time has not come."

"Your time?"

Jesus waved his hand. "Nothing, let's get over to the fire before I freeze to death."

When John saw Jesus and James approaching the fire, he ran to meet them. "We were worried about you," he said to Jesus.

Looking at James from the corner of his eye, Jesus said, "Maybe I should stand here and wait until everyone is done worrying."

"I don't think that's amusing," John said harshly.

Jesus put his hand on John's shoulder. "I went to meditate and pray to prepare myself."

"Prepare for what?" John asked.

"That I accept whatever will come," Jesus answered as he shook the dust out of his robe. "There are too many distractions in the camp. I needed time to think--to clear my mind." He raised a finger and added, "But most of all, to listen."

"Oh."

Jesus gestured to the others to seat themselves around the fire. "We're glad to see you," Andrew announced as Simon-Peter and Mark moved apart to make room for Jesus.

Simon-Peter continued to stare into the fire after Jesus sat down. "Is something wrong, Simon-Peter?" he asked.

"We wondered if you would come back," John interjected.

"Here I am..."

"This time!" John shouted. "But what would happen if you didn't come back? We need a leader for the camp when you go away."

Jesus seemed slightly amused by their concern. "Did you decide on a leader?" he asked.

"No," John replied. "First Simon-Peter said he would take your place, then Judas said he understood how to run a business and..."

James brought a hot bowl of soup to Jesus, cutting John off in mid-statement. Jesus wrapped his hands around the warm bowl and held it next to his nose to savor its aroma. Then he put the bowl to his mouth and drank it down. As he handed the bowl back to James he asked, "What were you saying, John?"

John's face reddened. "What can I say? They're older than I."

"Does that make a difference?"

"Of course it does. I'm only twenty and my brother James and Simon-Peter's brother Andrew are closer to your age. People will follow them despite..." His voice trailed off.

"Despite what?" Jesus prodded.

"Nothing."

Jesus looked at James. "What about you?"

James replied, "I want to follow you, not them. It's a stupid argument as far as I can tell."

Jesus smiled. "You're right, my friend. If anyone in this camp wants to be first, he must be the very last, the servant of all. Which reminds me; James, would you mind bringing another bowl of soup?" James nodded and headed for the cooking tent. While he waited for his soup, Jesus pulled James's cloak tighter and pointed to a circle of children playing in the sand near the fire. "In other words, you must humble yourself like those children if you want to be great on earth or in heaven."

Mark wondered why Jesus always seemed to choose the dark of night for his profound statements. Mark seldom carried his pens and papyrus to the sessions around the fire and he silently cursed himself for his bad memory and signaled Judas to join him in their tent. There, they spent an hour talking about the meaning of the things Jesus told them.

* * *

By the end of that week, Jesus and his chief followers decided they would finish their work in Bethabara and move to a camp near Jerusalem in time for the Feast of Passover. Although Passover was nearly two months away, they reasoned it would take at least a month to finish their work and move the camp. The next day, Jesus sent Judas and Andrew to Jerusalem to arrange for a camp large enough to shelter the pilgrims from both Galilee and Bethabara. He also had Mark write a long note to Zebedee in Capernaum explaining what he was doing and asking Zebedee to include the Nazareth people in his Passover caravan.

"Do you think Zebedee will agree?" Mark asked Jesus after he finished writing the note.

"I don't know," Jesus replied. "Someday...someday, Zebedee will see the light."

Mark was about to ask another question, but stopped when Jesus called to James. He gave the note to James who was preparing to return to Capernaum with his son, Aaron. "I'm giving you a note for Zebedee," Jesus said to James, "so you won't have to explain things to him."

James shot Jesus a cynical glance. "You mean argue with him."

"I suppose," Jesus replied. Taking James by the arm, he added, "Thank you for helping lead the Nazareth people to our camp. I appreciate your quiet cooperation."

After James left for Galilee, Jesus, John, and Thomas went to call on the Jewish communities of northern Perea. Mark wanted to go with them, but Jesus said he wanted to keep one Latin speaking person in the camp while they were gone. Later, when Andrew and Judas returned from their trip to Jerusalem, Andrew joined the crew working on the irrigation project, leaving Simon-Peter in charge of the camp. It was during this time that Mark began to teach Simon-Peter. Mark told him about Alexandria, Rome, and Cyrene, and taught him to read simple words. Simon-Peter, in turn, told Mark about Bethsaida and Capernaum as well as his experiences with Jesus. Mark enjoyed these sessions. The smell of wine no longer saturated Simon-Peter's clothes and breath, nor did he give in to the sudden flashes of anger that had marked his previous behavior. "I've been writing about you for over a week," Mark said one afternoon, "yet I still feel I don't know you."

Simon-Peter smiled and looked at the ground. "What is there to know? I'm only a fisherman. Judas and Thomas are smarter than me. Maybe after you teach me to read and write..."

Mark interrupted, "Reading and writing have little to do with knowing a person." Mark remained silent for a while, preferring to watch the women sitting in circles grinding barley collected from the surrounding fields, while other women sewed freshly tanned animal skins into clothing, tents, and bags. Finally, Mark snapped back to attention. "Why," he asked Simon-Peter, "did you come back after you argued with Jesus and left the camp at Scythopolis?"

"I don't know," Simon-Peter answered. "There's something about Jesus that draws me to him." Simon-Peter watched a small caravan traveling from Jericho toward Bethabara disappear behind a hill. Then he turned to Mark. "What do you think?" he asked.

Mark held his hand over his eyes to block the sun. "About what?"

"Do you believe in Jesus?"

"My only interest is writing about him..." Mark poked Simon-Peter on the arm. "...and you."

* * *

Jesus, John, and Thomas returned from the towns of Perea in a melancholy mood. It seemed the people of Perea were no more prepared to welcome Jesus than the people of Galilee and Judea. That news came as no surprise to Mark who reasoned that, if Jesus could not totally convince his immediate followers, he would have even less success with strangers.

That night they gathered around the fire to celebrate their last Sabbath at the Bethabara camp with readings and prayers. Before the ceremony, Jesus made a point of going to his tent with Andrew to find the exact scroll he wanted. Now he stood before a hushed group of worshippers, unrolled the scroll, and read the words from the prophet Isaiah:

> *See, my servant will act wisely; he will be raised and lifted up and highly exalted. Just as there were many who were appalled at him--his appearance was so disfigured beyond that of any man and his form marred beyond human likeness--so will he sprinkle many nations, and kings will shut their mouths because of him. For what they were not told, they will see, and what they have not heard, they will understand.*
>
> *Who has believed our message and to whom has the arm of the LORD been revealed? He grew up before him like a tender shoot, and like a root out of dry ground. He had no beauty or majesty to attract us to him, nothing in his appearance that we should desire him. He was despised and rejected by men, a man of sorrows, and familiar with suffering. Like one from whom men hide their faces he was despised, and we esteemed him not.*

Surely he took up our infirmities and carried our sorrows, yet we considered him stricken by God, smitten by him, and afflicted. But he was pierced for our transgressions, he was crushed for our iniquities; the punishment that brought us peace was upon him, and by his wounds we are healed.

We all, like sheep, have gone astray, each of us has turned to his own way; and the LORD has laid on him the iniquity of us all. He was oppressed and afflicted, yet he did not open his mouth; he was led like a lamb to the slaughter, and as a sheep before her shearers is silent, so he did not open his mouth.

By oppression and judgment he was taken away. And who can speak of his descendants? For he was cut off from the land of the living; for the transgression of my people he was stricken. He was assigned a grave with the wicked and with the rich in his death, though he had done no violence, nor was any deceit in his mouth.

Yet it was the LORD'S will to crush him and cause him to suffer, and though the LORD makes his life a guilt offering, he will see his offspring and prolong his days, and the will of the LORD will prosper in his hand.

After the suffering of his soul, he will see the light of life and be satisfied; by his knowledge my righteous servant will justify many, and he will bear their iniquities. Therefore I will give him a portion among the great, and he will divide the spoils with the strong, because he poured out his life unto death, and was numbered with the transgressors. For he bore the sin of many, and made intercession for the transgressors.

(Isa 52:13-53:12)

After he finished reading, Jesus carefully rolled the scroll and handed it to Andrew. He faced the people for a moment and slowly walked to his place next to the fire. There he sat down and pulled his shawl over his head to pray.

Andrew knelt next to him. "Will you say something? Explain this scripture to the people?"

Jesus shook his head. Mark noticed that Andrew's face turned alabaster white when he saw the look on Jesus' face. The scroll slipped out of Andrew's hand as he gestured to the others that the service had ended. Then he picked up the scroll, sat near Jesus, and pulled his own shawl over his head.

* * *

On the afternoon after the Sabbath, Jesus received a message from Martha of Bethany stating that she feared Lazarus would die soon. Jesus showed the message to John and shrugged. “I tried to help. I asked Mary--Mark’s mother--for medicine but apparently it didn’t work.” He looked at the sky. “It’s too late to travel today, and tomorrow we need to finish organizing the camp. We’ll go to Bethany the day after tomorrow.”

CHAPTER THIRTY-SIX

Jesus wept.

John 11:35

Upon reflection, it seemed to John that Jesus deliberately delayed their trip to Bethany. First, he had trouble deciding who to take, then wondered if he wanted to travel to Ephraim between his visit to Bethany and the Feast of Passover. That question made no sense to John who couldn't understand why Jesus would want to visit another strange community so soon after their disappointments in Perea. Jesus finally picked John and Judas to accompany Thomas and himself, and decided to leave for Bethany two weeks before the beginning of Passover to allow himself time to visit Ephraim.

They took the highway between Jericho and Jerusalem, turning to the narrower and less traveled road leading to Bethany before they reached the Mount of Olives. As they passed recently planted fields of vegetables and grain, Jesus kicked at the dirt on the road and said, "It's no wonder our people are disheartened. They struggle to work this hard ground only to see the crops burn in the sun or drown in the rain." He pointed toward a group of women gathering the last winter figs and men foraging for grayish-yellow flax in the fields. "Look, they work all day for a basket of figs or a bundle of flax. Then after the traders in the city squeeze them for the lowest price, the tax collectors take their portion."

"When I watch farmers bending over rows of beans and peas, I feel good about fishing," John commented, shaking his head. "I don't understand people who grow crops."

"I'm sure they feel the same about fishermen," replied Jesus.

"That's because they don't know any better," John retorted.

Jesus laughed. "Spoken like a true son of Galilee." His words were still hanging in the air when he saw Levi, the tailor, walking toward them with a glum look on his face.

Levi didn't trouble himself to greet Jesus. Instead, he pointed over his shoulder. "There's no need for you to hurry," he muttered. "Lazarus is already dead."

Jesus appeared paralyzed for a moment. "When did Lazarus die?"

"Two days ago." Rolling his sleeves to his elbow, Levi continued, "You need to talk to Martha and Mary, they're beside themselves with grief."

"Hurry," Jesus said to the others as Levi continued up the hill, "we have no time to waste."

Upon reaching Bethany, they found Martha, the sister of Lazarus, standing outside her house. Sobbing, she ran to Jesus and said, "Why didn't you come when we sent the message about Lazarus." Her face showed disillusionment as well as grief. "My brother would still be alive if you had," she admonished.

Jesus embraced her and whispered, "Your brother will rise again."

Eyes downcast, she pulled Jesus toward the house. "I know you told us those things about the kingdom of God, but..."

"Where is Mary?" Jesus interrupted.

"In the house...she hasn't stopped crying since Lazarus died."

"I'm sorry to hear that," Jesus commented to no one in particular. Then he took Martha's hand and said, "Bring Mary to me. I want to see the place where Lazarus was buried."

Martha and Thomas went into the house and returned moments later with Mary, her face filled with anguish and apprehension. Collapsing in Jesus' arms, she cried, "Why didn't..."

Jesus, not able to contain his own tears, said, "What could I have done for Lazarus that you did not do." He held Mary by her shoulders. "Did you pray?"

Mary nodded.

"Did a physician treat him?"

Mary nodded again.

"When caring for Lazarus, did you follow the physician's instructions?"

Mary nodded a third time.

Jesus threw his hands in the air. "Then what could I do?"

Martha cast a wary glance at Thomas and shrugged. "We heard stories about how you healed strangers, cured their blindness, and helped them walk again. We naturally thought you would do the same for your friend."

"And with Lazarus dead, you will lose your right to live in his house?"

"Levi will become master of my brother's house," replied Martha.

Changing the subject, Jesus asked where they buried Lazarus and Martha gestured to a series of small caves located beyond the plowed fields and olive groves east of Bethany. "We'll go there now," he said, taking Mary's hand.

"Why?" John asked. "Lazarus has been dead for two days. What good can we do now?"

Casting an admonished glance at John, he replied, "I want to pray at my friend's tomb."

The tombs were cut out of rocky outcroppings at the base of a series of low hills a short distance from Bethany. The late afternoon sun, reflecting off the tombs and the stones rolled in front of the tombs, cast menacing shadows on the ground. John, Judas, Thomas, and the women held back when they came to the place where Lazarus was buried, while Jesus went to the tomb and touched the heavy stone covered the opening. He stood there for a long time, seemingly lost in grief. Eventually, he stepped back and gestured to John and Thomas, saying, "Help me move this stone."

"Get away from that tomb!" Martha cried out. "Didn't you hear; it's been two days since we buried Lazarus?" Stamping her foot, she added, "Mourn here where there is no smell."

Jesus ignored her as they groaned trying to move the heavy stone away from the opening. Mary of Bethany looked away. Then looking at Judas, she asked, "Why?"

Judas' answer, if there was one, was lost to the sound of the three men grunting as they inched the stone away from the opening of the tomb. Once they moved the stone, Jesus cupped his hands around his mouth and shouted into the tomb. Only a hollow echo returned his call.

Martha's grief turned to rage when Jesus bent to look through the entrance. "Stop him!" she screamed. "He'll make himself and the tomb unclean! And the smell..."

Jesus backed out of the tomb and signaled for Martha to cease talking. Then he looked inside the tomb and shouted, "Lazarus, Come out!"

Shocked at Jesus' actions, Judas tried to raise his arms in protest, but lacked the strength to do so. Martha clutched Thomas' sleeve, while Mary cried softly. John shook his head and turned his back to the tomb.

Martha, fearful that Jesus would defile the tomb, turned away. She quickly spun to face the tomb when she heard Mary scream. It was then that the two women saw something moving within the shadows of the cave. Mary and Martha clutched at each other while Thomas said a silent prayer of thanks that the surrounding trees muffled the sudden outburst of noise around the tomb.

Judas was the next person to see someone moving inside the tomb. Words choked in his throat as he tried to call to John who was moving toward the women. It seemed to Judas that John was moving slowly, as if his feet were mired in clay. For their part, the women continued to scream, frozen in the spot where they first saw movement behind Jesus.

When Judas recovered his voice, he shouted, “Unclean; Jesus stay away!”

Thomas ran near the tomb intending to pull Jesus away, but Jesus entered the tomb before Thomas could reach him. At that point, everyone froze, stunned by the events unfolding before them. Not one person moved until Mary groaned and collapsed. John tried to catch her, but she slipped through his fevered hands as she slumped to the ground.

Still standing near the tomb, Thomas saw two shadows moving in the darkness. He quickly looked back at the others who gaped at him and the tomb. Their eyes and mouths opened even wider when they saw Jesus come out of the tomb, then Lazarus, still partially covered by his burial wrap. Thomas moved sideways toward the group, never taking his eyes off the figures emerging from the tomb.

John and Judas were horrified, while Martha and Thomas continued to back away from the tomb. They felt themselves losing control, afraid to stay where they were and too weak to run.

Judas grabbed John’s sleeve. “I see a light coming from the tomb,” he whispered. Then he released John’s sleeve and stumbled past the other disciples to where Jesus and Lazarus stood. He stood in front of them, legs shaking like a willow. After a long pause, he stammered, “You...are...the...anointed oh-oh-one!” With that, Judas fell on his face, grabbed Jesus’ ankles, and wept.

Jesus held Lazarus with one hand and touched Judas’ head with the other until Judas stood. He motioned for Judas to take Lazarus’ other arm. Together they walked toward the others, but the people backed away. John took Martha’s hand and looked over his shoulder toward Bethany, but Martha shook loose and ran to revive Mary.

Jesus raised his hand and said, “Don’t be afraid.” Gesturing to John, he said, “Here, help Lazarus. He’s weak--he can hardly stand.” As soon as John took Lazarus’ arm, Jesus wiped his forehead with his sleeve. “So am I. I need to rest for a minute.”

Once they revived Mary and seated themselves, Jesus talked to them. “This upset you. I understand your fear.” He glanced back at the tomb and continued, “I can’t explain...I hardly understand what happened.” He rubbed his hands together. “For now, I have to ask you to promise that you won’t tell anyone what you saw here...”

“What?” John shouted. “We see a dead man come out of a tomb and you want us to stay quiet?”

Judas gestured toward Jerusalem. “This is the very thing we need to convince the people at the temple.”

“Convince them of what?” Jesus asked.

"That you are the Messiah, the Anointed One," Judas shouted. "They can't deny your claim when we tell them about this. We have witnesses!"

"I haven't claimed anything," Jesus replied defiantly. "Don't put words in my mouth!"

"But..."

"Now hear me!" Jesus replied. "I don't care who it is, the Sanhedrin, the high priests, or whoever. They're not ready to hear these things." Looking at Martha and Mary, he asked, "Do we have proof that Lazarus even died?"

"I touched his cold body," Martha gasped. "Dead is dead."

"The high priests would deny it," Jesus countered.

"The people in Bethany know he died," Martha insisted.

Thomas looked at Martha. "Jesus is right. This is not the time or place to tell what happened. The real problem is what do we do with Lazarus?"

"What do you mean?" Judas asked.

Standing between Jesus and the tomb, Thomas said, "We can't take Lazarus to Bethany, it would frighten the townspeople. We certainly can't leave him here, living in the tomb." Thomas chuckled. "Can you imagine someone coming to visit the grave of their ancestor and suddenly they see Lazarus taking his afternoon walk?"

John added, "And we can't take him to Jerusalem. Someone might recognize him there as well."

Tears ran down Martha's cheeks. "I don't understand," she cried. "First my brother dies. Now he is alive. Then you tell me we have to hide him." She looked at Lazarus. "What do you say?"

Lazarus, still sitting where John and Judas left him, gave Martha a vacant gaze and opened his mouth, but only coughed lightly.

"I still don't understand why we have to hide him," Judas persisted. "This is proof that Jesus is the Messiah and he lives among us just as the prophets said he would!"

"What?" Thomas asked.

"Proof that Jesus is the Messiah," Judas repeated.

"This is not the time to talk about messiahs!" Jesus interrupted. "We can't tell people about this, not yet." Looking at Thomas, he asked, "What do you think we should do?"

"Let me take him someplace where no one knows him," Thomas replied. "Maybe Damascus or Antioch until the time is right. That way Martha and Mary can visit him from time to time."

Jesus nodded. "I agree, but what can we do with him until he's strong enough to travel?"

"We could take him back to our house," Martha replied.

"Too risky," Thomas countered.

John said, "We certainly can't..."

Suddenly, Jesus gasped and jumped up.

"What's wrong?" John asked.

"I forgot about the stone," Jesus hollered as he headed toward the tomb. "Help me push it back before someone sees us." John and Judas rushed to help Jesus, and after much groaning and grunting, they pushed the stone in front of the opening. "That stone seemed heavier than before," Jesus commented as he sagged to the ground next to Lazarus. "Where were we? Oh yes, what to do with Lazarus." He looked at Martha. "Is there a place near here where we can hide Lazarus until he's strong enough to travel?"

She thought for a moment, and then pointed to the low hills to the east. "You could hide him in one of the caves near the Salt Sea."

"Of course," Thomas interjected. "We can keep him hidden until dark, and then I'll take him to one of the caves and stay with him." He spread his arms. "Mary and Martha can bring us food and clothing."

Jesus nodded. "Done!" Then noticing that Judas was still seated with a downcast look on his face he asked, "What's wrong?"

"I don't understand why we can't tell anyone about this."

"I'm sorry, Judas. We need to do these things in their proper time."

"What if Lazarus dies *again* before people see him?"

"Then he dies and God will choose another way to reveal his glory to us," Jesus replied as he held Judas by the shoulders and looked into his eyes. "What happened here is a mystery, a miracle. I'm not sure this will ever happen again, yet people would expect it from us every time someone died." He shook Judas lightly. "We need time to make sense of this before we tell the world."

* * *

That night, John, Thomas, and Judas took Lazarus on a donkey to a cave hidden in the hills overlooking the Salt Sea. The next morning, Jesus and John left Bethany to tour the area around Ephraim before returning to Jerusalem for the Passover observance. At the same time, Judas left for Jerusalem with a message from Jesus to Joseph of Arimathea. As they parted, Jesus took Judas aside and said, "Say nothing to Joseph about Lazarus. Do you understand? Nothing!"

Judas nodded, too weak to argue with the man he now believed to be the Messiah promised to Israel by the prophets.

Later that morning, after they crossed the slopes of the Mount of Olives and started on the road to Ramah, John glanced at Jesus. “Will you tell me,” he asked, “What trick you used to bring Lazarus out of the tomb?” Then he scratched his head. “Or...was that really Lazarus?”

CHAPTER THIRTY-SEVEN
(Sunday)

"Do not be afraid, Daughter Zion; see, your king is coming, seated on a donkey's colt."

John 12:15

Jesus and John returned to Jerusalem from Ephraim the week before the Passover celebration. They went directly to the camp located on the Mount of Olives where Simon-Peter and Andrew set twelve large tents, anticipating a sizable influx of pilgrims from Galilee. Jesus reported that he had no better luck with the Jews in Ephraim than he had with those in Perea. Although he didn't realize it until later, Simon-Peter saw a change in Jesus demeanor. Jesus seemed less positive about his mission, perhaps even less enthusiastic since his trips to Perea and Ephraim. Simon-Peter didn't worry, though, for he knew the return of James and Philip from the camp at Bethabara would lift Jesus' spirits. For his part, Simon-Peter counted the days until Naomi's arrival from Capernaum. It had been too long since he shared his bed with Naomi and he was feeling edgy. For him, the Passover celebration would have more than one meaning.

At dawn on the Sunday before Passover, a large crowd of people gathered near the Water Gate waiting for the guards to let them in the city. Jesus, John and Judas were waiting next to a donkey near the middle the crowd when a group of young Israeli Jews noticed Jesus blue bordered robe. "Rabbi, tell us a story while we wait," a young woman asked.

"What kind of story?" Jesus asked.

"Oh, tell us about Elijah or Moses," she replied.

Jesus thought for a moment, then looked in the woman's eyes. "I think I know what they would say today," he said, glancing at the others. "Do you know the Law?"

They nodded.

"Then there's no need to talk about that," Jesus smiled. "The priests will remind you of the Law during the week." He touched his chin. "Listen, what would you say if I told you I'm here to announce the Kingdom of God?"

Judas and John, remembering the reaction to that question from the people in Galilee, left Jesus alone with the donkey and melted into the crowd.

"God's Kingdom is *here--now*--in us!" Jesus continued as he gestured for a boy to stand next to him. "Blessed are you who are poor--nothing stands between you and the Kingdom. Blessed are you who hunger for the Word of God--you will be satisfied. Blessed are you who weep--for you will also laugh."

Putting his hand on the boy's shoulder, he continued, "And bless all of you when men hate you. Bless you when they push you away and call you evil because you believe in the Kingdom of God."

Then waving to the people, Jesus said, "Rejoice and leap for joy, for your father in heaven has already called you." The donkey licked his hand as some of the people drifted away, but he spotted some people carrying kinnors and flutes and called them to the front of the crowd. Holding one of the musicians by the sleeve he hollered, "Sing! Sing! Praise Yahweh!" Within minutes he was pumping his arms, leading the crowd in singing traditional songs. Even people from Babylon and Gaul joined the singing. The joyous mood spread from group to group and soon the valley resounded with a thousand voices singing praise to God.

A broad circle opened about a hundred yards from the gate, giving space for the musicians to play and the people to dance. Jesus gave the donkey's rope to Judas, who by now had returned to his side. Then Jesus danced in a small circle near the gate as more people came across the hillside, drawn by the music and dancing. Some joined the dancers while others sat on the ground and clapped their hands.

At first the crowd amused the guards at the gate, but they decided to send for reinforcements when the music grew louder and the dancing more frantic. Additional guards arrived just as the shofar announcing daybreak sounded from the temple causing people to surge toward the gate.

Jesus jumped on a makeshift platform and signaled for order when he felt the mob pushing the dancers and musicians against the gate. "Wait--wait," he shouted. "We can worship God right here. The Temple will wait for us. I tell you now...Love each other and everything else will come to you."

He stretched his arms and yelled, "Love! Love! Love!" The crowd instantly picked up his chant, "LOVE! LOVE! LOVE!"

Jesus sang out, almost lifting himself from the platform, "God is light--not darkness. God is joy--not sorrow." Those who understood Aramaic or

Hebrew cheered raucously. After they translated his words to Greek and Latin, the others cheered in turn. The cheers started as a chant among a few hundred people, then escalated until everyone stood clapping and cheering outside the gate. Their frenzy catching even those people who could not understand what Jesus said.

Jesus glanced at the guards as if to reassure them, then signaled for more music, leading people of all ages to dance and sing in a delirious celebration of life. Soon, young women took flowers from the crowd, put them in their hair, and rode toward the gate on the shoulders of young men.

The guards opened the gate, but the crowd stayed outside the wall until a party of women carrying palm leaves entered the city. Behind them, several men threw flowers on the ground and the musicians entered the city with a blast of trumpets and drums.

The guards stared in amazement. It was as if someone organized hundreds of people to pass through the gates in perfect order--no urgency, no jostling. Several hundred people had passed through the gate by the time a group of Galileans found Jesus singing and dancing outside the wall. They took the donkey from Judas and hoisted Jesus on the animal and led him through the gate.

The people sang traditional Passover songs as the procession snaked from the gate to the temple. At the gate, women waved their palm leaves at Jesus while children danced around him and waved their shawls. Tears came to his eyes when he heard familiar songs of praise to Yahweh with new words.

"HOSANNA!" They screamed. Then, "HOSANNA!" again. He thought the force of their praise would shatter the walls. "HOSANNA!" His donkey shook with fear as the crowd drew closer. He raised his arms and shouted back, "Praise Yahweh, the Creator God--Our Father! Praise!"

They responded, "HOSANNA! HOSANNA! HOSANNA!" as another group of young men and women danced around the donkey. One young woman caught Jesus eye as she danced in perfect time to the music, circling his donkey, always moving beyond his sight. He was struck by her brightly colored robe and royal purple shawl drawn over her head as if she were praying while she was dancing.

Startled by the tumult, Pontius Pilate watched the procession from a window in the tower of the Antonia Fortress. He had arrived from Herod's Palace only moments before Jesus rode through the gate, and saw the thick plume of dust raised by the crowd. He slapped his riding crop on his thigh and said something to a man standing next to him. The man disappeared as Pilate continued to watch the procession twisting from the gate to the Temple.

The procession continued to the south wall of the temple where more than a hundred priests waited to bless the men and women before they entered the temple grounds. Inside the Hulda Gates, merchants lingered at their stalls, waiting to exchange foreign money and sell animals.

When Jesus dismounted, the young woman wearing the brightly colored robe and royal purple shawl took his hand. She pulled him toward herself and started to whisper in his ear, but the crowd pushed them apart. Jesus noticed as she backed away that she was an exceptionally beautiful young woman...and she was blind. Turning quickly to Judas, he asked, "Did you see that woman who helped me off the donkey?"

Judas shook his head. "No, why?"

Shrugging Jesus replied, "I feel I met her before, but I can't remember where."

Jesus gave the donkey's rope to Judas, who by now was pulling at his sleeve as he walked toward the ritual baths. With tears running from his eyes, Judas said, "You see? The people will follow you. Why do you deny your destiny?"

John added, "This will show the priests and scribes who God favors in Israel. Call out to them--now--they will listen to you! Only you know how to free Israel."

Jesus tried to reply but the crowd swept him toward the temple. Judas shook his head and quickly pulled the donkey away and started toward Mary Marcia's house. His heart pounded when he heard the sounds of singing and praying all the way to the Upper City.

A hundred armed men on horseback and another hundred, armed with spears and thick leather shields, waited for Pilate's signal in the courtyard of the Antonia Fortress. Tribune Manius Decius returned to the tower and told Pontius Pilate they were ready to charge the crowd on his order. Pilate slapped his crop and watched the crowd twisting through the narrow streets of the Lower City. Shafts of dust rising from beyond the gate warned him that thousands more waited to enter the city. Finally he shook his head and put his hand on the tribune's shoulder. "Not yet," he muttered, "not yet."

* * *

When Judas arrived at Mary Marcia's house, he gave the donkey to Mark and arranged with Mary to use her upper room for a special meal on Thursday. Per Jesus' instructions, he told Mary there would be about twenty guests including Jesus at the supper.

Judas started to tell Mark and Mary about the events at the Water Gate when Mark interrupted him. "Can I go back to the camp with you?" he asked.

"I'm not going back until tonight," Judas replied.

"Can I go when you do go back?"

"I'm not sure when I'm going." Judas glanced at Mark. "Why don't you wait until tomorrow? There won't be as much chaos as today." Then he patted his short beard and grinned. "I think this will be an exciting week," he said as he left their courtyard.

* * *

Later, Jesus' other disciples reached the temple. By that time, Andrew, Simon-Peter, and Mary of Magdala realized they had little chance of finding Jesus or John in the crowd that had now swelled to forty thousand people milling around the temple courts. Once Simon-Peter saw Jesus at a distance and started toward him, but he slipped on some wet tiles and barely avoided a trampling by the mob. Later, people who saw and heard Jesus told his disciples that they were more excited about Passover than ever before. "Truly," one man said, "that man is one called by God. Maybe he *is* God's Anointed One--the Messiah."

* * *

Pontius Pilate dictated messages to his personal aide, Adrien, for Annas, Caiaphas, and Herod Antipas. Then he left the Fortress and returned to Herod's Palace to eat his mid day meal with his wife, Claudia Procla.

* * *

Judas stopped at two houses in the Upper City after he left Mary Marcia's house. First, he left a message from Jesus at Joseph of Arimathea's house. Second, he approached the house of Caiaphas, the Chief Priest of the temple, but backed away when he spotted a group of soldiers standing next to the gate. He turned before anyone noticed and headed back to the Temple. As he walked through the streets of the Upper City, he recalled that there were times when his heart and head were filled with joy over Jesus.

CHAPTER THIRTY-EIGHT
(Monday)

And as he taught them, he said, "Is it not written: 'My house will be called a house of prayer for all nations?' But you have made it a den of robbers."

Mark 11:17

Adrien noticed that Pontius Pilate seemed unnerved during the week before he went to Jerusalem. He assumed Pilate's condition was caused by the last message Pilate received from the Prefect of the Praetorian Guard. Tiberius Caesar had not specified the length of Pilate's tenure, leaving him with a free hand to remove Pilate in the event he failed to fulfill his expectations as Procurator of Judea and Samaria. Pilate knew that if he governed well, his term of office might extend as long as ten years. Now, after six years, he saw his position threatened through the actions of peasant mobs and the inactions of the Jewish leaders.

Early Monday morning, at his administrative headquarters, Pilate slapped his riding crop on his thigh as he circled Annas, Caiaphas, and Herod Antipas. He looked at each man and grunted, then fixed his gaze on Annas. "Tell me again why you refused to heed my summons yesterday?"

Annas coughed politely. "It's not my place to accept your summons." Gesturing to Caiaphas, he added, "He's the Chief Priest."

Adrien noticed veins protruding from Pilate's forehead as he turned to Caiaphas. Putting his face as close to Caiaphas as he could without kissing him, Pilate asked, "Alright Lord Chief Priest--you tell me why you allowed Herod Antipas, my tribune, and me to wait for you in vain without as much as a message?"

Caiaphas shifted in his chair to avoid Pilate's glare. "To be honest, Procurator, it took time for the message to reach us, and..."

"And?"

Caiaphas fingered his breastplate. "We were needed at the Temple. Everything was in chaos."

Pilate turned away for a moment. "In other words, things were normal." Then he faced Caiaphas. "Go to the window and look at the mobs around the Temple," he ordered. "We could have a riot at any time."

Caiaphas remained seated.

Pilate almost slapped himself on the forehead with his crop. "What keeps you in that chair? Get over there!"

Caiaphas fidgeted, not accustomed to being treated like a household servant. "I can't," he mumbled. "Our Law forbids us to enter the inner chambers of a Gentile house." He wiped his forehead. "People would stone me if they saw me looking down at them from the Fortress." Annas nodded his agreement.

Pilate's voice softened. "Alright, who was the man who led the procession through the Water Gate yesterday?" he asked.

Caiaphas shrugged.

"You don't know," Pilate interjected. "I can tell you this; my guards saw people waving palm branches when that man came through the gate. I'm sure you know the symbolism of that demonstration."

Still no answer from Caiaphas.

Pilate looked at Herod Antipas. "What were those people doing?"

Herod twisted a large gold ring on his finger and looked at Pilate. "The palm branches are a symbol of Jewish independence, the..."

Pilate spun and faced the high priests. "See! Thousands of people marching to the Temple..."

"Maybe twenty thousand," Herod interrupted. "Only twenty thousand, Procurator."

Pilate slammed his riding crop on the table and released a sigh.

Annas grunted, "What do you want from us?"

"Identify the troublemakers and either imprison them or drive them out of the city," Pilate replied. "That's what we agreed upon during our meetings in Caesarea. You are responsible for policing your people."

"How can we identify these people?" Annas queried.

Pilate smiled. "For the sake of Jupiter, I'm not blind--you have spies everywhere."

Caiaphas looked at Herod. "My people think this man came through the Water Gate with a group of Galileans."

Avoiding Pilate's glance, Herod replied, "We have bandits, rebels, and terrorists operating in Galilee and Perea. Of course, they also travel freely between my provinces and Judea."

"Not to mention Samaria," Pilate added.

"Yes, I..."

Pilate ignored Herod and continued, "A few weeks ago, our patrols from Jericho fought a band of rebels along the Jordan River and later in the Judean Hills. They fought a battle near Ramah and killed more than twenty rebels--a fairly large group." He flicked his crop in his hand and added, "The patrol brought four captives to Jerusalem."

Herod smirked, "Did you give them the usual treatment?"

Pilate nodded. "We tortured them to see if we missed anyone, and then gave them forty lashes with the flagra." He looked at Caiaphas. "We crucified them the next day."

"They lived for a few days, hanging on their crosses." Pilate said as he looked out the window at the crowds milling in the Temple area. "By now the vultures have eaten the flesh off their bones. There's nothing left but a few grinning skeletons."

"Actually, we took the bodies down," stated Adrien.

"Are the posts still in the ground?" Pilate asked.

"Firmly, sire."

Pilate looked away. "Good, we're ready." He looked at the priests. "Do you remember what I said last time we met?"

"You mean, about the Temple?"

"Yes. I'll close the Temple to everyone including you and your priests. Do you understand?"

Caiaphas started out of his chair, but Annas stopped him. "You make things difficult for us," he said.

Pilate waved his arm. "There'll be no problems if you control the troublemakers as you promised you would. I'll take care of the rest." He gestured to Adrien. "Show the priests out." Pilate reached for Caiaphas' sleeve as he passed by, "It's in both our interests to catch the man who led the rabble through the gate yesterday."

The High Priest nodded and followed Annas out the door.

* * *

Near mid-day, Jesus and John went to the Temple, situating themselves at the foot of the broad stairway leading to the ritual baths and Hulda Gate. They remained there for several hours, teaching and healing the waiting pilgrims in full view of the priests near the Hulda Gate. Jesus prayed with people who were blind, lame, sick with lung disease, and feeble of mind. Several people left them claiming that Jesus had cured their illness.

Later, Jesus and John went to the area directly underneath the Royal Stoa. The area was already filled with noisy crowds of people exchanging their foreign money for Jewish coins at the money booths on one side of a wide aisle, while others queued up to booths stocked with sacrificial animals and birds on the other side.

When Jesus heard an exchange between a poorly dressed man and a coin dealer, he grabbed John by his sleeve. "That merchant only returned half the man's value in coins," Jesus whispered.

John shrugged as if to say that that's the way things work.

Jesus and John sauntered past several booths, listening as people bargained in strange tongues with the merchants. When they circled back to the money changing area, Jesus caught sight of an old woman exchanging her coins. The merchant showed the coins to his partner when she left and they both laughed. Jesus stopped the woman and took her back to the coin dealer.

When the dealer saw Jesus approaching his booth, he said, "You're out of place. Go to the back of the line."

Jesus put his hands flat on the counter and looked at the man. "I'm here because you cheated this woman out of what little money she has."

The coin dealer looked at the woman, then at Jesus. "Is she your wife?" he asked with a leer.

"No."

"Ah, then she's your mother?"

"No."

"Your aunt?" he asked acidly.

"Wrong again."

"Then why are you concerned with this woman?"

"You cheated her and I want you to give her money back." Jesus replied, waving toward the other booths. "You're all thieves, using the House of God to line your purses."

The man looked at him in amazement and laughed loudly. He pulled his partner's sleeve and said, "Did you hear what he said? He accused us of cheating."

Jesus gave the merchant an angry stare. "When you're done laughing, give her..."

The merchant gave Jesus a rude shove. "Get out of here!" he shouted. He pointed behind Jesus. "These good people want to exchange their money and you're in the way."

Jesus stood firm.

The man's partner came over and shoved Jesus as well. "Are you deaf?" he shouted. "Get out of here before I call the Temple guards!" He pushed Jesus against a pillar and made a threatening move toward the woman.

Jesus pulled the man away. The merchant turned and, in one motion, swung at Jesus at the same time his partner jumped on Jesus' back.

John snatched a staff from an old man and clubbed the merchant hanging on Jesus' back. The man fell to the ground screaming. Hearing the melee, the other merchants came to help their associates.

The pilgrims waiting to buy sacrificial offerings cleared a large area to give the men enough space to fight. They watched, sometimes hurling insulting comments, until Jesus and a merchant fell against a coin booth and tipped it over. When bags of money hurled to the floor and burst, the people gaped for a moment, then started a tumult as people dropped to their knees and fought over the money.

The fracas extended to the booths selling doves, pigeons, and sheep. Throngs of men pushed the merchants aside, broke the cages, and freed the animals and birds. The market area suddenly became a bedlam of flying birds, squealing animals, screaming merchants, and men and women brawling with the merchants and each other.

Once they freed the animals, the people knocked the booths over and threw the broken pieces across the shop area. Jesus, mortified by the riot, shouted, "This place is a house of prayer!" He raised his fists in the air. "You've turned it into a den of thieves!"

The people looked at him for a moment, shrugged and continued to pillage the booths. Before long, the crowd thinned as people snatched animals and birds and ran toward the Temple to make their sacrificial offerings.

John caught Jesus' sleeve and pulled him away from the melee. "Let's get out of here before the guards come," he shouted.

Jesus hesitated for a moment, then followed John down the stairs and out the Hulda Gate. Running for their lives, they ascended the steps next to the western wall of the Temple and crossed the arch running from the Temple to the Upper City. When they reached the Upper City, John stopped for a moment to catch his breath and looked at Jesus. "That was a big mistake," he snapped.

"What? Trying to get the lady's money back?"

"If you say so," John replied sharply. "I meant the riot you started. The Temple guards will surely search for you."

Jesus smiled. "John, you worry too much. The Temple guards never saw me. They don't know me from Moses."

"There were witnesses. Someone must know who you are."

Jesus snapped his fingers. "I have an idea. Let's go to Mark's house, I need to arrange our Passover celebration with Mary Marcia."

* * *

Simon-Peter chewed into a snack made with bread, slivers of lamb, and lettuce. Bits of food sprayed from his mouth as he announced, "I bring you word from Jesus of Nazareth. He's here to announce the good news to the poor, freedom for prisoners, and a recovery of sight for the blind." Simon-Peter had no idea of what he was saying or how the words came into his head.

The line of pilgrims moved slowly from the Water Gate to the Temple past the place where Simon-Peter stood, so they had no choice but to listen before they moved on. Other preachers competed for their attention, giving people a choice of preachers and beggars on the road to the Temple.

Simon-Peter shouted to a group dressed in the style of the Galileans and waved them to his spot. Young James and Mary of Magdala poured cups of water while Simon-Peter pointed to the Temple. "Do you see that building? The day will come when not one stone will remain on another. Jesus of Nazareth will build a new Temple to serve the common man instead of the priests." Again he had little understanding of his ideas as he looked into their eyes. "Watch out!" he yelled. "The priests and scribes deceive you! Yes, and watch for those who claim they're sent from God. Only one man comes from God--Jesus of Nazareth!"

Simon-Peter paused, sipped from a cup of wine, then continued, "Hear this, the Messiah is here in Jerusalem."

A swarthy man in the middle of the crowd shouted, "Fish bait! You don't know about Messiahs. I saw you at the inn drinking wine." The man's eyes darted around the crowd as he roared, "It's wine talking, not the Messiah."

"I saw Jesus cure lepers," Simon-Peter shouted back. "I saw fish come out of the sea when he called." He wiped his mouth with his sleeve. "I even saw him walk on water!"

The swarthy man laughed. "You poor sot. What do you know of gods and Messiahs?"

"You fool," Simon-Peter retorted. "The end of the world is at hand and Jesus of Nazareth will lead the angels to collect his people from the four winds."

"Ha-ha-ha, the only wind I see is the hot air coming out of your mouth." The man waved his hand. "Go back to Galilee where everyone is as stupid as you."

Simon-Peter looked at the people. "Aren't you Galileans?"

"We came here from Greece," the man answered. "We dressed this way because the wagon carrying our clothes fell into a ravine." He rubbed his fingers on his robe. "We bought these at a cheap market north of here."

Simon-Peter looked at the people and shook his head. "But you understand Aramaic."

The man laughed harder. "Wrong again, sot. I know Aramaic because I travel to Israel." He gestured to the people. "These people only know Greek."

With clenched fists, Simon-Peter started toward the man, but stopped when he felt a hand on his shoulder. He turned, fists still raised, to see Judas standing behind him. Judas beckoned him aside and stepped on the crude platform.

"What this man says is true," Judas said to the crowd in Greek. "I saw Jesus' miracles. I believe he is the Messiah!" Judas motioned to the swarthy man. "Come closer."

The man hesitated before coming to Judas.

Judas touched his lip with his finger and asked, "What is our prayer at Seder?"

The man gave him a perplexed look. "We do several prayers. What's your point?"

Judas touched the man's robe. "We raise our cup and say, `next year in Jerusalem.' Do you know what that means?"

The man nodded.

"Well, my friend, there is no next year in Jerusalem as long as the Romans occupy Israel. We may as well be in Egypt with Moses." He pointed to the guards watching the gates. "Everywhere you look, the Romans shove slavery down our throats. Taxes, laws, soldiers, and worse of all, Pagan practices."

"The same is true in Greece," the man replied.

"Jerusalem is not Athens," Judas replied acidly. "Jerusalem is the City of God and we are his chosen people. What's more, Jesus of Nazareth is God's Anointed One. He will lead us to freedom. He'll return Jerusalem to its rightful God."

"That's all very good. Where is this man?"

Judas looked at Simon-Peter and asked him the same question in Aramaic. Simon-Peter shrugged and pointed to the Temple. "Maybe at the Temple," Judas said to the man. The man gave him a funny look and walked away.

Simon-Peter and Judas preached from that place for several hours, with Simon-Peter preaching in Aramaic and Judas preaching in Greek or Hebrew. They finally quit in mid afternoon because of the dwindling crowds and mid-afternoon heat.

Judas patted Simon-Peter's back as they walked back to the camp on the Olive Mount. "Simon-Peter, I have new respect for you," he said. "I watched the people when you talked and they believed what you said."

Simon-Peter lifted his shoulders and lengthened his stride but remained silent. Later he told Judas, "Thank you for helping me. I was making a spectacle of myself until you came."

"I believe in Jesus," Judas replied. "He's inspired all of us to do things we never thought we could do." Judas stopped, held Simon-Peter's sleeve, and asserted, "I believe in Jesus so much I'm willing to die for him."

That night, Simon-Peter told John about what he and Judas had done. Simon-Peter said that regardless of what Judas said, he did not understand the business of kingdoms and messiahs.

* * *

Toward sundown, Andrew walked past the priests watching the Nicanor Gates and entered the Court of the Israelites. He spotted a group of Essenes milling in the crowd and greeted them.

A man named Joel asked, "Where have you been? We miss you at Qumran."

Andrew replied, "For the last two years, I've been traveling with a man named Jesus of Nazareth. I became his follower after I left the monastery."

Joel threaded his fingers through his beard. "That was three years ago."

"I visited Qumran a few months ago, but you weren't there," Andrew countered.

"I travel often," Joel muttered. "They keep sending me to help our communities in Syria and Greece." He put his hand on Andrew's arm. "Tell me about this Jesus of Nazareth."

"Do you remember John the Baptizer?" Andrew asked.

Joel thought for a moment. "I think so. Was he the one killed by Herod Antipas?"

"Yes," Andrew replied. "As you know, John would baptize along the Jordan River. I happened to be there the day he baptized Jesus." Andrew looked into Joel's eyes. "After talking with Jesus that night, I realized he was no ordinary man."

"What do you mean?" Joel asked as the other Essenes drew nearer.

"Jesus is either a prophet or a messiah," Andrew replied.

Joel shook his head. "A prophet I can believe, but a messiah I have to see." He looked at a man sitting next to him who nodded in agreement.

Andrew looked away. "He could also be possessed."

"Why do you say that?"

"He says things that make people so angry they drive him out of their homes and synagogues."

Eyebrows raised, Joel asked, "Did you say synagogues?"

"Yes."

"He worships in synagogues?" Joel's eyes darted among the Essenes.

"Yes."

"Then this man is not the Messiah." Joel pointed to the floor. "The Messiah will appear here--in this Temple. That, of course depends on which Messiah we talk about." He gestured toward the Holy of Holys. "The Messiah of Aaron will appear here and cleanse the Temple before he redeems our people. I don't know where the Messiah of Israel will appear. I only know he will lead us out of bondage--by military force if necessary."

"Are you sure about what you say?" Andrew asked.

Joel stiffened and answered, "The Teacher of Righteousness wrote the scrolls describing the Age of Tribulation. You know the Teacher of Righteousness is second only to Moses as a prophet." Joel slapped his hands together. "Maybe you have a prophet on your hands. The Messiah will never defile himself by congregating in a synagogue with Pharisees."

"That's what you say," Andrew retorted.

"That is what we teach at Qumran. We teach that the Pharisees and Sadducees have defiled our Temple and our faith. God will curse them for seven generations." Joel came face to face with Andrew. "The Temple has not been properly cleansed since the time of the Maccabees."

"Perhaps not," Andrew replied. Looking at the Essenes, he added, "Perhaps the Messiah will look at us and judge us unworthy. Then what?"

"Impossible," Joel snorted.

Smiling, Andrew said, "I would think that the Messiah will deal very well in the realm of the impossible." With that, Andrew bade a courteous farewell to Joel and the other Essenes. Covering his head with his shawl, he retired to a quiet place to meditate on whether Jesus could be the Messiah. As he prayed, he wondered how an obscure Galilean could presume to lead the Jewish nation out of its bondage to the Romans and to its past. Perhaps *that* is in the realm of the impossible, he thought.

* * *

As Andrew left the Temple at dusk, he drew his wool cloak close to his body and glanced at the campfires already visible on the hills overlooking the city. Soon, the entire countryside would come alive with fire and shadow as the pilgrims cooked their meals and exchanged stories. The sight of the hillside fires and the people crowding the Lower City filled Andrew with joy. To him, the presence of so many human beings confirmed the reality of God in his life.

On the way to the city gate, Andrew passed several gaily decorated merchant's stalls that reflected the realities of commercial life. The broad smiles on the merchant's faces reminded Andrew that the Passover celebration was an event of great monetary importance to the city of Jerusalem. Thus, the merchants routinely bribed the guards to keep the gates open later than usual so the pilgrims would have more time to sample their wares.

CHAPTER THIRTY-NINE

(Tuesday)

"Among my people are the wicked who lie in wait like those who snare birds and like those who set traps to catch people. Like cages full of birds, their houses are full of deceit; they have become rich and powerful and have grown fat and sleek. Their evil deeds have no limit; they do not seek justice. They do not promote the cause of the fatherless; they do not defend the just cause of the poor."

Jeremiah 5:26-28

Jesus and John accepted Mary Marcia's invitation to stay at her house instead of the Mount of Olives on Monday night. John, fearing that someone from the Temple might recognize them in the streets, said a silent prayer of thanks when Jesus accepted. They lingered long enough the next morning to eat their morning meal with Mark and Mary Marcia after the other guests had left the house.

Mark and Mary Marcia listened with wonder when John told them the details about the Sunday procession into the city and the Monday riot at the Temple. Frowning at Jesus, John warned, "I saw Roman soldiers looking at us from the Fortress on Sunday. And yesterday at the Temple..." He shook a finger at Jesus. "Do you realize they might have stoned us for what you did?"

"I don't see why," Jesus replied. "I wasn't the one who cheated the people."

"That's not the point," John retorted. "The authorities punish people who start riots in the Temple."

Jesus grinned at John. "Do you know that for sure?"

Mary slammed her cup on the table. "Stop it!" She shouted, looking at John, then Jesus, and finally Mark. "All you men think of is working and fighting." Her eyes narrowed to slits as she added, "One of these days..."

"I know--I know," Jesus said. "One of these days one of us will get hurt."

"Hurt!" she snapped. "Who cares about hurt? They might kill you." When Jesus saw the fire in her eyes, he touched her arm, but she pulled away. "I take back what I said to you about Mary of Bethany," she said. "You have no right to make her suffer."

John's eyes widened. "What Mary of Bethany?"

"Mary the sister of Lazarus," Mary Marcia replied.

John looked at Jesus. "You never said anything about her." "I don't tell you everything," Jesus replied, smiling. "Besides, it's time you opened your eyes and noticed things."

Playfully, John demanded, "Tell me more."

Jesus blushed, "I can tell you're jumping to a judgment. Mary of Bethany is a friend, like Mary Marcia and Mary of Magdala."

Mary Marcia raised her finger. "You can't fool me with your talk about friends." Casting a warning glance at Jesus, she continued, "That's not my point. I think you take too many risks."

Sensing an ally, John said, "I've been trying to tell him that all along. For one thing, he picks the wrong friends."

"Like who?" Mark asked.

"Judas for one," John quickly replied.

Mary Marcia smiled. "Judas?" She looked at Jesus and whispered, "I think he's cute. Don't you think he'd make a nice husband for Rebecca?"

John stood and stretched. "Isn't it time to go somewhere?"

"Are you returning to the camp today?" Mark asked.

"I will after I meet with Joseph and Nicodemus," Jesus answered. He looked at Mary Marcia and added, "Maybe I'll visit Bethany later on."

"Can I go to the camp with you?" Mark continued.

Jesus rolled a pomegranate in his hand. "Of course. You can camp with us as long as you wish."

Jesus said to John, "I asked Mary Marcia last night if she would prepare a special Seder meal on Thursday for our friends. She agreed to do that. I promised her that you and Mark would help prepare the upper room for our feast."

"What about the people at the camp?" John asked.

Jesus replied, "There will be a celebration at the camp as well." After breakfast, Jesus went to a quiet corner in the courtyard, pulled his shawl over his head, and prayed.

* * *

Manius Decius crouched as he crept through the secret passage connecting the Antonia Fortress with the Temple. He felt uncomfortable and vulnerable, dressed in a robe common to the city. After a few moments, he passed through the concealed entry and entered the colonnaded portico on the north side of the Temple Mount. Standing in the shadow of one of the massive white columns, he scanned the Courtyard of the Gentiles.

Eventually he spied a Temple guard and handed him a message. "Give this to the High Priest, Caiaphas," he instructed in his best Greek dialect. "Tell him I'll wait for his reply." The guard looked at Manius Decius suspiciously, then hurried to the gate leading to the Court of Women.

While he waited, Manius Decius thought about the contents of the note from Pontius Pilate to Caiaphas.

> *"We have a suspected rebel in our dungeon. Do you want to see him? What happened yesterday? Was there a riot in the Temple?"*

Manius Decius continued to stand in the shade behind the columns to slow the perspiration spreading beneath his woolen robe. He concluded that this day would be as warm as the previous days--not good weather for peace and quiet in Jerusalem.

Looking up, he saw Caiaphas running toward him across the Court of the Gentiles. He grinned at the priest's skinny legs pumping beneath his uplifted robe. Caiaphas slowed to a walk and waved when he spied Manius Decius. "What happened?" he asked breathlessly.

"What the note says, your people turned a man over to us this morning and told us he was the one who started the riot yesterday afternoon. Not only that, he fits your description of the man who led the people into the city on Sunday."

Eyes narrowed, Caiaphas replied, "I gave you no description."

"I don't know whose description it is," Manius Decius replied with a wave of his hand. "This man is a criminal, probably the one who caused the trouble in the Temple yesterday."

"What is his name?" Caiaphas asked.

Manius thought for a minute, and then answered, "Bar Abbas."

"Bar Abbas?" Caiaphas sneered. "Is that all? Bar Abbas?"

Manius Decius looked confused. "I have trouble with names. I don't know his first name." Manius Decius shook his head. "Give me time, I'll think of his name." Then he snapped his fingers and asked, "Meanwhile, can you tell me what happened yesterday, or would you rather talk to Pontius Pilate?"

"I don't have time to meet with Pilate. Besides, there's nothing to tell. Some criminals started a riot underneath the Royal Stoa. Probably thieves out to steal the merchant's money."

"Yes, well we have one of them in our dungeon and we'll get the names of the others from him," Manius said, rubbing his chin. "We do have a small problem, however. He claims he wasn't near the Temple yesterday. Would you know him if you saw him?"

"I didn't see him yesterday," Caiaphas replied impatiently. "Nor did I see the man who led the crowds on Sunday. Is this the man *you* saw on Sunday?"

"We didn't see his face from the Fortress. The Lower City is a long way from the tower, and the dust and haze blocked our view." Manius looked past Caiaphas' shoulder. "At least the Temple grounds are quiet today."

"We won't have a repeat of yesterday's problems. I assigned extra guards to the Temple as well as the Royal Stoa. This time we'll stop trouble before it starts." Caiaphas fingered his breastplate. "Also, I sent guards to inspect the camps outside the city. One of the money changers swears he'll recognize the men who started the riot if he sees them."

"In that case, he can take a look at our prisoner."

"Good idea, will you bring the prisoner to your courtyard?"

Manius Decius nodded. "Oh yes, you have your rules about--what do you call us?"

"Gentiles?"

"Yes, about going inside our buildings. Tell your man to ask for me. I'll send the prisoner to the courtyard."

Caiaphas gestured toward the Temple. "Please excuse me, I must return to my duties."

"Of course, I'm sorry I detained you." They separated until Manius slapped his hands and ran toward Caiaphas. "Wait--I remember his name. It's Joshua bar Abbas."

Caiaphas frowned when he heard the name, but gave no other sign of recognition.

* * *

On Monday, Judas had left a message for Jesus at Mary Marcia's house telling him that Joseph of Arimathea and Nicodemus would meet him at the house of Nicodemus at mid-day. When Jesus arrived, Nicodemus ushered him into his courtyard. Before closing the gate, he carefully looked at the street in both directions. Then he took Jesus' arm and led him to a quiet corner of the courtyard where Joseph waited.

Nicodemus offered Jesus a cup of white wine which he declined. Instead, Jesus looked at Joseph and Nicodemus and said, "You look worried. Is something wrong?"

"Did you lead that procession through the Water Gate on Sunday morning?" Joseph asked curtly.

Jesus shrugged. “I went to the Temple on Sunday along with twenty thousand other people.”

“What about the riot in the Temple yesterday?” Nicodemus asked.

Jesus’ eyebrows rose. “I was there too.”

“Did you cause it?” Joseph continued.

“No, one of the merchants started it. He cheated a woman and, when I caught him, he started a fight. Before long, the whole place was in an uproar.”

Joseph and Nicodemus exchanged glances. Nicodemus pointed in the direction of the Temple. “The place is still in an uproar. Caiaphas called an emergency meeting of the Sanhedrin to bring matters under control.”

Jesus gestured toward the wine decanter. “Maybe I will have some wine.”

Joseph stared at Jesus while Nicodemus poured a cup of wine. “They’re looking for you,” he said. “Caiaphas sent the money changers along with several Temple guards to the Mount of Olives to find you.”

Jesus smiled. “There are too many people out there. How can they expect to find one man in that crowd?”

“They guessed you’re from the north,” Joseph replied. “Galilee, Samaria, or Decapolis. They also know the leader is a rabbi about your age.” Joseph stood with a groan and added, “This is not a matter for humor. We have serious problems at the Temple and with the Roman Procurator.”

Jesus ran his finger around the rim of his cup. “They’re looking in the wrong place. We stayed in Jerusalem last night.”

“That may be, but they believe you’re a rebel or a thief.” Joseph took a deep breath and sipped from his cup. “What are you trying to prove?”

Jesus shifted on his bench. “I was the one in the Temple,” he replied. “And to tell you the truth, I wanted to drive the thieves out of there. What kind of people are we to use a sacred observance to cheat poor people?”

“I don’t think it’s quite that bad,” Nicodemus declared.

Eyes flashing, Jesus replied, “It’s worse. Our leaders treat people like animals. They forget that God created us to experience joy as well as pain.” Jesus looked around the courtyard. “When people live in places like this, they lose their feeling for the pain an average person feels.”

“What do you want us to do? Give everything we have to those people so we can live like them?” Nicodemus asked indignantly.

Jesus shook his head. “I thought you understood more than the High Priests.”

Joseph interjected, “Don’t you know that if we gave our money to the poor it would return to us within a month? Nothing would change.”

“That’s not my point,” Jesus replied.

“What is your point?” Nicodemus asked.

"There are hungry people and others too sick to care for themselves. Landowners who pay workers as little as possible for their labor and after that, a tax collector takes all the money he can." Jesus paced around the benches. "Then people come here for a feast and the Temple demands a tax, and finally the merchants steal what little money they have left."

Joseph stroked his beard. "Assuming what you say is true, what can we do?"

As he replied, Jesus looked past the men as if he were looking into eternity. "We need to liberate people from their suffering and their acceptance of that suffering," he said. "We can start by treating everyone like human beings--children of God. Look outside the walls of your city. The Romans hang people on crosses, and leave their bodies to the vultures after they rot. At the same time, our own people push the sick and the poor--people they think are less than human--outside the walls where they live in filth and poverty."

Joseph frowned at Jesus. "I'm not a Roman lover, but most of the people they hang are criminals."

"Criminals according to Roman justice," Jesus shot back. "Where is the code of dignity Moses brought from Sinai? Who listens to the words of Isaiah or Amos? Go to the fields in Galilee and work with the people. Live in their shacks and caves. Watch their children die because they can't pay a physician. See what happens to a family when a lawyer takes everything they have to pay a debt." The men cringed when it appeared that Jesus' anger was about to explode.

"Again--how do we solve the problem? How can we change the system?" Joseph persisted.

"One person at a time," Jesus replied. "You change one person, then that person influences others who are willing to change. Soon, the whole world has changed...one person at a time."

"That could take forever," Joseph mumbled.

"We have the time--we are already living in forever. I know you can't change all the people at once. Look at Moses or Samuel-- even David. They tried to change a nation, but things went back to the old ways after they died. My point is we have to start somewhere, and I need people like you to help."

Nicodemus looked at the sky. "I'm willing, but right now Joseph and I must return to the Temple. Can we talk about this after Passover?"

Jesus nodded.

"Stay quiet for now," Joseph pleaded. "We'll do what we can to pacify the Sanhedrin."

"What if the High Priests or the Romans ask you about what happened?" Jesus asked.

"They have no reason to suspect we know you. So far, they have no reason to suspect anything about us." Holding Jesus by the shoulders, Nicodemus warned, "For now, stay out of trouble."

"I'll be careful," Jesus replied.

Joseph called to Jesus before he reached the gate. "Before you go, I want to tell you I'm prepared to help you."

"Help me?"

"Yes. I'm willing to support you with money."

Nicodemus gasped and Jesus' eyes glazed when they heard Joseph's offer. "We will talk after Passover," Jesus answered. With that, he waved to the two men and exited the courtyard.

"Why did you do that?" Nicodemus asked Joseph after he was sure Jesus had left.

Joseph gave his friend a thoughtful look. "We depend on our political connections to cause change," he declared. "That's not enough. I realize now that Jesus has the ability to move people deeply." Joseph held Nicodemus' sleeve. "Didn't you see the intensity in Jesus' eyes when he talked to us? With some help, Jesus just might be capable of changing the way things are done."

"You sound as if you want to use him," Nicodemus said.

"Use is a harsh word," Joseph replied. "Let's say that Jesus could be a valuable partner."

* * *

Clouds riding a western breeze brought a promise of rain that would ease the untimely heat and settle the dust raised by the caravans of pilgrims coming to Jerusalem for the Passover observance. The guards at the walls and in the towers of the Antonia Fortress strained to watch the long lines of people snaking over the roads and paths of the Hinnom and Kidron Valleys. Despite their vigilance, there were times when an entire army could have crept to the walls of the city under the cover of dust and haze.

John and Andrew stationed themselves on a hill overlooking the Galilee Road to watch for Zebedee's caravan. John signaled to Andrew when he spotted Zebedee and Philip leading a procession of pilgrims from Galilee. John counted a few donkeys and wagons and at least fifty people from Galilee walking the narrow road.

Andrew and John shouted and waved at the small caravan as they slid down the hill to meet it. John scanned the column and spotted his brother, James walking with Jesus' brother, James bar Joseph. John hollered, "James bar Joseph! What a surprise."

"Why are you surprised? I always come to Jerusalem to celebrate Passover."

As he moved to greet his brother, John heard a gruff voice asking, "Are you going to greet your father as well?"

John hesitated for a moment, and then put his arm around his father. "You bless me with your presence," he said as he fell into stride with the group.

Zebedee looked at him from the corner of his eye and replied, "You should be amazed as well as blest. I don't know why I let Jesus and your brother James talk me into caring for these people." He touched James bar Joseph on the arm. "Better yet, I can't figure out how he convinced this fellow to help us."

John smiled. "Maybe now you understand why we followed Jesus to Jerusalem."

"I don't," Zebedee replied. "James and I came to celebrate the Passover. You and your brother came to forget how to work for a living." Before John could reply, Zebedee thrust a thumb over his shoulder and added, "Your mother's back there. She probably wants to see you."

The group split at the Fish Gate. James bar Joseph and Zebedee led a group into the city while John and Andrew led the rest to the Mount of Olives. Mary, the mother of Jesus, declined an offer from her cousin Salome to stay with her and Zebedee in the city. She chose instead to live with the people from Nazareth, the ones who camped on the hill outside the city.

* * *

The last rays of the sun cast reflections off the tents covering the hills behind the Hinnom Valley when Jesus reached the camp on the Mount of Olives. He saw his mother standing next to the fire to fend off the early evening chill and ran to greet her. They embraced, looked into each other's eyes, and embraced again. "Look," she said as she swept her hands across the camp, "we brought all these people."

Jesus quickly counted the tents. "There must be twenty tents. This is truly a week for celebration."

She took his hand and they walked to where Naomi and Leah were cooking the evening meal. She looked in his eyes and said, "I have a surprise for you."

Feigning concern, he asked "What kind of surprise?"

"Your brother James came with us."

"James? Here?"

"Not in the camp. He's staying with friends in the city."

"But he came with you?"

"Yes."

Jesus looked up and smiled. “Praise our Lord.”

Later, after finishing his evening meal, Jesus circulated through the camp and greeted the people who arrived from Galilee earlier that day. Afterwards, he met with his chosen leaders to discuss plans for their Passover celebration. Mark came to the camp in time for the evening meal and listened as Jesus talked to his people. He thought that Jesus seemed more preoccupied than usual. Later, much later, Mark realized Jesus was preparing his people for something more than a Passover celebration.

CHAPTER FORTY
Wednesday

Love the LORD your God with all your heart and with all your soul and with all your strength.

Deuteronomy 6:5

Do not seek revenge or bear a grudge against anyone among your people, but love your neighbor as yourself. I am the LORD.

Leviticus 19:18

Dawn on Wednesday brought dense clouds that hid the sun and left a continuing chill to cool Jerusalem and the city of tents outside its walls for a few more hours. James bar Zebedee had arranged a meeting at mid-day between Jesus and his father to be held at an inn in the Lower City. As Jesus and John left the camp on the Mount of Olives, Jesus' people gathered around the embers from the night fire to exchange gossip and prepare for the day.

Jesus and John came to the south wall of the Temple, entered through the triple Hulda Gate, and hurried up the stairs leading to the Temple platform. They pulled their prayer shawls over their heads when they reached the place where money was exchanged and animals sold to avoid recognition, then rushed past the money changing booths to a vendor at the far end of the market. There they bought two birds, then followed the crowd across the Court of the Gentiles to the Beautiful Gate.

Guards stationed at the gate carefully looked at each person as they passed into the Court of the Women. Neither Jesus nor John spoke, preferring instead to keep their heads low and stand with those waiting to present their sacrifice. As they shuffled toward the Court of the Priests, Jesus and John heard the scribes and lawyers talking with each other and lecturing the worshippers. They were using their own fidelity to God as an example of how people should live. Jesus poked John and said, "I have an urge to say something to those hypocrites. They..."

"Don't say a word," John interrupted. "Remember, I agreed to come with you because you promised not to start any arguments."

"You're right. We'll make our offering and meet your brother James and your father. Zebedee will present me with all the arguments I need."

When they reached the altar, a priest pointed to John. "Who are you and what is your offering?" he asked.

John gave the priest the small basket holding his bird and replied, "John bar Zebedee--Capernaum."

The priest took the bird and gestured for John to move on. Jesus handed him his basket and said, "Jesus bar Joseph--Nazareth."

The priest grunted and handed the baskets to another man. "These birds are from Galileans. Check for lice."

John moved as if he wanted to respond in kind, but Jesus cautioned, "Remember, we don't want any trouble here."

John frowned. "Right."

"Good, let's finish our meditation and meet Zebedee and James."

* * *

By mid-day the sun burned through the haze settled over the city leaving only a light chill when the clouds passed overhead. The marketplace, however, supplied its own heat because of the throngs of people and animals swarming through the stalls and narrow streets. Jesus carried his robe loosely on his arm until a young girl swept past him and grabbed it away. He snatched it back before she escaped, but John noticed a more cautious look in Jesus' eyes after the incident.

They found Zebedee and James sitting on boulders near a seedy looking inn and sat next to them. James quickly offered a share of his meal of apricots, dates and lettuce inside two pieces of flat bread but Jesus declined.

Later, James found two benches near a small cluster of trees and gestured for the others to join him. The men shared fruit, a few pieces of bread, and a skin of wine near the street where Simon-Peter and Judas had preached two days earlier.

Wiping crumbs from his beard, Zebedee pointed to John and said, "I thought you would've come home for good by now."

"Not yet," Jesus interjected. "We need him at our camps."

"I've been very patient waiting for you to come to your senses," Zebedee said to Jesus as he reached for the wineskin. "But soon it'll be spring and I need my fishermen." His face reddened slightly. "Yes, I've been very patient."

"Simon-Peter and James came back to help," John exclaimed.

Zebedee shook his head. “They came back too late and didn’t stay long enough.” He looked at Jesus. “I don’t know what you’re trying to do. In fact, I don’t know why I agreed to meet with you.”

“Mother,” John said with a grin.

Zebedee gave him a scornful look. “I make my own decisions. Your mother’s like you, no judgment. Why, if she had her way, this preacher would be living in our house.” Looking to Jesus, Zebedee growled, “Look, I’m a busy man. James said you wanted to meet with me.” As he wiped his hands on his robe, he said, “Here I am. Now get on with it.”

Jesus wiped his lips. “Are you leaving Jerusalem after the Passover?”

“Yes, and I’ll take my boys back with me.”

“We can talk about that then. Right now...”

Zebedee’s face turned bright red. “What do you mean--then? I said I’ll take my boys back with me. Do you understand?”

“I know what you mean,” Jesus replied.

“Good, we settled that,” Zebedee said with a glow of satisfaction. “Now, what is it you want to say?”

“I need your assistance.” Jesus answered.

“Help?” Zebedee yelled. “You want help from the man you called a self-righteous fool. What assistance could I give you?”

“There may be a time when your sons James and John will need your support and understanding. I want you to take charge of things in Capernaum--hold our community together.”

Zebedee looked at Jesus without comprehension. “What on earth are you talking about?” he snorted.

“I’m not sure why I’m telling you this. You’ll know when the time comes.”

“What makes you think I’d ever consider doing the things you ask for?” Zebedee replied.

Jesus spread his hands and replied, “You’ll do them because you have the Spirit within you.”

Zebedee slapped his forehead. “The more I hear, the crazier you sound. I won’t do a thing I don’t want to--spirit or no spirit.” Zebedee pointed to the Temple, looming over them as if it were suspended from the sky. “I’ll tell you again, that’s where The Lord lives, and that’s who I listen to.” He looked into Jesus’ eyes. “You are...a magician at best.”

“You will know who I am in time.” Jesus replied as he extended his hand. “For now, let’s leave in peace.”

Zebedee looked at John, who nodded and extended his hand. “I don’t understand,” Zebedee mumbled. “Sometimes you frighten me. But go in peace until I see you again.”

As they parted, Jesus spun and touched Zebedee's sleeve. "I almost forgot; will you join us for our Seder celebration tomorrow?"

Zebedee shook his head. "I would, but Salome and I promised to celebrate in Jerusalem with my sister. Perhaps we can share a meal after Sunday."

Jesus extended his hand to Zebedee. "I love your sons as much as you. May The Lord bless all of us on this sacred celebration." He felt the touch of Zebedee's wrinkled hands and sensed the old man had softened his feelings towards him.

As they headed back to the camp, John scratched his head and said, "Judas is acting strange lately."

"What do you mean?" Jesus asked.

John shrugged. "He told me yesterday that he believes you are the Messiah."

"What do you believe?" Jesus asked.

Frowning, John replied, "Judas will get us all in trouble before he's done."

* * *

Wary of the armed guards posted at the gates of the house of Caiaphas, Judas walked through the middle one of the three gates leading to the spacious courtyard. He gave a note of introduction to one of the guards and waited while a messenger went to the huge center complex that made up the living and working quarters of the Chief Priest, Caiaphas. The guard gestured for Judas to sit on a marble bench while he waited for a reply.

Judas scanned the courtyard, looking at the trees, bushes, and small porticos spread through the area. He spotted servants and slaves standing in a confined area to his left, while on his right, men dressed in expensive robes and wearing silk turbans talked next to the high columns surrounding the center complex.

The messenger returned and said to Judas, "The Chief Priest, Caiaphas, is in a meeting and cannot be disturbed. His aide said you should either come back tomorrow or talk to another priest."

Fingering his beard, Judas asked, "Who would I talk to?"

"You may, if you wish, talk to his assistant, Isaac ben Jonah."

"Fine, I'll talk to him," Judas said as he started toward the center complex.

The messenger pulled his sleeve. "Wait--Priest Isaac is at the Temple--the Court of the Priests. Go there and tell one of the guards that Caiaphas sent you. The guard will bring you to the priest."

As Judas turned toward the gate, the messenger called out, "Hurry, Isaac ben Jonah will only be at the Temple for a short time."

Judas nodded and ran from the house of Caiaphas to the Temple where he joined the crowd of people entering through the Hulda Gate. When he reached the Temple platform, he burrowed between the throngs moving toward the Women's Court. As he neared the Temple, he covered his nose and mouth with his sleeve when the smells from the sacrificial altars made his nose twitch.

Judas spotted a guard near the Nicanor Gate leading to the Court of the Israelites and signaled for his attention, gesturing and coughing as much as he could in that sacred place. The guard finally saw him and asked in a low voice, "What do you want?"

"The Chief Priest, Caiaphas, sent me to see Isaac ben Jonah."

The guard gave Judas a questioning look. "What is your business?"

"I came to meet with the priest at the request of Caiaphas." Judas hoped his evasive reply would get him an audience with the priest.

"Stay here," the guard muttered. Judas stepped back and watched the guard approach one of the priests taking sacrificial offerings. The priest listened, looked at Judas, and nodded. "Isaac ben Jonah will see you shortly," the guard said when he returned.

Judas held him by his sleeve. "Is he the priest ben Jonah?"

"Let go of my sleeve," the guard said darkly. "Yes, that is ben Jonah. Why do you ask?"

"He looks young. He must not be very important."

The guard glared at him. "I wouldn't tell him that if I were you."

Isaac ben Jonah washed his hands in a bowl and wiped with a cloth before walking over to Judas. "Caiaphas sent you?" he asked in a haughty voice.

"Yes."

"What do you want from me?"

"I...I came..."

"Why did you ask for me?" Isaac asked impatiently.

"I must talk with someone who is a leader..."

Isaac ben Jonah laughed. "You came to the wrong man. I have no charge over things. What is it you want?"

Judas looked at the people milling around them, jostling and calling for attention. "Can we talk someplace where it's quiet--no people? I don't want anyone to hear what I have to tell you."

Isaac ben Jonah sighed, "The Temple is the last place a person should come to for privacy during Passover week." Beckoning to Judas, he said, "Follow me." He led Judas out of the Temple area to the Court of the Gentiles where they found a deserted place near the west wall. "Now, is this quiet enough?" he asked.

Judas nodded.

"Can you tell me what you want, or are the crickets too noisy?"

Judas looked at the tile floor. "I know this man--a friend of mine--sent by God to free us from the Romans. I tried to see the Chief Priest, but he's too busy to listen..." Judas felt the words choke in his throat. He knew they were the wrong words, inadequate for what he wanted to say.

Isaac twisted his face into a huge question mark. "You came here to tell me that..."

"The Messiah is here," Judas murmured.

"WHAT?" Isaac shouted.

"I've been living with the Messiah for more than two years," Judas replied, his eyes darting from pillar to pillar. "I travel with him."

"Who is he--what does he look like..." Isaac ben Jonah slapped his forehead. "Why am I talking to you? You're another fanatic." He grabbed Judas' tunic. "Where are you from?"

"K-K-Kerioth."

"What did Caiaphas say when you told him this? And why did he send you to me?" Isaac demanded, rage creeping across his face.

Judas looked at the floor. "I didn't see Caiaphas."

"Yet he sent you to me?" Isaac rolled his eyes. "I'd think this was funny if I wasn't so busy."

"Listen," Judas pleaded. "I saw miracles!"

"What about it?"

"The blind see and the lame walk after he cures them."

"Who is he?"

"Jesus of Nazareth."

"I thought you were from Kerioth," Isaac hissed. "What do you know about Galileans?"

"I met him..."

Isaac raised his hand. "Enough! I have work to do." He tossed the last words over his shoulder as he walked toward the Beautiful Gate.

Judas watched Isaac disappear into the crowd surrounding the Court of the Israelites, then left the Temple platform. He stumbled down the steps next to the Royal Portico and left through the double Hulda Gate. People jarred him as he walked through the Lower City, but he didn't notice. Nor did he notice that Simon-Peter was preaching at the same spot he and Simon-Peter occupied on Monday.

"Who can I tell?" Judas muttered, half aloud. "Who can I convince that Jesus is the Messiah?"

* * *

After their meeting with Zebedee, Jesus and John returned to the Olive Mount and spent several hours on the hillside talking to people and leading them in prayer. Many people remembered Jesus from the triumphal procession on Sunday and encouraged him. Later a group of men came to him and said, "Teacher, we know you are a man of integrity. We saw you on Sunday, at the Temple, and again today on the hillside. Do you teach the true way of God?"

"I try," Jesus replied with a smile.

"Then tell us, is it right to pay tribute to Caesar?"

"Are you trying to trap me?" Jesus asked.

"Why do you ask?" the man countered.

"Because the Law forbids us to worship other gods, and Cacsar calls himself a god." Jesus looked at the men and shook his finger. "You'll have to do better than that. This is a question of civil law against holy law. Here, hand me a coin."

The man handed him a shekel.

"This is no good. Does anyone have a Roman coin?"

Another man gave him a denarius.

Jesus held the coin up to the sun, looked at it and handed it to the man. "Tell me, whose face is on that coin--and whose inscription?"

"Caesar's...and Caesar's," he replied.

Jesus took the coin back. "Then give to Caesar what is Caesar's, and to God what is God's."

Later on, a teacher of the law from Babylon heard Jesus debating. He tapped Jesus on the shoulder and asked, "Of all the commandments, which is most important?"

"The most important commandment," answered Jesus, "is this: Love the Lord with all your heart and with all your soul and with your entire mind and with all your strength. The second is this: Love your neighbor as yourself. There are no commandments greater than these."

"Well said teacher," the man replied. "You're right. To love him with all your heart, with all your understanding and with all your strength, and to love your neighbor as yourself is more important than all burnt offerings and sacrifices since Moses."

When Jesus heard his comment, he said, "You have discovered the Kingdom of God."

And so it went that Wednesday night, until Jesus returned to his camp and dined with his followers.

* * *

That same night, one of the money changers from the Temple went to the Antonia Fortress and identified a Joshua bar Abbas as the man who started the riot in the Temple on Monday.

CHAPTER FORTY-ONE

Thursday

On the twenty-fourth day of the first month, as I was standing on the bank of the great river, the Tigris, I looked up and there before me was a man dressed in linen, with a belt of fine gold from Uphaz around his waist. His body was like topaz, his face like lightning, his eyes like flaming torches, his arms and legs like the gleam of burnished bronze, and his voice like the sound of a multitude.

I, Daniel, was the only one who saw the vision; those who were with me did not see it, but such terror overwhelmed them that they fled and hid themselves. So I was left alone, gazing at this great vision; I had no strength left, my face turned deathly pale and I was helpless.
Then I heard him speaking, and as I listened to him, I fell into a deep sleep, my face to the ground. A hand touched me and set me trembling on my hands and knees.

He said, "Daniel, you who are highly esteemed, consider carefully the words I am about to speak to you, and stand up, for I have now been sent to you." And when he said this to me, I stood up trembling.

Then he continued, "Do not be afraid, Daniel. Since the first day that you set your mind to gain understanding and to humble yourself before your God, your words were heard, and I have come in response to them."

Daniel 10:4-12

Caiaphas adjusted his priestly robes and squinted at the morning sun reflecting off the gold and white facade of the Temple. He counted fifty one members of the Sanhedrin huddled in the apse at the eastern end of the Royal Stoa noisily reviewing the events of the week.

The murmurs died to a hush when Caiaphas spoke. "Tonight we will begin our solemn celebration of the Passover," he said. "As you know, the Romans warned they will take drastic measures to prevent a repeat of last year's troubles." Caiaphas fingered his breastplate and continued, "Fortunately, the money changers identified the man in the Roman dungeon as the man who started Monday's riot. That, for the moment, has satisfied Pontius Pilate."

They drew closer when he said in a low voice, "But the man they hold in the fortress is not the one who started the riot."

One of the priests interrupted, "How do you know? You said the money changer identified him."

Caiaphas waved at the priest. "The merchant lied."

"Why did he do that?"

"Because we paid him to lie," Caiaphas replied impatiently.

"Then who is the man we're looking for?" the priest asked.

"We wouldn't have a problem if we knew who the man and his friends were who started the riot," Caiaphas replied scornfully. "I called this meeting because I want you to watch every corner in the Temple and listen to every rumor in the streets for the next three days." He clapped his hands. "Notify me if you see or hear anything that looks like trouble. I will reward the man who finds him."

"What will the Romans do with the prisoner they have?"

"He's a criminal, just the type that would start a riot in the Temple." Caiaphas adjusted the sleeves on his robe, adding, "They'll torture him for names and execute him."

"What if he's innocent?" the questioner persisted.

Caiaphas looked away and muttered, "Better one man dies, than the entire nation of Israel."

Later, Isaac ben Jonah approached Caiaphas and told him about his conversation with Judas. "This man claimed his leader is the Messiah. He said the man has been healing and preaching from Galilee to Judea." Isaac ended by saying, "He's probably another religious fanatic trying to get attention."

Caiaphas grunted. "Is he the one who came to see me?"

"Yes."

Caiaphas touched his lips with his finger. "His name is Judas...something. Look for him--he might help us. And when you find him, bring him to me."

* * *

Pontius Pilate reviewed the latest dispatches from Rome while eating his morning meal with his wife, Claudia Procla. After a while, he pushed the scrolls aside and reached for a pear. "I wonder who reports this garbage to Rome. They seem to know events the day after they happen." He scratched his chin. "It's Herod Antipas. I know it's him. He has spies all over the place." Lips curled, he added, "Lucius Tullius told me that a whispered secret in Jerusalem is news all over Galilee the next day."

"Why would he spy on you?" Procla asked.

"Illusions of glory, probably inherited from his father. Herod thinks Tiberius Caesar will extend his territory to Judea and Samaria if he discredits me."

Procla touched his arm. "Does that worry you?"

"Not now. I want to make it through this week before I worry about Herod." Pilate wiped his mouth with a cloth. "Herod and I are allies for the time being. Neither of us has enough soldiers to patrol our territories, so we need to help each other."

Pilate pushed his food to the side and yawned. "I'm going to the Antonia Fortress this morning. In fact, I'll stay at my quarters at the fortress tonight and tomorrow night."

"Why do you have to stay there?" Procla asked. "What about Manius Decius?"

"He's there, but I don't want a repeat of last year's problems if the mobs got out of control."

"You're going to leave me alone?"

Pilate looked around the room. "This palace was good enough for Herod the Great and who knows how many of his wives, so it should be good enough for you." He looked in her eyes. "And another thing; I don't want you in the city today. Someone might recognize you and do something to embarrass us."

"I should've stayed in Caesarea," she whined.

"I agree, but you had to come to watch the Jews celebrate."

She pushed pieces of fruit around her plate with her bread. "Caesarea is tiresome."

Pilate frowned. "I'm sorry. Provincial affairs occupy most of my time. Perhaps you should've married a plebeian."

"That isn't what I meant."

"What did you mean?"

She adjusted the folds of her silk gown and lay back on the bench. "I prefer the excitement of Rome." She waved her scarf at him. "Jews are tedious. They can't do one thing because of their law, and they won't do another because the Gentiles do it."

"That may be," Pilate replied sharply. "But I'll still sleep at the Fortress tonight. That man who led the mob of Jews into the city on Sunday worries me."

"I thought you captured him."

"We did." Pilate paced around the table. "But there's more to this than Caiaphas is telling me. We've tortured the prisoner half to death and he still hasn't told us about his accomplices. Besides, there are others ready to make trouble when they see a chance." He slapped his hand on his thigh. "This time I'll be ready for them."

* * *

Jesus and his disciples stood at the edge of their camp on the Olive Mount and looked across the Kidron Valley to the Temple, anticipating their Passover celebration. Jesus put his hand on Andrew's shoulder. "We'll leave for Jerusalem in a little while. We should help Mary Marcia prepare for the Seder celebration as much as possible."

Andrew nodded and called to Philip. "We counted fourteen people who will remain in camp this evening," Andrew said while he waited for Philip to come over to where they stood. "That includes five men and four boys. That's enough to guard the camp." He looked at Jesus. "Philip and Nathanael will lead the Seder at camp. Two women from the camp next to us promised to prepare the meal."

"How many people will celebrate the Seder at Mary Marcia's house?" Philip asked.

Andrew and Jesus counted the names. "About sixteen or seventeen, including the women," Jesus replied.

"Counting the women?" Philip asked with raised eyebrows.

"Yes," Jesus replied. "Do you have a problem with women celebrating the Seder at the same table as men?"

Philip frowned but said nothing.

"Good," Jesus said. "I need a little time to prepare myself, and then we'll go to the market."

Hearing their conversation, Judas caught Jesus before he entered his tent. "Can I talk with you before you leave?"

Jesus nodded and leaned against a tree.

Judas hesitated for a moment, searching for words. Then he said, "Yesterday, I saw one of the priests at the Temple and I told him about you."

"What did you tell him?"

"I told him you are a prophet, or maybe even the Messiah."

"You told him that?"

Judas looked at the ground. "Yes."

"What did he say?"

"He didn't know whether to laugh or hit me." Judas replied with downcast eyes. "His name is Isaac ben Jonah."

"What else did you tell him?"

"Nothing, he was too busy to talk to me." Judas looked into Jesus' eyes. "Who are you--really?"

Jesus put his arm around Judas. "Why ask me? You already claim that I'm a prophet or even the Messiah. There's not much I can add to that."

"Do you deny what I say?"

"I can't ignore what God calls me to do," he replied as he ducked into his tent. "I am who I am."

* * *

On the eve of Passover, the marketplace in the Lower City of Jerusalem defined chaos. Merchants screamed at buyers. Buyers screamed at each other while cart drivers screamed at anyone who was in their way--which meant they screamed at everyone. Children and thieves scoured the stalls, looking for distracted merchants who wouldn't notice that they were stealing every manner of trinket and food. Dogs, drooling from the heat, scavenged the ground, ready to pounce on anything that fell off a merchant's shelf. Jesus and his people stayed as close to the buildings as possible, for the streets were only wide enough for the carts and carriages full of meat and vegetables rumbling dangerously close to the crowds. To complete the chaos, beggars, cripples, and blind people hung at the edges of the market, nearly blocking the streets as they competed for donations from the passing crowd.

John scraped his sandal on the pavement to loosen a wad of offal and glanced at Jesus. "I hope we leave this place in better shape than we left the Temple on Monday."

Jesus smiled at John. "These people don't pretend to help others worship God. Their greed is well known to those who enter the market." Rubbing his chin, Jesus added, "How can I put it? In this marketplace, the buyer must be careful, but in the Temple, we should never need to fear being cheated. Why should there be a temple if it has no special value?"

Quickly passing between the stalls, they bought lamb's meat, lentils, peas, lettuce, and fruitcakes. John held his nose when they passed a booth where stacks of fly covered meat and cheese rested on flimsy tables. He tried to ignore the next booth, which displayed fresh venison collecting the swirling dust and sand kicked up by people walking past the booth.

Jesus stopped at a stand where a bushy faced merchant sold jewelry. "I want to buy a bracelet for Mark's mother as a gift for preparing our Seder," he said.

The merchant shouted above the din of crying animals and screaming competitors to extol the virtues of his jewelry to Jesus and Philip. After a few minutes, Jesus agreed to buy two bracelets, but Judas caught him and pulled his arm.

"Don't buy them," he said, looking at the merchant from the corner of his eye. "These are low quality bracelets." Judas shook his head. "He wants too much money for this trash."

The merchant kicked at Judas and tried to chase him away.

Jesus frowned at the merchant. "This man is my friend and a better man at bargaining than I." He turned to Judas. "Here, you buy the bracelet."

"Do I have to buy them here?" Judas asked.

"Do as you please," Jesus replied as he and Philip turned away. Soon they heard Judas and the merchant screaming at each other as if they were mortal enemies.

Jesus looked over his shoulder and asked Philip, "What do you think of Judas?"

"I don't know him," Philip replied. "I haven't been alone with him that often. Why do you ask?"

"Some of our people distrust him."

"Has he done anything to earn their distrust?"

"Everything," John interrupted.

"I don't think so," Jesus retorted, casting an angry glance at John. "I put him in charge of our money when we lived at Beth-Shan and he has done well. The only problem I see..." Jesus stopped talking and put his hand on Philip's arm when he spied two Temple guards walking toward them, helmets held high and capes flowing. The soldiers passed them without a glance and stopped at a nearby stall. Jesus glanced at Philip. "What were we talking about?"

"Judas," Philip responded, "but you had a strange look in your eyes when you saw the soldiers. Is something wrong?"

Jesus shrugged. "I felt a sense of dread when I saw them."

Before long, a triumphant Judas caught up to them and displayed the bracelet. "Beware to the person who follows me into that booth," he bragged. "That merchant will charge him double to recover the profit I took."

"Well done," Jesus smiled. "I knew you could do the job." Looking over the crowd, he added, "We need to find Simon-Peter and Andrew. They'll take the food we purchased to Mary Marcia's house once we have our supplies and we can..." The shofar from the Temple announcing the time of prayer interrupted Jesus. The market fell silent for a moment. To John, the silence sounded eerie, almost deafening, after the noises he heard since entering the marketplace.

Jesus spied Andrew and Simon-Peter among the throng after his prayer. Giving his supplies to Andrew, he said, “Take these to Mary Marcia’s house, the women are waiting for us.”

Andrew and Simon-Peter looked at each other and shrugged. “I forgot where she lives,” Andrew muttered.

Jesus pointed to the Upper City. “There’s a well near the Zion Gate where people in her neighborhood draw water. Ask any man or woman carrying water from that well where Mary the daughter of Isaac lives. Someone will lead you there. Once there, tell her that we’ll come to prepare her upper room soon.” They nodded and left the market.

* * *

Jesus left John, Philip, and Judas at the market and went to the Temple where he joined a line of people waiting to enter the ritual baths. He thought he heard someone call his name, but saw no one he recognized when he scanned the crowd. He pulled his robe over his shoulders and shuffled closer to the baths where he heard someone call his name again. He looked at the people around him but saw no one he knew. He passed through the bath and presented himself to one of the priests who looked at him strangely, then waved him on.

The voice called once more as Jesus approached the Triple Hulda Gate. He spun and saw a blind woman sitting on the end of the steps. He approached the woman and asked, “Did you call my name?”

The woman gazed at him through sightless eyes and nodded. Then she raised her arm and said, “Take my hand.”

“Where do you want to go?” Jesus asked, noticing the woman’s robe. Her robe, now faded, but once brightly colored, and her shawl, once royal purple, but now dull red reminded him of something he couldn’t quite recall.

“Inside the wall,” she answered.

Jesus wondered, as they walked through the gate, why the priest took no notice of the blind woman. This was the same priest who looked at him twice when he presented himself after his bath. Once inside, the woman gestured to a dark corner.

When they were alone the woman asked, “You are Jesus of Nazareth?”

Jesus nodded.

“Speak up!” she said. “I cannot see.”

“I’m sorry--yes I am Jesus.”

“Your friend Judas is right.” The woman adjusted her shawl so Jesus could better see her face. “And he’s wrong.”

“About what?” Jesus asked.

"He called you the Messiah, the Anointed One. He's right, but he doesn't understand who the real Messiah is."

Jesus wiped his forehead. "How do you know about Judas?"

The woman smiled. "I know all your friends."

"Who are you?"

"A prophet--like you."

"And you call me the Messiah?"

The woman sighed, "What has been veiled from you since your birth must now be told. This is why Yahweh called you to on Mount Hermon--to fulfill the promises of the patriarchs and prophets."

Jesus caught his breath. "What will happen?"

The woman looked at Jesus through her sightless eyes, seeing him as well as any sighted person. "You will die at this hour tomorrow."

Jesus recoiled. "How do you know?"

"The Father has called you. There is no more you can do."

Jesus sighed. "Then my life is wasted."

"Jesus, you are blinder than I. You wasted nothing. You did what your Father asked of you." The woman took Jesus' hands in hers. "You will celebrate the Seder with your friends tonight?"

"Yes."

"After that, they will continue the work you started. Set them free tonight if you can."

Jesus tried to sort the flood of questions running through his mind. Suddenly he stiffened and asked, "How is this going to happen?"

"The authorities have promised a reward for the man who finds you. Some one you trust will turn you over to them."

"Why do the authorities want me?"

The woman grunted. "All along, you've taught seditious ideas in the Temple. On Monday you started a riot. And as we both know, you made a spectacular entrance into the city on Sunday." She paused for a moment, then added, "You've frightened them."

"How will I die?" Jesus asked.

"They will raise you on a cross."

"How--why? What will happen?"

"One who is close to you will give you to the authorities as a gesture of conciliation."

"Someone will betray me?"

"A man who shares bread with you tonight will give you up."

Jesus put his hand on the woman's arm. "What man? Who?"

The woman ignored his question. "You will suffer and die," she continued without emotion.

"What good will that do?"

"Very little on the surface. However, your disciples will go into the world using your name to establish the Kingdom."

Jesus looked up. "So this is what it comes to."

"This is what God asks of you. You have the freedom to turn away--to say no."

Jesus shuddered. "Why didn't I know this before?"

"Maybe you did," the woman replied. "Maybe you didn't see things as clearly as now. As you've often said, spiritual blindness is a terrible disease."

Jesus turned away when he heard a commotion on the stairway leading to the temple platform. Then he asked, "What..." But he saw no blind woman. He whirled and strained his eyes in every direction but saw no one except the crowds of pilgrims trudging up the stairs. Suddenly he remembered the blind girl dancing around him on Sunday. She tried to tell him something. He snapped his fingers. This was the same woman! But so much older. What happened to her? Jesus' head spun as he thought about his visions in the desert. The loaves and fishes. The lepers. The light on Mount Hermon. Bar Timaeus. Lazarus. He would later tell John and Andrew that he felt as if his entire life had been played out before him underneath the Temple.

Jesus left the Temple and walked to Mary's house, thinking about what the blind woman had said. As he stepped over spring weeds sprouting between the cracks in the pavement, he noticed the freshly planted fields beyond the city walls and savored the smell of blossoms carried on the humid breeze. His eyes moistened when he remembered that Passover promises renewal, as nature promises hope and rebirth every spring. Even the occasional breeze blowing across the fires of Gehenna failed to tarnish the agreeable sights and sounds coming to his senses.

He rubbed his shoulder, still tender from his fight at the Temple as he approached several children playing in a pile of sand. He stooped and asked, "Will you celebrate Pesah tonight?"

"Yes, my grandfather is here to recite the Haggadah," answered a boy with swirling blond curls.

"Who will hide the afikomen matzah?" Jesus asked.

"Grandfather." The boy replied laughing. "But he hides it in places where it is easy to find."

Within minutes after leaving the children, Jesus found himself at the gate of Mary Marcia's house.

Mark greeted him at the gate and pulled him toward the atrium. "Abraham and Anna arrived from Alexandria this morning," he said cheerfully. Jesus followed Mark to the atrium and heard Mark's words. "Abraham and Anna... this is Jesus of Nazareth."

Abraham moved to greet Jesus but held back when he saw a dreadful look in his eyes. Jesus quickly realized what was happening and took Abraham's hand. "Mark has a mission of doubtful value, recording the comings and goings of Galileans, but perhaps the scholars at Alexandria are wiser than we."

"I know a few of them," Abraham replied. "They're not as wise as they want us to believe."

"Few people are," Jesus answered.

* * *

The people staying at Mary Marcia's house spent the next hours preparing for the Seder. After Jesus met Abraham and Anna, Mary Marcia took him to the room where she stored the kittel. "This is the kittel once worn by my father," she said sadly. "You will honor our house if you choose to wear it during the celebration tonight."

Jesus gave her his robe and pulled the kittel over his head. "It fits. I consider it an honor to wear this kittel tonight." He fingered the fringe and looked at Mary. "Strange thing, these kittels. Few things symbolize both life and death the way they do."

Her eyes moistened. "I remember they buried my brother in a kittel as a symbol of rebirth. I didn't understand what they meant at the time."

Jesus picked up a candle. "Our oldest traditions tell how the generation from Egypt died in the desert so the new generation could claim the Promised Land." He removed the kittel. "Old attachments must die before new ones can develop."

* * *

Mary Marcia led the procession of servers to the upper room with the makings of the Seder meal. She carried the matzoth, Mark and Mary of Magdala helped with the Seder plates, and Mark and Rebecca took the wine and cups to where several reclining mats and two large tables faced each other with a passage between them.

Jesus signaled for quiet and gestured to Mark. "Bring a pail of water and towels," he commanded. Jesus then removed his kittel and wrapped a towel around his waist. After he poured the water into a basin, he washed Andrew's feet and dried them with the towel around his waist. He did the same for all his disciples in the room.

When Jesus came to Simon-Peter, he asked, "Are you going to wash my feet?"

"Yes," Jesus replied.

"No," Simon-Peter said. "You will never wash my feet."

"You will not be my disciple unless you allow me to wash your feet," Jesus replied.

"Then, not just my feet, but my hands and head as well," Simon-Peter shouted.

When Jesus finished washing their feet, he dressed with the kittel and returned to the Seder. Standing between the two tables, he asked, "do you understand what I did for you?'

No one answered.

"You call me Teacher and some say I am the Anointed One. You do so correctly, for that is who I am. Now that I, your Teacher, washed your feet, you also must wash the feet of the people you wish to lead."

He looked at each person before he continued, "I set an example for you to follow. I tell you; No servant is greater than his master, nor is a messenger greater than the one who sent him."

During the meal, Jesus sat between John and Simon-Peter. After he recited the sanctification, they drank from the first cup of wine and dipped a vegetable into a dish of salt water to symbolize the bitter tears shed by the slaves in Egypt before the Exodus.

Jesus took the middle of three matzoth, broke it, and wrapped the larger part in a napkin to be set aside as the afikomen. Mark took the afikomen to a hiding place since there were no young children at the Seder. Jesus mentioned for all to hear, that when they retrieved the afikomen at the end of the Seder, the broken piece of matzoh will symbolize the Messiah and the future redemption of Israel.

Then he started the maggid, the heart of the Haggadah or story of the Exodus. Aaron, the son of James bar Zebedee, asked the same Four Questions asked by a young person every year during the Seder celebration. From there, they passed through questions and recitations to the Dayyeinu, the song that recounts the great deeds God performed for the Israelites. This section of the Seder ended with a blessing that praised God as redeemer of Israel and spoke of their hope for future redemption. They concluded with a second cup of wine.

During the next part of the Seder, they washed their hands in basins brought to the room earlier and recited another blessing. Then they ate from the top and middle matzoth. When they reclined to eat the festive meal after the ritual commemorating the Exodus, the room vibrated with the noise of eating and celebration. Mark, seated at the opposite table, noticed that Jesus seemed distant, often staring into space and unconscious to conversations around him.

Finally, Mark went over and asked Jesus, "Are you alright?"

Jesus looked at him sadly and replied, "I'm fine."

"You look troubled."

Jesus gestured for Mark to lean closer. "Some one at this table will betray me to the authorities," he whispered. "One of those who dipped his bread into the bowl with me." Jesus held Mark's tunic and pulled him closer. "Woe to that person who betrays the Son of Man! It would be better for him if he had not been born."

John overheard the conversation and leaned on Jesus' shoulder. "What are you talking about?"

"I told Mark that one of you will betray me to the authorities."

"Who?" John asked angrily, "and why?" He wiped his lips with his sleeve. "How do you know?"

Jesus shrugged. "I don't know the answer to the first two questions, but I can tell you that a prophet told me." Then he stood and called for everyone's attention. "I wanted to eat this Seder with you," he said in a low voice. "I'll tell you now that I will not eat another Seder again until what it represents has occurred in the Kingdom of God."

Jesus took a loaf of bread and offered thanksgiving, broke it into pieces and said, "This is my body given for you; eat this in remembrance of me." They stared at him in disbelief but took the bread he offered from the loaf.

Then he raised his cup and gave thanks to God. "Take this wine and share it among yourselves. For I will not drink wine again until the Kingdom of God has come." Not understanding, they drank from their cups as he instructed.

Finally he looked at his mother and his friends and raised his cup of wine. "This cup is the new covenant of my blood which is poured out for you. You do not understand now, but you will when you discover the Kingdom of God as I have."

Jesus put his hand on John's head. "You did not choose me, but I chose you and now I appoint you to go and bear fruit--fruit that will last. The Father will give you whatever you ask in my name." Jesus put his cup back on the table and said, "Love one another."

Jesus reclined and watched as his disciples murmured among themselves, trying to discern what their leader had just told them. Later, Jesus saw a shadow emerge near the top of the stairs. His heart jumped when he saw it was his brother, James.

He quickly went over to James and together they went to Mary's table. While they were talking with their mother, Jesus glanced back to the other table and saw Simon-Peter engaged in a heated argument with John. At the same time, Andrew and Judas shook their heads and moved away. Jesus turned back to James and his mother. "James, thank you for coming. I know I've caused you trouble in Nazareth." He touched James on the shoulder. "How long were you at the top of the stairs?"

"I heard everything you said from the time you raised your cup," James replied, shaking his head. "You're a mystery to me, yet I want to know what you mean by the things you say."

"That will come in time," Jesus replied. "How long are you staying in Jerusalem?"

"Until the end of the Passover observance. I'm staying with friends a short distance from here. I do want to meet with you before I leave Jerusalem."

"Monday or Tuesday will be fine," Jesus said as he headed back to his table. Suddenly, he had a vision of the blind woman at the Temple and wanted to go back to James and his mother. "How could I explain," he asked himself. He shook his head and sat between Simon-Peter and John.

"I saw you and John arguing," he said to Simon-Peter. "Is something wrong?"

Simon-Peter's face reddened. "We talked about who would replace you if something happened. John and James bar Zebedee say they are better leaders than Andrew and I."

"We talked about this before," Jesus said, frowning. "After all this time, you still don't understand what I want from you."

Simon-Peter shrugged. "I know--you want us to act like children. That sounds stupid to me."

"Not act...be like them." Jesus made sure John and James bar Zebedee heard him. "The kings of the Gentiles lord it over their people, and the people have no choice but to like it. But you will not be like that. Instead, the greatest among you will be like the least, and the one who rules must be the one who serves."

Simon-Peter stretched and yawned, "I can do that." Staring at Jesus, he asked, "By the way, what were you talking about when you said someone would betray you?"

Jesus replied, "The man who will betray me to the authorities shared bread and wine with me at this table tonight."

Simon-Peter and John looked at each other, then at the other people seated at the table. "Who is it?" John asked casting glances in the direction of Judas.

"Certainly not I," Simon-Peter mused.

"Simon-Peter," Jesus said. "Satan will test all of you like a farmer separates wheat from chaff. I pray that your faith will not be tested."

Simon-Peter replied, "I'm not going anywhere without you. I'm ready to go with you to prison and even to my death if necessary."

Jesus answered, "I tell you, Simon-Peter, between now and tomorrow morning when the rooster crows, you will deny me three times."

Simon-Peter laughed. "Where do you think of this stuff? Why would I deny you?"

Jesus gestured to the others. "You will all fall away." His eyes brightened for a moment. "I remember now, one of the prophets wrote; `I will strike the shepherd, and the sheep will scatter.'" Jesus looked into Simon-Peter's eyes. "I am the shepherd and you are the sheep."

Jesus called to Mark. "Bring the afikomen to me."

Mark looked at him with sparkling eyes. "Not until you pay the ransom."

Jesus shouted to Judas, "Pay this man a ransom so we can eat the afikomen."

Judas called Mark to his side and pursued an earnest negotiation before he took some coins from his purse. "Bring it to me," he instructed. "Together we will present the symbol of the Messiah to Jesus."

After they ate the afikomen, the last food eaten at the Seder, Jesus rose and recited a blessing. Then everyone drank from the third cup of wine. Mark placed another cup on the table to stand as the Elijah cup and went to the stairs to see if Elijah was waiting to enter the room to herald the Messiah and the final redemption. Disappointed, he returned to the tables and announced that Elijah was not at the door.

Jesus recited the last of the Hallel and ended with a blessing over the fourth cup of wine. They reclined on the couches and drank the cup, then began the poem from the days of the Babylonian exile known as "Hasal Siddur Pesah." Together they recited, "le-shanah ha-ba-ah--Next year in Jerusalem."

The Seder ended when Jesus, John, and Andrew led a procession to the courtyard. Jesus gave Mary Marcia the bracelet Judas bought and embraced her. "Thank you for offering your house to us," he whispered.

She looked into his eyes and replied, "You blessed my house when you came to celebrate our Seder. I'll remember this night the rest of my life." She held his hands. "Now I see what the others see. You are truly blest by God."

"Thank you for your kindness. Right now, pray that you all will withstand the pain of the coming days and months."

Judas caught Jesus' sleeve. "I'm going to find the priest I talked to yesterday," he said, fired with enthusiasm. I'll return to camp from his house." Jesus nodded and started to walk away, but Judas held on to his sleeve. "Jesus, are you willing to talk to the Temple leaders if I can arrange it?"

"Is that who you plan to meet?"

"There are people in the Sanhedrin who will listen to you. I want them to hear what you say and see that you are the Messiah."

"But why tonight?"

Suddenly, Judas looked confused. "I don't know why. I just feel I have to do it."

"Go ahead if you must."

As Judas ran through the gate, Jesus and Andrew lit their torches and led the disciples through the city and the gate leading to their camp. Mark went with the group which now consisted of Simon-Peter, James and John bar Zebedee, Andrew, and himself. Mary the mother of Jesus, Mary of Magdala, and Naomi returned to a friend's house a few blocks away.

CHAPTER FORTY-TWO

Thursday Night

I told them, "If you think it best, give me my pay; but if not, keep it." So they paid me thirty pieces of silver.
And the LORD said to me, "Throw it to the potter"—the handsome price at which they valued me! So I took the thirty pieces of silver and threw them to the potter at the house of the LORD.

Zechariah 11:12-13

Judas muttered to himself as he hurried through the moonlit streets between the house of Caiaphas and Mary Marcia's house. He wondered as he walked, why he was driven to bring the Temple priests and Jesus together. What difference would it make if a Galilean teacher exchanged opinions with the Jewish leaders in Jerusalem? Judas didn't know these people. Furthermore, he had no idea whether he could trust them. Perhaps his father was right; maybe he was too rash. Halfway there, he convinced himself that his idea to see Caiaphas was a mistake. He stopped, looked around, and turned back to Mary Marcia's house.

Judas walked a short distance, still consumed by his internal argument. "What if Jesus really is the Messiah," he asked himself. "I would sit at his side instead of proud John or weak Simon-Peter" Judas snapped his fingers and turned back toward Caiaphas' house, convinced that God wanted him to be his messenger. At that moment, Judas felt the prophet's call. Judas knew the prophets had doubts, but they did what God asked. Moved by his latest insight, Judas turned and ran toward the house of Caiaphas.

Once there, he approached a guard. "I need to talk to the Chief Priest Caiaphas," he announced in a stiff voice.

Looking at him with disdain, the guard replied, "I doubt whether he would talk to you, but it doesn't matter. He's celebrating at the home of his father-in-law, Annas."

"Where's that?"

"Two blocks south and three blocks west," The guard answered. He raised a hand. "But you're wasting your time. He will allow no one to disturb him."

"Not even the Messiah?" Judas asked.

The guard laughed. "Not even the Messiah."

Judas rushed to the house of Annas and found it surrounded by servants and guards. He walked up to a guard and announced, "I'm looking for the High Priest Caiaphas."

The guard looked at him sternly and asked, "What do you want from him?"

"I want to give him a message."

"About?"

"It's a private message." Judas hiccupped. "Tell him that Judas of Kerioth wants to arrange a meeting between him and Jesus of Nazareth."

The guard sniffed, "That can wait until after the Sabbath. Go away before I set the dogs on you."

"You must listen," Judas pleaded.

"Go away!" The guard pushed him with his spear.

"Please." The guard was about strike his head when Judas noticed Isaac ben Jonah, the priest he met at the Temple walking through the courtyard. Judas grabbed the guard's arm. "Stop!" he yelled. "Call that man over here."

The guard pondered for a moment, then signaled to Isaac ben Jonah. The priest nodded and came to the gate.

He looked at Judas for a moment then asked, "Should I know you?"

"I am Judas of Kerioth--we met at the Temple yesterday."

Isaac frowned. "You and fifty thousand other people." Then he snapped his fingers. "Now I remember; what was it you wanted?"

"I want to arrange a meeting with Caiaphas and the Messiah."

"Guard!" Isaac snapped his fingers.

Judas clutched his sleeve. "You saw him!"

"What?"

"You saw him on Sunday when he rode into the city on a donkey," Judas whispered.

The priest waved the guard away. "Are you saying that you know the man who rode in with the crowd?"

"Yes."

"Where is he now?"

"He just left for his camp on the Mount of Olives."

Isaac led Judas to a small room next to the courtyard and raised a finger. "Wait here," he instructed.

Judas shivered as he leaned against the wall and looked over the courtyard. Next to the courtyard at the house of Caiaphas, this garden was the most magnificent he'd ever seen. He counted seven palm trees before the sound of footsteps captured his attention. It was Isaac returning with Joseph Caiaphas.

Caiaphas' eyes flashed with anger. "This better be good," he snarled. "What about the man on Sunday?"

"His name is Jesus and..."

"Where is he from?"

"Ah--Nazareth, Galilee," Judas stammered.

Caiaphas looked as if he didn't know whether to laugh or slap Judas in the face. "Galilee? No one of importance ever came from Galilee." He turned his back and said to Isaac, "Get rid of him."

"What about Monday--the Temple?" Judas yelled.

Caiaphas spun and faced Judas. "What about Monday?"

"He was there."

"So were ten thousand other people."

Pushing his luck, Judas declared, "He raised a man from the dead."

Caiaphas put his face close to Judas. "Are you drunk from too much wine...?" Caiaphas wheeled and looked at Isaac. "I heard a rumor about that..." Back to Judas. "Wait! You told Isaac that he came into the city on a donkey?"

"Yes."

"On Sunday?"

"Yes."

Caiaphas rubbed his chin. "Did he start the riot in the Temple on Monday?"

Judas shuffled his feet. "Yes, but the merchant..."

Caiaphas stared at Isaac. "He's the one."

Judas smiled for the first time. "I told you he..."

Caiaphas grabbed Judas by the shoulders. "Do you know where he is right now?" Caiaphas shuddered when he realized what Judas was telling him.

"Yes."

"Bring him here--to me! Now!" Caiaphas' pupils dilated to twice their normal size.

"Now?"

"Yes--now!" Caiaphas pulled Isaac's robe. "You--go with him and bring this...who is he?"

"Jesus," Judas replied weakly.

"Yes--Jesus. Bring him here tonight."

For the first time, Judas noticed the odor of wine on Caiaphas' clothes. Backing away, Judas protested, "It's late, let's wait until tomorrow."

"No!" Caiaphas growled. "I want him here tonight."

Isaac led Judas out of the courtyard and rushed to the city gate only to find it closed. "Open the gate," Isaac shouted to the guards.

"The gate is closed," they replied.

"I'm a priest of the Temple--on official business."

"The gate is closed for the night," the guard repeated. "Besides, high-born people like you wouldn't make it fifty feet past the gate."

"What do you mean?" Judas asked.

"Bandits, drunks, the usual. Once they rob you, they'll kill you and dump your body into the fires of Gehenna."

Isaac gestured impatiently. "We must go to the Mount of Olives tonight. The Chief Priest Caiaphas ordered us to bring a man back to the city."

The guard shook his head. "If it's the Chief Priest who wants this, have him send the Temple guards with you. I'll let soldiers through the gate." He poked Isaac's robe. "Besides, you need protection."

Isaac brushed his robe and looked at Judas. "He's right. We can collect the Temple guards and leave through the Golden Gate." He called to the soldier. "I'll do as you say. We'll leave from the Golden Gate and return through this gate. Will they let us enter?"

"As long as your soldiers know the password."

"The password?"

The guard looked at him with disdain. "Anyone can dress as a soldier. Your guards need to know the password."

* * *

Jesus, John, James bar Zebedee and Simon-Peter went to a place located within sight of their camp called Gethsemane. Jesus pointed to a large olive tree and said to his three companions, "Sit here while I pray. My spirit is crushed. I need people to watch with me."

He went a little farther and fell to the ground, filled with fear and horror. After a while, he leaned against a boulder and called James to his side. Whispering, he told James about his experience at the Temple earlier in the day. "Do you think," he asked James, "that Satan would tempt me at the Temple as he did in the desert?"

"You said it was a woman who talked to you," James remarked.

"I'm confused, I don't know if it was real. It was more like a dream." Jesus shook his head. "Leave me alone to pray."

James crawled near John and Simon-Peter who were sleeping against a tree. Troubled by Jesus words, he sat next to them and listened as Jesus prayed.

"Father, my Father!" Jesus moaned. "All things are possible for you. Take this cup away from me." He looked up. "Yet I want your will, not mine."

When Jesus returned to his disciples a little later, James pretended he was asleep so Jesus wouldn't know he heard his prayer. Jesus nudged Simon-Peter with his sandal and said, "Can't you keep awake for one hour?" John and James stirred when they heard Jesus voice. "Keep watch, and pray that you will not give in to temptation. Your spirit is willing but your flesh is weak."

Jesus prayed again, saying the same things as before. And as before, James listened. When Jesus came back a second time, he found them sleeping. They could hardly keep their eyes open when he woke them. When he returned the third time, he said, "Are you still sleeping and resting?" James wanted to console Jesus, but could not do so without revealing that he had listened to Jesus prayers. As for Jesus and the story of the blind woman, James brushed it off, assuming that Jesus had met a fanatic at the Temple.

Jesus reached for a cup of water but stopped when he saw torches flickering on the road to the camp. "Enough!" he said. "My hour has come. The Son of Man will be turned over to the authorities." Jesus touched each man on the shoulder. "Get up, the man who will reveal me to the world is coming into our camp."

James, still troubled by Jesus' earlier story, felt helpless as he saw the torches bobbing closer to the camp. Upon hearing the noise from the procession, people came out of their tents and stood in small circles, pulling their robes closer to keep warm.

They continued to watch as the torches drew nearer until a woman recognized the man leading the group. "Judas," she called out. "What are you doing?"

Judas ignored the woman and walked directly to Jesus, embraced him, and gave him a ritual kiss of friendship. "Rabbi, I have great news. The Chief Priest Caiaphas wants to meet with you tonight."

Jesus looked at the guards following Judas and asked, "Why are these men armed?" Before he said another word, Isaac ben Jonah ordered the guards to surround Jesus. Simon-Peter drew his sword and slashed at Malchus, a servant of the high priest, cutting his ear. At the same time, John and Philip jumped two guards and knocked them to the ground.

Jesus grabbed Simon-Peter's arm and pulled him from the servant. "Put your sword away!" he said. "This man means no harm to me." Then he dodged the guards and pushed John. "John! Philip! Stop!" Hearing this, Simon-Peter threw his sword on the ground and stared at Jesus with a mixture of anger and confusion. Jesus looked at his friends for a moment, then went to the servant Malchus to bind his wound.

When Jesus finished, he looked at Isaac. "Did you have to come with swords and clubs to take me to meet Caiaphas as if I were an outlaw? I worshipped and taught in the Temple and you didn't arrest me. Now you treat me like a criminal." As he started to leave the camp, he said to the Temple guards, "Keep your hands off me, I'll go with you in peace."

Jesus' frightened followers hid near their tents when Jesus, Judas, and the Temple guards started on the road to the city. Mark trembled, wearing only a light blanket as he watched the proceedings from the edge of the camp. When the group passed Mark too quickly for him to move, one of the guards pulled his blanket away, leaving him naked. He stood paralyzed for a moment, then ran into the darkness.

Simon-Peter staggered to his tent and shook Andrew awake. "Hurry, take your sword and follow me," he yelled.

"Where are we going?" Andrew asked.

"To the city. Quick, give me a clean robe." Within moments, Andrew and Simon-Peter left the camp and hurried to catch up with Jesus and the guards. As they ran down the road, Simon-Peter muttered, "All that talk about standing up to the authorities. Now look at him--he's as weak as a woman." Jabbing at Andrew's sleeve, he added, "Hurry, the only way we'll get in the city is to sneak in with the Temple guards."

* * *

The guards at the city gate recognized Isaac and acknowledged the password from the Temple guard, allowing the entire group, including Simon-Peter and Andrew, to pass through without question. The group, led by Isaac, Jesus, and Judas wound its way to the house of Annas. When Isaac banged on the gate, a crabby looking guard opened a small door and peered out. "What do you want?" he asked.

Isaac answered, "We are here on the official business of the Chief Priest Caiaphas."

"He's gone," the guard snorted. "He told me to send you to his house." The door slammed shut.

Isaac looked at the captain of the guards and shrugged. "Rclcasc all but two of your guards and follow me."

The captain gestured to the troop and the guards melted into the night. Simon-Peter and Andrew, trailing a short distance behind, hid in a doorway when the soldiers passed by. Then they hurried to catch the procession, reaching the house of Caiaphas in time to see Jesus and Judas enter the courtyard and walk with Isaac to the atrium. Andrew saw a group of people standing next to a fire and pulled Simon-Peter over to join them. After a short conversation, Simon-Peter learned they were servants and guards for various Temple officials. They told him Caiaphas called an unusual conference to meet with a man who claimed he was the Messiah.

* * *

Jesus and Judas gasped when they entered the meeting room of the Sanhedrin to find a group of tired, angry men waiting for them. They looked as if someone dragged them from their beds after an evening of feasting and drinking, which is exactly what happened. Jesus whispered to Judas, "This was not one of your better ideas."

Judas had kept his eyes to the floor since they entered the room, but now his eyes darted between the foul smelling oil lamps and elongated shadows cast on the walls by large candles. "I have a bad feeling. I...I'm sorry," Judas mumbled.

"What is your name?" Caiaphas shouted to Jesus.

Jesus took a long look at the men assembled in the room before he answered, "Jesus bar Joseph."

Caiaphas gestured for Jesus and Judas to sit on a bench near the middle of the chamber. He half smiled when he looked at Jesus. "You created quite a stir in the city this week. First, your grand entrance on Sunday, then a riot at the Temple on Monday. You were the one, weren't you?"

"If you say so."

Caiaphas laughed. "If I say so? Look here Galilean, this is a serious matter." He looked at Judas, then Jesus. "Your friend says that you claim to be the Messiah. Is that true?"

Judas started to object but Jesus held his arm and replied, "I am a teacher. My friend is excited about the Kingdom of God."

One of the officials seated on a bench near Jesus spoke up. "I recognize this man. He was at the Temple during the Festival of Lights. He argued with me and claimed that he could destroy the Temple and rebuild it in three days."

Caiaphas looked at Jesus. "Is that true?"

Jesus stared at his accuser. "I think I talked with him at the Temple," he replied.

"What about..."

Jesus rubbed his hands. "Let me think...I said the real Temple of God is not one made by man. And yes, it can be built or restored in three days if you wish."

Caiaphas looked at the other men. "What are we doing here...with this primitive Galilean?" He looked back to Jesus. "Did you know that Pontius Pilate threatened to close the Temple if our people riot or rebel against Roman rule as they did last year?" Pacing nervously in front of Jesus, he said, "The things you did on Sunday and Monday nearly drove him to do that. Do you know what that would mean to us?"

Jesus nodded.

* * *

In the courtyard, a man warming his hands next to Simon-Peter offered him a drink from his wineskin. "Are you a follower of the man meeting with the high priests?"

Simon-Peter grunted, "I was once."

"Not now?"

"No more." Simon-Peter reached for the wineskin.

The man rubbed his hands. "They called my master in the middle of the night to talk to this man. He must be important."

"I don't think so," Simon-Peter replied.

* * *

Gesturing to a man sitting three benches above Jesus, Caiaphas said, "Caleb, tell me what you heard."

The man pointed to Jesus. "I heard him preach in the Temple and near the Fountain Gate. He said we don't have to go to the Temple to worship our God. He said Yahweh is everywhere."

Caiaphas asked Jesus, "Are you a Pharisee?"

"Yes."

"Then you believe we can observe the Law at the synagogues."

Jesus shifted on the bench as he considered his answer. "There are many places we can worship. The Temple is one, the synagogues are another."

* * *

A woman servant of the Chief Priest brought trays of juice to the people waiting by the fire. She offered a cup to Simon-Peter, who refused with a wave of his hand. Putting the tray down, she asked, "What's happening in there?"

"What do you mean?"

"Caiaphas called those men to talk to someone. Who is he?"

"Probably Jesus of Nazareth."

"Then you know him."

"Yes," Simon-Peter replied, eyes downcast.

"Is he your leader?"

"He was once. But now he's joined Judas and the priests." Simon-Peter belched. "He's a traitor in my eyes. I don't know the man." Andrew pulled Simon-Peter's sleeve to quiet him, but Simon-Peter jerked it away and stared at the fire. "He sure fooled me," Simon-Peter mumbled to no one in particular.

* * *

Caiaphas rubbed his eyes and said to the council, "It's too late to do any more tonight." Looking at Jesus, he said, "I want you to stay in this house tonight and meet with us again in the morning."

Jesus replied, "I have a friend in Jerusalem who will let me sleep in her house."

"No," Caiaphas answered. "We spent too much time looking for you. I don't want to lose sight of you."

"What about Judas?" Jesus asked.

"What about him?"

"Where will he sleep?"

"In the street if he wishes," Caiaphas replied coldly.

* * *

"I'm leaving for Mary Marcia's house," Simon-Peter said to Andrew. "Are you coming?"

"I'll wait until Jesus comes out," Andrew replied. "Something is wrong, I know it."

Simon-Peter laughed. The only thing that's wrong is that Jesus made us look like fools. He's not one of us." Simon-Peter spit on the ground. "Judas has convinced him to join with the high priests."

With that, Simon-Peter waved to Andrew and started through the gate where a guard pulled him aside and asked, "Aren't you the one who came with the Galilean?"

Simon-Peter nodded.

"Aren't you going to wait for your master?"

Simon-Peter spit on the ground. "He's not my master," Simon-Peter growled. "He's not even my friend. What happens in there is between him and his Temple friends." He waved to the guard. "I know a house where the owner has some wine stashed. Wine is the only friend I have."

* * *

Isaac yawned and looked at Caiaphas.

Caiaphas, exhausted and past patience, pointed to Jesus and asked Judas, "Who is he?"

"Jesus of Nazareth," Judas answered.

Caiaphas slapped Judas' face. "You know what I mean. Does he claim that he is the Messiah?"

Judas looked at the floor and mumbled, "In so many words, yes."

"Good." Smiling, Caiaphas gestured to Rabbi Helcias, the Temple treasurer. "Pay Judas thirty pieces of silver and escort him to the gate," he said with a flourish.

Judas blinked. "What for?"

"That's your reward for bringing this dangerous criminal to our attention." Before Judas could leave, Caiaphas grabbed his arm. "I recall that you know Joseph of Arimathea."

"He's an acquaintance," Judas replied, "a friend of my father's."

"Does Joseph of Arimathea know this man?"

"They've met."

"How often?"

"I don't know."

"Is Joseph of Arimathea plotting some sort of Messiah trouble for us at the Temple?"

"Leave Joseph out of this," Jesus snapped. "I talked to him a few times, but it came to nothing. Joseph is loyal to the Sanhedrin."

"Anyone else?" Caiaphas asked.

Jesus pointed to the men assembled in the chamber and shrugged. "Why don't you ask them?"

Helcias handed Judas a pouch and said, "Count the money."

Judas shook his head and replied, "I don't want the money."

"Take it," Caiaphas urged. "Surely you can do some good with it." He patted Judas' shoulder. "Good night."

* * *

Simon-Peter staggered against an ivy covered wall, almost falling to the ground when he heard a rooster crow. He regained his balance and walked a little further, then realized what happened. Tears rimmed his eyes as he staggered through the streets, his path lit by the bright moon directly overhead. He shook his head and wondered how Jesus knew.

* * *

A temple guard escorted Judas from the house and pushed him down the steps to the courtyard. He stood at the top of the stairs until Judas collected himself and started toward the gate. When Judas felt a hand squeeze his shoulder as he neared the gate, he shook uncontrollably and urinated on the spot. Then he slowly turned to see Andrew's face.

"What happened in there?" Andrew asked.

Judas sobbed, "Something bad. They don't believe Jesus is the Messiah." Judas pulled Andrew closer and whispered in his face, "But he is! I know he is!"

"What will they do with him?" Andrew asked.

Judas shrugged. "Talk him to death for all I know." Judas pulled the bag of silver from his side. "Look at this; they gave me silver because I found Jesus for them."

"They rewarded you because you brought the Messiah to them?"

"I don't know," Judas answered as he clutched Andrew's arms and looked at him with woeful eyes. "Something bad is happening in there. The authorities want a scapegoat for Pontius Pilate." Judas' eyes grew large as he looked at the sky. "Oh my God!" he stammered. "I betrayed Jesus just as he prophesied."

* * *

Caiaphas stood in front of Jesus. "For the last time: Do you call yourself the Messiah as Judas claimed?"

Jesus gazed into his eyes and replied, "The time will come when you will see the Son of Man sitting at the right hand of God and coming on the clouds of heaven."

Caiaphas drew back in horror. "You blasphemed!" He put his face next to Jesus and sneered. "You fool!" Then he turned to the others and tore his robe. "You heard him--he calls himself the Messiah. We need no witnesses to prove his guilt. Praise be God!" Caiaphas waved his arms in the air. "Praise be God!"

The men stood on their benches and screamed, "Praise be God! The Almighty God of Israel! Praise! Praise!"

* * *

Judas sucked on a cup of wine next to the fire until he regained his strength. Then, looking at Andrew he said, "I'm going to Mary's house."

"I'll stay here," Andrew replied.

"All night?"

"If I have to. Jesus may come out at any time and I want to be here when he does."

Judas leaned against Andrew. "I'll come back at dawn. Maybe..." His voice trailed off as he left the courtyard.

* * *

Caiaphas called two guards over and whispered, "Take the Messiah to a room at the back of the house and guard him closely. Stay with him until I call for you." He pushed them toward Jesus, and then momentarily pulled them back, adding, "Talk to him. I want to know who his friends are, especially the ones who are members of the Sanhedrin. Do you understand?"

The guard tightened his grip on his staff and replied, "I understand."

"Be careful, though. I don't want him to look like a beggar from the Dung Gate in the morning."

The guard saluted and led Jesus out of the room.

Caiaphas sat on a bench and signaled to a servant. The servant brought a tray with several decanters while another servant brought a tray of cups. After everyone filled their cup, Caiaphas raised his cup and proclaimed, "Praise God--we solved our `Pontius Pilate' problem tonight. The Temple will remain open during our Passover observance." He drained his cup. "I want you back here at dawn. We'll take this Jesus to Pilate and present him as the man who started the riots."

Isaac ben Jonah asked, "What about the man they captured the other day?"

"We'll worry about him later," Caiaphas answered. "Pilate will have more interest in our boy when he learns Jesus thinks he's a king." Caiaphas snickered, "You know what the Romans think of kings."

"But he didn't say he was a king," Isaac persisted.

Caiaphas rolled his eyes. "Funny, I heard him say it." Caiaphas looked at the men near him. "Did you?"

They nodded.

After the men left, Caiaphas pulled Isaac aside and said, "We're doing God's work here. God called us to protect the Temple. And we must follow his command or forfeit our heritage."

CHAPTER FORTY-THREE
Friday

But he was pierced for our transgressions, he was crushed for our iniquities; the punishment that brought us peace was on him, and by his wounds we are healed.
Isaiah 53:5

A harsh wind blowing from the northwest kicked whirlpools of dust in the faces of the men walking from the house of Caiaphas to the Antonia Fortress. Caiaphas led the procession dressed in the robes of the Chief Priest, his features contorted with anger and frustration. A troop of temple guards pulled Jesus behind, followed by a small cadre of temple officials.

Caiaphas had risen two hours before dawn to call Jesus to his private quarters to talk, but learned little about Jesus activities or his people. Jesus' inability or unwillingness to explain recent events in Jerusalem or justify his actions incensed Caiaphas. He still had no understanding of who Jesus was or what his motives were. Most of all, he feared the crowds who followed Jesus through the Water Gate on Sunday Morning.

Jesus walked slowly, eyes downcast, prodded by the guard's small clubs when he stumbled. Aside from a black eye and a swollen jaw, he showed few signs of the harsh treatment given him during the night.

* * *

Andrew had remained in Caiaphas' courtyard after Simon-Peter left. He dozed a little before dawn, but woke when he heard the commotion from the priests gathering in the courtyard. Hurrying to Mary's house, he found Judas near the gate, drinking grape juice from a small clay cup. Prodded by Andrew's concern, Judas put the cup on a table and immediately followed Andrew to the Antonia Fortress.

* * *

The procession led by Caiaphas stopped at the large open plaza in front of the Antonia Fortress. Caiaphas beckoned to the Roman guards at the top of the stairway. "Tell Pontius Pilate that the Chief Priest Caiaphas is here to see him on official business," he shouted.

The guards hesitated for a moment, surprised at seeing a crowd of people standing in the square so early in the morning. Caiaphas glared at them until one nodded and hurried into the fortress. Meanwhile, the priests and other members of the Jewish ruling body milled around the plaza to keep themselves awake. Caiaphas mixed with the priests while the guards watched Jesus as if he were a legion of soldiers rather than one man suffering from exhaustion.

Caiaphas looked at the sky, blazing red at the eastern horizon, but slate gray overhead. "We need to finish our business before it rains," he mumbled. "It looks like more clouds moved in during the last hour." As if on cue, a few drops of water fell on his turban and rolled across his forehead. He rubbed his sleeve across his forehead, all the time casting appraising glances at Jesus trying to raise his head to catch a few drops of water on his parched lips.

The Roman guard came out of the fortress and ran to Caiaphas. Half saluting, he said, "Pontius Pilate is unavailable. Tribune Manius Decius will meet with you right now."

Caiaphas replied angrily, "This is business for the Procurator, not the Tribune."

"I'm sorry," replied the guard. "I am not permitted to disturb the Procurator."

Caiaphas was about to scream at the guard when he spied Manius Decius hurrying toward him. Brushing the guard aside, he growled at Manius Decius, "I demand to see Pilate!"

Manius Decius raised his hand to calm Caiaphas. "I notified Pilate's aide," he said as he scanned the group of people with Caiaphas. "I came to escort you into the fortress."

"Where will he meet us?" Caiaphas asked.

"His chambers in the southwest tower."

Caiaphas glared at Manius Decius. "You know better than that. Our Law forbids us to enter the living quarters of a Gentile."

"Are you willing to meet him in the courtyard?" Manius Decius asked.

Caiaphas looked at the others who nodded their approval. "Yes that'll be fine."

"What is the nature of your business?" Manius Decius asked.

"We caught a terrorist last night."

"Hmm."

"What does that mean?"

Manius Decius grinned. "He must be an important terrorist if the Chief Priest chooses to personally escort him to Pilate."

"This is the man who started the riot in the Temple on Monday," Caiaphas replied impatiently.

"But why..."

Caiaphas grabbed his sleeve. "Listen young man, your job is to deliver a message--that's all! I'll discuss the details with Pilate."

No one noticed that two extra men followed Jesus and the Temple officials into the courtyard. Andrew distracted the guard at the gate with a ritual chant and herded Judas to an unoccupied corner of the courtyard, covered by the shadow of the colonnades. They watched from there as Manius Decius went between two pillars, disappearing behind a heavy red curtain while Caiaphas and the other officials remained in the center of the courtyard. Andrew tried to catch Jesus eye without attracting the guard's attention, but failed.

After a few moments, they saw Manius Decius emerge from behind the curtain accompanied by Pontius Pilate dressed in a military uniform. Pilate immediately walked over to Caiaphas, offered him a restrained greeting, and then talked to him and the other priests. Andrew couldn't hear what they were saying, but from the look on Pilate's face, the conversation appeared less than friendly.

Pilate left them, snapped his fingers at a soldier, and signaled to his assistant, Adrien. The soldier immediately sprung into action, taking two other soldiers behind the pillars and returning with a wooden platform and a curule chair.

Andrew, sensing what was about to happen, turned to Judas and whispered, "I think Pilate is convening a tribunal."

The color drained from Judas' face. "A trial?" he asked.

"Probably."

"They're going to try Jesus?" The words caught in Judas' throat. "For what?"

Andrew jumped when Pontius Pilate snapped his crop. Silently, they watched as Adrien went to Pilate's side and handed him a wax tablet. Pilate looked at the tablet, almost smiled, and nodded his approval. Turning to the sparse crowd surrounding the platform, Adrien called the names of two men.

Nodding, Andrew said to Judas, "It's a tribunal."

"At this time of morning?" Judas asked. He realized that events had moved beyond his control and now felt a dread about what might happen next.

"Apparently the priest requested a trial for Jesus," Andrew continued.

"Caiaphas," Judas replied quietly, shaking his head. "But why Jesus?"

Within moments, Andrew heard groans and the sound of shuffling feet as the soldiers dragged two prisoners across the courtyard and threw them on the ground in front of Pilate. Both prisoners remained in a fetal position, drooling as Adrien shouted a proclamation in Latin. Looking at the sky, Pilate said some words to the men and gestured to the soldiers. They saluted, pulled the ropes tight around the prisoner's necks, and dragged them from the courtyard. Andrew saw, as the men stumbled in front of him, that they had been flayed and tortured to the point where they no longer resembled normal human beings.

Judas nudged Andrew. "What happened?" he asked.

"These men were condemned to death at an earlier trial," Andrew replied. "Apparently this Prefect gives condemned criminals a second hearing." Andrew paused as he looked toward the steps leading to the dungeon. "This was the hearing," he continued. "Pilate said he wants them crucified early today because of the weather."

Next, Pilate heard several guardianship cases involving the widows of soldiers. Adrien read (as translated by Andrew), "Our ancestors established the rule that all women, because of their weakness of intellect, should be under the power of guardians. The Julian-Titian Law provides that the guardians of such persons in the provinces be selected by the Governors, or in our case, by the Prefect."

He then read a list of five widows and the names of the people recommended for guardianship. Pontius Pilate waved his crop in approval and waited for the next case. Adrien looked over to the High Priest Caiaphas shuffling his feet, alternately nervous and angry over the pace of the proceedings.

Adrien read from his tablet. "The Chief Priest of the temple, Caiaphas, requests that you judge his prisoner on the grounds of treason and insurrection against the State of Rome."

Pilate looked first at Adrien, then to Caiaphas and gestured for the priests and Jesus to move to the front of his chair. He stared at Caiaphas. "Who is the man you accuse, and what has he done?"

"Jesus bar Joseph, and he..."

Pilate raised his hand for silence. "We already have one like him in the dungeon."

Adrien bent over and whispered in Pilate's ear.

"Oh," Pilate muttered, "you say we have the wrong man?" He gestured to Caiaphas. "You may continue."

"He's a criminal," Caiaphas said. "He started the riot in the Temple on Monday and his followers have been preaching sedition in the streets all week." Suddenly, Judas remembered how he and Simon-Peter preached in the streets near the Temple.

Pilate scratched his head and beckoned to Adrien. As Adrien leaned over, Pilate pointed to Caiaphas and said, “We already have a criminal in custody for the same activities.”

Overhearing Pilate, Caiaphas interrupted, “The man in the dungeon is not the one you want.” He pointed to Jesus and added, “He is.”

“But your merchant identified the man,” Pilate persisted.

“He lied,” Caiaphas retorted.

“How do you know?” Pilate asked sarcastically.

“He was afraid,” Caiaphas said. “I know he was afraid.”

Pilate cast a condescending glance at Jesus and asked Caiaphas, “So now you say this man is a criminal?”

Caiaphas nodded.

Pilate shifted in his chair and gazed at Jesus. After a few minutes, he said to the guards, “Bring him closer,” and two guards pulled Jesus to the platform. Laughing, Pilate flicked his riding crop on his thigh. “How many legions do you command, little man?” he asked. Then he pointed to Caiaphas. “Temple riots are your business, my friend. How many times have you told me that Roman soldiers defile your Temple and that Roman law has no place there? You judge him!”

“We have, and we found him guilty,” Caiaphas replied without hesitation.

“Guilty of what?” Pilate snapped.

“Blasphemy.”

Pilate threw his hands in the air. “Dear High Priest, pray that you never face charges in a Roman court. Your arguments are without merit or logic.” Looking back to Jesus, he asked, “What are they really accusing you of?”

Jesus shrugged and remained silent. For a moment, he reminded Pilate of the wretch who murdered Tribune Vehilius Gratus, except that Jesus still had ten fingers.

“Excuse me, Prefect,” Caiaphas interrupted, “there’s more.”

“Good, let’s hear it.”

Caiaphas pointed to Jesus. “He and his people are opposed to the payment of taxes to Caesar...”

Pilate almost smiled again. “Doesn’t everyone?” he interrupted.

Caiaphas paused long enough to draw the attention of the crowd, then continued, “...and he claims he’s a king.”

“What?” Pilate asked Jesus with raised eyebrows. “Are you a king?”

“Is that your idea...or his?” Jesus asked.

“Do you think I’m a Jew?” Pilate sneered. “Your people and your Chief Priest brought you here.” He walked down the steps to Jesus. “Do you understand there are no kings in Rome?”

Jesus stood straight and gazed at Pilate. "My kingdom is not of this world. If it were, my people would fight to prevent my arrest."

Pilate returned to his chair. "What you have here my dear Caiaphas is a maniac, not a criminal. I might add that you're almost as crazy as he, bringing him here to disturb my morning schedule." Pilate yawned, adding, "Where did you find him?"

Caiaphas puffed his chest. "He started in Galilee and..."

"Did you say Galilee?" Pilate shouted, suddenly alert.

"Yes, but..."

"That's Herod's province." Pilate stated. Turning to Manius Decius, he continued, "Escort these people from the fortress. Their guards can take this dangerous criminal to Herod Antipas at the Hasmonean Palace." Then he gestured to the priests. "You go with him. I'm sure you'll see to it that Herod renders a fair judgment."

Caiaphas raised his hand to protest Pilate's abrupt dismissal, but Pilate waved him off and disappeared behind the curtain. Once there, he muttered to Adrien, "Tell the others to wait. I need to relieve myself after dealing with those fools."

A small crowd had collected around the courtyard, some waiting to start their morning's business, others drawn by the early morning procession from Caiaphas' house to the fortress. Attracted by the intensity of the Temple officials and their sense that a good story was about to unfold, several of those people followed Caiaphas and Jesus out of the fortress. Andrew and Judas mixed with the crowd and followed Jesus to the Hasmonean Palace where they entered the courtyard to wait for the appearance of Herod Antipas. Judas continued to hang in the shadows, keeping a shawl wrapped over his head to keep the priests and temple authorities from recognizing him.

* * *

Shortly after he arrived from camp, John sat at a small table in the courtyard with Mary Marcia and Mark. He picked at a dish of apples, cheese and barley bread, lazily lifting the food and dropping it back on the plate. His voice echoed in the courtyard, "Where are they?" he asked for the third time since he arrived. The house seemed quiet, almost tranquil, in sharp contrast to the joyous celebration of the previous night.

"Andrew and Judas left early this morning," Mary Marcia replied, standing next to John with a steaming pitcher. "Here, have some tea while you wait."

"Left for where?" John asked.

Before Mary could answer, a commotion in the far corner of the courtyard alerted them that Simon-Peter was awake. John watched Simon-Peter rouse himself off the floor, noted his torn clothes and dirty hair, and shuddered. "You'll need more than a ritual bath to clean yourself today," he shouted across the courtyard.

Simon-Peter shuffled over to a bench and leaned heavily against the wall. He twisted his nose when Mary handed him a steaming cup of tea. Looking at John through his bleary eyes, he asked, "What happened to you last night?"

"What do you mean?" queried John.

"Why didn't you follow us into the city?" Simon-Peter asked in a tone more muted than usual.

John felt the lump on his head. "One of the guards knocked me out. I came to the city as soon as I recovered, but I couldn't get through the gate until this morning." Sipping his tea, he asked, "What happened here? Where did you go last night?"

Simon-Peter gestured for another cup of tea to wash the cobwebs out of his mouth. "Judas and Jesus went to the high priest's house after they left the camp," he answered after a while.

"Judas!" John spat the name out as if it were poison. "What did they do there?"

"I think they joined the Temple gang," Simon-Peter mumbled.

"What do you mean?" Mary Marcia asked.

"What I said," Simon-Peter responded. "Jesus spent the night with Caiaphas and his friends." He waved his arms. "All that stuff about kingdoms for the poor was just talk."

"Not Jesus," John shouted. "That Judas serpent tricked him." Pounding his fist into his hand, he added, "I should have been there to help. Jesus can't handle those snakes like a Zebedee can." He looked at Simon-Peter. "Certainly a sot like you..."

Simon-Peter jumped off the bench and stumbled toward John but halted when Mary, the mother of Jesus, shouted, "Stop it; we have to wait for the truth until Andrew and Judas return."

Simon-Peter waved his hands in the air. "I left Andrew at the high priest's house last night."

Mary Marcia tapped her lip. "Something happened. That's why Andrew and Judas left this morning. Andrew talked to Judas for a minute and they ran out of the courtyard."

"Where did they go?" John asked again.

Mary Marcia cast an impatient glance at John and shrugged. "I don't know. I was just coming into the courtyard as they left. Andrew said something about going to find Jesus; that we should wait until one of them comes back."

Simon-Peter yawned and scratched his head. "I'm going back to sleep. Wake me as soon as you know something."

Mary Marcia gave him a towel and a dish filled with water. "Here," she said, "at least clean your face. You can use one of the rooms in the back of the house. I'll wake you as soon as Andrew returns."

* * *

Herod Antipas was staying at the old Hasmonean Palace as he always did when visiting Jerusalem. The palace stood in the center of Jerusalem, only a few minutes walk from the fortress. The Herods stayed at this smaller residence rather than the lavish palace built near the western city wall by Herod the Great. That palace was now used as the living quarters for visiting Roman dignitaries, including Pontius Pilate.

Andrew carried his robe on his arm as he listened to the exchange between Herod Antipas, Caiaphas, and Jesus in the courtyard of the Hasmonean Palace. Judas, still hanging in the shadows, kept his shawl pulled tightly against his head.

Herod circled Jesus, occasionally probing his soiled and bloody robe with a small staff. He seemed as angry as Pilate for being disturbed at such an early hour.

"You say he called himself a king?" Herod asked Caiaphas.

Caiaphas nodded.

"And you say he's from Galilee?" Herod continued.

Again, Caiaphas nodded, shuffling his feet like a schoolboy. He didn't know why, but he felt uncomfortable in the presence of Herod Antipas. All the Herods seemed to carry a superior attitude, looking down at everyone including the high priests and the Roman officials.

"King of what?" asked Herod.

"I don't know, maybe Idumea," Caiaphas answered with a grin.

Herod gave Caiaphas an angry look then poked Jesus. "King of Nothing from Galilee. Galilee--the land of fools." Herod gestured to Caiaphas. "What else? After all, we have plenty of pretenders in Galilee. Why should I care? We are in Judea--Pilate's territory." Swinging his arms in a circle, he added, "Why should I worry about this one?"

"He claims he's the Messiah," Caiaphas answered.

Herod shot an incredulous glance at Jesus. "Ah, now we're getting somewhere. The Messiah--here--and from Galilee." With that Herod laughed and signaled his people to do the same. Then looking back at Jesus, he said, "Say, are you the one I heard the wild stories about? You know, walking on water, curing the blind--what was it? Oh yes, feeding hundreds of people with food out of nowhere?" Herod stood, legs spread and hands at his waist. "Are you the one we heard about?"

Jesus remained silent.

Andrew went over to where Judas was standing and whispered, "Why doesn't he talk--defend himself?" Andrew shook his head. "He's done no wrong."

"Do a miracle for me," Herod teased, growing impatient with Jesus' silence and the whole idea that this motley parade was interfering with his morning routine.

Judas felt Andrew stiffen and put his hand on his arm. "Don't start anything," he cautioned.

"No miracle?" Herod continued. Then he called a servant and whispered in his ear. Turning to Caiaphas, he said, "Pilate must think I'm a fool. The last time I dealt with one of these fanatics, he lost his head. His followers still haven't forgiven me for that. Now Pilate wants me to do it again."

The servant returned with one of Herod's old purple robes and, at Herod's signal, removed Jesus soiled robe and placed Herod's robe around his shoulders. Andrew wondered if there was something wrong with Jesus that he would submit to such degrading behavior. At the same time, he felt angry that people would treat his friend in such a way.

Herod flicked the robe with his staff and said, "Now you look more like a king." Drawing closer to Jesus, he added, "Tell me, King Messiah, would you mind if I married my brother's wife? Would it matter to you that she is also my niece?" He paused, and then followed with a wicked smile. "After all, what are these minor affairs in the grand scheme of things?" He waited for a reply but none came. "No answer? I guess they don't mean much." He hit Jesus on the buttocks with his staff and announced so everyone in the courtyard could hear, "Off with you, Messiah. Tell Pontius Pilate this king is no threat to Herod."

* * *

Pontius Pilate thought his eyes had deceived him when he saw the procession of priests, temple officials, and Jesus entering the courtyard of the Antonia Fortress. He quickly gestured for Caiaphas to meet him on the platform.

"What happened?" Pilate asked Caiaphas. "Did you take the prisoner to Herod Antipas?"

"We did," Caiaphas replied.

"And?"

Eyes downcast, Caiaphas replied, "He said to tell you that this man is no threat to him. Do with him as you please."

Pilate shook his head. "You brought this man to me as a criminal and a rebel," he declared in a low voice. "You didn't prove your charge to me or

Herod Antipas. As far as I can tell, he's done nothing to deserve death except play the fool. Therefore, I'll punish him for the disturbance you say he caused at the Temple and release him."

"He blasphemed," Caiaphas shouted back. "That's a crime punishable with death."

"Only for the Jews," Pilate retorted. "So it's up to you to execute him."

"We can't," Caiaphas sighed. "Have you forgotten that we signed an agreement forbidding us to conduct public executions?"

Walking in a small circle, Pilate stroked his chin. "Yes, well..."

Caiaphas, now more sure of himself pressed on. "Have you forgotten so quickly our meeting at Caesarea? It was there that we promised to manage our own affairs and, in return, you promised to enforce our judgments."

Adrien caught Pilate's eye and Pilate pulled him aside. "What is it?" he asked stiffly.

"I have a message from your wife," replied Adrien.

"So?" Pilate felt his patience running thin.

Adrien pointed to Jesus. "She dreamt about him last night," he whispered. "She said you should leave him alone. He's an innocent man."

"And?" Pilate's morning deteriorating with each new surprise.

Adrien continued, "She suffered terribly this morning because of that dream."

Pilate shook his head. "By Jupiter, I should've left her in Caesarea. What do women know about innocence and guilt?" Then he looked around to see if anyone heard them. Satisfied they were out of hearing range, he added, "I wouldn't be surprised if the brainless rabble from the streets won't come here soon with some advice on how I should handle this case." Pushing Adrien away, he added, "Send the messenger back to Procla and tell her to take a nap. Tell her to leave me alone."

Pilate turned his attention back to the priests, asking, "And what do you want me to do with this man?"

Caiaphas pointed to the Gabbatha Gate. "You said you have posts set outside the walls ready for more crucifixions."

"You want me to crucify him?" Pilate asked.

"Yes," Caiaphas and the priests chorused, "crucify him."

Pilate looked at the sky. "Look, you turned my schedule into a mess with your foolishness. I'll have him flogged and kept in the dungeon with the rats for a few days, and then we'll release him."

"We want him crucified--today! By sundown!" they shouted even louder.

Still failing to understand why the priests were so adamant about Jesus, Pilate raised his hands as a gesture of conciliation. "Look, we've got this

Joshua bar Abbas in the dungeon. We've already tortured him. Let's hang him instead."

Caiaphas looked at the other priests, then back to Pilate. "You have a custom at our feasts to release a prisoner chosen by us. We want you to release Joshua bar Abbas and crucify Jesus in his place." Caiaphas raised a finger to emphasize his point. "This Jesus claims to be a king. It was he who came through the Water Gate on Sunday. As you saw, he has thousands of followers to back his claim. What could your small cohort do to stop him if he chooses to attack Jerusalem?"

Glancing at Jesus, Pilate answered, "What you say could be true of anyone. But be reasonable; this is not the type of man who would attack Jerusalem." Pilate wondered for a moment whether Caiaphas was a little too hysterical in his condemnation of Jesus, or if there was more to this case than he knew. "I agree with Herod Antipas."

"You are no friend of Caesar if you let this man go," Caiaphas snapped. "He is a threat to Rome. Anyone who claims to be a king opposes Caesar."

Pilate shot an angry glance at Caiaphas. "Don't tell me what Caesar wants, or who his friends are." Calming as quickly as he angered, Pilate asked, "Are you sure this is the man we saw on Sunday?"

"Positive," Caiaphas replied, wiping the sweat from his face.

Pilate sat back in his chair and called to Jesus. "Why don't you say something in your own defense? Will these people send you to your death without you saying a word?" Without waiting for an answer he added, "What have you done that irritates these people so?"

"I told them the truth," Jesus replied.

"What is truth?" Pilate asked.

"The Word of God." Jesus looked into Pilate's eyes. "Also, the truth is you have no power over me. What I do here, I do willingly and in obedience to my father."

Somehow, Pilate sensed that Jesus was no ordinary zealot or petty thief. He shrugged and said to Caiaphas, "This Joshua bar Abbas is a known criminal. He murdered Jews. Yet you want us to free him and crucify this man."

"Yes," Caiaphas answered.

Pilate stood and waved his riding crop in a circle over his head. "THEN SAY IT!"

"CRUCIFY HIM!" the crowd screamed under Caiaphas' direction. "GET ON WITH IT!"

Pilate signaled to Adrien, at the same time pointing to a jug of drinking water standing on a nearby table. At Pilate's signal, Adrien poured water on Pilate's hands. "I am innocent of this man's blood," Pilate yelled to the crowd. "He is your responsibility now."

The priests answered in a chorus, “Let his blood be on us and on our children!”

With that, Pilate stood and proclaimed, “Take him to the dungeon, remove that silly robe, and flog him until his skin covers the floor. Then crucify him on the sixth hour with the two thieves I condemned this morning. We’ll see what he thinks of obedience then.” Gesturing to a guard, he added, “Release Joshua bar Abbas and throw him down the stairs if you wish.”

Finally, Pilate called Adrien over and whispered, “I’ll fix those pompous asses.” Eyes narrowing to a slit, he continued, “Make a sign to carry in front of that unfortunate creature. Have it read, `KING OF THE JEWS’ in three languages; Latin, Aramaic, and Greek.” Then he left the courtyard without an acknowledgement or glance toward Caiaphas and the temple officials.

As they left the plaza, Caiaphas turned to Isaac ben Jonah, and said, “This is not a good day for us. If I had my way, not one Jew would die at the hands of the Romans.” He raised his hands in a hopeful gesture. “Maybe now his followers will melt away.” He shook his head after they walked a little farther. “No, It won’t work that way,” he muttered. “There’ll always be people who want to destroy the Temple.”

“I feel the same as you,” Isaac said as he pointed to the sky. “Look, even the sky is gray, as if it also felt sorrow. It looks like we’ll have little time to prepare for our Sabbath before the rains come.”

Caiaphas rolled his sleeves toward his elbow and looked at Isaac. “Yes, it will rain before sundown, but at least we’ll have that pest out of our way.”

* * *

Andrew went to where Judas was cowering in the shadows. “Did you hear that?” he asked Judas. “Pilate condemned Jesus to death!”

Judas said nothing in reply, although his face looked like he was carrying the weight of the world on his shoulders.

I’m going to Mary’s house to tell the others,” Andrew continued. “You stay here to see if they bring Jesus back to the courtyard.” Andrew looked into Judas’ eyes and put his hands on his shoulders. “Are you alright?”

“Yes,” Judas replied softly. “But...”

“I don’t know what Jesus plans to do,” Andrew said as he started to leave. “All I know is that someone better do something fast.”

“I don’t think Jesus has a plan,” Judas mumbled.

“I’ll be back with the others as soon as I can,” Andrew yelled over his shoulder as he ran out of the courtyard.

Suddenly Judas felt totally alone as he watched Andrew run out of the courtyard.

* * *

By the time Andrew left the Antonia Fortress, the streets of Jerusalem were clogged with people shopping and preparing for the Sabbath. The markets, already strained to their limits from supplying the food and accessories for the Seder, tried to make room for carts filled with fruits, vegetables, and sheep. Andrew heard sheep bleating in the background as he ran, as if the sheep knew they were about to be sacrificed. When he entered the gate to Mary's house, he saw John who had just arrived from the camp, Mary Marcia, and Mark sitting on benches with expectant looks on their faces.

John jumped up. "What happened?" he asked. "Your face is as white as a priest's robe."

"I've been at the Antonia Fortress with Judas," Andrew replied between deep breaths. "Pontius Pilate just sentenced Jesus to death."

John fell against the wall, unable to believe his ears. When he caught his breath he asked, "What are you saying?"

"I said Pontius Pilate...sentenced Jesus to death...by crucifixion on the sixth hour. He is to be hung with two criminals." Andrew wiped the sweat off his forehead and slumped on a bench. "I left Judas at the fortress to watch for him."

"You left him at the fortress?" John screamed. "What is he doing?"

Andrew sighed, "Pontius Pilate sent Jesus to the dungeon..." He held his breath and tried to regain his composure. "...the Romans usually flog prisoners before they execute them."

John pulled at his hair and screamed, "What happened? My God! What happened?" Tears spilled from his eyes.

"Apparently the high priests took him to..."

John grabbed a handful of Andrew's tunic, pulling him off the bench. "No! No!" he yelled. "You're lying! They wouldn't dare crucify Jesus!"

Andrew, seeing the passion in John's eyes pried John's hands off his tunic and quickly moved to the other side of the table.

John sank to the bench and looked at Andrew with baleful eyes. "Judas, I knew from the beginning he was no good. Where is he?"

"I told you, he's at the Fortress," Andrew replied. Seeing the almost insane look on John's face, Andrew kept his distance and signaled the others to do the same.

John's eyes darted around the courtyard. "I have to find Jesus' mother."

"Why?" Andrew asked. "What can she do?"

"She's staying at a house near here," John said absently. "I'll get her." He looked at Andrew. "Where are they going to crucify him?"

"Caiaphas mentioned the hill west of the city--Golgotha?" Andrew looked into John's eyes. "Did you hear what I said?"

"When will they crucify him?" John continued, gazing past Andrew into a distant void.

Andrew came closer to John, hoping to calm him, but John seized Andrew's tunic again and shook him. "Why didn't you stop Judas? Why didn't you come back and get me?" Harsh words fell from John's mouth with the same passion as tears flowed from his eyes. Releasing Andrew as suddenly as he grabbed him, he ran through the gate.

Andrew, Mark, and Mary Marcia stood in silence, confused by the events around them. As he pushed the gate closed, Andrew asked, "Where are the others?"

"Abraham, Anna, and my cousins from Bethsaida went to the Temple this morning," she recited in a melancholy voice. "Simon-Peter is in the back room sleeping. Mary of Magdala is with Jesus' mother."

"The others are still at the camp?" Andrew asked.

"I suppose," She replied, looking toward the house. "Should we wake Simon-Peter?"

"Not yet," answered Andrew. "Wait until John comes back with Mary." Then Andrew scratched his head and asked, "What's wrong with Simon-Peter?"

Mary Marcia fussed with a pile of dishes on the table. "Something about Judas and the high priests." She turned and looked sadly at Andrew. "He came here late last night and drank a half a skin of wine. He'll be sick for a week." Returning to her dishes, she added, "I don't understand what went wrong."

"Neither do I," Andrew replied. "I don't have any idea where the real problem lies. As far as I can see, Judas is as upset as everyone else." Andrew took Mary Marcia's hand. "Stay here. Keep Rebecca with you and keep the gate locked. Wake Simon-Peter and tell him what happened. He can go with John when he returns. I want to get back to the camp before the rain starts to warn the others. Mark can come with me."

Mary turned to him with tears in her eyes. "Be careful. Please be careful."

* * *

The air in the courtyard of the Antonia Fortress had turned still and hot, yet Judas shivered as he stood alone in the crowd of people waiting for the prisoners to return from the lower level. When he heard noises from the stairs leading to the dungeon, he turned his head in time to see the soldiers dragging the prisoners up the stairs with ropes.

At first Judas didn't recognize Jesus. His face was a mask of pain, his body stripped of its flesh, and his blood leaked through the stripes left by the flagra. Judas blinked when he noticed a crown made from branches squeezed on Jesus head. He retreated further into the shadows and wept. "What did I do?" he asked himself. "I thought Jesus was the Messiah."

Judas was about to follow the procession to Golgotha when a heavy hand gripped his shoulder, holding him in place. He stood perfectly still, except for his shivering, and waited for the other hand to end his life. Instead, a gruff voice behind him mumbled something in Latin. Judas slowly turned and found himself face to helmet with a Roman soldier. This time the soldier said in broken Greek, "Follow me," and started walking toward the stairway to the dungeon. Now Judas was convinced it was his turn to die.

Along the way, the soldier collared two other men and the four men descended to the lower level of the Fortress. Judas took each step paralyzed with fear. His fright intensified when he saw the stone pillars the Romans used to tie prisoners for flogging. They looked so simple with a notch cut at the top to hold the prisoner's wrists. He spotted two bowls, one filled with brine and the other with water, and the sponge used to rub the brine into the prisoner's wounds.

Nothing in his life prepared him for what he saw next. The soldier led the men to a corner of the dungeon where a body, hacked like a piece of raw meat, lay in a pool of its own blood. The soldier pointed to the body. "Take this mess out of here and do whatever you Jews do to your dead." He kicked the body and rolled it over for all to see.

"Wh...Wh...What happened?" Judas cried.

The guard spit on the ground. "This man slipped past our guards and almost murdered our flogger. It took three of our soldiers to kill him." Growing impatient, he added, "Now get busy and take him out of here." The soldier pointed to a doorway leading to the east end of the fortress. "Take him out that door."

Judas tried to help but, by the time they reached the door, the dead man's body seemed to fall apart. Judas turned and vomited. The other men pushed him aside and continued up the stairs. After a few minutes, he spied another exit and ran through the courtyard and out of the fortress, toward the Upper City. As he ran, he tried to wipe blood off his hands on his robe. It had been less than one day since Judas shared his joyful Seder with Jesus and his friends. Now Jesus was on his way to Golgotha and Judas was on his way to uncertainty.

CHAPTER FORTY-FOUR
Golgotha

"Awake, sword, against my shepherd, against the man who is close to me!" declares the LORD Almighty. "Strike the shepherd, and the sheep will be scattered, and I will turn my hand against the little ones."

Zechariah 13:7

Soldiers led the procession of prisoners toward the west wall of the city. A small but noisy crowd followed the grisly parade of guards and bleeding, naked prisoners carrying cross pieces on their shoulders. The condemned men seemed insensitive to pain as the sharp stones laced between the pavement blocks cut their bare feet. A soldier rode on a donkey in front of them carrying a sign that read: "JESUS OF NAZARETH--KING OF THE JEWS," in Greek, Aramaic, and Latin.

The procession wound between the fortress and the Gabbatha Gate with additional spectators gathering on each block until the crowd numbered well over a hundred. The soldiers, fearing a disturbance, pushed the prisoners as fast as they could by whipping and jabbing them with the handles of their spears. After walking a few blocks, Jesus fell face down on the pavement. He lay there with the cross piece rocking on his neck until two soldiers scrambled to pull him up. Once on his feet, he stumbled forward, then twisted slightly and fell against one of the soldiers.

The soldier pushed him away, wiping Jesus blood and sweat from his armor and sleeves. An earlier drizzle now gave way to a light rain, and the soldier collected pools of water in his cupped hand to wash the blood from his armor. The spectacle reached a corner where two streets met. There the guards pushed the prisoners and pulled the ropes until they turned the corner toward Golgotha.

It soon became obvious that Jesus was too weak to carry his cross piece alone, so the soldiers pulled a man out of the crowd to help. The man pulled back, looking for a way to escape, but took the cross piece when a guard threatened him with his whip. The crowd hurled insults at people in the procession, some directed at the soldiers, but most directed at the prisoners. Women ran into the street, spit at the prisoners, and displayed suggestive gestures at the soldiers.

* * *

John reached Mary Marcia's house with his mother, Salome, Jesus' mother, Mary, and Mary of Magdala. Judas showed up moments later, exhausted and full of fear. John went over to Judas and held him by his arm. Pushing Judas against the wall he screamed, "What happened? Tell me what happened last night!"

Judas looked at him with sepulchral eyes and gasped, "I don't know. The men seemed interested in talking to Jesus, but then they got angry and told me to leave the room. All I know now is that the Romans are going to crucify him."

John went over to Mary and asked, "Did you hear what he said?"

"Yes," she replied sorrowfully.

"What should we do?"

She sighed, "I wish I were dead, but I must go to him."

"They plan to crucify him," Judas warned.

"I know, but I belong with him regardless of where he is or what happens to him. He is my son."

"I want to go with you," Salome said. Mary of Magdala nodded and took Salome's hand.

Mary Marcia was about to join the group when John stopped her. "When Simon-Peter comes out here tell him I couldn't wait, that we are heading toward Golgotha and he should get there as fast as he can."

* * *

Judas was sitting on a bench in the courtyard when Simon-Peter came out of the atrium. His bleary eyes focused on Judas as if he were a ghost, then he sprung at Judas like a panther. Squeezing Judas' neck, he shouted, "Where is Jesus? What did you do with him?"

Judas pulled at Simon-Peter's hands to break his grip and coughed, "High Priests--Romans..."

Simon-Peter let go when he smelled Judas' foul breath. "You turned him over to the Romans?" He slapped Judas' face with the back of his hand.

Judas tried to defend himself but Simon-Peter buffeted him on the sides of his head. Finally Judas ducked away, pleading, “Stop it...I didn’t do anything.”

Simon-Peter kicked Judas in the groin and battered his nose when he doubled over. Mary Marcia ran screaming into the courtyard to stop Simon-Peter, but swinging wildly, he sent her reeling over a bench.

Judas skulked against the wall, trying to summon the last of his energy. “You don’t understand, you...”

Simon-Peter, now in a full rage, hit Judas again. “Don’t call me stupid. I understand more than you do!” He stood back and watched Judas slump to the ground. His rage sated, he lurched out of the courtyard to find Jesus.

Judas brought himself to his feet and ran from the house.

* * *

John and the three women ran as fast as they could and reached the Gabbatha Gate just as the gruesome parade turned the last corner. Jesus’ mother almost fainted when she caught the first glimpse of her son. She found John and held on to his arm. She cried out when she saw Jesus’ torso, torn by his beatings and the weight of the heavy cross piece. Without thinking, Mary of Magdala removed her own robe and ran past the soldiers to put it on Jesus. A soldier grabbed her before she reached him and forced her back at the crowd. Only when some of the men in the crowd fondled her, did she realize she only wore a flimsy gown underneath.

Jesus slipped and fell on the wet pavement, dragging another prisoner down with him. One of the guards flailed his whip against Jesus to push him forward. When he reached back to hit Jesus a second time, the whip caught an onlooker’s face and the man fell to the ground. The guard, angered because the crowd was too close and afraid that they would get out of hand, flogged at the people. They responded first by dancing on their toes from the sting and yelled epithets at the guards and prisoners.

The lead guard stopped when he noticed lightning in the western sky and heard the distant rumble of thunder. Gesturing to the others, he shouted, “Let’s hurry, I want to get back to the fortress before we drown in the rain.”

* * *

Hearing the uproar, Rebecca ran into the courtyard and found her mother unconscious from Simon-Peter’s blow. Suddenly, lightening and thunder roiled the sky and heavy drops of rain splattered against the courtyard floor. The noise and the shock of warm water shook Mary Marcia's conscious. Pressing Rebecca's arm, she said, "Thank God you're safe."

"What happened?"

Mary Marcia looked at Rebecca. "Did you see anything? No?" She rubbed her eyes. "It was Simon-Peter; he was beating Judas. I ran into the courtyard to stop him and he hit me." She shook her head as if to shake her grogginess. "That's the last I remember."

* * *

John and the women followed the grisly procession at a safe distance. By now at least two hundred noisy, sweating people gathered around the spectacle of near dead prisoners and angry soldiers passing through the Gabbatha Gate. One of the prisoners fell when he stepped on a sharp stone and the guards hit him with the handles of their spears to keep him going. Kicking the stone aside, another guard mumbled, "They feel different on your feet than they do in your hands." Then he shouted at the prisoner, "Why don't you pick up the stones and throw them like you people do when you riot?" John noted the distant sound of crows cawing a warning of impending doom.

As they approached the hill, the guards wrapped the ropes around the chests of the prisoners to pull them up the incline more easily. John watched Jesus submit to the guards and shook his head. He remembered that less than twenty four hours earlier, Jesus washed his disciple's feet and presided over their community celebration in the full flush of manhood. Now Jesus was an object, a straw man tortured by Pagan guards.

The two Mary's and Salome shuffled behind John in grief and shock. They didn't hear the crowd or the thunder that hung over the city like a furious god passing judgment.

The procession stopped when one of the prisoners fell to the ground. "This man is almost dead!" a guard shouted. "Help me drag him up the hill." Two guards grabbed the thief's arms and pulled him toward the hill, leaving his crosspiece rolling unevenly to the side.

The air boiled with the noise from the crowd and the moans from the condemned men as they trudged up the hill toward Golgotha, although some of the crowd started to drift away, driven by the rain and the pall of violence that fell over the parade. John felt a pain in the deepest part of his stomach.

Slate gray clouds fingered the grotesque procession as it made its final turn up the hill. As the crowd quieted, only the sound of the guard's taunts and the crack of whips hung in the humid air. Another prisoner stumbled. A guard kicked his back as he fell on the sharp stones littering the path. The man rose slowly, first on one leg, then the other. Somehow he managed to stand on his wobbling legs to continue his journey.

John, intently watching every move Jesus made, thought he saw a look of serenity on Jesus face, but he knew better. "It's my imagination," he thought, like watching a dead person and thinking they were still breathing.

The procession stopped at the top of the hill where the crucifixion posts stood firmly in the ground, waiting for new victims. "The ever efficient Romans," John thought as he scrutinized the execution site.

The posts, braced from the rear, connected to each other about three feet off the ground with a long piece of wood. In addition, heavy boulders surrounded the base of each post to keep them in place. Blocks of wood placed near the middle of the posts served as seats to support the victim, delaying suffocation. Notches at the top of the post received the cross pieces after the executioners attached the victim to the cross piece on the ground. Ropes and pulleys raised the victim to the post where soldiers stood on ladders to tie the cross piece to the post. Later, when the victim died, slaves would cut the ropes and let the body fall to the ground. The slaves, used by the Romans for their dirtiest work, then dragged the corpses away for disposal.

John and the women stared in horrified silence as the guards prepared each man for hanging. The soldiers decided to hang the thieves first and threw the first one on the ground. They tied his arms to the cross piece with a heavy rope and left him there. They did the same to the other man. It seemed to everyone standing on Golgotha that the thieves were so close to death that their crucifixion was almost an afterthought.

John edged as close as he dared when the soldiers started on Jesus. "He's still alive," one guard said. "The other two are from the dungeon, but this one only came to us this morning."

"What should we do?" another guard asked.

The first guard looked at the sky. "I don't want to wait. He'll die right away if we take the seat off the post and break his legs." The second guard shook his head. "We only have orders to hang him. Why should we make it easier for him to die?"

"What do you want to do?" asked the first guard.

"We'll use nails to fasten his arms and feet. That way he'll bleed more." He shrugged and added, "If he hangs on too long, I'll run a spear through him and end his agony." The other guards looked up from their work, amused by his play on words.

Next they pulled Jesus to the ground where two guards lifted his shoulders and a third put the cross piece underneath. They tied his arms to the cross piece with a rope first, then held his body while another guard brought a crude mallet and a pouch of spikes. He sat on Jesus chest, took a spike from his pouch, and pushed it through Jesus wrist. Then he pounded it with the mallet until the oversized head caught Jesus flesh, causing his blood to spurt every time the blunt head of the mallet hit his arm.

Jesus lifted off the ground slightly each time the mallet made contact with the spikes. John felt the dull, deadening pain as if it were happening to him. The guard moved to the other wrist and hit the spike. It snapped away and pinged against the rocks. He cursed, spit in the direction of Jesus face, and then drove a new nail into his wrist.

John, moved beyond reason, seized a rock and started toward the guard nailing Jesus wrists. Two other guards walked past him as he straightened, and the scabbard of one caught the side of his head. He reeled until Salome pulled him away. "Stay out of this!" she cautioned. "There's nothing you can do." John looked at her, bleary eyed, and backed away.

Now the men pulled the prisoners up the posts with the pulleys and ropes while another guard ran up a ladder to guide the cross pieces into their slots. Below, the prisoner's legs hung loosely until a guard tied them to the post. Only Jesus had a spike driven through his feet.

The soldiers did their job well. Three prisoners hung with legs bent, seated on small pieces of wood. When they looked up, they saw dingy clouds almost touching their heads and when they looked down, they saw the murky outlines of people staring at their torn bodies. The people watched them writhe and gasp in their dance of death with a mixture of pity and fascination.

Mary, the mother of Jesus, looked at her son with eyes that seemed to see things beyond the horizon. John took her arm, asking if there was anything he could do. She licked her lips, dry and parched, and said, "I wonder what Jesus did so wrong that he should hang on a Roman cross." She looked away from the cross for a moment, adding, "I remember our days in Nazareth when Jesus worked in the carpenter shop with Joseph, and later, when we went to the wedding at Cana together." She gave John a sideways glance. "That was the first time he treated me as the head of the family--and it was so soon after Joseph's death."

As the soldiers continued their watch, John heard them bet on who would die first and who would last the longest. It didn't take long to pay the first bet, for soon one of the thieves choked, convulsed, and slumped in death. The soldiers took note and paid the winner.

One of the onlookers, a man John recognized as a Temple priest, taunted Jesus. "So! You would destroy the temple and rebuild it in three days," he shouted. "Come down from that cross and save yourself." The priest turned to a man standing next to him. "Is this the King of Israel--the Messiah?" he laughed harshly. "What a funny looking Messiah," he added as he turned away.

Other men approached the cross where Jesus hung and spit at him, then made lewd gestures at John and the women. "Be careful, Galilean," the priest said as he threatened John with a clenched fist. "You might be the next pig to hang here."

* * *

Simon-Peter blind with rage, ran the wrong direction from Mary Marcia's house and left the city through the Zion Gate. Realizing his mistake, he circled through the Hinnom Valley until he came to a hill a short distance from Golgotha. Hiding behind a clump of nettles, he watched the soldiers throw the prisoners on the ground to prepare them for crucifixion. The rain and fog prevented a clear view of the proceedings, so he decided to move to the next hill, cursing the prickles from the nettle bushes as he crept down the path to the valley.

The guards had hoisted one man on his post by the time Simon-Peter reached the bottom of the next hill. He shuddered when he saw the second body slowly rise up the post, guided by the pulley assembly on top and ropes tied to his legs. It looked as if the man was floating to the post. He had seen other people milling around the area when he watched from the top of the hill, but in the valley, he saw only the victims and a soldier on a ladder.

Simon-Peter slowly worked his way up the hill directly across from Golgotha as the guards hoisted the third man. He rubbed his arms when he thought he saw spikes in the man's wrists. The dreary scene left him with a sense of dread. He remembered when Jesus said the Son of Man would be lifted up. "What a twist," he whispered to himself. "To think I came back to him a second time. Judas is right. I am stupid."

He stood for a moment on the side of the hill, gazing at the three men writhing on their crosses. He whispered to himself, "If that's Jesus, where are the rest? James? John with his smart mouth? My brother Andrew who always knew more than I?"

He continued to indulge in self-pity until he looked at the crosses again. Now he could focus on the man in the middle, the one nailed to his cross. At the same time, the man looked back to him. His stare sent chills up Simon-Peter's spine. Jesus! The Romans hung Jesus! Stupid Jesus! Traitor Judas!

Simon-Peter's eyes opened large the next time he looked at the victims. Several soldiers were looking in his direction and gestured. Stumbling in fear and confusion, he turned and ran into the deep brush of the Hinnom Valley.

* * *

The death watch on Golgotha continued into the eighth hour. John turned his head when the second thief convulsed as if he were about to die, but the man recovered with a deep breath. Pointing to the thief, one of the guards asked, "Did anyone bet he would die last?"

They all shook their heads.

"Shall we do it?" he continued.

They nodded and a guard took a heavy club and slammed it against the man's legs. John covered his eyes as bone and flesh ripped apart. When he took his hands away, he saw the man perched crazily on one good leg. The guard stood back for a moment, then slammed the club again. The thief shuddered and screamed when the impact lifted him off the seat. The scream died abruptly when his chest collapsed and crushed his lungs. Blood and bile drooled out of his mouth as his twisted body hung by its wrists.

As the rain turned to mist and drizzle, John squeezed his eyes when he thought he saw a look of serenity on Jesus face. John's eyes asked, "Why?"

Jesus' eyes returned an answer John couldn't understand. John only knew that life had gone beyond reason. Seeing Jesus lips move, he edged closer to the cross. As the soldiers moved aside to let him pass, John listened to the hushed words forming on Jesus' swollen lips. "I...am thirsty," Jesus gasped.

Salome heard Jesus and found a pail filled with sour wine. She gestured to a soldier who put a sponge on the end of his spear, dipped it in the wine, and lifted it to Jesus' lips. It seemed a wasted effort; most of the wine dribbled down Jesus' chin.

Now the sky opened, crying swollen drops of rain that pelted people's faces and splattered on the ground. By now, only the small group of followers and a few soldiers remained under the cross. Most of the spectators lost their enthusiasm for the sight of people hanging on Roman crosses, especially Galileans who thought they were the anointed messenger of God.

Jesus mother touched John's arm and pointed to Jesus. The driving rain had washed much of the blood and dirt off him. Only the bruises, open cuts, and an occasional trickle of blood soiled his clean body. She screamed and clutched John when the sky lit from horizon to horizon, followed by a howling thunder that roared through the valley.

Thinking he heard a loud shriek from the city, John spun on his heels. He saw lightning dance across the roof of the Temple and arc over its gold plated sides, followed by another bellowing thunderclap. He felt a rush of excitement when the pattern repeated. It was as if an army of luminous soldiers were attacking. Why the Temple, he thought. Why not the fortress? That's where the pagans live.

John held Mary of Nazareth by the arm and looked up to Jesus. "Why did God allow you to die?" he screamed, trying to make himself heard over the storm. "Why didn't God kill the Romans or the priests...or Judas?"

Then he noticed that, in the midst his pain, he felt the cleansing power of light and water as he and Mary consoled each other under the cross. His feeling of tranquility vanished when John felt a hand on his shoulder. He released Mary's arm and slowly rotated to face...Zebedee. He saw the grief stricken face of his father in the driving rain, water running off his beard and soaking his robe. Zebedee slowly put his arms around John and Mary and held them in a tight circle. Later, Mary of Magdala and Salome joined them in their ring of grief and love.

One of the soldiers, water soaked and impatient, picked up a spear and walked to the cross. John saw him from the corner of his eye and ran over to stand between the soldier and Jesus. The soldier gestured for John to move but he stood firm until Zebedee pulled him away. "There's no reason for you to die today as well," he told John.

John almost fainted when the soldier plunged the spear into Jesus side. But there was no movement, no quiver, and no sign of life. Jesus, the Anointed One, the Son of Man, had died on the cross. The soldier with the spear walked toward the other soldiers. He said something in a language John didn't understand and followed with a thumbs down gesture. With that, the soldiers who broke the legs of the two men crucified alongside Jesus ordered the slaves standing off to the side to cut the victims from the crosses, then picked up their weapons and tools and left for the city. The slaves lifted the broken bodies of the two criminals on to a wooden pallet then went to take Jesus, but John stopped them. They shrugged and turned away to lug the pallet down the hill.

CHAPTER FORTY-FIVE

(Ninth Hour)

When the people of Jabesh Gilead heard what the Philistines had done to Saul, all their valiant men marched through the night to Beth Shan. They took down the bodies of Saul and his sons from the wall of Beth Shan and went to Jabesh, where they burned them. Then they took their bones and buried them under a tamarisk tree at Jabesh, and they fasted seven days.

1Samuel 31:11-13

To the rain soaked people standing under the cross, it seemed as if an eternity had passed since Jesus presided over their Seder meal. Totally consumed by grief, they hung on to each other. They shared their loss, ignoring wet clothes, strands of hair hanging over their faces, and the blood from the victims mixing with the water running past their feet.

Four men pulling a pallet up the hill passed the soldiers on the road between Golgotha and the city gate. John strained to see their faces through the rain, but only saw that one man was gray and heavy-set, older than the others. Zebedee, however, quickly recognized the man as Joseph of Arimathea and met him half way up the hill.

Joseph told Zebedee, "I received permission from Pontius Pilate to take Jesus and bury him before Sundown according to our custom." Gesturing to the other men, he continued, "This is Nicodemus, and the other two men work for me. They will help me carry his body to my private tomb."

Overhearing their words, John interjected, "We will bury Jesus."

"Let them do it," Zebedee countered. "There is no way an old man and a group of crying women can help in this situation."

"I heard that Jesus' mother is in Jerusalem," Joseph said.

Zebedee gestured toward the women. "Over there. Do you want to meet her?"

Nodding, Joseph answered, "Yes, if she'll talk to me."

Zebedee and Joseph went over to Mary. "I'm sorry," Joseph said to Mary. He seemed to have trouble finding the right words. "Nothing worked the way we thought it would."

John thought he saw a mixture of guilt and sorrow on Joseph's face as he talked to Mary.

"We need to hurry so we can bury him before sundown," Joseph continued. "You're welcome to come to his tomb the day after the Sabbath. It's in my garden. Zebedee and Judas know where I live. I'll meet you there to mourn Jesus' death if you wish."

Mary looked at Zebedee.

"Let him do it," Zebedee counseled in response to her glance.

Jesus' mother bowed her head and embraced Joseph. "Please do as you say," she said, her words punctuated with soft sobs that seemed to come from an inexhaustible well of tears. "I don't know why you came, but you are a blessing from God."

Tears flowed into Joseph's beard, mixing with the soft drizzle fading to the east.

Then the three women, along with John and Zebedee started down the hill, arms and hearts locked in grief. As they left, Joseph watched as two young men gently placed Jesus' body on the pallet and covered him with a blanket. Mercifully, the angry skies were starting to clear and the western horizon carried a hint of sunlight surfacing beyond the clouds.

* * *

By sundown, only a few torches lit the streets as the people of Jerusalem settled down for the evening. After a while, only the sound of heavy Roman sandals echoed in the deserted streets as wary patrols watched for new signs of trouble.

That night two men, sick and exhausted, wandered through dark alleys and deserted places in and around Jerusalem. One, a Galilean named Simon-Peter shuffled toward the Upper City looking for a safe house. Greeted by Mark at the gate, he stumbled into the courtyard and collapsed in a mound of grief.

The other man, a Judean named Judas, staggered through a deserted field outside the North Wall scrounging for garbage. The rays from the cloud shrouded moon offered no warmth to his beaten and hungry body, nor did he rest safely in a tomb as his Messiah now did.

There was a time when both men believed Jesus was the Messiah promised by the prophets; when both men would have sacrificed their lives to save his.

EPILOGUE

On the first day of the week, very early in the morning, the women took the spices they had prepared and went to the tomb. They found the stone rolled away from the tomb, but when they entered, they did not find the body of the Lord Jesus.
While they were wondering about this, suddenly two men in clothes that gleamed like lightning stood beside them. In their fright the women bowed down with their faces to the ground, but the men said to them, "Why do you look for the living among the dead? He is not here; he has risen! Remember how he told you, while he was still with you in Galilee:
'The Son of Man must be delivered over to the hands of sinners, be crucified and on the third day be raised again.' "

Luke 24:1-7

APOSTOLIC SELECTION

There are fourteen rather than twelve named original apostles in the four Gospels. This has been explained by assuming that Thaddaeus and Nathanael were the same persons as those identified as Jude and Bartholomew.

*

Andrew – May have spent time with the Essenes in Qumran. Possible disciple of John the Baptist. Jesus may have fit into their idea of the imminent coming of the Messiah.

Simon (Peter) – Andrew's brother. Became an apostolic leader after a turbulent beginning. Married; one child named Jepthania.

James – Son of Zebedee and Salome. Married; son named Aaron. Some traditions identify Salome as Mary's (the mother of Jesus) sister or cousin. James was beheaded by Herod Agrippa I in 44 CE.

John – James' brother. Credited with writing the fourth Gospel and several letters (epistles). Known for his intensity.

(Jude) Thomas – Thought to be a cousin of Jesus. Called Didymus (twin) because of his resemblance too an unidentified person, possibly Jesus. Credited with writing the Gospel of Thomas.

Judas – Son of Simon of Kerioth. Judas was a Judean who was often out of place among the Galileans who followed Jesus. Jesus meets him in Capernaum and mentors him until he joins the mission. He was resented by some of the other apostles because he was Judean and educated.

Matthew (Levi) – Levi was a tax collector until he met Jesus and changed his name to Matthew. May be the author of the first Gospel.

Philip –Met Jesus in Jerusalem or Bethsaida. May have introduced Nathanael to Jesus.

James (The Lesser) – Son of Alphaeus. His mother, Mary was present at the cross on Good Friday. There is no information about James after the death of Jesus.

Thaddaeus (Jude) – Possible author of the Letter of Jude. Calls himself the brother of James, but no information on which James.

Nathanael – (Bartholomew) Introduced to Jesus by Philip. Nothing known about his history or ministry.

Simon (Zealotes) – May have been an anti Roman rebel. No information about Simon after the death of Jesus.

SIMILAR NAMES

There are several people in the New Testament who have the same or similar names. There are at least five Mary's and five Simon's who participated in Jesus' journey during his lifetime and after his resurrection. Note: The word "bar" or "ben" in a man's name means "son of." Bar was used where people spoke Aramaic. Ben was used where people spoke Hebrew.

*

James bar Zebedee – Apostle; son of Zebedee and brother of John.
James bar Alphaeus – Apostle; son of Alphaeus and Mary. Known as "James the Lesser."
James bar Joseph – Jesus' brother. A leader of the early Christian community in Jerusalem. *Matt 13:55, Mk 6:3. Gal 1:19.*

Joseph – Father of Jesus.
Joseph Caiaphas – High Priest; religious and political leader.
Joseph of Arimathea – Gave his tomb for Jesus. Mt 27:57, Lk 23:50.

Judas of Kerioth – Apostle; Son of Simon. AKA Judas Iscariot.
Jude bar Joseph – Jesus' brother. *Matt 13:55, k 6:3.*
Jude – Sometimes referred to as the son of James (?). *Ac 1:13.* Possibly the person known as Labbaeus or Thaddeaus. *Mt 10:3, Mk 3:18, Lk 6:16, John 14:22.*
Judas – Disciple. *Ac 9:11.*

Mary – Mother of Jesus. Present at the Crucifixion.
Mary Magdalene – Disciple; Present at the Crucifixion
Mary of Bethany – Sister of Lazarus and Martha.
Mary Marcia – AKA Mary bas Isaac. Thought to be the mother of Mark. The Last Supper, the meeting place for the apostles after the Crucifixion and Pentecost were thought to be held in the "upper room" of her house. Certain events recorded in The Acts of the Apostles were also held at her house. *Ac 12:12.*
Mary – Mother of James the Lesser. Widow of Alphaeus. Present at the Crucifixion.

Simon Peter – Apostle; Brother of Andrew.
Simon of Kerioth – Judas' father.
Simon Zealotes – Apostle; AKA Simon the Zealot.
Simon of Cyrene - Helped Jesus carry the cross.
Simon – A leper. *Mt 26:6, Mk 14:3.*

THE HERODS

1. **Herod the Great** (73 - 4BCE.)[4]

- Married eleven times. Enterprising, keen intellect, builder of the Temple. Bloodthirsty and cruel.
- Son of Antipater, appointed governor of Coele-Syria, eventually became king of an extensive territory. Ordered the death of sons whom he viewed as disloyal. Connected to the 'slaughter of the innocents.' (Mt 2:1, 3, 7)
- The Kingdom of Herod the Great was divided between his sons after his death.
    - o **Archelaus** (23 BCE – 18 CE) became the ethnarch of Samaria, Judea, and Edom from 4 BCE to 6 CE. He was the son of Herod the Great and Malthace, the brother of Herod Antipas, and the half-brother of **Herod Philip I.** Deposed 6 CE.
    - o **Herod Antipas** (before 20 BCE – after 39 CE) was a first century ruler of Galilee and Perea, who bore the title of tetrarch ("ruler of a quarter"). He is best known today for accounts in the New Testament of his role in events that led to the executions of John the Baptist and Jesus of Nazareth. (Mt 14:1, 3; Mk 6:14; 8:15; Lk 3:1, 19; 9:7: 13:31; 23:7, 11; Ac 13:1)
    - o **Herod Philip II** (4 BCE–34 CE), or Philip the Tetrarch, was son of Herod the Great and his fifth wife Cleopatra of Jerusalem (no relation to Cleopatra of Egypt) and half-brother of Herod Antipas and Herod Archelaus. Philip inherited the northeast part of his father's kingdom and is mentioned briefly in the Bible by Luke (3,1): He married his niece, the daughter of Herodias and Herod Philip I. She appears in the Bible in connection with the execution of John the Baptist. He rebuilt the city of Caesarea Philippi, calling it by his own name to distinguish it from the Caesarea on the sea-coast which was the seat of the Roman government.
    - o **Herodias**: (c. 15 BCE-after 39 CE) Around the year CE 1 or 2, she married her uncle, Herod Philip I, the son of Herod the Great and Mariamne II. Although seen for a while as the successor to Herod the Great, he fell from grace after his mother's implication in a plot to kill the king. Herodias had a daughter with him. After Herod Philip died, she married another uncle, Herod Antipas, tetrarch of Galilee and Perea. Although Herod Antipas and Herodias may really have loved each other, political considerations were probably of more importance

4 BCE and CE represent *Before Common or Christian) Era* and *Common or Christian era.* These replace BC and AD in most contemporary literature.

to them in this marriage. However, the ambition of Herodias proved the ruin of Herod Antipas. Being jealous of the power of Herod Agrippa I, her brother, she induced Herod to demand of Caligula the title of king. This was refused through the machinations of Agrippa, and Herod was banished. But Herodias kept faithful to her husband during his exile. (Mt14:3; Mk 6:17; Lk 3:19)

2. Later Herods

- **Herod Agrippa I** (10 BCE - 44 CE), King of the Jews, was the grandson of Herod the Great, and son of Aristobulus IV and Berenice. He is the king named Herod in the Acts of the Apostles, in the Bible. (Acts 12:1, 20; 23:35).
- **Herod Agrippa II** (b. 27/28 CE), son of Agrippa I. He was the seventh and last king of the family of Herod the Great, thus last of the Herodians. (Acts 25:13; 26:1, 27)

3. Herodians: The Herodians were a sect or party mentioned in the New Testament as having on two occasions; once in Galilee, and again in Jerusalem, manifested an unfriendly disposition towards Jesus (Mark 3:6, 12:13; Matthew 22:16; cf. also Mark 8:15, Luke 13:31-32, Acts 4:27). In each of these cases their name is coupled with that of the Pharisees. According to many interpreters they were the courtiers or soldiers of Herod Antipas. The Herodians were a public political party, who distinguished themselves from the two great historical parties of Judaism (Pharisees and Sadducees) by the fact that they were and had been sincerely friendly to Herod the Great, the King of the Jews, and to his dynasty.

DISCUSSION POINTS

Chapter 1-4: How did Jesus view his mission? Religious, political, or social?
Chapter 5: The Wedding at Cana only appears in John's Gospel? What is John telling us?
Chapter 9 What do you think about Jesus, Peter, James, and John leaving home for two weeks without telling anyone about where they were going, and why?
Chapter 11: Why were the people angry with Jesus? Was their anger justified?
Chapter 13: Did Jesus do the right thing, calling people away from their work and families?
Chapter 15: What does it mean to be unclean? Was isolating people with communicable diseases or mental problems okay?
Chapter 16: Has human behavior changed since Jesus' time? Do we still view the poor as lazy and unmotivated? Why did Jesus, Judas, and John go to Tiberias?
Chapter 17: What do you think Jesus and the apostles did on a normal day?
Chapter 18: Who are the Samaritans and what was the cause of the enmity between the Jews and the Samaritans?
Chapter 26-31: These chapters tell us about a conflict between Pontius Pilate, Herod Antipas, Caiaphas, and Annas. What was the root cause of the conflict? Go to *http://www.livius.org/ja-jn/jewish_wars/jwar01.htm* to learn the background of the initial Roman/Jewish relationship.
Why are these events important to Jesus and his followers?
Chapter 36: The account of raising Lazarus from the tomb is only told in John's Gospel which was written after the Gospels of Matthew, Mark, and Luke. How should we interpret this story? Why didn't the news of this event become public?
Chapter 38: Why was the Temple used to sell animals and exchange currency?
Chapter 40-42: Did Judas deliberately betray Jesus? Did anyone else betray Jesus?

CPSIA information can be obtained at www.ICGtesting.com
Printed in the USA
BVOW070744241011

274373BV00002B/1/P

9 781593 307448